Praise for the Very Cherry Mysteries

Cherry Pies & Deadly Lies

"The first in an amusing new series features a fearless, reckless sleuth who unravels a complicated mystery while juggling her sex life and her future plans."

—*Kirkus Reviews*

"Whitney is a well-drawn, sympathetic character, and the small-town frame, with a close-knit community and a cherry orchard, will appeal to cozy readers who enjoy Joanne Fluke's Hannah Swensen mysteries."

—*Booklist*

"Hannah displays … talent."

—*Publishers Weekly*

"Great fun and extremely well-written. The crime, the characters—everything comes together … an extremely 'tasty' story you will definitely devour in one sitting."

—*Suspense Magazine*

Cherry Scones
& BROKEN BONES

Cherry Scones & BROKEN BONES

A VERY CHERRY MYSTERY

DARCI HANNAH

MIDNIGHT INK
WOODBURY, MINNESOTA

FIRST EDITION
First Printing, 2019

Book format by Samantha Penn
Cover design by Kevin R. Brown
Cover illustration by Greg Newbold/Bold Strokes Illustration

Midnight Ink, an imprint of Llewellyn Worldwide Ltd.

This is a work of fiction. Names, characters, places, and incidents are either the product of the author's imagination or are used fictitiously, and any resemblance to actual persons living or dead, business establishments, events, or locales is entirely coincidental.

Library of Congress Cataloging-in-Publication Data
Names: Hannah, Darci, author.
Title: Cherry scones & broken bones / Darci Hannah.
Other titles: Cherry scones and broken bones
Description: First edition. | Woodbury, Minnesota : Midnight Ink, [2019] |
    Series: A very cherry mystery ; 2.
Identifiers: LCCN 2019001043 (print) | LCCN 2019003037 (ebook) | ISBN
    9780738758503 (ebook) | ISBN 9780738758381 (alk. paper)
Subjects: | GSAFD: Mystery fiction.
Classification: LCC PS3608.A7156 (ebook) | LCC PS3608.A7156 C49 2019 (print)
    | DDC 813/.6—dc23
LC record available at https://lccn.loc.gov/2019001043

Midnight Ink
Llewellyn Worldwide Ltd.
2143 Wooddale Drive
Woodbury, MN 55125-2989
www.midnightinkbooks.com

Printed in the United States of America

For John,
my husband, partner in crime, and best friend.

One

I read once, probably while skimming through ads in an *O* magazine, that true success doesn't come from one's ability to dream big and shoot for the stars like some jacked-up mythological arrow, but rather from one's ability to thrive where you are. Right where you are. And to be content. God help me, I was trying. But waking up day after day in the overdone Victorian love nest my mother had created out of my old bedroom was not bringing me contentment. It was, quite frankly, giving me a headache, and probably a rash as well.

I turned off the alarm and rolled onto my back, staring up at the pink chiffon canopy suspended above my bed. It was ridiculous, sleeping in a bed cocooned in flowered chiffon and hung with fresh sprigs of lavender. I mean, how was a practical, twenty-eight-year-old overworked modern woman supposed to thrive in her childhood bedroom that had been purposely renovated by the queen of modern Victorian chic? Baby steps, I reminded myself. I took a deep breath and was just about to roll out of bed and put my plan into action when Mom's voice floated through the bedroom door.

1

"Whitney. Are you awake, dear?" She sounded excited. She also didn't bother waiting for me to answer. The door burst open and Mom fluttered in just as I was propping myself higher on the absurd mountain of decorative pillows.

"Oh good, you're awake." She beamed, peering beneath a swag of flowery curtain. "I've the best news. I've just heard it. Margaret left a note for me at the front desk. I saw it on my way back from the kitchen. Guess what?"

I yawned and rubbed my eyes. "What?" I replied, lacking enthusiasm. My alarm had just gone off. Nothing enthused me at 5:45 in the morning.

Mom's soaring spirits plummeted at my lackadaisical tone. But she wasn't one to be deterred. Her round blue eyes twinkled as she pinned on her brightest smile. "Silvia Lumiere just booked a room with us, from Saturday through Labor Day weekend! Nine whole weeks! Isn't that marvelous? She's never stayed at the Cherry Orchard Inn before, and now she's staying with us for the remainder of the summer. See? I told you, Whitney. You're a genius. Your new ads are working. We're back in business, and in a big way. Silvia Lumiere!" Mom shook her head, sending the single flaxen braid down her back wiggling like a dog's tail. "I would never have dreamed it, and you've done it. Oooh, everyone's going to be so envious that she's staying here!"

I was genuinely tickled by Mom's enthusiasm and the fact that she was proud of me. But the obvious reason someone would book a room at the Cherry Orchard Inn for nine weeks had escaped her. Murder, however craftily one could spin it, still tended to taint a business. And, quite frankly, I hadn't spent a lot of effort trying to explain away, in clever advertisement or any other form, all the chaos that resulted when Jeb Carlson, our orchard manager, got killed this spring. Even

2

though it was what had brought me back home from Chicago. What I'd done instead was lower our prices to the point of absurdity for the peak of tourist season in Door County, Wisconsin. If I'd learned anything over the last few weeks, it was that affordable luxury accommodations during the height of a Cherry Cove summer was the only force on earth powerful enough to combat the horrors of murder. And, if what Mom was telling me was true, it appeared to be working.

I sat up a little straighter and cleared my throat. "Mom. That's great news. But who is this Silvia Lumiere, and why is everyone going to be envious?"

Mom was from hardy, cheerful, perpetually polite Midwestern stock and it took a lot to disappoint her. But I'd done it within two minutes of waking. It was a new record. I'd have to remember to text my younger brother, Bret, and rub it in. It took me a second more to realize that Mom was still talking.

"You don't know who Silvia Lumiere is? She's a Chicagoan, Whitney. I'm surprised. How could you live in Chicago for six years and never have heard of Silvia Lumiere?" Apparently the thought was as preposterous as it was disappointing.

"I was busy, Mom. And obviously not moving in the right circles. Is she an actress or something? Is she in commercials?"

Mom gave a dismissive twist of her lips. "No, she's a painter, dear. A famous one, known primarily for her portraits. She discovered Cherry Cove five years ago and since then has spent every summer here, painting her portraits and creating quite the buzz. She's part of our local artists' community. She's also the darling of the Cherry Country Arts Council. Oh, Whitney," she breathed, filling with a new wave of delight. "She'll be here, at the Cherry Orchard Inn, painting on the lawn! Such an honor. Oh!" she exclaimed as another, even more titillating thought popped into her head. "We should have her paint a family portrait. Why not? She'll be right here. We'll have plenty of opportunity to pose for her. Oh, drat." The quasi-expletive dropped from Mom's lips as disappointment swiftly toppled delight. "Bret's still out of the country," she said. "I suppose I could call him and have him fly home for the sitting, if he's not too busy."

Bret was somewhere in Europe chasing ghosts … literally. I wished to God it was metaphorically. That would be a heck of a lot easier to explain to people than telling them that your promising younger brother was traipsing across Europe, barging into haunted castles and stirring up the spirits that lived there. It was all for a reality TV show he was filming.

I glanced at the time on my iPhone. It was swiftly approaching six o'clock, so I needed to get a move on. I got out of bed, looked at Mom, and smiled. "Bret doesn't have to be here, Mom. This woman's a portrait painter, right? We can just show her a picture of him and tell her to paint him in. In fact, I'd be happy to choose the picture."

Mom didn't like the grin on my face and swiftly declined. "No. I'll pick it out. It's a portrait, after all. You can't just delete it if you're not happy with it. It's there forever. For posterity. But you're right. Although I'd love for him to come home, Bret doesn't need to be here. Anyhow," she continued, "since Silvia will be arriving Saturday evening, I think we should plan a tea in her honor for Sunday afternoon. I'll rally the Cherry Cove Women's League and have them pass the word around. I want you and Grandma Jenn to plan the menu."

I'm not going to lie. The thought of planning a fancy high tea reception for a celebrity guest was scintillating. The wheels of my mind were already spinning as I grabbed my running clothes off a lavender wingback chair. "Sounds like just the challenge I need," I told her as I excused myself and headed for the bathroom. "I'll get on it straight away … after my run."

"Run? I didn't know you liked to run, dear?"

"I don't. I mean, who does like to run, right? I'm just embracing it for now as a way to stay in shape." And a way to ambush the one man I couldn't stop thinking about. But this I didn't tell Mom. Mom had her own ideas about my love life. She still adored my ex-boyfriend Tate Vander Hagen despite the fact he'd cheated on me when I lived in Chicago. However, since his recent heroics during the Cherry Blossom Festival last month, I'd started seeing him again, strictly on a trial basis. But this time my heart wasn't entirely in it. Which I blamed on the other man in my life, a man who wanted nothing to do with me. It was this attitude that had really gotten under my skin.

"You should try goat yoga," Mom suggested, standing at the bathroom door. "I saw it on the internet. It's all the rage." Apparently she was serious.

I wrinkled my nose. "Mom. You can't believe everything you see on the internet. I know goats. Goats aren't exactly Zen-friendly. Nobody in their right mind would do yoga with goats."

I was about to shut the door on her when she added, "Hannah's considering it."

It was all that needed to be said. Hannah Winthrop, one of my best friends, owned Yoga in the Cove. She was tall, blonde, and bendy ... and perpetually hyped-up on caffeine. I could almost picture her trying such a class. The thought made me laugh.

"Thanks, Mom," I said. "But today I'm just going to stick to running." I cast her a wink and shut the door.

Two

It was my good fortune that the Cherry Orchard Inn sat atop a modest bluff across the bay from the picturesque lakeside village of Cherry Cove. Not only was the view spectacular, but, more importantly, it was a downhill coast to town—which was about all I could manage in my current non-runner's physical condition. And I didn't want to appear out of shape. Not in front of him.

As I struck a moderate jog down Cherry Bluff Lane—the long, meandering driveway that connected the inn and the orchard to the main road—I was a little taken aback by the accuracy with which my plan was unfolding. I had studied this man's movements for the past month, noting what time he passed Cherry Bluff Lane, how long it took me to jog from the inn to the end, and what time I needed to leave to make it look like ours was a chance meeting. Was that stalking? I hoped not! But if it was, I had to admit that I was darn good at it.

The moment the main road came into view my heart beat a little faster. Certainly, it was already beating fast. Recreational running wasn't my thing. But this new frenetic pounding was entirely due to the sight of the tall, fit, redheaded man running down the road with his faithful dog beside him. He was the one person in all of Cherry Cove that kept popping into my thoughts like an annoying cyber pop-up ad—and at the most inopportune times. I tried to blame it on my overtly romantic bedroom, but the truth of it was, it went far deeper than that. The runner, Jack MacLaren, was an old high school friend of mine and Cherry Cove's only police officer.

We had lost touch after high school. Then this past May, after years of pursuing our own careers, murder had thrown us together once again. It had even pitted us against one another, because Officer Mac-Laren hadn't appreciated the fact that I was bound and determined to sniff out the killer myself. He eventually came around. In fact, he came around to such an extent that, having been swept up in the heat of the moment, he kissed me. And it was this kiss that haunted me by night and ambushed me by day. Because, dummy me, I'd walked away from it, and him.

Jack had been humiliated and was avoiding me. Our friendship was in peril, and Jack's friendship, I realized, was one of the things I valued most about returning to Cherry Cove.

The moment I hit the main road, MacDuff, Jack's adorable floppy-eared springer spaniel, made a beeline for me. If Jack couldn't stand the sight of me, at least his dog could. We were pals. Besides, I had cheese.

MacDuff was the first to spot me. I loved that dog nearly as much as Jack did, and the feeling was mutual. The moment I hit the main road, MacDuff dashed away from Jack's side.

I stopped running and gave the dog a long-overdue hug, slipping him a piece of his favorite snack as I did so. Jack ran past us, giving a dead-fish flop of a wave in greeting. He then called MacDuff to his side and took off down the hill, heading for town and his turf-roofed troll-cave of a police station.

He wasn't about to stop for me.

MacDuff, clearly torn, was above all else faithful. After a mournful stare the black-and-white pooch ran back to Jack's side. But I hadn't stalked Jack MacLaren just to be blown off so easily. I picked up my pace and ran after them.

"Hey," I said, catching up to him at the bottom of the hill. Jack had a very long stride, not to mention the fact that he was a habitual runner. My five-foot-seven-inch frame was no match for the trim six-foot-four running machine. I was winded and plagued with a stabbing side cramp by the time I had his attention. "How … how've you been?" I forced a smile through the pain. "Haven't seen you lately."

"Been busy," he replied. "Tourist season, ya know. How's Tate?"

That was unfair, but understandable under the circumstances. "Haven't seen much of him," I replied truthfully. "Been a little busy myself." We had come abreast of the public beach and were running through the parking lot side by side. I sucked in a lungful of much-needed air, adding, "Tourist season, ya know." I looked at him, flashed a grin and fell to the unyielding pavement with a painful thud. At nearly the same moment every resting seagull leapt into the air with frantic wings and angry cries.

Jack stopped running. "Whitney! Christ, are you okay?" He grabbed hold of my arm. MacDuff was licking my face, and I was paralyzed with embarrassment from tripping over a rogue cement parking block. Then I noticed Jack's look of genuine concern. It was nearly enough to dull the throbbing pain consuming my hands and knees.

"Yeah," I said, attempting to spring to my feet. I fell a little short of the mark. "Totally," I assured him. "I haven't gone for a run in a long time and I forgot how dangerous this sport can be." Jack let go of my arm as I counted off the dangers on my fingers. "Uneven pavement, exposed tree roots, curbs, parked cars, and the occasional rogue cement parking block."

"You're bleeding," he said, suppressing a grin.

"Oh? So I am." It was the first time I realized it. My knees were a bloody mess, skinned and peppered with gravel. Yet remarkably, they looked worse than they felt. I gingerly brushed them off and looked up at Jack. "You have an impressively long stride. You make it look easy."

"Whitney, you should have told me it was your first day running."

"I was trying to, but I get the feeling you're still mad at me."

He was going to say something to that but instead closed his eyes and took a deep breath. He exhaled through his nose. That's when I noticed the sweat. He was covered in it. It dripped from under his bright copper hair and rolled down his handsome, flushed, frustrated face. Jack had stopped running too soon.

I touched his arm, causing his honey-brown eyes to spring open. "Let's keep walking," I suggested. "Would you mind it very much if I came with you to the police station? I could use a couple of bandages, and I'd like to pick your brain. Do you recall ever hearing the name Silvia Lumiere?"

Jack looked puzzled. "The portrait painter?"

"Ah, so she is real and not a figment of my mom's imagination."

"What's Silvia Lumiere got to do with you?" he asked as we headed for the Scandinavian-replica log home that was the Cherry Cove Police Station.

"Apparently, Ms. Lumiere has just booked a room at our inn through Labor Day weekend. That's nine weeks."

A ruddy brow lifted as Jack considered this. "That's great. I thought you were having trouble booking guests after … you know, the incident?"

I did know. And, until my madcap rate reduction, we'd had very few takers. I met Jack's questioning look with a nod. "Yeah. It's great for business. Still, most people don't stay at the inn for more than a week. Mom thinks it's a huge honor to have such a guest, but frankly, I'm a little suspicious. What's she like, this painter?"

Jack gave a noncommittal shrug. "Artsy. Very artsy and very Gold Coast Chicago. You two should get along just fine."

I wrinkled my nose at him. "Just because I worked in advertising when I lived in Chicago doesn't make me artsy or Gold Coast. I'm a baker."

This made him laugh. "And a darn good baker at that. Okay, Bloom," he finally said, leading me toward his police station. "Let's get those knees of yours cleaned up. And I need a shower. Do you think you could manage a pot of coffee while I do? Oh, and if you wouldn't mind, the kids are out back. I know how you love my kids. I promised them they could play on the roof this morning. Do you think you can handle that as well?"

I wasn't exactly gloating, but I was happy. Jack was talking to me again. He was at ease in my company, and that was a huge victory. "Of course," I said, regarding the coffee. Coffee brewing was second nature to me. Jack's kids, however, were another matter altogether. Getting those two hellions on the roof? I wasn't entirely certain the roof was the best place for them, but, for the sake of our friendship, I would give it my best try.

Three

Jack's kids weren't really kids at all, well, not in the human sense of the word at any rate. They were two little billy goats, brothers he'd inherited when taking up residence in the odd little police station. The picturesque building had been a Scandinavian boutique and gift shop, and somewhat of a tourist attraction before the village purchased it. That was shortly after Jack's father had fallen ill. Jack, an up-and-coming police detective in Milwaukee, had resigned from his job to be with his parents during what was undoubtedly a hard time for the MacLaren family. Shortly thereafter, at the urging of the village, Cherry Cove hired its very own police officer and presented him with the iconic building, where he now both lived and worked. Everyone knew Jack was overqualified for the job, but from all accounts he didn't seem to mind the change of pace, or being back in Cherry Cove where he could better look after his widowed mother. The goats, however, were a little more than he had bargained for.

If Jack's goats had real names I didn't know what they were. He simply referred to them, albeit ironically, as Thing One and Thing Two—a nod to the whirlwind duo in *The Cat in the Hat*. Jack swore that he didn't know which goat was which but claimed MacDuff did. Naturally, after setting up the coffee pot to brew, I called MacDuff. The dog ran to the back door and nosed a couple of leashes hanging there. I got the hint and grabbed them, following MacDuff into the garden. He ran to the little goat shed that was a miniature version of the police station.

Two little be-horned brown-and-white heads poked out of the framed window. They looked innocent enough with their long floppy ears and inquisitive eyes. Their chins were tufted with a hint of a beard—one white and the other brown. The fact that Jack couldn't tell them apart was just laziness. As MacDuff and I approached the velvety ears began twitching, preceded just slightly by excited head bobs. Soft bleating came next, and then, as if a switch had been flipped, they both began to scream.

I had forgotten about the screaming.

Jack didn't know why they did that, but suspected they were narcissists and loved the attention. Screaming goats on a police station roof were hard to ignore, and, as if Mac Duff's barking wasn't enough, the goats always managed to alert Jack that someone was approaching.

After a short bout of wrestling with each kid, the leashes were finally secured. However, like two demons possessed, the moment we left the shed the goats bolted for the garden gate, dragging me along with them. MacDuff, barking excitedly, ran after us.

It occurred to me the moment Thing One and Thing Two decided to split up and head in opposite directions—One for the lake and Two for the town—that goats might not be leash-ready pets. In fact, shortly before both my shoulders were torn from their sockets, I was positive. I had no choice but to let go of one of the leashes, and I was sorry to think that my decision was driven solely by the arm that was about to go first. The lucky goat was Thing Two of the brown beard. He wasted no time dashing down the street, aiming for the large, shiny object bounding down the front steps of Cheery Pickers, the eclectic antique boutique owned by one of my best friends, Taylor Robinson. Thing One of the white beard was pulling me toward the lake where MacDuff, having shot across the street the moment he realized my hands were, literally, tied, was now racing up and down the beachfront spooking seagulls into the air. The goat began to scream at the dog while bouncing at the end of the leash like a caffeinated child on a pogo stick.

My newly bandaged knees had just stopped bleeding and the palms of my hands had a bad case of road rash, and all I could think to do was pray that Jack was still in the shower. It had taken weeks to get the man talking to me again. If I lost his goats and his dog on the same morning, he'd never forgive me.

MacDuff, thankfully, responded to his name on the third try. By then every seagull had been thoroughly terrorized and was nervously circling the beach. With that job done—because it was obvious he thought it his duty—he next set upon the goat with the same enthusiasm. The goat, with horns lowered, made a run for the dog but MacDuff was quicker. He got a hold of Thing One's tail, gave it a good yank, and then ran for the police station garden. Thing One took the bait and ran after the dog. Because I was still holding the leash, I ran after him too. Once the garden gate was firmly shut with both animals secured, I set out for Thing Two, now in the possession of the large shiny man in front of Tay's shop.

My jaw dangled in disbelief as I approached.

"My Lady! Would this noble creature belong to you?"

The man, a large fella, was encased in a full suit of medieval armor. I was utterly dumbfounded. For the flash of a second, I thought I'd crossed some invisible time barrier, falling back five hundred years and onto a different continent. I had read my share of time-travel romances and was, unfortunately, open to the possibility. But I was clearly still in Cherry Cove. The man was holding Thing Two by the horns. To be totally honest, I was a little disappointed that time travel hadn't taken place. It was just an eccentric dude in shiny armor parading outside Tay's store.

Wrangling the wayward goat, however, was the feat of a real hero. And the knight, for that's what he was, was in character. Maybe *he* was the time traveler, I mused, a little breathless at the thought. Of the man himself, I could see nothing. His armor, on the other hand, was magnificent. The polish of the metal was near mirror quality, and there were intricate flourishes of cobalt blue on the breastplate and visor. It must have cost a small fortune, in any century. Then I noticed the two little dents on his left thigh. It didn't take a huge leap of the imagination to guess what had made those. I cast Thing Two a look of disapproval.

"My Lady? The goat?"

"Ah, yes. No." I fought to regain my composure. "No. It's not mine. I'm just goat-sitting for a friend." As I took the leash, I wondered why armor had fallen out of fashion. It was such a good look on a man. "Sorry about those dents," I said, and gestured to his thigh.

"Dents?" The helmeted head bent while at the same time the thigh in question rose. A moment later came the muffled cry, "Holy shit!"

So much for the chivalric code. It hadn't occurred to me that he didn't know the little horns had left marks. I looked at Thing Two with newfound respect.

"What I meant to say," the knight continued, slipping back into character, "was never worry, fair maiden. Your little beast has the heart of a lion and the aim of a dangerous child. Is he meant for the grill? If so, I claim the head."

The knight, only partially joking, took off his helmet. The moment he did, a fall of lustrous, caramel-colored hair emblazoned with summer highlights tumbled to his shoulders. It suddenly dawned on me who this man was.

"You're Lance Van Guilder, Tay's boyfriend!" I'd nearly forgotten. Lance was Tay's current man. I'd been living in Chicago when they'd met but had heard all about him. Tay said that he was a jouster on the Renaissance fair circuit. I guess I'd thought she was just being meta-phorical about his abilities. I now realized she'd been serious. I had to hand it to her—Lance fit her type to a tee. Tay liked her men long-haired, muscly, and shirtless. I assume she made an exception for the armor. I know I would have. "I'm Whitney," I told him, extending a hand. "I'm one of Tay's friends."

"Whitney Bloom!" he cried, his eyes creasing with delight. "Of course. I've heard all about you." He lowered his voice and added, "and all about that terrible incident this spring. Sorry I missed it." He gave the air a violent swipe with his imaginary sword, as if slaying a foe. I appreciated the gesture. "Tay said you've moved back to Cherry Cove. Said you're helping your parents run their inn. Sweet. Great to finally meet you. Want some help with that goat?"

We arrived at the police station in time to see Jack, dressed in his po-lice blues, leaning against the doorway with a cup of coffee in hand. He was clearly enjoying the spectacle of the long-haired man in full battle armor carrying his wayward goat, and me beside him holding the leash. Jack raised a ruddy eyebrow, then came out to retrieve his naughty pet.

"I see you didn't get my kids onto the roof, Bloom, abandoning the task for a knight in shining armor instead. Typical."

Ignoring his sarcasm, and both sets of grins, I introduced the man in question. "This is Lance Van Guilder. He's Tay's boyfriend. He's a professional jouster."

"Ah!" Jack said and shook the man's hand. "Now it makes sense. Nice to finally meet you, Lance. Hope this little guy didn't cause you too much trouble. He's not exactly working with a full set of horns, if you get my meaning. I once saw him head-butt a rock. Oh, damn." Jack's eyes had settled on the two glaring dents in Lance's armor. "Did he ...?"

"Came straight at me. At speed, no less. Didn't even know what hit me until it was too late. On a brighter note, I think I stunned him."

"Serves him right, the little brute." Jack cast a wary eye over his goat. "Come inside." He beckoned with a gracious sweep of his hand. "Whitney's made coffee. I'll join you in a minute, as soon as I get the kids safely on the roof."

While Jack was tending to his animals, Tay came over to the station and joined us for coffee. She was positively beaming. From the roots of her chic, deep-red hair down to her gold-painted toenails, she radiated happiness. Like Hannah, Tay was one of my oldest friends. We'd all met in third grade. Hannah, who displayed more volatile emotions, had wildly varying tastes where men were concerned. Not Tay. She had a type. But still, a Renaissance fair jouster? A man perhaps as eccentric as she was. How strange the heart is, I mused, casting a covert glance at Jack.

After introductions and a bout of pleasant conversation, the knight excused himself to go change out of his armor. Although Lance was a metal artist himself, Tay explained, and worked in the off-season creating metal sculptures, he also made his own armor. However, having recently come into a bit of money, he just couldn't resist purchasing a top quality suit from a renowned armorer. It was the equivalent, according to Tay, of an up-and-coming fashion model splurging on a Versace gown. Lance was in town for the summer, she happily informed us. He was performing at a nearby Renaissance fair just outside of Sturgeon Bay. The armor had arrived at her shop yesterday and Lance had been trying it on for size.

"Isn't he something," she remarked, smiling like a cat who's just won a long battle with a very wily mouse. Knowing my own issues regarding Jack, she was watching us closely. Obviously, the fact that I was there meant that Jack was talking to me again. Emboldened by this phenomenon, Tay added, "I'm excited that Lance is finally getting to meet my friends. Hey, I have a fabulous idea. Why don't we all go to the Renaissance fair together and watch him joust? This Saturday he's up against the Green Knight. Lance is the fabled Black Knight. He's the favorite to win, but one never knows. Jousting's a fickle sport. It should be exciting to watch. And if jousting's not your thing, you two can eat turkey legs, drink mead, and get hit on by busty wenches."

"Busty wenches," Jack repeated with the ghost of a grin. "Sounds like a dream, but I need to take a rain check. I have to work. It's the height of the tourist season and I'm the only cop around here."

"Lame excuse." She rolled her eyes and turned to me.

"Honestly, I'd love to. But I'm going to have to take a rain check as well. We have an important guest arriving on Saturday and Mom will kill me if I'm not there to greet her. I promise I'll go see him joust, but not this weekend. Can we reschedule in a week or two?"

"Sure." Tay leaned over her mug, her brown eyes sparkling with intrigue. "Important guest? Who?"

"Some painter named Silvia Lumiere."

"No way," she said, striking a look somewhere between awe and disbelief. "She's really staying at the inn—even after what happened in the cherry orchard?"

"I think she's staying at the inn *because* of what happened," I confided. "Very sensational, and she's getting quite a deal. You obviously know her. Jack knows her too, but he's not one to gossip."

"Damn right," he said, and got up to retrieve the coffee pot. Refilling our mugs, he added, "In most cases I think it's best that people form their own opinions of others, unless, of course, the person is known to be dangerous. In that case it's a matter of duty. You can rest assured, Whitney, that Silvia Lumiere is not dangerous."

"No, she's not," Tay agreed. "I'm surprised you don't know her. She's been coming to Cherry Cove for years. She's a big deal in the artist community. A very talented, very well-known painter."

"So I gather. Mom's been gushing over the news."

Tay grinned. "If I was pressed to offer an opinion on the lady, I'd say that her one glaring flaw is that she's very aware of her talent."

The fact that Jack was smirking into his steaming mug was a sure sign he agreed.

"Gotcha. Noted. Years of working in advertising has taught me how to 'manage' the talent. We're hoping to rebuild the image of the Cherry Orchard Inn, and I think having Ms. Lumiere as our guest will do wonders for the morale of our staff as well as our guests."

"I hope so," Tay agreed. "The Cherry Orchard Inn should have nothing to fear. You're a top-notch establishment, but I would think she'll only stay a week or so. You're pricey, and rumor is that although Ms. Lumiere likes to fly first class, she doesn't like to pay for it."

Now Jack was smiling. It was an outright grin of silent revenge. I ignored him. "Actually, she's staying a bit longer than a week."

"The rest of the summer," Jack informed Tay. "Which means that Whitney is going to be very busy."

"I like being busy," I told them both. "In fact, I've volunteered to do all the baking for the high tea we're throwing in Ms. Lumiere's honor. It's this Sunday. I hope your knight isn't jousting on Sunday as well? I want you to come."

"He is," Tay said, rolling her eyes. "However, as much as I like staring at him, I can't watch every jousting match Lance is in. It's not healthy. So count me in. And I'll let Char know as well, if she hasn't already heard."

Char was Tay's mother. Up until last year we'd always referred to her as Mrs. Robinson, but then we were told not to. The name Mrs. Robinson, of course, is rife with connotations of an older woman seducing a younger man, and since that's exactly what Tay's mom had done with Todd—a man four years older than her daughter—she'd insisted that we start calling her by her first name.

"Char will rally the troops," Tay added. "Which, I'm afraid, also means Todd will be joining her." She made a face at this last remark.

"Excellent. Jack?"

Jack looked up from his coffee and grinned. "Not my cup of tea, I'm afraid. But I'll tell Ingrid." Ingrid was his mom, a lovely woman who had come to Cherry Cove from Sweden when she was just sixteen. Jack, in a slightly mocking tone, added, "She's not one to miss such an important event."

As soon as Tay left, Jack offered to drive me home. It was a quiet ride until the moment he pulled up to the inn's entrance. I was about to get out of his police-issue SUV when he spoke.

"Hey. Do you want to run downhill again with me tomorrow?" The question was tentatively spoken, and for a minute I thought he was joking. But he wasn't. This was his olive branch.

"I would," I replied, sincerely. "A girl's got to start somewhere."

"Yes, she does. But not many get to start at the top of the hill." He grinned. Jack had a heart-melting grin. "Want me to text you when I'm ten minutes out?"

"Not necessary. Your movements are like clockwork. You should really mix it up a bit if you don't want people tracking you. See ya tomorrow at 6:15."

Jack looked amused. I watched as he drove away, then walked inside the inn, realizing that for the first time in weeks I was excited to get to work.

Four

Saturday evening I was in the kitchen with Bob Bonaire, the head chef for the Cherry Orchard Inn's renowned dining room, when a tall, blond-headed teenager barged through the kitchen door, breathing heavily and holding a pair of binoculars.

"She's here! She's here, Ms. Bloom."

Having just pulled eight cherry pies from the oven, the inn's signature dessert, I turned and looked at the boy. His body was full of drama while his voice held a hint of scandal. "You said you wanted to know as soon as she was spotted. Well, I have ... spotted her, that is. She's coming up the drive. And I should warn you, she doesn't travel lightly ... or alone." This last bit he added with a weighted look, clarifying the reason for the scandalous tone.

I set down my knife and looked at the young man.

Erik Larson and I had a short, tumultuous history together. He'd previously been employed on our cherry orchard and had gotten into a bit of trouble. It was Tate, using his cheek-dimples to their fullest effect, who had convinced me to keep the boy on at the inn. Erik, for his part, understood my hesitation and was trying his hardest not to make me regret my decision. I had to hand it to him, he was becoming a model employee. Every task I threw at him he embraced with his eighteen-year-old zeal. If I was simple I would have believed it redemption. But the real motivation behind the remarkable transformation was a pretty eighteen-year-old waitress named Kenna McKinnon, who also worked at the inn.

Erik was waiting for me to be scandalized. I wasn't going to bite. "When you say that she's not traveling alone, are you implying that she's brought an entourage with her?"

"No. Well, maybe. She's got a man with her."

Bob, consumed with a searing hot pan of brandied cherries, turned from the stove long enough to give a short hoot of laughter. "And that's why your tighty-whities are all in a bunch, boy? Because an eccentric old lady's brought a man with her? I thought you millennials were open to all forms of gender identities and sexual preferences, even the kind where a lady likes a man. And really, it's none of your business."

"Don't mean to contradict you, Mr. Bonaire, but it kinda is my business, sir. I'm handling the lady's luggage, and there's a whole truck and trailer of it. It's going to take me all night." This he added with a resigned sigh. "And the man she's with is too young for her. He's got a scraggly brown beard and likely a man bun as well. Ms. Lumiere is an old bat of a thing—and she's only got the one room. I know, because I've checked."

"A man bun, you say?"

"Can't tell for sure, but he looks the type."

"And we didn't put her in one of the double queen suites?"

"Whitney showed me her room," he said. "It's only got the one bed, and it's on the second floor."

21

It was true. Since Ms. Lumiere was going to be with us for a long time I had decided to put her in one of our cozy couples' getaway rooms. She'd have a king bed, a generous closet, a dresser, two comfy chairs by a fireplace and an en suite bathroom. Dad had even erected a beautiful white gazebo on the lawn for her to paint under. I looked at the young man's concerned face and smiled.

"Shouldn't be a problem," I told him. "And use the elevator for the luggage."

"I'm planning on it."

"And flash her your dimples," Bob added, looking amused. "If what you've seen through those binoculars is correct, we've got ourselves a cougar. Play your cards right, Larson, and she'll be lavishing you with money and gifts. She'll maybe even invite you in for a—"

"No-no-no," I said, cutting Bob off before he had time to expound on that thought. "Don't do any of those things!" I took off my apron, slapped it on the counter, and cast Bob a deprecatory look. The man was a gifted chef, but a total rogue as well. We had worked on tonight's menu together. Bob had pulled out all the stops, insisting on roast duck in a brandied cherry demi-glace with a side of butter pecan baked sweet potatoes and oven-roasted Brussel sprouts. Dessert would be the inn's signature cherry pie. Silvia Lumiere, cougar or not, was going to be dazzled by her first meal at the Cherry Orchard Inn. Not only was it important to Mom, Dad, and Grandma Jenn that she enjoy her stay, but I strongly felt that the fate of the inn depended on it.

"Okay, you two, enough. No more speculating on this mysterious young man, Erik. It's not our job to judge our guests. And you, Bob, just concentrate on dinner, okay? Come on," I said, pulling Erik out of the kitchen with me. "We have an important guest. Let's go and give her a warm Cherry Orchard Inn welcome."

Although the inn was nearly booked for the coming week, the wide veranda out front was unusually crowded. Cherry Cove was a small, close-knit community, and word had gone around that Silvia Lumiere was due to arrive for her annual summer visit. From the look of it, she was a popular visitor. The entire Cherry Cove Women's League had turned out with their husbands in tow, and a few of Dad's closest friends were there as well, enjoying pre-dinner drinks and nibbling hors d'oeuvres. Among this last group, I caught sight of a bright blond head looming above the crowd. His sun-bronzed face was bent in lively conversation. Somehow, in the whirlwind of activity over the last few days, I had forgotten Tate would be here; I had forgotten I'd asked him to come.

It was a little strange even to my own ears, but for the first time in my life, I'd finally figured out that I belonged in Cherry Cove. After years of trying to make a living in Chicago, I realized that I thrived when surrounded by family and friends, working at the place I loved most. But I wasn't certain Tate was my future anymore. And, quite frankly, it was too much to think about, especially now. I pushed all thoughts of the hunky man aside and redoubled my grip on Erik's arm, pulling him to the front steps of the inn with me. Because if he spied Tate, I knew he'd abandon me in a heartbeat.

We were just in time to see the huge white Cadillac Escalade, towing an equally huge white trailer, pull beneath the portico. I was too distracted by the sight to react to the elbow nudge in my side or the look of *I told you so*. The lady was a portrait painter, after all. She obviously needed a place to put her canvases, brushes and paints. I only hoped she wasn't planning on keeping them in her modest room.

The driver's door burst open and the young man Erik had described nearly to a tee ran to get the door for his passenger. I'd seen plenty of his type in Chicago, tall, pierced, thin, and dressed in a combination of clothes that could only be described as modern hippie. His shirt was blousy, the top buttons left undone to better display his bony chest and the handful of dangly necklaces he wore. His jeans were black, distressed and frayed in strategic places. And, yes, all the long brown hair had been pulled off his bearded face and fastened into a prickly man bun. The guy oozed hip: chill: artsy. But it was the portrait painter herself that I couldn't pull my eyes from.

Silvia Lumiere sat perched on her seat, framed in the blackness of the SUV. The moment the evening sun hit her, colors sprang to life—the silver-white of her short, stylish hair; the merry black eyes; the red lips and the vibrant silk wrap of a blue so pure it nearly hurt the eyes to look at it. I had lived in Chicago for six years and marveled that I'd never seen this woman—this plump, petite, pixy of a woman. As the young man helped her out of the car her eyes settled on me. I was genuinely smiling when I welcomed her to the inn, feeling that this small, lively woman just might be the real thing—the talisman that the Cherry Orchard Inn needed to overcome the stigma of death.

"You must be Whitney," she said, taking my hand. "Jani's told me all about you. You're far lovelier than she described. You look like that weather girl on that morning show. So pretty. My dear, you must allow me to paint you."

I didn't quite know what to say to all the flattery, but I didn't hate it. Ms. Lumiere flashed an impish grin and put a foot on the first step. It was a small foot, encased in a shimmering silver pump that matched her pixy-cut hair. She then turned to Erik.

"Fetch me a sour cherry martini, sugared rim and two cherries. Peter will have a fresh-pressed carrot juice with a splash—just a splash, now—of Worcestershire sauce."

Erik, suppressing a grin at this last order, gave a nod and was about to run off to the bar when Ms. Lumiere stopped him.

"And I want my luggage brought to my room immediately … immediately, do you hear? But not the green duffel bag. That will go in Peter's room. It should be next to mine. And there's quite a bit so you'll want to hurry. I suggest you use a luggage carrier."

Erik, clearly at a loss of what to do first, hesitated a bit too long. Peter, swooping in at the pause, dropped the keys to the Escalade in his hand.

"And, like, park the Lade in the way back, dude. Don't scratch it, and don't freakin' touch the trailer. I handle the trailer. Now, how 'bout those drinks, bro? The lady is parched."

The old Erik Larson would have laughed in the guy's face. The new Erik Larson did something even more terrifying. He simply replied, "Yes, sir," and then dashed off in the direction of the bar. A wave of relief washed through me, and, perhaps, a little welling of pride as well.

I turned my attention back to Ms. Lumiere. She was struggling to get up the front steps. It suddenly dawned on me that she was elderly and heavyset, all of it masked by a glittering facade and charismatic smile.

"I've been in the car too long, and the old legs aren't what they used to be," she breezily explained as she waved to her fans on the veranda. "Thank Heavens I'll be on the first floor."

My heart gave a silent, chest-crushing lurch. Two rooms! And on the first floor? Holy hand grenades, had I screwed up! I didn't have any rooms on the first floor. Although the inn wasn't quite full, all the rooms on the first floor had been booked for weeks. And there hadn't ever been any mention of a second room until now.

"Peter. Your arm," she demanded of her millennial hippie. I was about to take the other when Tate, appearing out of nowhere, beat me to it.

25

"Ms. Lumiere. Such a pleasure to see you back in Cherry Cove." His tone was personal and full of sincerity.

"Oh, Mr. Vander Hagen! What a pleasant surprise!" Her glossy black eyes narrowed in what one might term a coquettish manner as she added, "My, you're looking as fit and tan as ever."

Tate cast me a private wink, then turned to the painter. "And you're looking as lovely as ever. I see you've met Ms. Bloom. You couldn't be in any better hands. And wait until you taste her cherry baked goods. They're the best in Cherry Cove. Whitney's even won the coveted Gilded Cherry trophy this year for her pie." Tate, pouring on the charm, had whisked the lady up the front steps before she knew it.

"Look," he said, "here comes Mrs. Lind."

I looked up in time to see Grandma Jenn waltzing out the front doors. She was elegantly dressed in a long, shimmering skirt of light gray and had two sugar-rimmed, sour cherry martinis in her hand.

"Silvia!" she exclaimed and came forward to greet the portrait painter. "Welcome to the Cherry Orchard Inn, dear." Gran, ever the hostess, handed Silvia one of the sour cherry martinis. "And who's your charming young friend?"

Silvia took the drink and replied, "Peter McClellan, my new assistant."

"Oh, how wonderful it must be to have such a handsome young man at your beck and call. You'll be the envy of the women's league and the arts council to boot! Come along, Mr. McClellan, there are a lot of friends on the porch who are just dying to chat with your talented employer."

The moment they left for the veranda I turned to Tate.

"Thank you."

"That's why I'm here, Whit. For moral support, and to make sure the old girl succeeds in making a grand entrance. She's an artist. Mrs. Cushman told me they all like to have their egos stroked." This made me smile. Mrs. Cecilia Cushman was Tate's elderly housekeeper and the closest thing he had to a grandmother. She was in her late sixties and a hoot of a lady. Mrs. Cushman had quite recently moved from Tate's house by the marina to an abandoned yacht moored in one of his slips. The yacht was named the *Boondoggle II*. "And I have to wonder," Tate continued, "in a world of smart phones and selfies if she doesn't realize that her work is irrelevant."

"Irrelevant?" I stared at him. "Is that what you think? I don't think so at all. A portrait is not so much a picture as it is a work of art. It's as much about the subject as it is the painter's interpretation of it. Besides, a portrait doesn't fade with age, or disappear with your lost cell phone, or get hacked in the cloud and passed around the internet. It endures. Your grandchildren's grandchildren will look upon it and see you exactly as you were in the very space and time your portrait was painted."

He looked at me, a soft smile touching his lips. "I never thought about it that way before. But you're right. Maybe that's why she's a bit of a handful, because she believes she holds the power of immortality in her paintbrushes."

I returned the smile. "It's quite a power to wield. And here we are: you rent sailboats and slips to tourists while I wow them over with cherry baked goods. There's no immortality in that."

"No, but we make people happy, too. Ms. Lumiere, truth be told, usually makes people a bit miserable, but it's nothing you can't manage. Didn't Jani warn you?"

"Mom never said a thing," I confided. "I wish that she had. She was so overjoyed at the prospect of Silvia staying with us that it must have slipped her mind."

"Or, more likely, she didn't want to worry you."

"Well, I'm a little worried now. Silvia has one room and it's on the second floor. Hopefully I can find something suitable for Mr. McClellan." We were walking through the foyer to the front desk when I suddenly turned to Tate with an irrepressible grin. "Erik saw them in the car when they were driving up. He thought they were lovers."

"They probably are," he said. "Wouldn't put it past her. Last year she whispered to me during a rather public event that she wanted to paint me. I was flattered until I realized she meant in the nude. You may not believe it, but I do have my standards. The trick with Silvia, Whit, is that you don't give her everything she wants. Keep her on the second floor. She's perfectly capable of using the elevator. Give lover-boy the broom closet if you have to. Chances are good he's not going to be sleeping in there anyway."

"How can you say that?"

"Because I've been subjected to Silvia for the last five summers. I know what I'm talking about." He leaned over and gave me a kiss on the cheek. "We're having dinner tonight, babe. Remember? Save me a seat." He turned to go.

"Where ya going?"

"To help out a bro. Erik's got a mountain of luggage to move and I thought I'd give him a hand. Oh, and Whit, if that kid lasts the next week here with that woman, forgive him anything."

"Anything?" I frowned. "We're talking about Erik Larson here. A prodigy of teenage angst and underage partying."

"Okay." He relented with a dimpled grin. "Nearly anything."

Five

While Ms. Lumiere drank sour cherry martinis and mingled with her summertime friends on the veranda, Tate and Erik moved three carts of luggage to her room. Her trust in the Cherry Orchard Inn was implicit, and the pull of martinis and free hors d'oeuvres had been too great. While the alcohol flowed, and the guys were stacking luggage like cordwood in her room, I jumped behind the front desk with Margaret and scanned the inn's reservations. I was trying to find suitable accommodations for Mr. McClellan. Being a modest bed-and-breakfast, we only had ten guest rooms, and six of these were on the second floor. The good news was that our price-reduction rooms were booking fast; the bad news was that there was only one room available, and I hated to tie it up for the duration of the summer.

Erik materialized beside me and dropped a green duffle bag at my feet. "All done, boss. Mr. Vander Hagen's parking the Escalade and trailer. He said to tell you he'll meet you in the dining room."

"Thank you, Erik. But I'm going to need you to pick that thing up again." I handed him a room key. "Please take that to the Pine Suite."

His eyes flew wide. "Really? You know it's nowhere near Ms. Whatsherface's room, right?"

"Lumiere," I reminded him. "It's the only room we have. It's not next to hers, but it's on the second floor. It's the best I can do."

He gave a shrug and slung the large bag over his shoulder. Margaret and I exchanged a look as Erik headed for the grand staircase in the foyer. She shook her head. "It's like they always say, youth is wasted on the young. Oh dear, here she comes."

I looked up from the reservation computer. Silvia Lumiere was walking unsteadily toward me, another dark red martini in her hand.

"Point me in the direction of my room."

I came around the desk with her room keys in hand and gave her my brightest smile. "Ms. Lumiere, what a pleasure it is to have you with us for the summer. Your luggage has already been moved to your room. If there's anything else you need, please let us—"

"What?" she cried, looking at the painted key chain. "You have me in a room called the *Sailboat Suite*? And on the second floor!?"

I didn't know what I'd been expecting, but the screaming outrage took me by surprise. A moment ago, she had sparkled under the adoration of her friends and admirers. But the charming pixy had gone, swallowed, it appeared, by a diva-troll. A scathing tirade commenced. Didn't I know she had arthritis? Was I stupid or something? Could a human being possibly be more inconsiderate? Of course, she couldn't use the stairs! And elevators made her claustrophobic—even the ones that only serviced two floors.

Margaret, poor soul, had taken the original reservation. She very calmly reminded Silvia that she'd only booked one room, specifically requesting it be on the second floor because of the spectacular view. Ms. Lumiere shot her a look that would have knocked her off her feet had it been backed by anything other than bloodshot eyes. She then insisted that Margaret had gotten it all wrong and was obviously trying to cover her mistake with a lie. When we told her that there wasn't an available room on the first floor, she about flipped. I appeased her with the good news that we had found a room for her assistant. It was also on the second floor. However, when she learned that it wasn't right next to hers, she threatened to write a scathing review for the *Chicago Sun-Times*. What if she needed him in the middle of the night? Were we expecting her to walk all the way down the hall to fetch him? Margaret suggested she use a cell phone, and if that wasn't an option all she need do was ring the front desk. This helpful tip was met with open disgust. An establishment of our reputation should know better than to upset a guest, she reprimanded. She added a few choice lines before turning her black eyes on me with a malicious twinkle. I could see that she was prepared to take it further if she had to.

I hated the thought of lost revenue, but one had to know when to cut their losses. For Mom's sake as well as the inn's reputation, I offered Mr. McClellan's room free-of-charge for the duration of their stay.

"I guess that will just have to do," the painter said, and tottered off toward the elevator, careful not to spill her cocktail.

Tate had a glass of wine waiting for me at dinner. We were dining at our own private table. He had insisted. I suddenly realized, then, how great it was seeing both the wine and him sitting there. Although we had our differences, I couldn't deny that there was always something comforting about Tate—his kind smile, his ease of manner, the familiarity … the dimples. It was a big part of the reason I couldn't let go. That, and the fact that he was persistent.

"So," he began, staring at me over his wineglass, "now that you've met Silvia, what do you think?"

I glanced at the woman in question. She was sitting at the head of a large table, surrounded by her adoring friends, Mom, Dad and

Grandma Jenn among them. "What do I think?" I repeated and took a hefty sip from my own glass. "I think I want to strangle her. I want to like her," I told him honestly, "like I want to like a vicious bichon frise that bites me every time I try to pet it. Eventually you get bit so many times you give up. I'm being nice," I said to his questioning gaze. "Truly, I am. I'm even giving her a second room—on the house. And don't get me started about how poorly she treated Margaret."

"This, I believe, is what they call baptism by fire, Whit. You've only been managing the inn for a month and you've been saddled with the most difficult customer possible. Did I mention that she stiffed Erik after he brought all that luggage to her room, then turned and propositioned me, asking if I'd like to come back after dinner for a nightcap? Of course I said yes." He flashed his dimples.

"You had to," I said, playing along. "It's called taking one for the team. Maybe you can use your charm to woo her … or, better yet, take her out on your sailboat and toss her overboard. I'll take care of Erik."

"No need. I already have. Slipped him a couple of twenties for his efforts. And that woman's not stepping aboard the *Lusty Dutchman,* babe. I told you, I have my standards."

The duck in the cherry demi-glace was sublime, and yet Silvia, having eaten most of it, sent it back, stating that it was dry and gamey. An expertly grilled New York strip was brought out immediately in exchange for the duck, which seemed to please her better, although she couldn't keep from offering a few helpful pointers on the proper way to grill a steak to the chef via the waitress. I hoped the young woman had the foresight not to pass them along. It would never do to make an enemy of Chef Bob Bonaire.

Sunday the onus was on me. Well, Grandma Jenn and me. Since Mom had put us in charge of the high tea reception we were determined to make it the event of the summer. We'd been in the kitchen since five a.m. working on the food. Gran, having a passion for fancy finger-sized nibbles, headed up the savory treats, peeling hard-boiled eggs for her creamy egg salad, which was spread on ribbons of soft pumpernickel bread. She whipped up herbed butter for her delectable cucumber sandwiches on flattened farmhouse white bread, and shredded poached chicken for her scrumptious cherry chicken salad. This she served on soft King's Hawaiian dinner rolls.

While Gran worked on the sandwiches, I was busy preparing the mini desserts for the three-tiered plates. Classic lemon tarts were a must, as well as plump strawberries filled with sweet clotted cream. Other strawberries were dipped in chocolate and drizzled with a white chocolate flourish. I made little white cake squares covered in a smooth white gnash glaze. Although all the mini desserts were divine, my mini cherry scones with sour cherry drizzle were my favorite. I'd been perfecting the recipe for weeks until finally achieving a scone that combined the best of the British Isles with the taste of Door County. Like with Gran's award-winning cherry chicken salad, I used toasted pecan and dried tart cherries grown on our own orchard.

In the dining room Mom had worked a little magic of her own, transforming the tables into a vision of Victorian wonder. Each was covered with lacy white linen and adorned with a tall vase overflowing with gorgeous fat roses in shades of pink and white. Blue cornflowers and purple lilacs added splashes of color, while lily of the valley lent a certain nostalgic charm to the arrangements. The pretty china teapots and the delicate china cups and saucers completed the transformation. It was enough to make anybody feel special, including a diva artist like Silvia Lumiere.

"How do you put up with her?" I asked Grandma Jenn.

"Patience, dear, and a lot of flattery. Vain people demand it. But in Silvia's case I think you'll find it a worthwhile effort. She really does have quite an extraordinary gift," Gran added, slicing peeled cucumbers for her herbed cucumber sandwiches. "And she knows how to put on a show. Just wait. People will be hovering like flies to commission her for a portrait or a landscape. She has a knack for those too. But she can only take so many, you know. And people do love to watch her paint."

"So you're saying that I should just hold my tongue and keep kissing-up to her, even if I feel that she's taking us for a ride?"

Grandma Jenn's sky-blue eyes twinkled as she looked up from her finger sandwiches. "Think of her like a queen bee with a particularly sharp stinger. Drones will flock to her, but those drones must eat something. Keep Silvia on your good side, dear, and keep baking plenty of those delicious cherry treats of yours. Have fun with it. Set up a little Bloom 'n' Cherries! table on the lawn when she's painting and staff it with a couple of the high school waitresses. Don't be afraid to exploit Silvia's gifts, because you've already learned she's not afraid to exploit yours."

Bolstered by Gran's sage advice and her contagious optimism, I felt a little better about our difficult guest. The feeling continued when the French doors to the dining room were opened, revealing a throng of excited guests in their finest tea-toting attire. My spirits soared even higher when I saw my two best friends.

"Holy Victorian Splendor!" Hannah remarked, looking stunning in her mid-length floral dress and floppy wide brimmed hat. She ran her bright blue eyes over the dining room. "This place looks amazing. Jani's really outdone herself this time."

"It's a room meant to impress," Tay remarked, rocking a flapper-inspired ensemble that accented her chic red hair and large brown eyes. "So how's our celebrity?"

"Hopefully arriving soon. I'm told she likes to make an entrance."

"She does. Char does too," Tay informed us. "They should be here any minute. Last summer, Todd commissioned Silvia to paint their portrait as an engagement gift to Mom."

"How romantic," Hannah quipped teasingly.

"Isn't it just?" Tay agreed with a quick lift of her brow that held a hint of disgust. "Anyhow, they're both geeking out because Silvia's bringing it here. She likes to unveil all her commissions from the summer before in front of her adoring public." A mischievous look came to her eyes as she added, "Can't wait to see the masterpiece I've been referring to all year as *Mother and Son*. Hope it doesn't disappoint." Her grin was deliciously diabolical. It faded the moment she remarked, "Hey, where are the easels?"

"What?" A flash of dread shot through me.

"The easels. You know, those things that prop up the paintings?"

My jaw dangled a moment before re-engaging. "She never mentioned anything about easels."

"Well, if she never said anything, then you're off the hook."

"That's not the way things work with Ms. Lumiere," I told them, ushering my friends to their seats. "She doesn't tell, she just expects. Hopefully she's put her assistant in charge of the easels. But just in case I better go check. I'll join you in a minute."

I turned to go, then stopped as a tall, slender, immaculately dressed older woman stood before the podium, beaming from ear to ear.

"Ladies and Gentlemen, my name is Alexa Livingstone, president of the Cherry Country Arts Council. Today I have the great privilege of introducing my long-time friend and Cherry Coves' favorite summer artist in residence, Ms. Silvia Lumiere."

Six

Silvia Lumiere did know how to make an entrance, I have to give her that. She waltzed into the crowded room on the arm of her assistant, dressed from head to toe in black with a shimmering silver wrap draped around her shoulders. It set off her luminous, white pixy hair and matched her sparkly slippers. She appeared a fashion-forward superhero for the elderly, and, judging from the looks on the mesmerized faces, that's apparently what she was. Peter McClellan, for his part, had brushed out his man bun of the night before, letting his magnificent mane of brown hair tumble down his back in silken waves. He was wearing an embroidered tunic over white baggy pants, and sandals on his feet. His face, in contrast to Silvia's bubbling rapture, appeared bored, his eyes gentle yet distant. I was staring at the pair of them when an elbow in my ribs demanded my attention.

"Who's the hot Jesus," Hannah whispered.

"What? Oh, that's Peter McClellan, Silvia's assistant." I frowned. "The fact you think he's hot is a little disturbing."

Hannah, ignoring my mild disgust, brightened. "So he'll be here for the summer?"

Tay, grinning from ear to ear, nodded. "He's got 'yoga guy' written all over him, doesn't he? I bet he's as bendy as you are, Hannah."

"He does look bendy," she mused, staring at the man in question. "And doesn't HJ just ooze sexual enlightenment? I'm calling him HJ now because Whit finds Hot Jesus offensive." She rolled her eyes at Tay, who was giggling.

"Can we just call him Peter?"

"You can," she said. "But I call dibs. You all heard it. You already have Tate," she continued. "Besides, rumor on the street has it that you've been making early morning visits to the police station as well." Her weighted look was beyond insinuating. "Two men should be enough for you."

"He's my jogging buddy," I hiss-whispered.

"How's that going?" Tay, with elbows on the table and chin plopped between her hands, held me in a rapt, questioning gaze.

"Truthfully, not very well. I was only able to make it out twice. I've been too busy to think about running the last few days."

"Or Jack?" she teased. "I don't believe that for a moment. And what about Tate? Mrs. Cushman over there"—she gestured to Tate's housekeeper, who was sitting with Grandma Jenn—"was just telling me how happy he's been since you've moved back home. Said you've been to his house a time or two but haven't yet set foot on the *Lusty Dutchman*." She raised an accusatory eyebrow at this.

The Lusty Dutchman was Tate's sailboat and his favorite make-out spot. That boat held a lot of memories. I wasn't ready to climb aboard it just yet. I banished the thought and waved to Mrs. Cushman. "Dear Mrs. Cushman. I'm surprised she's noticed now that she lives aboard that fancy yacht. But again, I've been so busy with all the baking and trying to get a handle on running this place that I don't even have time to give men, or romance, a serious thought. And now with Ms. Lumiere

37

staying here, it's likely to get worse before it gets better. My plan is to just forget about men for a while and concentrate on my career for the time being. I'm good at that. I've had plenty of practice. Besides, what we really should be focusing on is Tay and her knight in shining armor. How is your hunky warrior and his jousting?" I asked, glad to be changing the subject.

Tay grinned. "I went to the Ren fair yesterday, and it was awesome. I was propositioned by a dwarf dressed as a jester and pinched in the keister by the king. And Lance wasn't slain. He broke three lances."

Hannah wrinkled her nose. "That sounds tragic. Is he okay?"

"He's fine. And that's a great thing … not the proposition or the pinch," Tay clarified with an eye roll. "Unless you're into that sort of thing. But breaking a lance on your opponent is how a jouster scores points. Surprisingly, he's doing really well this year. Must be that new suit of armor, although he doesn't wear it for jousting. It's too fancy and way too expensive, but in an odd sort of way it gives him more confidence. And that reminds me. You two both promised you'd come with me to watch Lance joust. There's to be a tournament in three weeks. It's on a Sunday, which means both of you can come. No excuses. And bring dates … unless you want to be pinched by medieval creepers."

"We're coming!" Hannah declared, and grabbed my hand with more enthusiasm than I felt. "And I know who I'm bringing. I have three weeks to convince him. Who are you going to bring, Whit?" Her look had more of a challenge about it than a mere question. Tay leaned forward, curiosity gripping her as well. The trouble was I knew who I wanted to bring. His face sprang to mind, but I pushed the thought aside. I feared he would refuse the invitation, or worse, he would agree and Tate would find out. While all this played out in my head and my friends, delighting in my inner turmoil, eagerly awaited an answer, I was thankfully spared. Silvia had arrived at the podium.

"What a lovely reception," she began, gracing the audience with her impish, pixy smile. "And I can't get over the transformation of this tired old restaurant into this picture of Victorian splendor. We have three generations of the lovely Bloom women to thank for that." This was followed by a round of applause. I was clapping, too, until I happened to spy Bob Bonaire sitting at one of the far tables. He wasn't clapping, or smiling. Although cloaked in a compliment, the slight to his restaurant was something he wasn't about to ignore. Silvia, however, breezed right past it until finally coming to her big announcement. After introducing her new assistant, Peter McClellan, a promising young artist in his own right, she explained that this year she and Peter were going to personally deliver last summer's commissioned portraits and hold private unveiling ceremonies for the families.

Applause erupted, and I can honestly say that no one was more relieved to hear this than I was. It meant that Silvia hadn't needed the easels after all. I was off the hook, so to speak. She then announced that she would be taking new commissions for next year, limiting the number to twelve. They were on a first-come-first-serve basis. Peter would be handling the orders and schedule the sittings.

"Did you hear that?" It was Char. She and Todd had joined us shortly after Silvia had made her appearance. "She's coming to the house for a private unveiling! You girls have to come too. We'll have hors d'oeuvres, champagne and make an event of it."

"Wouldn't miss it for the world," I said, and cast Tay a private wink, thinking of the grand portrait lovingly dubbed *Mother and Son*.

The high tea reception was going along nicely. The guests staying at the inn seemed to be enjoying the event as much as Silvia's local admirers were, and of these there were plenty. Mom, Grandma Jenn and their friends from the Cherry Cove Women's League held their own against an impressive showing from the larger and slightly pretentious members of the Cherry Country Arts Council. I wasn't as familiar with these folks, mostly because only one of them lived in Cherry Cove, Gran's nemesis and the woman I shared the Gilded Cherry trophy with, Edna Baker. The rest of the arts council resided all over the peninsula, but it was just my luck that every one of them was familiar with Tay and her shop, Cheery Pickers. Hannah's yoga classes had attracted more than a few members as well.

"So who's the middle-aged man with her now?" I asked, noting a man dressed in a blazer and jeans bending close to Silvia. He was whispering something in her ear, making her giggle like a school girl.

"That's Fred Beauchamp," Tay informed me. "He's a potter. Has a studio near Gill's Rock, and he's quite the charmer. I sell some of his pottery at the store. He does exceptional work."

"And has been married four times," Hannah added. "Rumor has it that he means to make Ms. Lumiere number five."

I thought about that a minute, recalling what Tate had told me earlier about Silvia going after younger men and his suspicion of Peter McClellan. Fred Beauchamp, although not young, was definitely younger than Silvia. "I guess Mr. Beauchamp's going to be a frequent visitor at the inn. I'll have to introduce myself."

"Alexa Livingstone will be here a lot too," Hannah continued, setting down her tea cup. She gestured to the president of the arts council. "She's in my nine a.m. yoga class at the studio. Which reminds me, I need to talk to you about hosting a yoga class here … a goat yoga class. Jenn called me the other day and thought it would be a fun activity for the inn to host. I do too."

"Excellent idea!" Char exclaimed, looking totally enchanted. "It's all the rage on YouTube."

I'm sorry to say that I still found the notion more puzzling than enchanting. "I have no idea what goat yoga might be, and as far as I know you don't even own goats."

Hannah shrugged. "Minor issue. I can just rent them. Anyhow, back to Alexa. She moved up here five years ago and shortly thereafter became the president of the arts council. That's impressive, given all the local artists who'd love that title."

Char leaned across the table. "She also commissioned a portrait from Silvia last summer. Her sitting was before ours. Isn't that right, darling?"

"Absolutely," Todd answered, a little too quickly. He looked up, his large hazel eyes wide and clueless. Todd always reminded me of a nerdier version of an eighties teen movie bad boy—with his preppy attire, country club looks and attitude, and fluffy blond hair that was chronically a little too long. It was probably why Char was attracted to him, since she'd lived and partied in the eighties. Todd, meanwhile, was born in the late eighties. He was thirty-two and a full-blown millennial.

He now stopped playing Angry Birds on his phone and shoved it into his pocket. Then, placing a hand over Char's, he added, "The White Lady. That's what we called her. Remember, hon?" Tay's mom stared doe-eyed at her fiancé and nodded. "Get this," Todd continued, shifting his attention to Tay. "She wanted an outdoor portrait, like we did, with the lake in the background. But Alexa chose to stand beside the trunk of a knotty old tree, and she was wearing this outdated white gown from, like, the sixties or seventies. Might have looked virginal on a younger woman, but on Alexa it looked positively haunting." He manufactured a shiver for comedic effect.

"Maybe that was the point of it," Tay remarked. "A portrait by Silvia isn't cheap. Maybe old Alexa wanted it done to spite her daughter. I hear she's loaded, and I met her daughter once. Wouldn't it be the ultimate payback to have a creepy portrait painted of yourself, then state in your will that in order to inherit, the portrait must be hung in a place of prominence in the inheritor's house? Every time Alexa's spoiled-rotten daughter would walk past it, she'd feel the cold, dead eyes of her mother judging her from beyond the grave."

"Oh, for cripes' sake, Tay," Todd admonished. "That's disgusting."

"You're engaged to my mom and you think *that's* disgusting?" Tay genuinely liked Todd, but she was never one to miss an opportunity to torque him up a bit. They fought like brother and sister, which was slightly disturbing when, in reality, they were about to become stepfather and stepdaughter. "*My story's* funny, Todd," Tay went on. "*You're* disgusting."

"All right, you two," Char broke in. "Enough."

The conversation was once again brought under control. After a few more colorful descriptions of the local artists, I excused myself and went to check on Silvia. Hannah excused herself as well, but it wasn't to Silvia she was heading. Nope, my tea-besotted friend headed straight for the table where Peter McClellan was taking orders for Silvia's next round of commissions.

Seven

It was challenging enough for the owner of an inn to see to the needs of all their paying guests, but with a customer as vocal and demanding as Silvia Lumiere, something had to give. Unfortunately, over the first few weeks of her stay I wasn't the only one she harassed. Even more unsettling than our celebrity guest was the pool the staff had going in the kitchen. They were placing bets on who would crack first: Erik Larson, Bob Bonaire, or me.

After the success of the high tea, I honestly thought Silvia would settle down and be civil. After all, Mom had outdone herself for the event, and Silvia had been the center of attention. The dozen new commissions she'd put up for sale had sold out in a matter of minutes, and all her private unveilings had been scheduled and scattered out over the summer. This, I surmised, was another attempt to build drama and keep the air of excitement going. Silvia had openly praised Grandma Jenn for her delicious tea sandwiches and couldn't stop raving about my cherry scones. Of course this pleased me to no end. I took great pride in our cherry orchard and inn, but most especially in the cherry-inspired baked goods I had worked so hard to perfect while living in Chicago. The inn's bakery, Bloom 'n' Cherries!, was now booming. Cherry pies had always been a hot seller, but now, thanks to Silvia and the praise she'd lavished on my cherry scones over the first few weeks of her stay, we couldn't keep enough on the shelves. This was partially due to the fact that I'd taken Gran's advice, as well as to Dad's inspired gazebo.

The gazebo sat on the back lawn and offered a spectacular view of the Bay of Green Bay, an arm of Lake Michigan on the west coast of the Door Peninsula, and also the smaller, picturesque Cherry Cove Bay. Quaint white buildings, a lofty church spire, and the rustic log cabins of the village dotted the half-moon shoreline. The inn, built on the opposite shore and sitting on a gentle rise, had one of the best views in all of Cherry Cove, and Silvia Lumiere knew it.

On the days Silvia painted outside, a gallery of chairs was set up around the gazebo. There was a lazy sort of charm in watching a painter at work, whether it be on a landscape or with a new client during a siting, and the seats were always filled. Most who came to watch were Silvia's fans from the artist community, but I was happy to note that quite a few guests were enjoying the experience as well. The advertiser in me couldn't help but drum up a little more business on those days. Gran had planted the seed and I ran with it, setting up a little stand that sold coffee, tea, lemonade, and cherry scones. It was a simple stand, the kind that only required being polite and making change. Since the inn was getting busier than ever and the waitresses were already overworked, I decided to hand the stand over to Erik Larson. The boy was dependable, and also charmed by the idea of earning extra money.

"Whitney, dear, bring me one of those immediately!" demanded Silvia the moment she spied me carrying a tray of fresh scones out to Erik. "And don't be mean with the lemon curd and clotted cream. My blood sugar's dipping. And tell that lazy ingrate of yours that my coffee's gone cold. The brute just sits there, flirting with the waitresses."

I had to admit, this wasn't far off the mark for Erik. Especially if Kenna was working.

"He hasn't even bothered to refresh my mug," the painter continued from her chair under the gazebo for all to hear. "This may be one of the most beautiful inns I have ever had the pleasure of staying at, but the help leaves something to be desired." She lifted her head and glared down her nose in the direction of the boy through her zebra-striped glasses. All heads turned in our direction.

"That old dried-out sack of paintbrushes needs a lesson in manners," Erik growled under his breath the moment I set the tray down on the table. I cast him a stern, watch-your-step look.

"What?" he said defensively. "It's the truth. She's had three scones already and insists she doesn't have to pay. And it's not like I have a pot here that I can just pick up and carry over to her easel. It's a self-serve push-pot! It's for all my customers. I'm not going to upset the flow of business by picking it up and lugging it over there for that dolled-up hag at her easel."

"Enough with the names, Erik. It's not appropriate to sink to her level. And did you ever think about picking up her mug, dumping out the cold coffee and refilling it?"

"Why should we treat her any differently than we treat the other guests? If I let that nasty woman dump out her cold coffee and get a refill at no charge, I have to let everyone else do the same. Everyone staying here already gets complimentary breakfast with all the coffee they can drink, but breakfast is over. This is a stand. It's a separate business, Ms. Bloom. My customers are actually tipping me for the service." He gestured to a large, brightly painted jar on the table that was hard to miss. "And most of that lot aren't staying here anyhow."

"That's a very good point," I said, mildly impressed with Erik's burgeoning business acumen. I loaded a fresh scone onto a paper plate and, mustering a determined look, told him, "I'll handle this."

I honestly thought that I could. But when I explained to Silvia that after breakfast the scones were not complimentary and that she would have to pay for them, she threw a fit. It didn't matter that we were in front of her coffee-sipping, scone-nibbling admirers. If anything, it drove her on, inspiring her to fling such phrases as "overpriced rubbish" and "glaring lack of Midwestern hospitality" and, worst of all, "shoddy biscuits stuffed with subpar cherries."

The insults not only stung me, but also shamed me. My face grew hot and I had to bite my tongue. If I didn't I feared I would snap. My only recourse was to leave the painter with another complimentary scone with all the fixings and a fresh cup of coffee.

"Whitney, isn't it?"

I was nearly on the patio when the voice stopped me.

"Alexa Livingstone." The Cherry Country Arts Council president extended her hand. "I was at the high tea you threw in Silvia's honor."

I shook her proffered hand, noting she'd come alone. I had seen this handsome woman from across the room, but up close I could tell that her aging face had been given a youthful pinch from a clever plastic surgeon. Ms. Livingstone's lips were a little too plump, her smile genuine but stiff. And her brown eyes had a perpetually startled appearance in their wrinkle-free sockets. But the bone structure beneath was good. I assumed she'd been a model from her tall, lean frame and designer clothing. Her lustrous brown hair, cut and colored to compliment the long shape of her face, also spoke of a woman who prided herself on her looks. Alexa took good care of herself, yet judging from the sagging neck skin, I put her close to Silvia's own age.

"She's a trying woman," Alexa began in a distinctly Chicago accent. She waved a beringed hand nonchalantly. "Her little eccentricities can take a rather nasty turn. We've all been in your shoes at one time or another. What I came to tell you is how thankful we all are that you handled the situation like a professional. There's nothing to be ashamed of, Ms. Bloom. Silvia's meanness is only surpassed by her talent, and she's extraordinarily mean."

"Implying that her talent is even more extraordinary?" I raised a skeptical brow at this.

"Yes," she said, unflinchingly. "Especially in a backwater like Cherry Cove. Her technique is remarkable. Her use of shadow and light is sublime. And wait until you see one of her finished portraits. You'll understand what I'm trying to tell you then."

"What exactly are you trying to tell me?"

A forced smile rippled across her unnaturally taut face, an act reminiscent of a wave hitting a seawall. "Quite simply," she began, "that we at the arts council feel it's imperative we do nothing to lose Silvia Lumiere. An artist of her talent could summer anywhere they pleased, and yet she has chosen to come here. Regardless of her demanding ways, she must be treated with the respect her talent deserves. We owe that much to the community." Alexa paused. "I can tell that you don't like this idea."

"Honestly, no. I'm partial to the Golden Rule myself. You know, treat others as you would like to be treated? I don't believe rudeness should get a pass because of talent."

"But you are not an artist, Ms. Bloom." This was stated matter-of-factly and with a smack of condescension as well.

For some reason her presumption rankled me. "Not an artist?" I retorted and crossed my arms. "Some might argue that I am. Although my medium isn't as traditional as paint and clay. I work in cherries."

"That's baking, not art."

I exhaled a bit forcefully. "All right, look. We're all going out of our way here to treat that woman like a queen, and for our efforts she's stomping all over us like secondhand carpet. And she's under some misguided impression that the Cherry Orchard Inn is an all-inclusive resort, which we're not. We're strictly a bed-and-breakfast establishment here. But that doesn't stop her from ordering dinner every night, eating most of it, and then sending it back to the kitchen with scathing remarks only to demand another dinner—on the house! I've already given her a second room for Mr. McClellan at no extra cost—"

During my tirade, Alexa was fumbling with her purse. "I'll pay you for whatever she eats," she cut in. "Send me the bill."

"No," I blurted, placing a hand over hers. "What I mean is, that's very kind of you but not necessary. Honestly, I don't understand why you'd go to all this trouble for some ungrateful woman?"

"Let me put it to you this way. In the artist community, that woman is a superstar. She's the equivalent of an A-list actor. She could spend her summers anywhere she wishes, but she's chosen us; she's chosen Cherry Cove. Silvia is willing to paint our portraits and let us watch her stellar technique. In return our community is enriched, our reputation gains prestige. You're new here. Your mother obviously never told you, but Silvia Lumiere is the one guest that does get a pass on bad behavior. Really, Ms. Bloom, it's for the greater good."

Eight

For the greater good. I was still trying to wrap my head around that concept, and the fact that nearly every member of the Cherry Country Arts Council willingly allowed Silvia Lumiere to bully them, when Jack stopped by the inn. It was a Wednesday morning two weeks after Silvia's arrival. I was manning the Bloom 'n' Cherries! bakery counter and felt a welling of guilt at the sight of him. I hadn't met him for a downhill run since our demanding painter had arrived. Jack was checking in to see how things were going and, of course, to eat one of my cherry scones, having heard so much about them.

I assured him I was fine and teased, "You're finally giving up your donut habit for my cherry scones. Welcome to the club." I grinned and placed an extra scone in the bag for MacDuff, who was waiting in the car.

Jack, looking adorably smug, said, "Really? Does this look like the body of a donut-eating cop?"

I gave his well-fitting uniform the once-over. No, it certainly did not, I thought, and consciously refrained from licking my lips. Jack cleared his throat. Dangit! I had stared too long. What the heck was I doing? "You hide it well," I remarked, covering my guffaw.

"Only because I run. The only reason I'm here now is because word on the street is, your scones are to die for. You know my kryptonite."

"Cherry pastry, I believe, especially the type pushed on you by kindly old ladies."

"And young ladies as well. We've missed you," he added, all the playful flirtation leaving his voice. "Every time we come to the hill, MacDuff dashes off in search of you. Poor thing can't figure out where you're hiding."

"Here, I'm afraid. I'm sorry, Jack."

"It's that Lumiere woman, isn't it?" His soft, honey-colored gaze held mine. "Every summer she's been coming here it's the same story. She always manages to make life a living hell for some poor soul."

"Thanks for the warning."

"Surely not you?" he said, picking up on my sarcasm. When I didn't reply he pursed his lips, looking genuinely concerned. "Whit, that's not good."

"Oh, on the contrary, it's for the greater good, or so I'm told by the Cherry Country Arts Council. After all, the customer's always right. Right?" I was feeling a little giddy as I launched into a hushed tirade. Lack of sleep and a waking nightmare in the form of Silvia Lumiere was beginning to unhinge me. "Nothing's ever good enough for her," I hiss-whispered, leaning across the counter so only he could hear. "Every dinner she's ordered she's sent back. Every morning there's a new complaint about her room. She's accused the housekeepers of stealing her paints and demands repayment for what's gone missing from her room, never thinking that her assistant might have used them up by mixing her colors for her. She can't manage the stairs, and when her overworked assistant isn't available to hold her hand on the

50

elevator she insists Erik takes his place—all because she's afraid of elevators and refuses to use a cane or a walker."

I paused for a breath, then continued. "Sometimes it's that potter friend of hers, Fred Beauchamp, who escorts her to her room. He fawns all over her. It's disgusting. But I tell you, she's just humoring him. Anyhow, the moment Fred leaves, Silvia orders room service."

I threw a hand in the air. "She knows the kitchen's closed, but that doesn't stop her. Since she demands that Erik deliver it, I've gotten in the habit of making up either a charcuterie board or a plate of cherry scones with lemon curd and clotted cream. And she always orders a bottle of wine." I stared at Jack a moment to make my point.

"And she never signs for it, of course. And heaven forbid she actually tips that poor kid. I seriously doubt she'll even pay her bill when all is said and done. And she's terrible to that boy, Jack, calling him an ingrate one minute and pinching his behind the next like an old creeper. Erik's on the verge of quitting, and I don't blame him. For his sake I should have never hired him back. The only reprieve we get is a few precious hours on the weekends. And we deserve those! That's when her assistant loads up the trailer and whisks her away on her unveilings. She makes such a big production of it all... as if she wants everyone to be awed by her talent. The moment we see her leave we all want to lock the doors behind her and catch our breath, but we can't. We have a lot of guests arriving on the weekends. I tell you, Jack, we're all walking on eggshells here. Honestly, I don't know if I'm going to last until the end of the summer. A few more weeks of this and I'm going to strangle the old sack of paintbrushes myself," I declared, borrowing Erik's spiteful pet name for our guest.

"Jesus, Whit," Jack breathed, sweeping a nervous eye around the room. Other than a few couples eating before the fireplace in the breakfast room we were alone. "Don't say that, okay?"

"Oh, for the love of Pete, Jack! It's not like I'm going to do it or anything. It's only a fantasy—one I've been harboring ever since *that woman* arrived."

Jack, blanching, held up a cautioning hand. "Whit, seriously, you're in danger of becoming unhinged. I know the signs. I saw plenty of it in Milwaukee. Too much stress coupled with too little sleep and a person can snap. And snapping's never good. Dear Lord, you can't even sneak away for a morning run, or an hour of yoga with Hannah. I know, because she's told me."

I crossed my arms on the counter and hung my tired head. "My baking schedule's ramped up. As hard as it is to admit, Silvia Lumiere is good for business."

"That may be, but what you really need is a day off."

The moment Jack mentioned it, I perked up. Call it lack of sleep. Call it impulsivity. Call it totally turned on by his long, lean-muscled legs. Whatever it was I was driven to blurt out, "I do have one. This Sunday, in fact. Hannah and I are going to the Renaissance fair with Tay. Lance is jousting in a tournament."

Jack raised a ruddy brow. "Sounds fun."

"Come with me!"

The invitation was a shock to us both, and I silently cringed as he paused, giving my impulsive request more serious thought than it deserved. He was still thinking when Hannah came bounding around the corner from the lobby, dressed in her yoga clothes with her rolled up yoga mat under her arm. Beneath the long, light blonde hair, her pretty face was flushed with exertion.

"Hey." She smiled in greeting, her blue eyes shining even brighter due to the intense color of her cheeks.

Jack did a double take. "What the heck are you doing here?"

"Trying to steal Silvia's boy toy," I remarked, grinning at Hannah.

"Hardly." Her breezy laugh fooled no one.

"Peter McClellan," I told Jack. "Silvia's assistant. Have you met him?" Apparently, he hadn't.

"And he's not her boy toy," Hannah said with a mild air of disapproval. "More like an indentured servant if you ask me. But he handles the arrangement as best he can. He's very resourceful." Her brow wiggled as she leaned against the counter. She plucked a scone bite from the sample plate and popped it in her mouth. A dreamy look crossed her pretty face, compelling her to add, "He's a sensitive soul—a real deep thinker with strong, sensual hands and a very creative mind."

"Who's perfectly fine with the fact that he's being kept by an old lady," I added.

"Smart move for a starving artist." Jack grinned. "So what were you doing with him?"

"Giving him a private morning yoga class by the lake." Hannah's grin was positively impish, and highly inappropriate, indicating that a wee bit more than yoga had taken place this morning on the beach.

Jack and I exchanged a look, after which he said, "This guy must be something if you've come all this way to give him a private yoga class."

"He is, which reminds me, Whit. Jenn wanted me to let you know that we're hosting our first goat yoga class on the lawn Friday morning."

"You're having that here?" Jack questioned.

I shrugged in defeat. "Why not? We've already got a painter on the lawn. What's the harm in adding another spectacle?"

"Nothing,' Jack said, an odd smile touching his lips. "Only I doubt Hannah's told you that she's borrowing Thing One and Thing Two for the class."

"What?" I cried and shot Hannah a look. "You're using those little hellions?"

"Relax, Whit. They're adorable little creatures. The serenity of the setting will be good for them and precisely what they need. And they're not afraid to engage. Peter thinks it will be quite freeing, for all parties involved."

"I'll bet he does," Jack concurred with a look of mild concern. "And speaking of Peter, be careful, Hannah. If I know anything about Ms. Lumiere it's that she can be very possessive of her things, her assistant included."

Hannah pooh-poohed the warning. "He's not her thing, Jack, just an employee. And he's going to try to come with us to the fair on Sunday. You're coming too, right?"

"Yeah. Of course," he said, which I believed surprised us both. A thoughtful smile came to his lips as he took his pastry bag off the counter. "Wouldn't miss it for the world."

"Good. Whit's probably already told you that we're meeting here at eight. She's driving. And if we're real nice to her she's even threatened to provide some of her delectable cherry baked goods for the trip. Oh, and come in your best medieval attire. We're all dressing up for the occasion."

"Sounds entertaining. And good luck Friday. The kids are really looking forward to their field trip to the Cherry Orchard Inn."

Nine

riday morning, after a short night's sleep, a long pre-dawn bout of furious baking, and a busy morning shift at the bakery counter of Bloom 'n' Cherries!, I was beginning to have my doubts about Sunday's outing. It was sheer lunacy, but I honestly didn't know if I was ready to spend the entire day in Jack's company. Oh sure, I wanted too, but there was still the problem of Tate. If he got wind that we were all going he'd insist on coming too. And that would be a disaster. Not only would it be awkward for all parties involved, but Jack and Tate would be putting their bromance to the test. One could only guess what that might mean at a Renaissance fair.

No, my plate was already full to bursting. The frenetic pace of the inn was really beginning to wear on me, making me believe that Jack might have been right. I needed a day off or I'd snap. But the staff was already overworked, and who else was there to handle the problem of our celebrity guest? Grandma Jenn was semi-retired and preferred to use her talents in the kitchen. Mom was our social chairman and event planner and was already spread very thinly between her duties at the inn, the orchard, the Cherry Cove Women's League, and the

Chamber of Commerce, not to mention the demands of being married to Dad. She was often on her own planet. Therefore, it came as no surprise when she popped into the kitchen while I was glazing three trays of warm cherry scones and demanded I appear on the back lawn at five p.m., washed, dressed and wearing some outfit laid out on my bed. I had no idea what that was about, and, honestly, I was too tired to care.

After a long morning of baking I went out to the lawn to make sure Silvia had all she needed to begin her morning painting. The chairs had been set up near the gazebo and Erik was already manning the stand, arranging the plates, silverware and mugs for easier self-service.

"Geez, Ms. Bloom," he remarked upon seeing me. "Sleep much? You look like you could use some serious caffeinating yourself." I was about to demure when he handed me a mug full of hot black coffee.

"Dear Lord, this smells like heaven," I mumbled and took a good whiff. I didn't even bother to protest when he placed a plate in my hand. The scone, surrounded by a spoonful of lemon curd and a dollop of clotted cream, looked delicious, reminding me that I hadn't eaten a thing all morning.

"Go ahead," he said, directing me with his head to the patio. "Take a load off. I've got it from here."

I was on the patio finishing my coffee and contemplating basking in the glorious sunshine all day, when Hannah appeared on the lawn. She was leading Jack's two little goats. A sizable class of twelve followed, including Tay and her mom, Mrs. Cushman, Edna Baker, Ingrid MacLaren and Peter McClellan along with a handful of brave guests. Mom and Grandma Jenn, dressed in their brightly colored yoga outfits and carrying a tub full of yoga mats, brought up the rear.

The moment Tay saw me she veered from the group and came over to join me on the patio.

"How's she doing that?" I marveled, gesturing to Hannah. The goats were following her and behaving remarkably well.

"Bribery, of course," Tay remarked, pointing to the bucket Hannah was carrying. "It's full of sliced carrots. Aren't you going to join us?"

I had just eaten a cherry scone washed down with two mugs of black coffee. I wasn't about to do yoga with goats, no matter how bizarre it sounded. In fact, watching the yoga-pant-clad menagerie heading to a quiet spot near the lake, I felt the whole idea was mad. I looked at Tay. "I just ate a scone. I'm going to have to take a pass on this one."

She grinned. "That's a great excuse. I think I'll grab one of those as well and join you."

While Tay and I ate scones and chatted about men, Renaissance fairs, and why it was imperative she keep our outing on Sunday from Tate, it became obvious that Ms. Lumiere wasn't too pleased about the competition unfolding on the other side of the lawn. The rapt attention of her loyal following was waning as laughter and joyous goat-screams caused heads to swivel. And who could blame them? It was quite the spectacle.

Tay and I had never laughed so hard in our lives as we watched Hannah conduct a yoga class while Thing One and Thing Two pranced and bounded around and on top of the bodies on the mats. Their curiosity was endearing, especially when rewarded with a carrot for thrusting a velvety nose in the face of an unsuspecting yogi doing a downward dog or jumping on the back of a person in plank.

As all food-motivated creatures do, they caught on quickly. Bodies crashed to the mats in fits of giggles. Cloven hooves frolicked on Lycra-covered flesh. Laughter inspired chaos, and everyone was having a great time … until the treats ran out. That's when Jack's goats really showed their true colors.

Peter McClellan, as flexible as we thought him to be, was displaying an impressive skill on the mat and didn't flinch when Thing One landed on his back. However, when no carrot was forthcoming the goat decided to eat Peter's man bun. The neatly coiled hair was chomped with such gusto that Peter yelped and crashed on the mat. Thing Two took umbrage with Char's backside when she was in downward dog. That's when the stubby horns, swaddled in tape for the event, were employed.

Tay was laughing so hard she could barely breathe. "Oh my God, that goat just … butted my mom's butt! Did you see that?" I did but was laughing so hard all I could do was nod. "Knocked her to the mat! A most undignified way to get out of that pose. And look," she continued, stifling her giggles. "Char does not look pleased."

I stopped wheezing long enough to remark, "It's the risk you run whenever goats are involved."

The laughter was contagious. Even Char had succumbed to it when Thing Two bounced off after his next victim. In fact, I was having such a great time with Tay, watching our friend conduct her first-ever goat yoga class, that I had nearly forgotten about all the pressure I'd been under since Silvia arrived. It all came flooding back, however, the moment the goats decided to abandon the class. Hannah yelled out to us in warning, but it was too late. The goats had already smelled the cherry scones.

Tay and I jumped to our feet and tried to head them off before they reached the stand, but the little creatures moved like ninjas on

crack. We tried to warn Erik until we realized that he was more interested in recording the unfolding chaos on his iPhone than stopping it.

"Put that damn thing down and help us!" I cried, which he eventually did, but not before the scones had been reduced to crumbs and
every coffee mug sported hoofprints. The goats themselves evaded
capture. They took off again, this time heading for Silvia and her
easel.

Silvia had been so put-out by the boisterous yoga class that Fred
Beauchamp gave her a pair of noise-canceling headphones. What had
probably been a romantic gesture on his part was now a threat to the
woman's health. She had her back turned to the oncoming goats, con-
centrating instead on a stunning landscape of Cherry Cove Bay. All
warning cries fell on deaf ears. Silvia, oblivious, kept painting.

Her admirers, taking action, began leaping from their chairs, attempting to stop what was certain to be a calamity. Jack's goats, master escape artists, continued bounding through the throng of bodies
desperately trying to grab a pert tail or spindly leg. Thing One was
finally apprehended by Inga MacLaren, Jack's mom. Thing Two, however, had scrambled free of potential captors. He was the scrappier of
the two, a little alpha-male as well, and was determined to rattle Silvia's masterpiece. With horns lowered, he charged.

Silvia turned, saw the goat, and screamed.

Thing Two, undeterred, leapt for the painted canvas.

A collective gasp rose from the crowd of onlookers as Fred Beauchamp, embarking on another chivalrous gesture, also leapt. Man and
beast collided in midair. They also collided with Silvia. All three fell to
the ground with a cringe-worthy thud. The painting was spared but
not, unfortunately, Hannah.

The moment Silvia was helped to her feet the tirade began. It was
an ugly, ugly scene. Hannah was publicly shamed and reduced to tears.

And the only resolution that would appease Silvia and her friends was banning Hannah (and the goats) from the inn for the duration of the portrait painter's stay. It was unconscionable, but for the greater good I was forced to go through with it. I'd never hated anyone as much as I hated Silvia Lumiere in that moment. She had made me banish my own friend. It was going to be a long summer.

∞

I had barely recovered from the calamity of the morning when I was called out to the back lawn for my five o'clock meeting. Dressed in the red blouse, navy skirt, and yellow scarf Mom had laid out for me, I soon realized that my entire family was similarly dressed and standing in front of Silvia's easel. I wasn't ready to face the portrait painter. Yet it was the sight of Tate, standing there as well, that really set off the alarm bells.

"What's going on?" I demanded. Dad, having been summoned from the orchard, and wearing an outfit that matched Mom's, looked about as excited to be there as I was.

"Oh, for the love of simpleminded idiots!" Silvia boomed, spinning on me. "What does it look like we're doing, Ms. Bloom? Having tea? Do you see a teapot?" She cast me one of her infamous snooty glares, a look that began with her aging pixy head thrust straight back while her beady black eyes shot down her nose and through her zebra-striped glasses. "I am painting your family's portrait. Think of it as a thank you gift." A charming smile appeared on the painter's lips as she spoke. She looked at Mom, Dad, and Grandma Jenn with a kindness I never believed she'd been capable of had I not witnessed it myself. Once again, I thought that maybe I was wrong. Maybe I was misinterpreting Ms. Lumiere and her demanding nature.

"I'm impressed with your generosity," I told her. "I understand that your portraits go for a premium."

Her lips pulled into a smile that didn't reach her eyes. "Oh, this isn't free, Ms. Bloom," she whispered so that only I could hear. "What it means is that I've managed to squeeze you in to my very tight schedule. You should be thankful for that alone."

I narrowed my eyes, determined to make a stink, when Silvia held up a cautioning hand.

"Do not sully this occasion with your petty issues, Whitney. Your poor judgment and that ridiculous friend of yours with the goats have done quite enough damage for one day. And stop staring at me like that. Your face is turning red. It's very unbecoming. My suggestion, if you do not wish to upset your mother's dream of a family portrait, is to forget this conversation, smile and get over there by your brother."

It was unbelievable. Silvia was pointing at Tate. What had Mom done? Tate, grinning at me as if it were all a big joke, beckoned with a playful finger.

"He's not my brother," I hissed.

"Duh," she said, adding a look that made me feel even more stupid.

Mom, visibly overjoyed that her dream of a family portrait was finally becoming a reality, was also blind to Silvia's true nature. I wasn't entirely certain her attitude toward Ms. Lumiere was all part of the 'greater good' mentality but rather because Mom was a charitable Christian, a model of true Midwestern hospitality, and slightly out of touch with reality. She also couldn't fathom anyone being purposely mean and manipulative because she didn't have a mean bone in her body. "I've called Tate over to stand in for Bret," she explained. "I just couldn't ask your brother to fly in from Europe for a sitting. It's such an imposition."

"Mom. What about using a picture, like I suggested? Ms. Lumiere could just paint him in."

"Terrible suggestion," Silvia remarked. "I could, of course, but I won't."

"She's right," Mom agreed. "This seems so much more natural, dear. And Tate's a shoo-in, isn't he? It was Silvia's suggestion. Once she has the pose and our physical dimensions all fleshed out she'll just switch out Tate's face with Bret's." Mom cast her loving, motherly gaze on Tate.

Grandma Jenn, not so easily beguiled as her daughter, cast me an ironic grin. "Lucky Bret," she remarked. "He's grown four inches and put on fifty pounds of sculpted muscle, all without lifting a finger. Not to mention that he now towers over his father. I wish I had a stand-in. Younger, of course, and bustier."

"Yes, lucky Bret," Dad muttered. "Come on, Whitney. Jump in beside your *brother*. The sooner you do, the sooner we all get to carry on with our lives."

Silvia—and I had to believe it was out of pure spite—demanded that I stand hip to hip with Tate, place my hand on his shoulder, and tilt my head toward his with a fake smile plastered on my lips. While she worked away, sketching the details of our family portrait against a spectacular evening sky, it took everything I had to not erupt in a fit of exhausted giggles and run away. I kept reminding myself that I was doing this for Mom and Dad. I tried not to think about the tons of things yet to do on my daily list. Tate, bored to tears as well, entertained himself by whispering inappropriate things in my ear and tickling me with the arm Silvia insisted he place around my waist. It was a highly unbrotherly pose. Really, the only thing that made it bearable was the thought of Bret and what he was going to say when he saw his head on Tate's body.

"Eyes forward, head still!" Silvia yelled at me. It was her mantra, and I was, quite frankly, getting a little tired of hearing it. I had looked away for only a moment, but it was long enough. A blur of blonde hair moving at speed caught my eyes. I turned for a second look, confirming my suspicions that the hair belonged to Hannah. Apparently the term "banned for the summer" had a different meaning for her. She was behind a row of tall bushes, dressed in black and running as stealthily as she could for the beach. I nudged Tate, directing his attention to our friend.

"You two!" Silvia shrilled, pointing her sketching pencil at us. She was at her wit's end. "For the love of all that's holy—"

"We know. We know." Tate cut her off with a disarming grin. "Eyes forward, head still. But here's the thing, Silvia. If you're as good as you claim you are, you should have it by now. And if not, you always have the picture Mr. McClellan took earlier, for reference. Where is he, by the way? Slipped off an hour ago and never came back. Which reminds me, Whitney and I have a dinner engagement." I looked at him and nodded, playing along.

Grandma Jenn concurred with a wry grin. "Yes, Silvia. I'm quite done as well. Can't expect a lady my age to stand here forever. It ages a body."

"Good man," Dad whispered to Tate. "There's an hour of my life I'll never get back." He then grabbed Mom's hand. "Come on, Jani. Fun's over. I'm starving."

Silvia threw up her hands in disgust and bellowed for her assistant. But Peter McClellan was nowhere to be seen. Having spied Hannah slinking down to the shore minutes before sunset gave me a pretty good idea where her faithful assistant had disappeared to. What they were up to was anyone's guess.

Jen

"Come on," Tate said, taking my hand. "They've ventured a little farther afield than the inn's beach." He pointed down the rocky shoreline in the direction of the Cherry Cove Lighthouse, an old abandoned structure belonging to my family. It sat on a modest bluff, rising forty feet above the water. My brother, Bret, having once claimed to have spied the ghost of the old lightkeeper on the beach below, believed it was haunted. Dad, harboring a fancy to start a winery, believed it would be the perfect site to age his secret batch of cherry wine. And now Hannah, after the humiliation of the morning, was heading there as well. Obviously her flavor-of-the-month, Peter McClellan, had something to do with it. Yet it was the fact that she hadn't bothered to tell me what she was about that I found highly suspicious.

"Nothing like a walk along the shore at sunset," Tate remarked and gave my hand a little squeeze. "There's something about the way the sun reaches out across the darkening water one last time—as if it's reluctant to give way to the night. It stirs my blood, I tell ya. It's my favorite moment of the day. Used to be yours as well, if I remember correctly." It was an intimate statement, yet before I could reply, he asked, "Why didn't you tell me about the Renaissance fair?"

I stopped walking, my throat suddenly unnaturally dry. "How … how did you hear about that?"

"I ran into Lance. He was having a bite to eat at Swenson's this morning while Tay was at Hannah's yoga class. He mentioned that you were all going to watch him joust in the big tournament on Sunday. I was just wondering when you were going to get around to asking me?"

Inwardly I cringed. Dangit! So much for trying to rebuild my relationship with Jack. And now Tate was going. What was I to do? I turned to Tate. "I've … been a little busy lately."

"That Lumiere woman. She's getting to you, isn't she?" His strong, square-jawed face was wrought with disapproval.

"She is," I admitted. "She's driving me nuts with her demanding ways and snide, belittling remarks. If she was our only guest I could probably handle it, but she's not. We're fully booked at the inn, Dad's working his hands to the bone at the orchard, and the bakery is doing better than ever. We sell out of baked goods every day, and our cherry products are flying off the shelves. The truth is, Tate, I'm not even sure if I'm going to the Renaissance fair myself."

He stopped walking. "What? You have to go! Tay's counting on you." I wasn't used to being reprimanded by Tate, and I didn't like it now. He continued. "Look, I know jousting's a weird way for a dude to make a living, but she really likes this guy. As her friends, it's important we all support her."

"True, but I'm busy."

"Let Jani and Jenn handle it. They've always done so before."

"I know. But they had Dad to help, and they've never had anyone like Silvia staying at the inn, as far as I know."

"But it's Sunday, Whit. Silvia won't even be at the inn. She'll be driving all over the peninsula with her traveling art show doing her big reveals. Besides, I've never been to a Renaissance fair. I'm intrigued."

As Tate rambled on about the Renaissance fair, making a strong case as to why I had to go, I grew increasingly uncomfortable. Silvia wasn't the real problem. It was Jack, but I could hardly tell Tate that. Not wishing to dwell on how catastrophic Sunday was going to be, I continued walking and changed the subject.

"What do you suppose they're up to?"

Even with my troubled mind, I had to admit it was a spectacular evening. The last rays of light glittered across the darkening sky, throwing its fading colors on the underbelly of the cottony clouds. While shades of luminous purple and bright indigo rippled across water and sky, Tate replied, "Probably what anyone gets up to on a private beach at sunset, babe."

I stopped walking. "We shouldn't be following them."

"Normally, I'd agree. But we're talking about Hannah here. Something's not adding up. She could meet McClellan anywhere . . . why the old lighthouse at this hour? And why all the black?"

"I thought men found black attractive on a woman."

"Black dress, maybe. Black yoga pants, definitely. But from what I could tell she wasn't wearing either of those things. She looked . . . baggy."

That was a puzzle. Hannah seldom looked baggy. However, a short while later our questions were answered when we rounded a rocky outcrop and landed on the lonely stretch of beach beneath the lighthouse. It was the same rocky beach where Bret had seen the ghost of the old lightkeeper. The thought sent a chill up my spine, or perhaps it was the three figures dressed in black huddled around a flickering fire. The one in the middle was wearing a hooded robe. The youngest of the three had what looked to be a joint pinched between his fingers.

"What the devil is going on here?" I cried, louder than anyone had been expecting.

Erik, eyes closed and blowing smoke from his mouth like a chimney, choked at the sound of my voice and flicked the burning joint into the rocks, hoping, no doubt, that I hadn't seen it. But I had. Tate had too, and he was flaming mad. Peter, witnessing the act as well, threw back his hood and cried, "Dude. Uncool!" as he scrambled after it.

The state of nirvana Hannah had nearly reached faded the moment her eyes met mine. "Geez, Whit, what the heck are you doing here?"

"I could ask you the same question. All of you!"

"Look," she said, "before you get all judgey on us, you should know that this isn't what it looks like."

"Really? Because it looks an awful lot to me like you two are corrupting a minor."

"Minor?" Peter looked at Erik. "Dude, how old are you?"

"Eighteen."

He grinned. "Not a minor." Peter then looked at Tate and gave a little nod in greeting. "Yo. Vander Hagen."

Tate darkened, clenched his jaw, and growled, "McClellan."

"And he is a minor," I continued undeterred, vividly recalling an earlier incident involving Erik and his underage proclivities. It didn't help that the boy was easily lured to the dark side. But we'd been making such great strides. Peter, straddling the chasm between hippie and hot Jesus, was what he was … but Hannah? She liked her fun, but smoking pot had never been a part of it. I glared at them both. "Recreational pot is still illegal in this state," I informed them.

"But this," Peter said, holding up the recently discarded joint, "isn't recreational."

"Oh, really? Because it looks pretty recreational to me."

"Whoa. Chillax, Whitney. It's medicinal," he admonished, resting his gentle, dark-eyed gaze on me. "We're cleansing."

"Cleansing?" I shouted. "What the heck could you possibly be cleansing with that?"

"All the toxic vibes Silvia lays on us," Peter calmly explained. "You of all people should know. Silvia is an emotional vampire who sucks the life from our souls with her foul spirit. Hannah is her latest victim. I'm surprised you haven't come to me sooner."

"It's true," Hannah was quick to say, having obviously smoked some of Peter's magical cleansing weed herself. "Peter's not only an artist, Whit, *he's a shaman*." This she whispered with eyes wide and glossy as lake stones. As if this statement wasn't wacky enough, she attempted to back it by thrusting her hand under Peter's black robe. I was aghast. Tate looked intrigued. A moment later we were both appalled when Hannah pulled out a six-inch doll.

"What the ...? Whoa!" Tate said, inspecting it a little closer. "Dude," he admonished. "That's seriously messed up. Why are you carrying around a pocket sized Lumiere ... with vampire fangs?"

"Holy cobbler!" I said, realizing Tate was right. The likeness to the portrait painter was unsettling—from the stylish cut of the white pixy hair down to the tiny, bedazzled shoes. The facial expression was hair-raisingly creepy, so dead-on but with fangs. There was no doubt in my mind that Peter had created a voodoo doll of his employer. The thought was bone-chilling.

Apparently, Hannah disagreed. "He's *sooo* gifted," she remarked, and let out a little sigh.

I was about to ask just how much of the medicinal herb she'd smoked but realized the question was unnecessary. She'd obviously smoked enough to be loopy as a loon. I felt betrayed, saddened even. I was so seething mad at them all. "I hate to inform you, but Silvia Lumiere is not a vampire."

"Not a blood-sucker," Peter clarified. "A soul-sucker. There's a difference."

"If you smoke enough pot I'm sure there is," I agreed. "However, rational people know that vampires, soul-sucking or otherwise, do not exist. This"—I held up the creepy doll—"is just an excuse to smoke pot."

"No." Peter stood, his calm, hippie demeanor fading like the setting sun. "She is, Whitney. She's a soul-sucker, feeding off the hopes and dreams of the young and beautiful. Look at yourself. You're a beautiful woman in the prime of your life. You run a business. You're successful, and yet she pecks away at your psyche, suckling off your confidence bit by bit with her foul elitism. Look what she did to Hannah today. And need I remind you how she torments yon strapping young dude?" He gestured to Erik. "Don't you think it odd that she treats your mother with respect and your grandmother like an old friend but treats you like dirt? Youth is the fuel that feeds her craven soul."

"Holy mother of evil," Tate uttered, and crossed himself.

I wasn't buying it. "What about Bob Bonaire?" I challenged. "He's neither young nor beautiful by any standards, and yet she torments him as well."

"That's different," he said with a wave of his hand. "That's her little game. She's a cheap-ass food snob who believes that if she makes enough noise she won't have to pay her bill." He flashed a malicious grin. "Apparently, it works."

"I'll grant you, she's not a pleasant woman. But if you truly believe she's a vampire, why are you still with her?"

"I've no choice," he said. "We made a deal before I realized what she was. She found me fresh out of art school. I was flat broke and suffocating under the burden of crippling debt. Silvia offered to pay off all my student loans if I came to work for her. Crippling debt's a vampire as well, Whitney, only debt is a hell of a hard vampire to slay. Silvia, I can manage." He grinned a little unsteadily and held up the smoldering joint. "You might say I've chosen the lesser of two evils. Here." He held out his medicinal vampire slayer. "Join us. Both of you. Take a hit and cleanse your wounded souls. It's either this or risk being overcome by the desire to murder the old bitch." His pointed stare, as if looking into my own soul, made the hair on the back of my neck stand on end.

Tate, utterly creeped out as well, shook his head.

"Look, you two are old enough to make your own decisions," I told Hannah and Peter. "Do whatever you like, but I'll be damned if you subject Erik to your ridiculous cleansing ritual of pot and voodoo. He's coming with us."

I left Tate to deal with Erik and stormed back down the beach toward the inn, my fists balled in anger, my mind swirling with the desire to strangle the soul-sucking vampire myself. I didn't believe in vampires, but I had to admit that there was a thread of truth to what Peter had said. Silvia was a merciless tyrant to the young and promising in Cherry Cove, and she was driving my friends and employees to corruption. The "greater good" had just met its match, because I was determined to put a stop to it, one way or another.

Eleven

Sunday morning I was awakened by the buzzing of my iPhone. I thought it was my alarm and instantly filled with dread. The Renaissance fair! Holy hand grenades, what had I gotten myself into? Tate didn't know Jack was coming; Jack didn't know Tate was coming; and I was too much of a chicken to be honest with either of them. Then there was Hannah. She was still miffed at me for nearly everything that had transpired Friday. All I'd received from her since was a text telling me that I was to pick her up, and, yes, she was still planning on bringing Peter—which added a whole new level of uncomfortable to the mix. Never mind that the entire voodoo vampire cleansing fiasco beneath the old lighthouse had shaken me to the core, or the fact that since the goat yoga debacle Silvia had launched into full-blown diva mode, sparing no one. Tate was unshakable in his conviction that we were still dating; Erik was still employed but avoiding me; and Jack, popping into the bakery the last several mornings, was positively flirtatious. I was romancing a nervous breakdown and felt that a day at the Renaissance fair might throw me over the edge. But what choice did I have? It was too late to back out now.

Just as my thoughts were spiraling out of control, I happened to look at my phone. It was five in the morning. Not my alarm. I wasn't baking this morning, having stayed up late into the night preparing the dough for the cherry scones ahead of time. They were already rolled out, cut into triangles, and placed on parchment covered baking sheets. Gran said she'd come in early and bake them for me. Obviously she had a question.

The moment I answered my phone, she blurted, "Whitney, are you all right, dear?"

It was an unusual greeting, but Grandma Jenn was a bit of an eccentric. "I am, Gran." I stifled a yawn. "Just tired. The scones are in the walk-in. Is there a problem?"

"You might say that. Are you in your room?" Her voice was a near-whisper as she spoke. When I told her that I was she said, "Good. Throw on some clothes and meet me at the front desk." Without elaborating further, she ended the call.

Since I was dead tired I gave a thought to calling her back but decided against it. Gran sounded agitated, which wasn't like her. Resigned to another day of sleeplessness and frustration, I threw on a pair of jeans and an old sweatshirt and proceeded down the hallway that connected the family wing to the main office behind the front desk. I had no sooner walked through the office door than I saw Gran. Although the lobby was dark her face appeared ashen beneath the soft lights over the reservation computer.

"I don't blame you, dear, but we can't just leave her like this."

I had no idea what she was mumbling on about, so I just stared at her.

"Silvia," she stated, gesturing to the darkened foyer as if I should have known. At first glance I didn't see anything out of place. She then pointed to the wide, sweeping steps that rose to the second floor. I came around the desk. The moment I did I saw the body, tangled in layers of pink satin and white faux fur, sprawled indignantly on the floor. The short puff of silver-white hair could only have belonged to Silvia Lumiere.

My hand flew to my mouth. "Oh, dear heavens! Is she ...?"

"As a doornail, I'm afraid." Gran's face was awash in a look of pity. "Death is ghastly in all its forms. I only wish I felt something other than relief. What a terrible thing to have admitted out loud. Well, we'll have to call Jack, of course, but first it might be best if we remove the scone."

I had a paralyzing fear of dead bodies. It was a real thing, a gripping panic. It didn't help that while Gran talked in her steady, level-headed way, my own head was spinning. Dear God! A DEAD BODY! On the floor of the Cherry Orchard Inn! My mind ground to a stupefied halt, the words "we're not supposed to have dead bodies here" looping in my thoughts like a broken record.

"Dear?"

"What?" I shot back, nervously wringing my hands.

"Latex gloves. Grab two pairs from behind the desk. And hurry. We don't have much time. The sun rises early this time of year. It would never do if one of the guests saw us."

"What? No-no-no. I'm not going near that thing! That thing is *DEAD.*"

"Whitney," she hissed. "This is no time for a weak stomach. Especially since this is your doing."

"Wha ... Wha ... What?" It suddenly dawned on me what Grandma Jenn was saying, and, quite frankly, I found it a little insulting. "Wait. You think I had something to do with this?"

"Look, my love, I think the world of you. You're my favorite grandchild, don't tell your brother, and when not sleep-deprived and driven mad by some uppity artist, you're capable of so many great things. That's why I'm not about to stand by and watch you spend the best years of your life rotting away in some prison cell, all because some wretched old fool goaded you into choking them with a scone and pushing them down a flight of stairs."

I stared at her, mouth agape. "But I didn't ... What?" I was still struggling to comprehend what she was saying.

"A scone, dear. You've been making so many of them lately, it's no wonder."

"But ... I didn't choke her with a scone," I said, hoping I was correct. A terrible thought flashed through my mind. What if I had? In my sleep? Was that a thing? I banished the thought as soon as it came and braved another glance at the body on the floor. "Is that even possible?"

"Apparently, yes," Gran remarked. "At least I think that's what happened. I saw the pile of pink satin when I came in, and when I went to investigate I got the shock of my life. Silvia's dead, her poor old mouth stuffed to bursting with a cherry scone." Gran's eyes softened. "Whitney, are you sure you had nothing to do with this? Because if you did, dear, I hope you understand that your secret's safe—"

"I'm not a liar, Gran! And I'm certainly not a murderer. How can you even jump to that conclusion?"

Her lips pulled taut. "If you'll recall, you seem to have jumped to that very same conclusion about me when Jeb was murdered."

"That's because it was *your* blender!"

"Well, that's *your* scone, isn't it?" She gestured to the splatter of crumbs on the floor.

"I make a lot of scones. Sure, I might have daydreamed about strangling the woman. Who didn't? But I'd hardly waste a quality cherry baked good on that." I wiggled my hand at the rumpled heap of pink satin, white fluff and scone crumbs on the floor, my arm being too overwhelmed to work properly. "That is not my doing."

Grandma Jenn had an uncanny resemblance to Helen Mirren, only she was taller, livelier and not one bit English. She was a proud American of Scandinavian descent, and yet her round blue eyes held me in an icy Norwegian stare. A moment later she relented. "Good. That's what I wanted to hear. I thought as much but figured it would be best to make sure. Also, it doesn't hurt to be prepared for some hard grilling. Everyone knows you didn't get on with the woman, just as everyone knows you're the queen of cherry scones around here."

"But … who would do such a thing … I mean, for real?" Murdering an old lady was bad enough, but the thought that someone had used one of my scones to do it seemed either desperate or diabolically evil. Whoever wanted Silvia dead had either grabbed the closest object in reach, which, knowing Silvia, really might have been a cherry scone, or the real killer was trying to frame me. Either way, the fact that a dead body was lying in the grand foyer of the inn wasn't sitting very well with me, and it certainly wasn't going to help the Cherry Orchard Inn brand any. I hated to admit it, but Silvia Lumiere had been good for business. Taking a step toward the body, I offered, "Maybe it was an accident."

"Maybe it was." Gran hooked her arm in mine. "She was a bit unsteady on her legs," she added, walking with me to the foot of the stairs. "She insisted on using the elevator, but maybe she got brave in the middle of the night."

"I don't think so, Gran. She was arthritic. She'd never take the chance. However, if she was sleepwalking and didn't know where she was … ?"

"And eating a scone while doing it?" She cast me a deprecatory look. We both knew it sounded absurd.

75

We stood beside the body. The petite, plump form was swaddled in an elaborate dressing gown. I'd only seen one other body before and that had been in the morgue. It was a ghastly sight that had resulted in me passing out. However, staring at Silvia's body in so familiar a place felt surreal. "Maybe she isn't dead at all," I offered. "Maybe she's just been knocked unconscious." Before Gran could stop me, I knelt beside the body and tugged on the sleeve of Silvia's dressing gown. The fleshy form rolled into my legs, spilling crumbs and knocking me onto my backside.

"Dead! Dead!" I squawked, scrambling backward. There was no question in my mind: Silvia Lumiere had been murdered, and I was nearly certain I had nothing to do with it other than baking the murder weapon. But was that a crime? Hopefully not.

Then cold, hard reality set in. The inn would be thrown into a tizzy. A lengthy murder investigation would commence. And I would be working double-time to try to put things right once again. The only upside to a calamity of this scale was that I now had a legitimate excuse to bail on the Renaissance fair excursion.

Twelve

"My God, this is like a bad dream," Dad remarked, peering at the lump beneath the white sheet. Grandma Jenn had raided the linen cart, not only covering the body but roping off the crime scene with a ribbon of knotted flat sheets as well. It was quick thinking. Mom was beside Dad, crying and mumbling something about the family portrait and how a dead body was really going to throw a wrench into the inn's complimentary breakfast routine. It definitely would, but I couldn't think of that now. I had a more pressing problem. Because, after the shock of discovering the dead body, I began to recall details of the previous night—including the last person to pay Silvia a visit.

The foyer suddenly filled with the reflection of flashing red and blue lights. Mom stopped crying.

"Jack's arrived," Dad said and went to unlock the front doors.

The rest of the morning unfolded like a poorly acted cable TV cop drama, with me both a disjointed spectator and the most likely suspect. It was a truly nightmarish feeling, especially since the man who was currently starring in all my romantic fantasies marched through the

77

door with an air that was all business. He was curt, professional and only looked at me when he absolutely had to. I had found it all so unnerving that I had chosen the moment he began tweezing up crumbs of the murder weapon for his evidence bag to make a bad joke.

"She always said they were to die for." Standing with arms crossed, I flashed him an ironic grin, knowing I'd get an impish smile if not an all-out chuckle.

Apparently, my timing was off.

Mom gasped.

Grandma Jenn blanched and covered her mouth.

Dad's normally calm face creased with angry disapproval. "Too soon, Whitney. Too soon."

Jack, who'd been kneeling beside the body, looked up at me. It was odd, but I couldn't detect a trace of humor in his unflinching gaze. "Are you confirming that you baked this scone?" he asked.

I had always been able to make Jack smile in the past. He smiled easily. The fact that there wasn't the slightest lift at either corner of his mouth was more than disturbing. "It's one of mine, yes. Jack—I mean, *Officer MacLaren*—you've eaten enough yourself to know that it is."

"Do you know when this particular scone was baked?"

"No. I mean, if I had to guess, I'd say yesterday morning. The scones for this morning are still in the cooler. They haven't been baked yet. I was only trying to lighten the mood."

"There's a dead woman in the lobby of your inn with one of your scones jammed so far down her throat that all I can pull out are crumbs, and all you can think to do is make a joke?"

"Obviously, I thought wrong. So is that what killed her?" I pointed to the scone crumbs trapped in the ziplock baggie.

"Possibly."

"Well, that's ridiculous. My scones are perfectly baked, crisp on the outside, moist on the inside."

"True. But what the scone didn't finish, the broken neck did. Ms. Lumiere took quite a nasty fall down the stairs." Then, for the first time, Officer MacLaren cracked. His face softened as his voice became a mere whisper. "Whit, you do realize that I have to bring you in for questioning? At the moment you're my prime suspect."

I lowered my voice too. "Oh come on, Jack. Just because I said a few negative things about the old woman doesn't mean I'm the murderer."

"I hope not. But here we are, kneeling at the foot of the stairs beside a dead body with a scone sticking out of her mouth. She was pushing you toward the edge. I believe you told me you were, and I quote"—he flashed a set of air quotes—"'going to strangle the old sack of paintbrushes myself.'"

I frowned. "True, I did say that. But I wasn't the only one to harbor the fantasy. And anyhow, you don't know that she's been murdered. She could have tripped," I offered, trying to look as if I believed it.

"She could have," Jack said. "But that wouldn't explain the scone. If she was eating it and got too close to the stairs, she would have dropped it in the fall or crushed it in her fist. At the very least there would be large crumbs scattered all over the steps as she fell down them. But there's just a small trail of fine crumbs here," he said, pointing a gloved finger up the stairs. "The impact of her head hitting the stairs did that. But most are here, at the bottom, where she landed."

As Jack confirmed what Gran and I had suspected, my heart began to beat with the frantic rhythm of a hyped-up techno tune.

"Look," Jack began, holding me in a pointed gaze. "Sometimes the fine line between fantasy and reality gets blurred. A person might not even realize what they're doing because the act is so vivid in their mind. I'm not saying—"

I swallowed the lump in my throat, then sneered. "Don't bother. I know perfectly well what you're saying. And it's highly unflattering. You think I'm a nutter!"

"All I'm saying, Whit, is that I hope you have a rock-solid alibi, or it's going to be a rough morning."

Jack wasn't kidding. The morning descended from there. The Cherry Orchard Inn was declared a crime scene and all guests were ordered to stay in their rooms until further notice, which proved a near Herculean task. There's something about a dead body that piques curiosity, especially for the gentleman staying in the Swan Suite, who was caught gawking over the railing at the lumpy sheet on the floor no less than seven times. Jack was losing his patience. The inn resembled more of a prison lockdown than the beautiful Victorian bed-and-breakfast it was.

More squad cars arrived. Sergeant Stamper and Officer Jensen from Sturgeon Bay appeared and joined the growing number of police officers working under Jack. Grandma Jenn's cordon of clean linen was taken down and replaced by proper yellow crime scene tape. Truthfully, I preferred the linen. It wasn't nearly as jolting.

Bags of evidence were removed from Silvia's room before it was taped off as part of the crime scene. More evidence was gathered, and pictures were taken, until finally the ambulance arrived. The body was then removed from the indignity of the marble floor only to be transported to the indignity of the morgue at Door County General, a place I vowed never to visit again. There Doc Fisker, the county coroner, would conduct the required autopsy for suspicious death. Was it too much to hope that Jack was wrong? An accidental death due to a gluttonous midnight binge of cherry scones and a trip down the stairs would look better for me, as well as for the Cherry Orchard Inn.

Even more upsetting than being Jack's prime suspect was the fact that Dad had rolled up his sleeves and took control of the inn. This caused Mom to trip into hyper-hostess mode. She and Grandma Jenn called in a skeleton staff and proceeded to organize a mass effort to deliver coffee, sweet rolls, and fresh fruit to every room while doing their best to make sure every guest was comfortable, under the circumstances. Mom had even suggested that I make sure all the personnel working the crime scene had access to hot beverages and cherry baked goods as well, but she'd given strict instructions not to bake any cherry scones.

"And no more jokes, Whitney," she'd gently admonished me. "You're a suspect, dear. This isn't a laughing matter."

As if I needed reminding.

Once the body had been removed and all the guests had given their names, addresses and preliminary statements to the police, they were free to leave their rooms, minding that they stayed clear of the crime scene. Jack was ready to take me to the station for his version of "interrogation" (which likely wouldn't look at all like my fantasy version—dear heavens, what was wrong with me?) when another thought popped into his head. He spoke the name Peter McClellan, as if everything I'd been telling him had fallen on deaf ears.

"I haven't seen him this morning," I told him, half expecting him to throw me in handcuffs.

"He wasn't here to make a statement," Jack said. "What room is he in?"

I told him Peter was staying in the Pine Suite, a small room tucked away at the far end of the second floor. A moment later Dad produced the master key and the three of us went to check on him. When no one answered, Jack took the key and unlocked the door. We were instantly hit with a wave of stench that nearly knocked us over. To be honest, I'd seen messier rooms, but the smell was impressive, a potent combination of sweaty male, stale pot, cheap incense, and old paint. The man in question, however, was nowhere to be seen.

"Oh, for the love of Pete! That smell!" Dad covered his mouth with his shirt sleeve. "It's like a skunk sprayed up a locker room. Why didn't housekeeping report this?"

Dad was staring at me, waiting for an answer. The stern, unbending look undid me. "They couldn't report it, because they haven't been here since last Monday."

Clearly this wasn't what my father had wanted to hear. If Jack hadn't been standing next to me Dad would have given me an earful on proper inn management and why it was so important to keep tabs on housekeeping. Thankfully, he refrained.

"Sorry, Dad, but Silvia finagled this room from us at no cost," I explained. "Since she wasn't paying for the room, or much else, I made the executive decision to cut back on maid service to only once a week. I had no idea the guy was smoking pot in here." This wasn't entirely a lie. I knew the guy smoked pot. Friday night I had caught him on the beach pushing it as a cleansing herb to Erik and Hannah. I had no idea he'd be stupid enough to smoke it in his *non-smoking* room.

"McClellan's not here," Jack said, ushering us back to the threshold. "We can't legally enter or search this room without his permission or a search warrant. He's Silvia's assistant," Jack continued. "I was told that he worked very closely with her. We're going to need to talk with him. Whitney, do you have any idea where he might be?"

It was the intensity of the honey-colored gaze that prompted me to reply, "Um, maybe." That same intense look coaxed me into pulling out my iPhone and dialing Hannah's number. My open frustration with Silvia had caused Jack to consider me a prime suspect in her murder. While the fact that she'd been choked with one of my scones hadn't helped any, it could be argued that Peter McClellan had a stronger motive to see her dead than I did. And yet I silently prayed, as I dialed my friend's number, that he wouldn't be there. After the incident on the beach, which I'd never mentioned to Jack, I'd warned Hannah to keep her distance from Peter. But Hannah was obsessed with the guy and, unfortunately, my well-meaning advice had fallen on deaf ears.

The moment the phone was answered an over-caffeinated voice cried, "I'm so excited! We're just getting dressed for the Renaissance fair now. I'm going as a medieval nun and Peter's dressing as a hermit. Isn't that just perfect? He's wearing a long robe made of hemp and his sexy Jesus sandals. We've been *dallying*," she said, and burst into giggles. "We'll be ready in twenty minutes. You can pick us up then."

"Actually," I began, staring back at the two men staring at me, "there's been a change of plans. Can you meet us at the police station instead? Jack has something he'd like to ask Peter."

"Yeah. Sure. No problem. See ya there."

Jack, standing on the threshold of the room, began massaging his forehead in frustration. "You didn't tell her about Silvia. She still thinks we're going to the fair. You do know that we can't go now, not with an open murder investigation at the inn?"

Why did I feel nothing but relief at the thought? I looked up at Jack. "Of course. And I'm your prime suspect. Even if I wanted to go to the fair today I hardly think you'd let me."

"Sorry, Whit. I was really looking forward to our outing today too." He cast me a pointed look, continuing, "But murder changes things."

"Oh, fer cripes' sake, MacLaren! You don't seriously think Whitney had anything to do with that woman's death? The old witch had more enemies than teeth. Besides, my daughter's worked too hard trying to rebuild the inn's reputation after that last incident in the orchard. She'd hardly throw it all away again. Lord knows that painter tried her patience, but my daughter's no murderer!"

"Thanks, Dad." I looked at him with all the adoration I felt.

"Mr. Bloom, sir, regardless of my feelings for your daughter, I hope you'll appreciate that this is first and foremost a professional matter."

Dad looked at Jack as if for the first time. "Feelings?" he questioned. "And how exactly do you feel about my daughter, MacLaren?" Obviously, the thought that there might be something more than friendship between Jack and me had never entered his mind ... until now.

Unfortunately, what I felt for Jack was a little harder to disguise than my relief for our canceled outing. My cheeks burned under Dad's inquisitive gaze. Jack, under the same silent parental interrogation, was also in danger of combusting. Thankfully, he was more adept at handling such situations than I was. He chose to ignore Dad's inquisitive stare in favor of focusing on the problem at hand.

"You sent Hannah and Peter to the police station. Why didn't you tell her what's really going on?"

"Look. I'm a suspect, but that doesn't mean I don't have suspicions of my own. I'm conducting a little experiment."

Jack, bemused, crossed his arms and cocked his head. "What's that supposed to mean?"

"That I'm not the only one who had issues with Ms. Lumiere. She tormented Peter to such an extent that he actually believed she was a vampire." I was waiting for them to be shocked. Instead both men held me in a look of pity.

"Whit." Jack spoke first. "Vampires aren't real."

I shrugged. "Sure, you and I know that, but Peter doesn't. It's a long story," I said to his questioning gaze. "I'll tell you all about it in my interview, right after I tell you that I didn't kill Silvia Lumiere. For now, let's just see if Peter shows up at the police station. If he had anything to do with Silvia's death he would know by now that her body had been found. Pushing an elderly lady down the main flight of stairs in a hotel lobby is hardly a private murder. If she was murdered, it was meant to be a public display. Silvia never went near those stairs. Also, everyone knew that she loved my cherry scones. Have you considered that the murderer could be framing me? There isn't a person in all of Cherry Cove who isn't aware of how Silvia tormented me, or how much she loved my scones. But if I was really going to kill her, why would I be stupid enough to use one of my scones to do it?"

"Exactly my point," Dad said, looking vindicated.

Encouraged, and trying my hardest to put the blame on someone other than me, I continued. "Also, remember that Peter has a motive. He told me that he *had* to work for Silvia. You might not have known this, but she was paying off his student loans in exchange for his services. He also had access to her room and knew her habits. If Silvia needed him in the middle of the night, he was expected to be there for her. I can't say for sure, but judging by the sound of Hannah's voice, there's a pretty strong chance he didn't sleep here last night. We won't know the time of death until Doc Fisker does his examination. But the deed could have been done any time after midnight. That's when we lock the doors and dim the lights in the foyer. Hannah stays up late on the weekends and wouldn't say no to an early morning visit from Peter. He normally doesn't leave the inn, but he would if he knew Silvia wouldn't be needing him. And if he was responsible for Silvia's death and got wind that you wanted to question him about her murder, he might decide to take his chances and run."

"Wow!" Dad exclaimed, beaming with pride. "She makes a convincing argument, MacLaren. You should listen to her. As much as I hate to admit it, my daughter's got a real knack for this crime-solving business. Doesn't she?"

Jack crossed his arms, and, for the first time all morning, I caught a hint of a sardonic grin. That was never a good thing. "Well," he began, allowing his narrowed eyes to size me up, "I wouldn't recommend that she quit her day job just yet. It's an interesting theory, Whitney, but unfortunately, it's not backed by sound logic. Criminals are often under the belief that they can get away with murder. Running, hiding or refusing to talk to the police is seen as a sure sign of guilt, and therefore usually avoided. Often a criminal is so confident that they can actually get away with murder, they'll appear helpful, normal even. It's what makes my job so difficult. Criminals are also very skilled liars, but even a skilled liar will trip up eventually." This last statement was punctuated with an accusatory look directed at me.

"Whoa, fella," I said, taking offence. "I'm not a murderer, nor a skilled liar."

"Sometimes we don't know what we're capable of until our backs are against the wall," Jack added, pulling the door closed and making sure it was locked. "Whether McClellan is innocent or not," he continued, turning to face us, "I'm confident he'll show up at the station. Besides, Hannah is with him. She just might be able to give him an alibi for last night." Jack chanced a look at me again and shook his head. "I wish to God it was you at Hannah's place and not him. Because if you had stayed away last night I wouldn't have to apologize for what I'm about to put you through this morning. And I do apologize, Whitney."

Thirteen

It was the first time I'd ever felt trepidation about entering the welcoming turf-roofed, Scandinavian log building that doubled as Jack's home and the Cherry Cove Police Station. As I sat at the desk reserved for "interrogating," I stared at the man across from me and thought, what in the world did I ever see in this idiot? All the geeky charm of my old high school friend and academic nemesis had faded, replaced by a steely-eyed, robotic, humorless cop, albeit a hot one. The most disturbing thing was that Jack was treating me like he actually believed I had murdered Silvia Lumiere. He hadn't even offered me coffee or water, a courtesy performed by even the meanest cop on all the TV crime shows. Nope, I'd been unceremoniously ushered to the desk behind the front counter. There Jack plopped a tape recorder onto the table and started asking me a string of questions that were, quite frankly, insulting.

What did I do for a living? How long have I been employed at the Cherry Orchard Inn? How long had I known Silvia Lumiere? Seriously? Was he for real? When I cast him a look of pure exasperation, he shot me a glare of chiding disappointment, stating it was formality, part of police procedure. After a dramatic eye roll, the questions continued. *What was the nature of my relationship with Silvia Lumiere? Am I the only one who bakes the scones? Who else has access to them? Had there recently been any variation in the recipe that might make them dry?*

"What?" This got me. Jack had eaten enough of my scones to know that my recipe created a delectable baked good that was crisp on the outside and buttery soft and moist on the inside. I pursed my lips, stating that I wasn't even going to answer that question.

"Right." Jack scribbled something on his notepad that looked suspiciously like *uncooperative suspect*. Why he was taking notes when the whole conversation was being recorded was beyond me. A moment later the bright ginger head lifted. "And when was the last time you saw Ms. Lumiere?"

"Shortly before midnight, just after I left the kitchen."

"Where did you see her?"

"In the lobby."

"Was she alone?"

"Nope."

"Who was she with?" His eyes narrowed with impatience.

"If you must know, it was Fred Beauchamp, from the arts council."

The honey-colored gaze considered this. "What was he doing with Silvia?"

"Really, Jack. I thought gossip was the grist in the mill of every small-town cop." I leaned forward and rested my elbows on the table. "I'd like to say they were talking shop, but the truth is, Fred had a thing for Silvia. He was trying to worm his way into her heart via her bedroom. Silvia played along and had him buying her dinners, and a good deal of booze as well, thank goodness. It's lifted some of the burden off us, but it's really quite shameless the way she was using him."

He bit the cap of his pen as he ruminated over this little tidbit. The pen came away. The steely face cracked with the first glimmerings of emoting, which was, unfortunately, incredulity. "Were they, you know, doing it?"

I shrugged. "I doubt it. I don't believe she ever let him into her room. I would say it was sweetly old-fashioned, but it's not. Even you must know that her tastes run to younger men."

"But Fred Beauchamp *is* a younger man ... by at least a decade."

This was true, but I recalled what Peter McClellan had said that night on the beach. He believed Silvia was a vampire, feasting on the souls of the young and beautiful to fuel her great talent. Of course, he'd been super high at the time, and it was all a load of hogwash. But there was a sting of truth to her delight in tormenting the young and promising. The only reply I had for Jack was a noncommittal shrug.

"How did she treat him?" he asked.

"Kindly. But I do think he was beginning to get frustrated with her, having hit a wall, so to speak."

"Okay. Do you remember what Ms. Lumiere did after Mr. Beauchamp left?"

I did, but here I hesitated. "She, ah, came to see me."

The ruddy eyebrows lifted. "Why?"

And here it was, the question I feared. Part of me didn't want to tell Jack the truth, because the truth was damning. I hesitated. A ripple of concern crossed Jack's face. He schooled it and began drumming his pen softly on the desk.

"Okay," I finally said. "I wasn't the last person to see Silvia, but please don't read too much into this. She ordered room service."

A brow lifted. "Was this a regular request?"

"Yes. I think I've mentioned it to you before that it was."

"Who delivered it?"

"The same person who always delivers it. Erik Larson." As I spoke the boy's name, Jack's face fell. Obviously, Erik's name being connected to Silvia was upsetting. I couldn't say that I blamed him. Erik and Jack went way back, from the time the boy and his friend Cody Rivers were caught stealing bikes from tourists and selling them on eBay for cash, to the using and selling of performance-enhancing steroids. Erik Larson was clearly no angel, but I knew he wasn't a murderer either. However, if Jack's look was any indication, he was entertaining the idea.

"This was around midnight?" he asked. "Why was he still working at that hour?"

"It's summer, and he likes the extra money. Also, Kenna stays late to straighten up the patio and wipe down the tables. She and Erik help Bob in the kitchen. The three of them basically hang out and goof around until Silvia's room service is delivered."

Jack nodded. "I remember you telling me how she tormented Erik. Could the kid have snapped?"

"I think it's unlikely. Look, he's a good employee. I don't want to pat myself on the back just yet, but he's really turning the corner. I've told him many times that he didn't have to put up with Silvia. Last night I even offered to deliver her tray myself, but he insisted."

"Why do you think that was?"

"Because Silvia requests that he deliver it. I would have been perfectly happy to disappoint her, but Erik knew she'd have a fit. He didn't want to risk upsetting the other guests."

"What did she order?"

I took a deep breath and cringed slightly. "Two scones and a bottle of wine."

A fearful look crossed Jack's face. He lowered his voice and said, "She had scones in her room last night and you failed to mention it until now?"

"I ... I didn't think it was relevant."

"What?" he cried. "Not relevant? The woman had a scone shoved down her throat and you think that her room service order wasn't relevant?" The look Jack shot at me was deflating. It was followed by a furious bout of pen drumming. The pen stopped and he asked, "I thought you said that you sell out of scones every day."

"We do, but I always keep half a dozen in the freezer for emergencies, namely Silvia's room service order. They're fully baked. All Erik has to do is pop them into the microwave for thirty seconds and they come out smelling like they're freshly baked. A little secret of the trade. Jack, you're acting like scones were an unusual request for Silvia. They weren't. She ordered room service every night. I don't think the woman could get to sleep without downing a bottle of wine and a late-night snack."

"Are you certain Erik delivered them?"

"If you're asking did I see him, the answer is no, I didn't. But he said that he would, so I assume that he did. He's a very reliable employee."

"What did you do after talking with Erik in the kitchen?"

"I went to bed."

Jack lifted his eyes from the notepad. "Can anyone corroborate that?"

It might have been just me, but I detected a hint of challenge in the question. "What do you mean, 'can anyone corroborate that?'"

He set down his pen. "I mean, can anyone corroborate that you were in bed all night?"

"Is this your way of asking was I sleeping with anyone?"

He glared across the table. "It's a simple question, Whitney. Was there anyone in bed with you last night?"

How dare he even ask such a thing! Oozing sarcasm, I replied, "Hmm, let me think. As you know, I have so much energy at the end of my eighteen-hour day, and there are so many men who make regular visits to my bed, that I can't quite remember."

"This isn't a joke, Whitney. I need to know."

"Jesus, Jack!"

"Look, I'm not accusing you—"

"Really? Because it sure sounds to me that you are. You think Tate was in my bed, don't you?"

"I'm beginning to wish that he was. It would help establish your whereabouts at the time of death."

"Well, that's going to be a little hard to do, because I was alone, Jack. There's no one to corroborate my whereabouts. A nasty old woman was murdered at my inn last night and, unfortunately, I have motive, opportunity, plenty of scones on hand, and no alibi. But I didn't kill her. I don't have it in me. I was hoping that you of all people would at least understand that. But apparently you don't. I think we're done here."

Jack shot me a challenging look and turned off the tape recorder. "Are we?" he pressed. Clearly there were two meanings in that question.

I stood up so fast my chair tumbled to the floor. MacDuff, who'd been banished to the garden, began barking. I pressed the tape recorder back on and cried into the speaker, "It's unfortunate that your dog has more sense than you!" I turned it back off again and was about to storm out of the police station when Hannah and Peter came waltzing through the door. They both looked as if they'd just stepped off the dirty, dung-strewn streets of a medieval village. Hannah was in a long flowing robe of butter yellow with a chain of medallions around her waist and a wreath of wildflowers crowning her long, white-blonde hair. Peter looked like a grubby, pierced, pot-smoking Jesus. At the sight of me in jeans and Jack storming behind me in police blues, Hannah gasped.

"Whitney! Jack! You're not dressed!"

I looked at them both and had a sudden flash of clarity. Before Jack got the chance, I said, "No. Unfortunately, there's been a change of plans. Silvia Lumiere has been murdered."

If this news was a shock to Peter, he didn't show it. Then I realized he thought I was joking. "Impossible," he drawled. "Vampires are immortal."

"Not this one, sweetheart. In fact, Officer MacLaren will tell you all about it."

"Holy hand grenades! Are you serious?" Hannah shot Peter a look, then blanched white as a ghost. Peter merely looked thoughtful.

There was something troubling in the look that passed between the two of them. I knew my friend almost better than I knew myself, and I had never seen such a look before. It wasn't quite guilt, but more the look of unholy fear, and it shook me to the core. My fingers and toes went numb, and my entire body ached with dread. Much as I would have liked to stay and listen as Jack questioned Peter, I couldn't. Beside the fact that I had worn out my welcome, I was also overcome with a pressing need I knew I was going to regret the moment I came to my senses. Hopefully I wouldn't come to my senses anytime soon. I waved noncommittally to them all and shot out the door, fully aware that somewhere in Cherry Cove lurked a murderer and come hell or high water I was going to find them.

Fourteen

I tumbled into the morning sunshine and hungrily gulped the cool air, doing my best to ignore Thing One and Thing Two. They were frolicking near the edge of the turf roof, screaming at me. I had learned to accept Jack's goats, but the fact that he'd interrogated me as a murder suspect was beyond my comprehension. The nerve of him! It was unconscionable! A month ago he had kissed me, for cripes' sake, and now he actually believed that I was capable of murder? What an idiot!

Across the street, the lake twinkled like a sea of diamonds. It was amazingly beautiful and so at odds with the anger that consumed me that I bolted toward it, regardless of the oncoming cars. Ignoring goat screams and one motorist's choice comment, I headed up the shore-line toward Tay's shop. It was doubtful she'd be there, this being the day of Lance's big jousting tournament, but I needed a place to think. I also needed a way back to the inn and knew Tay wouldn't mind if I borrowed her ancient Vespa scooter.

As I walked along the calming waters of Cherry Cove Bay toward the charming Victorian building that housed Cheery Pickers, the nagging thought kept hounding me. Could I have actually murdered Silvia Lumiere while still asleep and not have known it—a lethal form of sleepwalking? Lord knows the woman had gotten under my skin. She was also the source of all my nightmares. As Jack had pointed out, there was nobody to validate the fact that I'd been in my bed all night. What if I had gotten up, crossed over to the inn side of the building, opened Silvia's door and shoved a scone down her throat? I had dreamed of doing something very close to that nearly every time I encountered the woman. Heck, my own grandmother had the very same suspicion of me but knew better than to interrogate me. Instead she'd been willing to tamper with the evidence, God love her. Perhaps she'd been a little too willing, but either way there was no doubt Gran had my back. But what if such a thing was possible? The thought was as curious as it was frightening. Reflexively, I pulled out my phone and called the one man I knew who'd entertain the possibility.

"Angel, it's Sunday morning," the languid voice complained. "Haven't I told you never to call me on Sunday morning?"

"Maybe. I don't remember. Listen, Giff, are you alone?" Gifford McGrady, friend and former assistant during my advertising days, still worked and lived in Chicago. He had an artistic eye, a knack for market analysis, and kept his finger on the pulse of everything chic in the Windy City.

Giff yawned into the phone. "Unfortunately, utterly alone. Through no fault of my own, I'll have you know. It's your old job. The workload! The pressure! And having Mr. Black breathing down my neck twenty-four seven has crushed any hope I had of finding love. I now understand what it's like to be you. In an odd sort of way it explains all the frustrated baking. How's the baking, by the way? Or have you already gotten your dough hooks into Officer McHottie?"

"I'm off him," I said angrily. "Honestly, I don't know what I ever saw in that ... that insufferable jerk!"

"I do, but that's beside the point. Whit, darling, what's happened?"

"Murder's what happened. Cold-blooded murder." This got his attention.

"Dear God, not again. I never dreamed that Cherry Cove was such a dangerous place. And here I was, about to pay you a visit. I still might. Two murders in one summer doesn't scare this Chicago boy. And anyhow, I want to bask in the magnificence of your renowned painter before you kick her out. You know she's going to adore me."

If the painter was still alive, this would undoubtedly be true. Giff was a handsome young man, charming and easily impressed by celebrity. We talked at least a couple times a week, and it was part of the reason I had delayed his visit. Moving in all the right circles of Chicago's artistic elite, Giff had known of Silvia Lumiere and her work. He would have just poured more grease on that already out-of-control fire. Silvia, being a soul-sucking vampire, would have eaten the poor man alive.

"Well, I'm afraid you're too late," I said. "She's the one who's been murdered."

A loud gasp rang out, followed by, "NO! Not Silvia Lumiere! Whitney, she's a *celebrity*." His tone was as horror-stricken as it was admonishing—as if I had something to do with her murder.

Why did everybody jump to that conclusion, including myself?

Stifling the scandal before it consumed him, I quickly filled Giff in on all the events of the morning, including my own unsettling thoughts regarding sleepwalking and murder.

The phone fell silent on his end as he contemplated my question. "Interesting," he mused. "She really got under your skin, didn't she, the nasty old girl. Well, it doesn't help that everyone knew how you felt about her. Makes you the most likely suspect. But have you considered that you're the easy target? Also, you being the murderer doesn't make sense."

"I know, right?"

"Look, even if I thought you were capable of murder I absolutely know for a fact that you'd never sabotage your own business for revenge. Your weird obsession with trying to prove yourself would absolutely forbid it. And even if you were a habitual sleepwalker and abusing Ambien, I feel that your deep-seated need for approval would kick in and supersede all your carnal sleepwalking desires. In a nutshell, darling, I don't think you have anything to worry about there. But just in case, I'll ring an old friend of mine, a neurologist who spends a lot of time at the sleep clinic conducting studies. Truth be told, it's what put me off him. Highly unsettling waking up next to someone who's staring at you and taking notes. *Creeeeepy*. But if sleep-murder is possible, Brad'll know."

"Thanks. Also, could you do a little poking around for me regarding Silvia Lumiere? It's odd, but for all the trouble she caused I know very little about her. See if you can find out if she was ever married, has children, any affiliations, police records or enemies we're unaware of. Also, did she have any strange behaviors, like soliciting young men or drinking blood?"

"Jesus," he admonished. "She's dead. No need to keep dragging the old girl thought the mud."

"Look, her assistant thinks she was a vampire. I'm just covering all the bases."

"How disturbing, and yet I'm intrigued. I'll see what I can do."

Tay lived in the same Victorian building as her shop, inhabiting a charming and utterly chic apartment above the retail space. Since Cherry Pickers wasn't open on Sundays, and Tay was most likely already at the Renaissance fair with Lance, I was hoping her mom was poking around inside the building. Char liked unpacking new stock. She also liked rearranging all the lovely pieces her daughter had already displayed to perfection. It drove Tay nuts, but she loved the fact that her mom took an interest in her business. I went to the back door and knocked, hoping that if Char was around she'd hear me.

A moment later the door flew open, but instead of Char, Tay was the one who stood in the doorway. We were both puzzled and a little confused by the sight of one another.

"Sorry," we both blurted at the same time.

"I should have called," Tay continued, looking upset. "I'm ... I'm not going to the Renaissance fair today."

"No problem," I replied. "I should have called you as well to let you know that I'm not going either."

She frowned. "Because of your Jack-Tate love triangle?"

"No. I mean, there is that. But the real reason is that there's been another murder."

We sat in Tay's airy living room, ensconced in puffy cream chairs and sipping black coffee. I insisted she tell me about Lance first, he being the source of her anxieties. Murder, however much it intrigued her, could wait.

"He's been very upset lately," she said, nervously wringing her hands. "Something happened, but he wouldn't discuss it with me. I mean, we've been dating for nearly a year! I tell him everything! The fact that he wouldn't even give me a hint as to what was bothering him was extremely upsetting. Anyhow, when I noticed that his mood wasn't improving, I kept pressing. All he would tell me was that it was a private matter and that he would handle it. Then, Friday night, he finally broke down and told me. That's the day two men came to his tent at the fair and repossessed his beautiful new suit of armor—in front of a crowd of onlookers! It's not his jousting armor, mind you. That armor he makes himself, but this was special, Whit. It's his parading armor; it's for the pageantry of the fair. It hadn't helped any that his greatest rival, the Green Knight, was laughing at him as the men hauled it away, mocking him for a fool and telling the crowd that such things happen when a knight falls out of favor with his wealthy patron. I tell you, Whit, that destroyed him."

"Holy cobbler," I breathed. "The poor man. What the heck happened?"

"Apparently, the money owed him by an old client he'd been after bounced. It was quite a hefty check, and poor Lance, a very trusting soul, just assumed it would be good. Unfortunately, he'd ordered the armor in anticipation of the funds, then paid for it shortly after depositing the bad check." She shook her head. "He's positively horrible with personal finance. He thought if I knew I'd be upset. Ha! I'll tell you what's upsetting me. I'm upset by the fact he's let that idiot Green Knight into his head. The jousting and tournament battling are mostly all staged. It's little more than playacting, kind of like a medieval version of WWE. However, last night when he came home I saw that his entire body was covered in bruises, and I think he has a couple of broken ribs as well. He refused to go to the doctor. Said it was just punishment for being stupid enough to trust this particular client." She picked up her coffee and took a meditative sip.

"He's off his game, Whitney, really badly this time. In the state he's in he's little more than a pin cushion for the other knights to impale during the tournament. I begged him not to go today, but he just ignored me and stormed out the door. He's so down on himself that I fear he's going to get himself killed. And I absolutely refuse to watch him sacrifice that gorgeous body for such a stupid cause."

"I agree," I said, giving a silent nod to Lance's stunning physique. "Such a terrible waste. So, who's this shoddy client and why does he owe Lance so much money?"

"That's the upsetting part. He won't say. It's all part of this mysterious past of his that he absolutely forbids anyone to dredge up, including me. I used to find it hot. Now it's just annoying. Anyhow, those are my demons at the moment."

"Pretty big demons. I'm sorry I'm not at the fair today offering moral support. I really was planning on going until Grandma Jenn found Silvia Lumiere lying dead at the bottom of the stairs in the foyer."

It was Tay's turn to be aghast. I quickly filled her in on all I knew, including the fact that Jack regarded me as a prime suspect.

"Really?" she quipped. "Just because she was found with a scone in her mouth? Every time I saw that woman she had a scone in her mouth ... or a sour cherry martini. Who's to say she didn't trip?"

"One can only hope, but I doubt that's the case. According to Jack, the scone was shoved pretty far down her throat. It was enough to choke her. Jack believes the tumble down the stairs finished her off by causing a broken neck. Anybody could have done the deed, but what really grinds my gears is the fact that Jack immediately assumed I'm the one who killed her."

"Right," she mused. "Because of the scone and the fact that she made your life a living hell."

"But anyone who knew me would know that I didn't do it. As much as the woman drove me crazy, I could never harm her let alone commit murder—if for no other reason than it would compromise the Cherry Orchard Inn brand. And Lord knows how hard I'm working to rebuild it since the debacle this spring."

Tay agreed. "So, was Jack serious?"

"Serious enough to pull me into the station and interrogate me."

"NO!"

"It's true. He didn't even offer me coffee or water. He just jumped right in with the insulting questions."

"The peckerhead!"

"Yep, but that's not the half of it. He actually asked me if anyone was in bed with me last night who could verify that I didn't get up and kill Silvia. Part of me believes the only reason he asked the question was because he thinks I'm back with Tate. And, for the record"—I added, noting the curiosity dripping from her eyes—"no, to both those questions."

"Damn," Tay remarked. "What are you going to do?"

"Oh, I'm gonna get him good. I'm going to find Silvia Lumiere's real murderer before Jack does and rub it in his face."

"Yes!" she cried, and set down her empty coffee mug. "Yes, my friend. You go girl!"

"Darn right," I affirmed, filling with self-righteousness. "I've done it before and I'll do it again. In fact, that's why I'm here. I came to retrieve my suspect board and my dry-erase markers. Do you still have them?"

"I do. They're in my office, right where we left them last time."

"Excellent. And I'm going to need a ride. Can you give me a lift back to the inn?"

"I'll do even better than that. I'm coming with you. I never thought I'd say this, but murder's just the thing to keep my mind off that stubborn knight of mine."

Twenty minutes later Tay emerged from her garage with two oversized helmets and her Vespa scooter. "Where's your car?" I asked, eyeing the scooter with suspicion.

"Lance took it this morning. He's afraid they might repo his car next, so we're leaving it in the garage just in case. All right, you know the drill. Put that on, and hop aboard."

A moment later, heralded by a loud PUT-PUT-PUT, we pulled into church-going traffic slightly above walking speed while trailing a cloud of thick black smoke. Motorists didn't love us, but it was a public road, and we were on a mission. I felt there was a good deal of honking for what was normally a polite crowd, yet even this couldn't shake Tay from her course. Sitting behind her with my giant whiteboard under my arm, I felt like a rage target. I pulled a marker from my pocket and scribbled a large *SORRY*, which I turned to the queue of cars stacking up behind us.

"I've got a plan," Tay cried over the noise of the scooter. "Nobody interrogates my friend! Get ready, Whit. We're about to rile up some roof-goats."

"I don't think that's such a—"

With a jerk of the handle bars, Tay veered off the road and into the police station parking lot. Someone clapped, but the sound was soon drowned out by the revving of the scooter's overtaxed motor. Thing One and Thing Two, frolicking on the thick turf roof, loved it. They bounded across the grass with screams of pure goat-joy. Inside the building MacDuff started barking. A moment later Jack flew out the door, red-faced and angry.

Rubbing salt into the wound, I flashed him my newly revised whiteboard as Tay threw the Vespa into gear. Defiantly I held it up. *SORRY, NOT A MURDERER!*

"Nice," Jack cried over the racket of the goats, dog and scooter. "But it's going to take more than a declaration on a whiteboard to prove your innocence. And I forgot to tell you, in case you were wondering. You're not to leave town, not until you're off the suspect list."

Tay gave Jack the back of her hand, then kicked the Vespa into gear.

It would have been awesome if we could have sped away, leaving Jack in the dust. Unfortunately, all our anticlimactic exit produced was more joyous goat-screams and some not so nice comments from the other motorists trying to navigate the bayside road.

Fifteen

The moment we pulled up to the Cherry Orchard Inn, Greta Stone, the statuesque reporter from Baywatch News (and Jack's former girlfriend) abandoned her current interview and ran down the wide steps of the front porch toward the sputtering scooter. The poor cameraman assigned to her had no choice but to run after her. The last thing I needed was to be questioned by Greta Stone, but this time there was no Jack to protect me from the press, and the scooter couldn't be relied upon to outrun the leggy blonde on stilettos, although Tay was willing to give it a try.

"Damn," she breathed when Greta jumped in front of the old Vespa, waving frantically.

"Whitney!" Greta cried as Tay hit the brakes. "Whitney Bloom!" she said again, reminding me that not only did she know me but, thanks to recent troubles at the orchard, we were on a first name basis. It was like bad déjà vu all over again, being accosted on the front steps of the inn by Greta. Grrrretah!

Truthfully, aside from the ditzy blonde act and the sensational angle she used to pump up her ratings, Greta wasn't all that bad. My issue with her stemmed more from the fact that she and Jack had a history together, and really, I knew very little about it. Jack never wanted to discuss it, and anyhow, what did I care about that now? She could have him back for all I cared. So why were the fingers of jealousy creeping up my spine? I shook them off and had to applaud the reporter's tenacity. The woman jumped right in with cameras rolling.

"Whitney Bloom, the current manager of the Cherry Orchard Inn, has just pulled up on a scooter with gal-pal Taylor Robinson, owner of the trendy boutique Cheery Pickers. Ms. Bloom, what is the meaning of that sign you're carrying?" Before I could register what she was saying, her cameraman moved in for a close-up of the whiteboard. Tay uttered a profanity and then ripped the sign from my hands, vigorously employing her shirtsleeve on the round letters. Unfortunately, Greta, her cameraman, and the greater Green Bay viewing area had seen it.

"'Sorry, not a murderer?'" she quoted with a probing look. "On the morning of yet another murder at the Cherry Orchard Inn, don't you find that a strange message to be toting around town? Or are you in fact proclaiming your innocence before a proper investigation can take place?"

I stared at her a moment. Then, urged by a sharp elbow in my ribs, flipped into damage control mode, something I had a good deal of experience with lately. The first and most important tactic was to deflect suspicion. "Greta, so glad you're here," I said, projecting a confidence I didn't feel. "As you can imagine, it's been a difficult morning. Everyone here at the Cherry Orchard Inn is saddened and traumatized by the loss of Silvia Lumiere. Today the art world has lost a huge talent."

"Is it true you're the head baker of this establishment?"

"It is."

"And is it true that Ms. Lumiere was found at the bottom of the main staircase with a cherry scone stuffed into her mouth—a cherry scone baked by you?"

"That is also true. But before we jump to conclusions I believe it's important to note that the authorities are still trying to determine whether Ms. Lumiere's death was accidental. Anyone who knew her could tell you that she wasn't very steady on her feet."

"Actually, Ms. Bloom, the coroner has determined cause of death. We just got word a few minutes ago. According to the coroner's office in Door County General, the famed portrait painter, Silvia Lumiere, died from a broken neck suffered from a fall down the stairs. Crumbs from the cherry scone stuffed down her throat were also found in her lungs, indicating aspiration as well as suffocation. Now do you see why that sign you're carrying is so suspicious?"

I didn't much care for her smirk, or the way her Barbie-blonde hair tumbled over her shoulder with the tilt of her head.

Tay jumped to the rescue. "We hadn't heard," she said, kicking the Vespa into gear. "And Ms. Bloom has nothing more to say to you on the matter."

I pulled Tay into the inn's kitchen with me and shut the door behind us.

"What are we doing in here?" she asked as I flipped on the lights.

"Brainstorming," I told her. "I'm a murder suspect. We need to think, and I always think better when my hands are covered in dough."

"Gotcha," she said and set the suspect board on the prep counter, propping it up against the open shelving. While Tay picked up a marker, I took down two glasses and proceeded to fill them with sour cherry juice topped with a measure of good old-fashioned ginger ale. I handed a sour cherry fizz to Tay and took a sip of my own.

"Whatcha making?" she asked, turning to the whiteboard.

As I rattled around the kitchen, pulling down mixing bowls, rubber scrapers, a pastry cutter, and a sack of flour, I replied, "I feel like I need to work with a really complex yeast dough, but I don't have time for that. Instead I'm afraid it's scones again."

"Fitting," she quipped with a slight grin. "Besides, I'm starving. There's nothing like a fresh scone out of the oven."

Scones were relatively simple to make, and that was fine with me. As I thought about the murder of Silvia Lumiere I measured out the flour, the baking powder, the sugar and salt, and gave it a good stir. Next I added the cold butter and cut it in to the dough with my pastry cutter until it was the size of small, crumbly peas. As I worked on the scones, Tay began scribbling names on the board as fast as I could say them.

"Fred Beauchamp," I said, adding the dried cherries and toasted pecans. "Silvia's romantic interest. I saw him leave the inn around midnight, but he could have come back."

Whisking the sour cream into the half-and-half, I added, "I suppose we should add Bob Bonaire as well."

"Good call. Silvia was so hyper-critical of his delicious food it's a wonder the man didn't strangle her in the middle of the dining room."

"Peter McClellan," I added next, sinking my hands in the moist dough and giving it a good kneed.

"Hot Jesus, her hippie assistant. Can't leave that wack job off the list." Tay grinned and scribbled his name on the suspect board.

"And Erik Larson," I said, less than enthusiastically. "I believe he was the last person to have seen Silvia alive after delivering a tray of scones to her room."

Tay grimaced as I said this, but wrote his name down as well. She turned to me, noting that my hands were covered in sticky, lumpy dough. "Do you really think he could have done something like this?"

As I shaped the dough on the floured surface, patting it in to a nice inch-thick disk, I shook my head. "I dearly hope not. But we're going to need to talk with him. Also, and I hate to even mention this, but I have another name that I think we need to consider."

"Who?" Tay remarked, looking quizzical.

"Hannah. You'll recall that after her goat yoga debacle on the lawn Silvia had her banned from the inn … and I allowed it." I gave a guilty shake of my head. "To keep the peace, mind you. But you know as well as I do that Hannah was mortally embarrassed, especially so because she's romantically involved with Peter. It all got out of hand, and Silvia would have been perfectly justified asking to have all goats banned from the lawn while she was painting. But she wasn't satisfied with that. She wanted her pound of flesh from Hannah and was going to take it come hell or high water. It was a personal attack on our friend, and I'm inclined to believe it was more the fact that Hannah had grabbed Peter's attention than her questionable yoga class. I was with Jack one morning in the bakery when he had warned Hannah not to get involved with Peter. He told her that Silvia was very possessive of her things, Peter included. Hannah, of course, just laughed."

"I would have too," Tay admitted, thinking on what I had just told her. "So, you think Silvia was in some private war with Hannah?"

The dough, now cut into six perfect pie-shaped wedges and brushed with a nice egg wash, went into the hot oven. I shut the oven door and answered. "I think Silvia was in a private war with nearly everyone that displeased her. In Hannah's case I believe Silvia's goal was to deny her access to Peter. Think about it? She banishes Hannah from the inn and runs poor Peter ragged with her petty requests. But our Hannah's not one to sit back and take that kind of thing lightly."

A fearful look crossed Tay's face. "But ... would she really kill the old witch?"

"I hope not, but ...?" I shrugged. Tay gave a nod and added the name *Hannah Winthrop*. I had just dumped the dirty bowls into the sink when I saw the other name she'd added—a name placed at the top of the list.

"What?" I cried, drying my hands and slapping the dishtowel on the rim of the sink. "You can't do that!" I protested. "You can't add my name to the list. I'm investigating this murder!"

"Right. But if you *were* the murderer, that would be the perfect cover, wouldn't it?"

"But I've already told you that I didn't murder her! That's why we're doing this!"

"Easy, Whit. I believe you. But to the rest of the world you're still a prime suspect. As Jack pointed out, you have motive, opportunity, and access to the murder weapon." Here she pointed to the oven where the scones were baking nicely. "Plus there's only your word that you were asleep during the critical time. That's why we have to add you to the list. We need to write your statement down, then prove beyond a shadow of a doubt that you didn't murder Silvia Lumiere."

"You do have a point," I grudgingly admitted. I crossed the kitchen, opened one of the drawers and pulled out a notebook full of hand-scribbled recipes. I flipped to a clean sheet, grabbed up a pen and handed both to Tay. "Here. It's best that you take this down—for the record." Then, while the scones baked and filled the kitchen with their heavenly cherry smell, I proceeded to walk Tay through every detail I could remember, from the last time I had seen Silvia alive talking with

Fred Beauchamp to the moment Grandma Jenn took me to the lifeless body at the foot of the steps.

"Damn, those smell good," she remarked. Then, studying her notes, she added, "Question. Would Jenn have any reason to want Silvia dead?"

"Not that I know of. Silvia and Gran were on friendly terms. The only plausible reason Gran might have to want her dead would be because of how Silvia treated me. But she'd hardly frame me for the murder by choking her with one of my scones. Remember the part when I told you that Gran thought I was responsible?"

"Right. But what if it was a little spat in the heat of the moment and there was nothing at hand but a couple of your scones?"

I shook my head. "First, Gran's too thoughtful and centered to ever lose her head like that. And secondly, if she was going to murder someone, I think she'd use poison."

"Yeah," Tay nodded. "Totally. You're gran's the clever sort, and devious. She'd definitely use poison."

We both knew it was a ridiculous line of conversation. Grandma Jenn was not a killer, but somehow the practice of thinking it through was cathartic. It helped soften the blow for the next name on our list.

"Okay. Let's talk about Hannah," Tay said, and drew a line under the name. "Do we know where she was when the murder took place?"

"Not yet. All I know is that Hannah and Peter arrived at the police station just as Jack was finishing up with me." I cast her a wan smile. "They were both dressed for the Renaissance fair. They looked great. I hadn't told them we weren't going."

"Whitney," Tay chided, giving a disparaging shake of her chic red hair.

"But here's the part I can't get out of my head. When I told them that we couldn't go because Silvia had been murdered, Peter barely reacted to the news. Hannah, however, looked scared. Really scared, and that's not like her. Hey. What are you doing?"

Tay looked up from her phone. "Calling her. She's our friend, Whit. Let's give her the benefit of the doubt. Okay?"

Fifteen minutes later, while eating warm scones topped with sour cherry icing and mulling over the names on our suspect board, we heard a knock at the kitchen door. It was Hannah. She'd changed out of her medieval outfit and was now wearing shorts and a sleeveless top. She was also carrying a bottle of wine.

"It's five o'clock somewhere," she proclaimed, raising the bottle. "Dang it, girl! Those scones smell yummy." As I plated one for Hannah, she continued. "Okay. I know what's going on here. There's been another murder, which means that Cherry Cove's top crime solvers are on it. Ladies let the brainstorming begin. Swingin' dingles!" she cried, noting the suspect board for the first time. "Would someone mind telling me why my name is on there … and Peter's?"

Hannah looked pissed. It was becoming an all-too-familiar look for her when visiting the Cherry Orchard Inn, and rightly so. "Relax," I soothed. "Mine's up there too. At the top, no less. The only one of us who didn't make the list is Tay. That's why she'll be asking the questions."

Although it wasn't quite yet noon, we unanimously agreed to open the bottle of wine and grease the skids, so to speak, before the uncomfortable questioning began. Tay, sitting on a stool before the suspect board, downed the remains of her wine. "All right, let's get this over with. Hannah, where were you between midnight last night and five this morning?"

Hannah had already been questioned by Jack; apparently her interview went a little better than mine had. At least she could vouch for the fact she had spent the entire night with Peter, providing them both with an alibi.

"Okay, so you two were together the whole night. Was this at your place or the inn?"

"Well, since I was banned from the inn," she said, flashing me a pointed look, "I guess it would have to have been at my place, wouldn't it?"

I studied her closely, noticing the crossing and uncrossing of her legs as if she were uncomfortable, and then came the nervous laughter. Hannah laughed easily, but this was a totally different kind of laughter. My friend was lying.

"You weren't at home," I said accusingly.

"Of course we were. That's exactly where we were when you called us."

"But that was this morning. You were at the inn last night, weren't you?"

"I never stepped a foot inside the inn, not since you banned me." She crossed her arms and glared at me.

There was something Hannah wasn't telling us. Unlike Tay, I had seen her face the moment she learned of Silvia's death. Hannah had been terribly frightened. She was hardly a murderer, so why was she so frightened? What did she know? I looked into my friend's wide blue eyes and understood it had something to do with her latest infatuation, Peter McClellan.

"Okay," I said. "You weren't at home all night, but you weren't at the inn either. So where were you?"

She wrung her hands as her eyes nervously shot around the deathly quiet kitchen. "Oh, all right," she relented. "But you can't tell Jack. Promise?"

Tay shot me a look. If Hannah didn't want Jack to know something, that was fine by me. We both nodded our agreement.

"Okay, we were here, but not at the inn."

I inhaled sharply. "You were down at the beach again! You were down by the old lighthouse! Hannah, how could you?"

"How could I not?" she cried. "You saw what she did to me. And, from the moment she caught us making out in his room, she's been merciless to Peter."

"Wait." Tay held up a hand, looking confused. "Silvia caught you two making out? When? Where?"

"A few nights ago," Hannah admitted. "Peter has no privacy in that room. Silvia had his spare key. And Peter failed to mention that she barges in whenever she pleases. It was two in the morning, for cripes' sake! Anyhow, last night Peter insisted we meet. Silvia was really getting under his skin."

"So what were you two doing down by the old lighthouse?" Tay inquired.

"They were smoking pot," I said, and crossed my arms like a disapproving adult.

"Well, yes, that was part of it. But we were also putting a hex on Peter's voodoo doll of Silvia." All the color drained from Hannah's face and her lower lip began to tremble. "We didn't mean to kill her, honestly … at least I didn't. I thought it was just a bit of spooky occult fun, but when we heard …" Hannah broke off with a sob. "Oh, the horror of it!"

Tay, utterly confused, jumped in. "Wait. What the dickens are you talking about? Who has a voodoo doll?"

"Peter," we both said in unison.

"Great Odin's beard! And why am I the last to know about this?" Tay's large brown eyes glittered with intrigue.

113

Once Hannah had settled down, and Tay was brought up to speed on the doings down by the old lighthouse, Hannah told us her mind-boggling tale. Peter, apparently pushed to his wits end by Silvia, had called Hannah and asked her to meet him at the Cherry Cove Light-house at midnight. There the two descended to the beach where they built a fire and partook of Peter's medicinal cleansing herb. Hannah listened patiently to Peter's latest diatribe against his manipulative employer. Having been banned from the inn by the nasty old woman, she agreed. That's when Peter took out the voodoo doll of Silvia.

"He said some words," she remarked. "I didn't understand them. He wasn't speaking English. Then, when he was done speaking, he held the doll up to the black sky and said he wished that the old bitch would trip and break her neck. That's when he grabbed the doll's head and snapped it right off at the neck. Peter's a pacifist. It was the most violent thing I've ever seen him do. Then he threw the head into the fire and put the body back into the pocket of his cloak. But that was it. That was all. He killed the doll, but we never believed it would really work. Oh, God, I never imagined that voodoo was real! I'm such an idiot!" Hannah buried her face in her hands and began to cry.

"Hannah," I said, placing a hand on her shoulder. "It's okay. But I have to ask you something else." She looked up from her hands, her fair face blotchy with tears. "You said that you met Peter at midnight. At any time between midnight and my phone call earlier this morning, did he return to the inn?"

She shook her head.

Tay, looking slightly amused, added, "And did Peter, by chance, try to shove a cherry scone down this voodoo doll's throat before he snapped off her head?"

I shot my friend a questioning look, not sure where she was going with this. Her reply was a patient nod. Hannah merely looked confused.

"No," she snuffled. "That doesn't make sense. It's a wooden doll. Wooden dolls don't eat scones."

"Does Peter?" I asked.

"Hardly. He's a health freak. He says your scones are too full of nasty sugars and fats."

"More like delicious sugar and fats," Tay quipped. "So, Peter doesn't eat Whitney's scones?"

"No, and what's that got to do with Silvia's death?"

"Didn't Jack tell you?" I asked. "Silvia was suffocated with a cherry scone before she tumbled down the stairs."

"Oh no," she breathed. "I didn't see that one coming." Hannah, fear-stricken, added, "He ... he did mention something about hoping the old bitch choked on a scone, or ... or maybe he said bone ... right before snapping off her head. Either way, he's one powerful wizard."

Or one clever murderer, I mused, but kept that thought to myself.

Sixteen

$\mathcal{W}$hile Tay went with Hannah to talk with Peter, I decided to head out to the old farmhouse on Stage Road where the Larsons lived. It was Erik's day off, and although he wouldn't be too happy to see me, I needed to talk with him before Jack did. Lori, his mother, answered the door. Her fingers were stained purple and she was covered from head to toe with flour.

"Baking pies," she proclaimed, looking frazzled. "I'm trying my hand at blackberries. Messy little things. What brings you out here on a Sunday?"

Lori, a single mother, real estate broker and an ambitious novice baker, was very likely the only person in Cherry Cove who didn't know there'd been a murder. For the love of me, I wanted to keep her in the dark, especially since her son was employed at the very site of the murder. However, she was a parent, and it was best she know all the details. Once inside the door I briefly described Silvia's suspicious death and my reason for the visit.

"That nasty old witch," Lori added. "Can't say I'm sorry to hear it. Erik's told me all about her and how horrid she was to you. He loves working at the inn, Whitney. I hope this doesn't change anything?"

"Nope. Everything's fine. But I do need to ask your son a few questions."

"Well, you're gonna have to wake him then. He got in very late last night. Good luck. That boy sleeps like the dead."

It was my second, and hopefully last, visit to the garbage dump known as Erik Larson's bedroom. And here I thought Peter McClellan's room had smelled bad. Stale and skunky was repulsive, but it still couldn't hold a candle to the taint of sweaty locker room bathed in dirty undies. I proceeded with caution. The boy was sleeping in his bed, buried under a pile of rumpled clothing.

"Erik!" I said loudly, not expecting him to react as violently as he did. He sprang up, eyes wide and gelled hair standing on end. Then, seeing my face, he flopped back down on the pillow. When I realized he wasn't moving or attempting to wake up, I said his name again.

"Oh. You're still here. I thought I was dreaming. What day is it? Am I late or something?"

"No. Listen, I don't want to alarm you, but Silvia Lumiere's been murdered."

He sat up again, this time making a serious attempt at waking. "What?" he cried.

"It happened last night," I told him. "Sometime between midnight and five in the morning. This is important, Erik. As far as I know, you were the last person to see her alive."

Above the clear blue eyes, his brow furrowed. "What ... are you saying, Miss Bloom? Do you think I ...?"

"No, but I do know she delighted in tormenting you."

"You too," he protested.

"True. She was an unpleasant lady. But I need you to think. You were the last person I saw last night. Do you remember what time that was?"

"You finished making your scones for the morning at around eleven thirty. I remember seeing you leave the kitchen," he said. "I was in there with Boner and Kenna cleaning up. You told us that you were going to the front desk. Said something about a Renaissance fair and Sunday morning checkout."

"Right. I was checking to see what guests were checking out and which rooms needed to be turned over. I was supposed to be at the Renaissance fair today and just wanted to get a handle on things before I went to bed. That's when Silvia came over and demanded that a plate of scones and a bottle of wine be brought up to her room. I popped into the kitchen and relayed the order to you. I assume you're the one who delivered it?" Erik nodded. "Okay, I need you to tell me what time you took it up."

Erik pondered. "She was like a short, fat, wine-guzzling Bob Ross, only Bob Ross was way more chill."

"And kinder," I added, smiling inwardly at his remark. "All right, Erik, I need you to remember. What time did you deliver her tray?"

Erik stared into the distance a moment, scratching his messy blond hair. "I didn't jump right to it, of course. I like to make her wait. If she'd been in the habit of tipping me, it'd be another matter."

"I understand," I said. "So what time *did* you go to her room?"

He shrugged. "Twelve thirty, quarter to one, maybe."

That surprised me. It seemed later than usual. I asked, "And how was she when you went there?"

"Angry, as usual. And nasty." The blond head tilted. "But she wasn't handsy. That *was* unusual." A troubled look crossed his face. "It's kind of a perverse dance we go through, Ms. Bloom. I've told you

118

of it, just as I've told you not to worry. I can handle Silvia's insults and the fact that she never signs for her bill. We all know her game. Last night she just called me a brainless twit, took the tray, and slammed the door."

"Was anyone else in the room with her?"

He shrugged. "I don't know. I didn't see anyone. But come to think of it there might have been." A sly smile came to his lips. "I thought I heard someone clearing their throat—in a manly sort of way. I thought maybe it was Mr. Beauchamp, ya know? But it could have come from the room next door."

I thought about that. "I saw Fred Beauchamp leaving the inn around midnight."

"He could have come back. Guests always use the side door after midnight. Maybe Ms. Lumiere gave him her key?"

"That's a very good possibility," I said, and wondered why I hadn't thought of it earlier. Probably because I was tired and overwhelmed by another death at the inn. I then asked if he'd seen anyone else at the inn at that late hour.

"Only the older dude staying in the Swan Suite and his lady friend. They were on the second floor too, trying to unlock their door. They were a little drunk," he explained.

Interesting, I thought, recalling events of the morning. The gentleman staying in the Swan Suite had been fascinated with the crime scene. So fascinated, in fact, that the authorities had asked him to stay in his room quite a few times. "Is there anything else about last night that seemed strange to you or stood out in your mind?"

His face darkened a measure as he shrugged. "Not really. Kenna and I were busy cleaning the patio. We left shortly after I delivered Ms. Lumiere's room service."

"Oh, and one more thing, did you happen to see Peter at the inn last night, or Hannah?"

Almost without thinking he gave a quick, dismissive shake of his head. Unfortunately, I thought it a little too quick. I repeated the question again and got the same reply. I had enough experience with Erik Larson to know that although it wasn't an outright lie, he was hiding something. But it would never do to press him. From years of studying armed forces commercials, I was aware that young men enduring hardships together formed an unspoken alliance. It was like the bro-code on steroids. And although Silvia Lumiere was hardly as dangerous as terrorist-infested streets, she was that psychotic taskmaster who'd put both men through their paces. Erik might be covering for Peter, and it was up to me to figure out why. But now was not the time.

"Anything else?" he asked. I shook my head and made to leave. I was almost at the door when he asked, "Hey, Ms. Bloom, how'd she die?"

"By cherry scone," I said, turning to face him. He almost laughed, thinking I was joking. I quickly elaborated. "It was stuffed down her throat before she was pushed down the stairs. She broke her neck in the fall. Grandma Jenn found her body early this morning."

His eyes shot wide, and his face blanched as gray as the undies littering his floor. "Oh, God," he breathed and flopped back down on his pillow.

Seventeen

I was in my red Ford Escape driving back to the inn when my phone rang. It was Giff. I pulled off the road and took the call.

"Okay, Whitney dear, I've done a little digging on our unfortunate portrait painter. It's amazing what a few phone calls and some pointed internet searching will do. Dredges up all kinds of skeletons in the proverbial closet. Get this. Ms. Lumiere's Gold Coast penthouse apartment is in foreclosure."

"Really?" I breathed, thinking that would explain all the penny-pinching behaviors Ms. Lumiere exhibited at the inn. "Any idea why?"

"Only the obvious one. The woman spent more than she made. Apparently, Ms. Lumiere liked living large—furs, jewelry, fine dining, expensive spa treatments—all of which she put on credit cards and didn't pay. And you're right. She had a nasty habit of propositioning younger men. Five years ago, there was a case brought against her by a young man whose identity has been protected. This man claimed he worked for Silvia at her studio, although there seems to be some disagreement whether she ever paid him for his work. This mysterious person—we'll call him Jonny Doe—claimed that he worked under constant sexual harassment and ill treatment. Now, you might not want to believe this, angel, but sexual harassment against males isn't taken as seriously as it is for female employees, especially five years ago, when this case supposedly occurred. It appears that it took our Jonny Doe some time before he spoke up about it. The straw that broke the camel's back was when Ms. Lumiere allegedly made him pose in the nude for an erotic portrait, stating that once he did she'd pay him all the monies owed to him. According to sources, Jonny Doe claimed to have posed in the nude, but there's no evidence that this painting exists. And if it did, Ms. Lumiere certainly never paid him. The entire case was thrown out of court when Silvia made a mockery out of this poor man by countering his accusation with a salacious one of her own, stating Jonny Doe was the real abuser and that he was just after her money. She must have been very convincing, because after the hearing there was never any mention of this person, or this case, again."

"Oh, the poor man," I replied, empathetically. "From what I know of Ms. Lumiere, he was probably telling the truth. In fact, Tate recently told me that ever since Silvia's been coming to Cherry Cove, she's flirted with him. She even tried to pinch his behind whenever he wasn't looking. Tate, being Tate, just laughed it off, until last year when Silvia tried to get him to pose in the nude for a portrait."

"My, my," Giff uttered. Then, with a little too much enthusiasm, added, "And did he?"

"Of course not! Tate has his standards."

"Well, good for him." Giff's voice was laced with a heavy dose of sarcasm as he said this. He cleared his throat, invoking "corporate Giff" once again. "Anyhow, I just thought you'd be interested to know that there's a Jonny Doe running around out there with a pretty big axe to grind against your unfortunate guest. She really was quite talented, though."

"So I hear. Anything else?"

"Yes. Two things. The first is that I'm on my way to the Cherry Orchard Inn. I'll be arriving in time for supper. And, if you're back on that delicious ex-boyfriend of yours, call him. I don't mind third-wheeling it with you two."

I was relieved to hear Giff was coming to Cherry Cove. He was a good friend, always entertaining, and had valuable skills that would come in handy when trying to crack this case. He also adored my family and valued my friends nearly as much as I did.

"I'll do better than that," I told him. "I'll call Tay and her valiant knight, Lance, as well. Hannah and her new man will most likely want to join us too. And Grandma Jenn, of course. There's always a crowd at the inn for dinner."

"Excellent! You know that Grandma Jenn's my spirit animal. As long as her pie-bribing nemesis Edna's not there, count me in."

"Will do. But I'm putting you up in the family quarters. There's a lot of crime scene tape hanging around the inn."

"Nothing ruins a party like a swag of crime scene tape, not to mention the fact that the color's God-awful unless you're a bumble-bee or a cop. And speaking of cops, crime scenes, and criminals, here's the second thing I wanted to tell you. Silvia has an ex-husband. Again, it should come as no surprise that the man had money. It only lasted seven years, though. Nasty divorce. No kids involved, but she did get a hefty settlement of two million dollars. However, this divorce happened ten years ago. Apparently the money's gone, and although Ms. Lumiere is a fine painter, her work doesn't demand the high prices it once did."

I sat a moment, absorbing this new information, and then thought to ask after the ex-husband's name.

"Stanley Gordon," Giff offered. "Owns a string of high-end car dealerships in the greater Chicagoland area."

The name sounded familiar. "Can you text me a picture?" A moment later, staring at the face on my iPhone, my suspicions were confirmed. Stanley Gordon was the middle-aged man gawking over the railing at the body this morning. Stanley Gordon was the name of the man staying in the Swan Suite.

Thanks to Giff and his dogged research we had another name to add to our growing list of suspects. As I raced back to the inn I was filled with a sense of excitement. Stanley Gordon was a weekend guest. I remembered the man checking in on Friday afternoon, booked for a two-night stay. How convenient that he'd be checking out today, I thought, especially after the mysterious death of his ex-wife. However, I doubted if anyone else but Giff and I knew of his connection to the dead woman. After securing the crime scene, Jack had conducted a preliminary interview of all the guests, which largely consisted of taking down names, permanent addresses, and any statements willingly offered. But Jack had been so focused on me as his prime suspect that I doubted he'd given Stanley Gordon a second look. And why would he? Well, I was going to give him that second look, and hopefully put an end to this troubling case. Another death at the Cherry Orchard Inn was not going to be good for business.

I was pondering business and the very real problem of damage control as I drove up to the inn, then stopped the moment I saw the parking lot. It was full, too full under the circumstances. The crime scene unit, police and news van had all left, having been replaced by what looked to be guests arriving for a black-tie event, or perhaps a group of misplaced churchgoers. A quick glance at the time on my iPhone told me that church was done for the day.

The men and women crowding the wide front porch, carrying flowers and teddy bears, small-framed pictures, and votive candles, made me suspicious. Then I spied Edna Baker lugging her insulated casserole carrier up the front steps.

"No," I hissed. My suspicions were further confirmed when I saw Alexa Livingstone dressed in black emerging from her white Audi. Beside her was the potter and romancer of Silvia Lumiere, Fred Beauchamp. I slammed the car door, dashed through the parking lot and pushed my way up the front steps.

"What the heck is going on here?" I demanded.

"It's her!" Alexa cried, her arms loaded with red roses, her face streaked with tears. "It's Silvia's murderer! We all knew you had it in for her, but why, WHY, did you have to kill her?"

"What? Wait." I was dumbfounded, and more than a little angry. "Please, all of you, listen to me. I'm not responsible for this! The notion's ridiculous."

"Is it?" Fred Beauchamp challenged. I didn't like the way he was looking at me. "The poor woman was choked with one of your scones and pushed down the stairs in the middle of the night. You knew she was arthritic and yet you made her stay on the second floor." Like Alexa, his eyes were red and his cheeks wet with tears.

"We ... we have an elevator," I reasoned, feeling fear nipping at my heels.

Fred rounded on me. "She was a difficult woman, I'll grant you that. But she didn't deserve to die like a pitiful beast, all alone on the cold, hard floor."

"How...how do you know how she died?" I asked, thinking it a bit odd that he knew all the specifics. I was also recalling what Erik had said about folks using the side doors after midnight. Silvia could have been making a show of teasing Fred and then sending him home, but not before slipping him her room key for a more private visit. Erik thought that somebody could have been in the room with Silvia...why not Fred? I swallowed my fear and gave him a hard look.

He threw it right back. "We all heard it. Greta Stone broke the story this morning. We all saw that picture of you holding your incriminating sign. It's all anyone is talking about—all thanks to you and your...your damn murderous cherry scones!" These last words were flung in my face like a rotten tomato.

"I did not kill that woman!" I averred, staring at the angry crowd. I soon realized that whatever I said was going to be judged harshly. I'd already been convicted of a crime I didn't commit by these people. I decided it best to go on the attack. "And would someone mind telling me what you're all doing here, the entire Cherry Country Arts Council—and Edna Baker—standing on my front porch?"

"We are honoring the memory of the renowned painter and our dear friend, Silvia Lumiere," Alexa called from within her circle of friends. "The police won't allow us into the building, so the inn's front porch has, by default, become the sight of our memorial to the beloved Ms. Lumiere."

"Oh no-no-no!" I cried. With anger pulsing through my veins, I grabbed Alexa Livingstone by the arm and pulled her down the steps of the front porch with me. Standing on the other side of the inn's iconic turret for privacy, I said, "Look, Alexa, this is a place of business. I know you're upset about Silvia. I am too, but your people cannot place flowers, teddy bears, lit candles, and...and..." I glanced back at the porch, where I caught a glimpse of a framed picture depicting Fred Beauchamp kissing Silvia Lumiere on the lips. I swallowed hard, choking back the bile, and continued. "And slightly inappropriate photos of Silvia Lumiere here!"

She looked at me, pity in her eyes and roses in the crook of her arm. "I thought, I truly thought, you understood, Whitney. It was about the greater good. Letting Silvia's unkind ways roll off your back."

"But I did," I told her. "I really did, Alexa." It was then that a thought popped into my head. She was, after all, Silvia's friend and the head of the arts council. "What about you? Where were you last night?"

The dark eyes nearly popped out of their too-tight sockets at this question. "What are you suggesting? Are you trying to cast blame on me now? Well, your little trick isn't going to work."

"There's no trick, Alexa. And I didn't kill your friend. All I'm asking is where you were last night."

She took a deep breath and adjusted the flowers in her arm. "Very well," she seethed. "Remember, I owe you nothing. You're not a cop and I shouldn't even respond to your stupid question, but I will. I will because Silvia was my friend and she deserves better than she saw here." A condescending smile touched her lips as she answered. "I was at home. I ate dinner in, attended to some work, then went to bed. That's all."

"It sounds remarkably similar to what I did," I remarked and crossed my arms. I imagined it was how Jack felt, heady with the power of interrogation. Unable to let it rest there, I pushed. "And do you have a witness who can verify that statement?" Knowing that, like me, she didn't.

"I do," she said, knocking me off my power trip. I stared at her, noting the chilling confidence with which she spoke. "Paulina, my housekeeper, can verify that I was in bed by eleven. Do you want me

127

to have her call you? Or will you take me at my word?" She was about to head back up the steps when she turned around again. "Perhaps I should let Officer MacLaren know about this little conversation. Does he know that his prime suspect is snooping around, asking questions of mourning civilians?"

"Don't call him," I said. "I'm sure he'll be calling you."

I had climbed the porch stairs as well and was about to enter the inn when Edna shoved her casserole carrier into my hands. It weighed a ton and I told her as much.

"You should have thought about that, sweetie pie, before you gave Silvia the old bumpity-bump-bump down the stairs. Now be a dear and bring that to Jenn. It's my tuna-funeral casserole surprise. Tell her to plate it up and bring it out with some forks and some lemonade. We're all getting parched out here. Mourning is tough work and your porch is getting hot. Also, Jeffery"—she indicated a sandy-haired young man on the other side of the crowd wearing tight jeans and a wrinkly T-shirt—"has brought his guitar. He's a knot-artist." She rolled her eyes as she said this. "Ties a bunch of knots in hemp rope and calls it art. Anyhoo, he thinks he can sing as well. I'm giving you fair warning because we're both Gilded Cherry trophy winners. Bring out the casserole soon or there's going to be a racket out here that'll raise the dead."

I closed my eyes, took a deep breath and opened them again. "Anything else?" I asked.

"You could bring us some of those scones of yours, if you've got any left."

"Really?" I said, staring at her with dripping incredulity. "Don't you think that's in poor taste, considering how the woman died?"

"Actually, it's quite fitting," Alexa broke in, aiming her pointed stare at me. "Under the circumstances."

∞

I was shocked to see Tate in the inn's office dressed as a Viking marauder. He was with my parents, Grandma Jenn, and Brock Sorensen, our accountant, who didn't usually work on Sundays. Today was obviously an exception. I had barged in on a discussion, a troubling one if the looks on their faces were any indication. And then my eyes settled on Tate. In all the commotion at the inn this morning I'd forgotten to call him and tell him that our outing had been canceled. Truthfully, I had never invited him to begin with, but seeing him standing there, dressed in camel-colored pants bound in leather strapping from the knees on down, shirtless, plastic horned Viking helmet atop his head and a bear skin rug draped around his thick shoulders, I couldn't help but smile. He looked good, and his look of genuine concern was just as attractive.

"Babe," he said to me the moment I came through the door. "What a tragedy. You okay?"

"I'm fine," I assured them all. "But we've got the arts council on our front porch to deal with, and they're acting a little batty."

"Indeed they are," Gran concurred. "They're acting as if that woman was a saint, the fools." Her eyes dropped to the object in my hands. "Dear heavens, that looks like Edna's casserole carrier." She eyed the hefty dish with suspicion, then scrunched her nose. "Smells like her tuna-funeral casserole surprise. Let me tell you, nobody wants that kind of surprise at a funeral. Spoiler alert! Funyuns! That's the surprise. Those nasty little onion-flavored cornmeal rings are crunched up and stirred in there. The woman's obsessed with the things. If you were wondering why she always smells like onions and garlic, now you

129

know. And she has some nerve bringing that here. Jani and I are top-rate cooks, and we have a smashing good chef on staff."

"Sure do," Brock was quick to agree. Brock Sorensen, a meat-eater at heart, had married a strict vegan. Needless to say, he ate a lot of his meals at the inn.

Dad shook his head. "What I can't fathom is the way they're all parading out there with that lynch-mob mentality, convicting our Whitney before all the evidence has been gathered—as if she could have done such a thing to that woman!" Although I knew Dad wanted to believe I was innocent, the vacillating expression on his face told me he was still struggling with the idea.

I was getting a little sick of having people think the worst of me, especially my own family. I gave them all a stern look. "You don't seriously still think I had something to do with Silvia's death?" Guilty looks all around confirmed my worst fears. "Oh, COME ON!"

"Look, babe, the woman was a total nut job. Some might say she had it coming. Whatever you did to her, I'll defend you with my life." Tate's spectacular bare chest heaved with Viking bravado. Dangit! Why did he have to look so smokin' hot at a time like this?

Brock cleared his throat, grabbing my attention. "We ah … just got off the phone with our lawyer," he informed me. "We thought it might be wise to cover all our bases. He suggested we go with temporary insanity."

"What? That's insane!" I shot Grandma Jenn a particularly wounded look.

"Dear, I believe you. I've been trying to convince the lot of them all morning that you're innocent."

"Listen up, people, because I'm only going to say this one more time. I did not kill Silvia Lumiere, but I think I can find the person who did." This got their attention. I told them a little bit about my morning, about my list of suspects, and informed them about the identity of the man staying in the Swan Suite. "So, you see? I have plenty of leads."

"I knew you were innocent!" Mom exclaimed in an ill-timed epiphany. Her round blue eyes shimmered with tears of joy. "And best of all, you're going to find Silvia's real killer! How dare Jack think that my girl could do something as cruel as push that arthritic old woman down the stairs?" They were all thinking the same thing, but I liked the fact they were turning on Jack.

"In Jack's defense," Tate chimed in, "he's just doing his job."

As much as I wanted to refute this, I knew it was true. Heck, I was at the head of my own suspect board, though strictly as incentive. It was a reminder of what would happen if I didn't throw my hat into the ring and find Silvia's real killer. I addressed them once again. "Look, time is of the essence. Does anyone remember if Stanley Gordon has checked out of his room?"

"Dear," Mom said, and shook her head. "And that's the other part of this tragedy. Everyone but Silvia's bedraggled assistant has checked out, and he's only here because of the complimentary accommodations. I don't think he has anywhere else to go."

Tate produced a Viking scowl. "Unless you're a member of the arts council, murder at the Cherry Orchard Inn's a total turn-off. I heard some of your guests have transferred to the Blue Heron."

That got me. I handed Edna's casserole over to Mom and Grandma Jenn. "This isn't for us, it's for them. Apparently, they've turned the front porch into a shrine to their favorite artist. I don't know if it's legal but they're doing it. Edna suggested we plate up her casserole and bring it out, along with some lemonade. If they ask, cherry scones are out of the question. I say we plate this up and quickly, or else some knot-artist named Jeffery is going to start singing."

With Mom and Grandma Jenn on the task, I turned to the men. "Dad, do you think you and Brock could hold down the inn a while longer? Tate, as much as I hate to ask this, would you mind throwing on a shirt? I need to take a look at the reservation book. We've got an ex-husband to track down!"

Eighteen

I sat in my car, gripping the steering wheel while staring out the window at the inn's crowded parking lot. I needed to talk with Stanley Gordon. My dilemma was that Stanley and his new wife had checked out of the inn a mere half hour before I arrived. Thanks to hotel records, I not only had Stanley's home address and email but also the make, model, and license plate number of his car. It was a lot of info, but unfortunately, unless I wanted to question him by email or drive all the way down to his house in Barrington, Illinois, none of it helped me. What I needed was the man's cell phone number, which I was pretty certain Jack had gotten as part of his interview. But did I really want to call Jack?

"Babe, let me handle this."

I looked beside me and saw that Tate already had his phone to his ear. His uber-tanned and perfectly muscled chest had been covered, thank heavens, but for some odd reason the horned helmet remained. I must have been staring. He cast me a seductive wink just before addressing the man on the other end of the phone.

"Hey, MacLaren, what's up, bro?" Tate listened to Jack a moment before replying, "Oh, right, busy investigating a murder. Bummer. So where are you now? *The Larson house?*"

This was news to Tate, unpleasant news at that. To me, however, it was music to my ears. Although I was unnerved by the fact that Jack considered Erik a suspect and would put him through his paces, so to speak, it also meant that my investigation was ahead of Jack's. And I wanted to keep it that way. Ignoring Tate's look of genuine concern for Erik, I urged him to continue.

"Yeah, all right. So, um, I was wondering if you had the cell number for of one of the guests who recently left the inn? A Mr. Stanley Gordon?" There was a slight pause on the other end. Then, in a flash of creativity, Tate lied. "He, ah, left in a hurry this morning and forgot one of his bags. I'm here at the inn. Baggsie asked me to call and see if you have it." Bringing Baggsie—aka my dad—into it was a nice touch.

I held my breath as Tate awaited Jack's reply. A moment later I heaved a sigh of relief as Tate gave me a thumbs-up. His lie had worked. He then asked Jack to text him the number before ending the call. With cell number loaded, he handed me the phone. "All right, babe, make the call."

The Gordons agreed to meet us in Sturgeon Bay. They were heading to their favorite supper club for lunch and would remain only as long as their food lasted.

Even though Jack was one step behind me, I had the feeling he was catching up quickly. As Tate and I drove, my iPhone kept lighting up with his number. Three times I let it go to voicemail. The fourth time, Tate, growing irritated, synced my phone with the car's speakers and answered it.

"Where are you?" Jack wasn't mincing words as his voice echoed down around us in my Escape.

"Um, at the inn," I lied.

"You're not at the inn. How do I know this, you ask? Because I'm there now, witnessing some bizarre vigil being held for Silvia Lumiere. The whole artist community is here, and Edna Baker. They're singing and are about ready to burn you in effigy."

"I hope you're joking."

"Not about the singing." It was true. A discordant choir of voices rose and fell in the background, struggling through the words and melody of what sounded like Amazing Grace with a twang of Old MacDonald thrown in. "Hear that?" Jack asked. "It's the second murder at the inn today." Tate and I almost laughed until Jack cut in with, "You've gone after Gordon, haven't you? He never left anything at the inn. My suspicions were confirmed when Alexa Livingstone told me that you tried to interrogate her."

"Interrogate is hardly the word for it. I asked a few questions. Is that a crime?"

"You're a suspect, Whitney. The entire arts council is convinced you murdered Ms. Lumiere, and you're further fanning the flames by sticking your nose in where it doesn't belong. I've already talked with Ms. Livingstone. She was Ms. Lumiere's friend and therefore maybe had some information on what happened last night. Unfortunately, she didn't."

"What if she did it, Jack?"

"Without motive, means, or opportunity, and with an alibi that checks out? Come on, Whitney. Now tell me why you used Tate to get Gordon's cell number."

"Not *used*, bro." Tate, slightly offended by the barb, stepped in to defend himself. "I'm on the case with Whitney."

135

"Tate's in the car with you?" Jack's voice sounded as shocked as it was reprimanding.

"Excellent deduction, Sherlock. All right," I said, having had quite enough of Jack and his attitude for one day. "I'll tell you why I'm interested in Stanley Gordon. While you and the lazy vigilantes are convinced I murdered Ms. Lumiere, I'm actually trying to solve this case by finding the real person responsible. You obviously interviewed Stanley Gordon earlier today. Nothing stood out to you?"

"Look, Whit, you're a suspect. I want to believe you're innocent, but I have to do my job. And regarding Stanley Gordon, he was upset. But so was everyone else I talked to."

"But unlike everyone else you talked to, Stanley Gordon had to be asked several times to get back to his room and not stare over the railing at the dead body on the floor."

"So he's morbidly curious," Jack parried, playing devil's advocate.

"I thought so too until I learned that Stanley Gordon had been married to the newly departed."

"What?" Jack's voice crackled over the car speakers. "Where did you learn that?"

Tate turned his be-horned head, looking impressed. "I have my sources," I told Jack. "Thanks for his number, by the way. The Gordons have agreed to meet us at Babette's Supper Club."

"Okay," Jack said, "I'm on my way. Keep them talking until I get there."

The Wisconsin supper club was a nostalgic blast from the past and, sadly, a dying breed. I'd grown up with supper clubs; my parents' and grandparents' most memorable meals had come from supper clubs;

and I was shocked that my Chicago friends had no idea what a supper club was all about.

A supper club was always a destination. The theme and style of the building was up to the owner, but it was usually set apart, nestled in a picturesque setting or just off the highway where its big neon sign was enough to draw in diners like moths to a flame. The menu was fancy and the prices reasonable. The drink of choice was a cosmopolitan or a brandy old fashioned, never beer or wine. A complimentary relish tray filled with carrot sticks and pickled delicacies was plopped on every table alongside a basket of bread and crackers and plenty of orange cheese spread to go around. Prime rib, perch, and chicken were the stars of the menu; everything came with soup *and* salad *and* potatoes *and* vegetables; and one dessert could feed the entire table. Every Friday was an all-you-can-eat fish fry. In a supper club the décor was circa 1950s, the service friendly but not fast, and few left the restaurant without a doggy bag. It was quintessential Wisconsin, and a dining experience that still spoke to older generations, but not so much to millennials. I, for one, however, was glad that the Gordons had decided to stop at Babette's Supper Club. It meant that they weren't about to leave the Door Peninsula anytime soon.

Tate was the type of man who stood out in a crowd; the fact that he was dressed like a Viking only exaggerated the effect as we entered the restaurant. "Take off the helmet," I whispered as every head turned. Stanley and his wife had been sitting at a booth beside a large picture window. Soup and salad finished, they were now on to the complimentary relish tray where the pickled beets and three-bean salad were currently under attack. Stanley recognized me immediately and stopped chewing.

"Mr. Gordon, thank you for agreeing to meet with us," I said, standing beside the table.

"We didn't know you were bringing a Viking with you," his wife added, clearly enjoying the spectacle. She was a pretty woman, at least a decade younger than her sixty-something-year-old husband and dripping with expensive jewelry,

"This is my friend, Tate Vander Hagen," I explained. "We're supposed to be going to a Renaissance fair today, but our plans got changed."

"I imagine so." A troubled look crossed Stanley's face. "Rough morning at the inn, Ms. Bloom. Please, join us."

"We'll only be a moment," I assured them, slipping in beside Mrs. Gordon. Tate plopped his helmet on the table and sat down next to Stanley.

Mr. Gordon gave me a hard stare from across the table. "I thought you were brought in for questioning?"

"I was," I told him. "It's a formality, of course. And that's partially why I'm here. I learned that you were once married to Silvia. I find it a little suspicious that you checked in to the inn on the weekend your ex-wife happened to be murdered."

A troubled look passed between the Gordons. "Ah," Stanley finally said. "So you found out about that. I thought that might be the case when you called and asked to meet with us here. It's tradition for us to come to Babette's. The last stop before heading back to Chicago."

"Nice choice," Tate agreed, as he lifted a sourdough roll from the basket. "May I?"

Besides the fact it was a bottomless roll basket, the Gordons would hardly want the fingered roll back. Without getting a reply, Tate began eating it. I took the opportunity to ask a few questions.

"I have a witness that says you were wandering around the inn after midnight. Is that true?"

"Is that a crime, Ms. Bloom?"

"No, but it is suspicious. We know that Ms. Lumiere was killed sometime between twelve thirty and five o'clock in the morning. Look," I said, casting a glance at Mrs. Gordon sitting next to me. "We all know that Silvia was a difficult woman. I also understand that your divorce wasn't a pleasant one."

"That's an understatement," the new Mrs. Gordon quipped.

"Therefore, knowing that you knew the deceased, I have to ask you both if you saw Ms. Lumiere any time after twelve thirty a.m.?"

Stanley set down his fork. To be fair, the complimentary relish tray had already been picked clean. "Okay," he said, his dark eyebrows merging together on his forehead like magnetically charged tufts of fur. "Let me explain a little something to you about Silvia. There might have been a time when I wished her dead, but certainly not now. Last night Carol and I went to a play, then went to Shenanigans for a couple of drinks and came home. Yes, it was well after midnight. Yes, we were fumbling around on the second floor, but we never saw Silvia until this morning. It was a real shock to see her like that, sprawled at the bottom of the stairs."

"But you said nothing about having been married to her when Officer MacLaren interviewed you. Why?"

"For the exact reason you think. It looks highly suspicious. Carol and I were scared and just wanted to get away from it all."

"It's true," Carol added, looking genuinely frightened. "Stanley and I knew that Silvia would be in Cherry Cove," she admitted. "But we never imagined she'd have the money to stay at the Cherry Orchard Inn for the whole summer." She lowered her voice. "I don't like talking ill of the dead, Ms. Bloom, but Silvia was having money problems."

A thought struck, and I asked, "Was she trying to blackmail you for money?"

Stanley nearly laughed at this. "Money, ha! It was always about money with Silvia. There's little doubt that she'd blackmail me if she could, but she had nothing on me. And there was really no need. Carol can attest to the fact that I've always thought it best to"—he put up air quotes—"'support the arts,' namely Silvia. Stay one step ahead of the game, y' know. Plus, I take the charitable write-off on my taxes."

It was then that Stanley decided to tell us about his marriage to the portrait painter. Apparently the marriage had been volatile from the start. He'd met Silvia twenty years ago at a fancy charity event and was instantly taken with the popular artist. Stanley owned a car dealership at the time and believed Silvia would be the perfect wife for an ambitious business owner who wanted to attract a wealthier clientele for his high-end cars. Silvia had been attracted to Stanley's money and stability. The marriage lasted for seven years and ended badly when Stanley found out that his middle-aged wife had been having a torrid affair with the pool boy.

"No kidding," Tate breathed, resting his elbows on the table and cradling his face between his hands. He'd just finished his second roll and was staring at the man beside him. "The cheating little bitch." Tate, no stranger to his own troubling indiscretions, received a gesture from me to zip it.

"A cougar is what she was," Stanley added. "It was highly upsetting. Truth be told, the most upsetting part was the huge divorce settlement she got from me. I was so angry at her at the time, I might have considered killing her. Now, oddly, I realize it was all for the best. Two years after my divorce from Silvia I met Carol. My business has been growing by leaps and bounds ever since, and I've never been happier." Stanley reached across the table and took his wife's hand, a gesture that received a smile of pure adoration from Carol.

"In fact," Stanley added, "to prove I have no animosity toward Silvia, I'll tell you this as well. Two months ago she came to me asking for money. As I've explained, this wasn't unusual. I've been known to help the old girl out from time to time, especially when she pulled back on her corporate accounts to concentrate on portraits. But this was different. Silvia was losing her condo and had sold off nearly all her belongings. I'd never seen her so desperate. Said she needed to get up to Cherry Cove for the summer and sort things out. I think she was seeing a man up here, another artist fellow. Only I believe she made it clear that the poor guy couldn't afford her. Anyhow, I told Silvia I couldn't give her the money she needed to save her condo, but I did do her a favor. Silvia may have been a terrible wife, but she was always good for business. I have to give her that. Her haughty attitude, her pretentious mannerism, her ability to butter-up a customer and make them believe they couldn't live without luxury were invaluable to me. So I paid for a two-year lease on a brand-new Cadillac Escalade, and bought a big trailer for all her worldly possessions to go along with it."

"Wait," Tate said, looking at Stanley. "You leased her that huge Escalade? Dude, that's generous."

Stanley smiled at the compliment. "Told her it was my parting gift and hoped she'd be able to buy the truck at the end of the lease. The old girl deserved to start out anew. Carol and I came up for a quick weekend getaway, and to check up on her, you know, make sure her new hippie assistant hasn't damaged the truck beyond repair."

"You know about Peter?" I asked.

Stanley nodded. "Silvia couldn't drive. She always had a younger male assistant drive her around and carry all her paints and supplies. Made her feel important."

"Did you ever wonder how she could afford to keep them?"

"No," he said. "I was always amazed that they'd put up with her."

I looked at Tate, suddenly thinking about Silvia's affinity for younger men and her desire to paint them in the nude. "Mr. Gordon, you said that Silvia was having an affair with the pool boy. Do you remember his name? Where he lived?"

"Of course I remember his name. I was paying the guy to mow my lawn, maintain my gardens and pool, and apparently entertain my wife! But he's no longer a kid. He's got to be in his mid-thirties by now. Jake Jones. The little bastard used to live in Palatine. I have no idea where he is now."

I checked the time on my iPhone. We'd been with the Gordons for fifteen minutes. Jack would be along any moment. We thanked the couple for their time just as two heaping plates of prime rib were served. It looked mouthwateringly delicious, causing my own empty stomach to growl. Tate picked up his helmet and ushered me out of Babette's before I decided to join the Gordons and order my own slab of prime rib.

I had to admit that there was an honesty about Stanley and Carol that would be hard to manufacture. Stanley had said that even though Silvia was a nightmare of a wife she had been good for his business, and I knew what he meant. I was convinced that they had nothing to do with Silvia's murder. Heck, Stanley had even gone so far as to help Silvia on many occasions, the latest act of charity being her huge white Cadillac Escalade. That was very generous indeed. I felt that a light had been cast on Silvia's little games and things were beginning to add up. But if the Gordons were innocent of her murder, they had still mentioned the name of a young man who might have reason to want Silvia dead. An unnamed young man had once tried to sue the portrait painter for sexual harassment. I wondered if Jake Jones had ever worked for Silvia after her divorce, and if so, had he been required to pose in the nude for a painting?

Nineteen

ecause I was starving and couldn't concentrate on anything but a plate of inch-thick prime rib, Tate and I stopped for a quick bite to eat at Ed's Diner in Sturgeon Bay. It wasn't a supper club, just a diner, and nearly everything on the menu was served with fries, hash browns or mashed potatoes, and gravy. Thankfully I was a French fry kinda gal. It was just our luck that Jack's favorite waitress happened to be working a Sunday shift. Marge, a stocky, no-nonsense woman in her sixties with bedazzled drugstore readers on a chain and bright pink painted nails, cast me a look of extreme curiosity as she took us to our booth.

"And will Officer MacLaren be showing up soon?" she inquired. Her tone dripped with innuendo while her manner, as she slapped an extra menu on the table, was pure mob boss warning. Marge had a real soft spot for Jack. Tate, oblivious to her look and her warning, handed the menu back.

"MacLaren's busy investigating a murder," he told her.

Marge feigned surprise. "Really? According to that leggy reporter on Baywatch News, it's already been solved. Apparently, the young lady you're sitting with did it." Her beady dark eyes turned to me.

"Marge," I said soothingly. "You know Greta Stone is a sensation monger who has no evidence to back up her claim. You can't believe everything you hear on the news."

"I know. But it's easy, ain't it?" She winked. "It's a wonder that Stone woman still has a job. But we all know why. Don't we, *Mr. Vander Hagen*."

"Sex sells, Marge. Never forget it!" He flashed her his cheek-dimples.

Marge, staring over her bedazzled readers, quipped, "Well, some of us don't need no fancy advertising degree to figure that one out."

While Tate and I waited for our cheeseburgers and fries, I decided to give Tay a call and find out what, if anything, she'd learned from her talk with Hannah and Peter.

"I'm not getting anywhere," she uttered before heaving a sigh. "Hannah believes the guy's some all-powerful wizard and, quite frankly, I find it a little spooky. She was so normal before meeting that hippie. Well, normal's a relative term, isn't it? I mean, she's always been impressionable, but never delusional. The trouble is, Whit, neither one of them is denying that they had something to do with the murder, but Hannah swears that Peter was with her all night. Peter swears that he was with Hannah all night. And I'm a little creeped out by the both of them."

I gave an involuntary shiver. "Holy cobbler," I breathed. "We've got to shake her out if it. But for now, let's just couch the whole Hannah, Peter, and their all-powerful-wizard voodoo-doll theory for a while. I've got some other leads I'd like to throw by you." I quickly filled her in on my conversation with Erik Larson and his suspicion that someone had been in the room with Silvia when he'd delivered room service. I told her about my conversation with Giff and our most recent talk with the Gordons at Babette's Supper Club.

"Wait. Giff's coming up to the Cove?" Tay's voice was full of excitement. "When?"

"Undoubtedly by dinner. He's not one to miss a free meal. And, in case I forgot to tell you, we're all dining tonight at the inn, you and Lance included. Listen, as I mentioned before, I don't believe Silvia's ex-husband had anything to do with her murder. However, he did tell me that the reason he divorced Silvia in the first place was because she was having an affair with a young man who was working for them at the time. His name's Jake Jones. It would have been about ten years ago. Jake is in his thirties by now, and we have no idea what he looks like. All I know is that he used to live in Palatine, Illinois. The reason I'm suspicious is because he might be the one who tried to sue Silvia for sexual harassment."

"Gotcha," Tay said, following my train of thought.

"So, would you mind doing a little poking around on the internet while I grab a bite to eat with Tate?"

"Whoa. Whoa. Whoa. You're with Tate?" Her voice rang with disbelief. "Do you think that's wise in your current sleep-deprived, man-deprived, murder-suspect state?"

"Definitely not with him dressed like a Viking." I smiled at the man across from me, adding a wink for good measure. "Let me know if you find anything."

"Whitney! That's a perfect storm of stupidity you're facing," she warned just before I ended the call.

Silly me, I should have heeded Tay's warning. The girl knew what she was talking about. Tate had always been my kryptonite. As we awaited our burgers and fries we discussed our conversation with the Gordons, painfully aware that a nosy old waitress was hovering nearby.

We were deep in conversation when suddenly Tate reached across the table and placed his hand over mine. The move was intimate; Tate's hand was strong and warm. But it was the look in his deep-set, clear blue eyes that gripped my heart. The whole wild-haired Viking thing he was rockin' only added more fuel to the already blazing fire.

"This is great, babe. I've really missed eating burgers with you and talking about murder suspects. Well, our burgers aren't actually here, and we've never talked about murder suspects before," he clarified. "But I like it. It's a total turn-on. I liked the way you took control of the conversation back there with the Gordons. You're really good at this."

The compliment served to further weaken my resolve, and I could feel myself blushing. "Thank you," I said and gave his hand an encouraging squeeze. After a moment of intense silence, I blurted nervously, "Do you know what's crazy? This morning when Jack interrogated me he actually said that he wished you were in bed with me last night. That way I'd have a lock-tight alibi." Why in the name of sweet pickles did I repeat that?

The dimples on the other side of the table were in full bloom; it took everything in my power not to reach across and sink my fingers into them. "Smartest thing MacLaren's ever said," Tate replied, cradling my restless fingers between his hands. "Tell you what," he continued, gently massaging my hands. "I could be in your bed tonight…in case there's another murder. Or, better yet, you could climb aboard the *Lusty Dutchman* and we could do a little midnight sailing. I'm always up for giving you an alibi, babe."

"I always thought that was a terrible metaphor, Vander Hagen." The voice, distinctly male and very familiar, broke the mood. I yanked my hands from Tate's grasp as Jack plopped down on the booth beside me. "And anyhow, it's too late for that now."

"Jack," I said, very aware that my face was on fire. "How did you find us?"

The look he gave me was chiding at best. "I saw your car in the parking lot. I've got a cheeseburger coming as well. I thought I'd join you. In fact, I distinctly remember telling you to wait for me at Babette's. I also distinctly remember telling you, Whitney, not to leave town." Jack turned his disappointed honey-brown gaze on me.

"When you said town, I didn't think you literally meant Cherry Cove." It was an honest reply, yet, apparently, this was not the answer he was looking for. "If it makes you feel any better we're heading back now ... well, after we eat."

"I'm here to make sure that you do. And why are you dressed like ...?" Jack was having a hard time figuring out what exactly Tate was dressed like.

"A Viking, bro." Tate looked mildly offended. "And I'm dressed like this because I was going to the Renaissance fair with Whitney, before murder happened."

"*You* were going to the Renaissance fair with Whitney?"

And there it was, the one thing besides murder that I'd been fearing all week. I thought I had escaped the social horrors of the Renaissance fair, but this was definitely worse. There were no diversions. There was nowhere to hide. I eyed the ladies' room longingly, knowing that they'd never buy that feeble excuse. Nope, the three of us remained pressed together in a little diner booth surrounded by awkward silence and hurt looks. Correction: the three of us and Marge.

"So, ya finally found out she was two-timin' ya." It was addressed to the table at large. Jack and Tate looked confused. Marge, her meaty arms holding three large plates, began doling out the burgers. "I suppose it shouldn't come as any surprise that she's a murder suspect as

147

well." The waitress then tossed out a cheeky wink, clearly finding the situation amusing. "Will anyone be needing ketchup? No? Okay. Enjoy your meal."

$$\infty$$

The cheeseburger sat like lead in my upset stomach as Tate and I drove back to the inn in silence. The meal had been a disaster. I even picked up the tab, hoping to smooth the feathers I had ruffled. But they'd been ruffled too far, Tate's most of all. I was forced to admit that I had invited Jack to the fair, which caused Tate to realize that he'd been invited by Hannah. It began to dawn on him, then, for perhaps the first time since my return to Cherry Cove, that he no longer was the center of my universe. It had been his mistake to assume that he could just slip back into my life like a familiar comfy sweater, entirely forgetting the episode of his indiscretion. It had taken me the better part of a year to put that behind me. I had sworn off men. I had watched a lot of bad reality TV. I had even lost my job in advertising. But now, back in Cherry Cove, I realized that it was finally behind me. The blaze of my first love had died out, left to smolder in the ashes. And Tate, poor Tate had finally understood that Jack MacLaren was more than just a friend.

Tempers had flared, words had been said, and I had ended up declaring that I was quite through with them both. They assured me that they felt the same. To make his point, Jack had shoved his last fry into his mouth, picked up his cap, and stormed off. Tate had been left with me. It was a long, painfully quiet ride back to the Cherry Orchard Inn.

"You know where to find me if you need me," Tate said, exiting the car the moment I parked.

"Tate. Wait. I'm sorry."

"Yeah. Me too." He shut the door and headed for his pickup truck.

I watched him drive away, suddenly conscious of the fact that I was crying. The sight of the pop-up shrine to Silvia Lumiere on the front porch kicked my anger into high gear, but the fact that the mourners still lingered as well helped quell my blubbering self-pity a measure. But it was the hastily drawn likeness of me pinned to the railing with the tagline *MURDERER* written across the bottom that really set me off. "Those cherry-stomping idiots!" I seethed and dried my eyes.

Disgusted, I left my car and walked up the front steps, ripping down the poster as I went. "You do realize that you're on my front porch?" I cried. "Not only is this libel, but it's a really terrible drawing!"

A muffled voice from the back of the crowd piped up. "All we had was black pens and a red crayon."

"Well, it's no wonder you all worshiped Silvia Lumiere," I shot back. "She actually had talent! Now go home, all of you, before I call the police."

I didn't wait to hear their replies. Instead I stomped back down the porch steps and marched around the three-story turret to the family wing.

Sad, angry and utterly depressed, I sat alone at the end of my bed and stared at the suspect board. Who killed Silvia Lumiere? Everybody had a motive, but only one person had actually crossed that threshold and killed the woman.

Before collapsing on my pillows, I had added the names Stanley and Carol Gordon, and that of Jake Jones as well, although any motive the Gordons had was weak at best. Even Jack had admitted this back at the diner. Jack also wasn't happy that I'd employed Giff and his researching talents to look into Silvia's background. I told him in no uncertain

149

terms that I would use whatever resources I could if it meant finding Silvia's *real* killer. I'd emphasized the word "real" because Jack, being a spiteful, pig-headed idiot, still refused to remove me from his suspect list. "Suit yourself," I had told him. Then, to poke the wounded bear with an even pointier stick, I reminded him of the last time we had a murder in Cherry Cove, and of my leading role in apprehending the killer.

Tate had piped up, reminding us that he had been there as well. We both looked at him. Tate blanched and fell silent. I fell silent then too, feeling terrible and guilty. They were both remarkable men, the best Cherry Cove had to offer, and I had hurt them with my coward-ice and indecision. The truth was, I didn't deserve either of them, and anyhow they were both quite finished with me.

Oh, what had I done? I asked myself as new tears began to flow. Was I going to turn into a mean, nasty old woman like Silvia Lumiere? Manless, penniless, with only my cherry pastry talent to cling to? I gasped at the thought and sobbed even more.

A good while later, I forced myself to focus on the problem at hand: namely, murder. Jack, my once dear friend and nemesis, was only one man. Damn his prideful, stubborn ways. I couldn't deny that he was a great policeman, but that also meant he had to work within the boundaries of police procedure. I was an overzealous ex-ad exec who now baked cherry pastry for a living. I didn't even know what proper police procedure was, nor did I really care. A murder had taken place at my inn; my own innocent pastry had been involved, and I was bound and determined to find the sicko who thought they could get away with it. Maybe Jack would even be wise enough to realize that he needed my help. And just to keep my advantage, I had never told him about the sexual harassment lawsuit or mentioned the name

"Jake Jones." Hopefully Tay, who was also happy to poke around on the internet, could find the guy for me.

I dried my eyes and saw the other name on my suspect board that jumped out at me. Stanley Gordon thought that his ex-wife was seeing a man in Cherry Cove, a man who couldn't afford her. Erik Larson thought that there might have been someone in the painter's room when he delivered her room service tray. He had also reminded me that if someone wanted to get back into the building after hours all they need do was go to the side entrance and use a key. Had Silvia given Fred Beauchamp her room key? Had Fred slipped back into the building without notice? Poor Silvia. It just might have been the biggest mistake of her life.

I would check at the front desk and see if we were missing a key to Silvia's room. Then I would pay Mr. Beauchamp a little visit. First, however, I was going to take a nap. Murder, being a suspect and losing the two men I wanted most, hadn't made for a very pleasant day. Hopefully my evening would go a little better.

Twenty

"Really, how can you sleep at a time like this?"

I awoke with a start only to find Giff leering over me, hands on hips and looking mildly put out. My heart was pounding in my throat as I sprang up, rubbing my swollen eyes. "What's happened?"

"Nothing yet, angel, but dinner's about to." A devilish smile played on his lips as he sat on the edge of my bed. He'd just driven up from Chicago, a five-hour drive in good traffic, but looked as if he'd just stepped out of a men's fashion magazine. His dark wavy hair, now streaked with blond highlights, was glued in place with a lot of expensive product. His khakis were skin-tight and rolled at the bottom to reveal his fashionable red sneakers. And his navy blue tee looked so soft I wanted to touch it. Of course, I refrained. "Jani's made her famous fried perch," he informed me. "We're dining alfresco on the patio. How intimate. Hannah and her hairy friend have just arrived, and Tay and her 'jouster' are on their way. I know all of this because I've been here a good half hour already, chatting with Jenn and helping Baggsie finish a bottle of his finest cherry wine. Not quite ready for general consumption, but he's getting the hang of it. Whoa!" he said and leaned back a foot. "Did you actually cry yourself to sleep?"

My reply was guilty silence.

"Your eyes," he said, wiggling his finger at my face. "So swollen and puffy. I'm guessing that didn't happen because of a dead celebrity painter. This looks like the work of a man, Officer McHottie to be exact. Am I right?"

"Partially," I said, then blubbered with a flow of fresh tears, "Oh, Giff, it's all my fault!" I proceeded to tell him my sorry tale of how Jack found me at a diner with Tate and how Tate realized I'd invited Jack to the Renaissance fair and not him. "I hurt them both," I sobbed, "because I'm too much of a chicken to break up with Tate and too scared of being rejected by Jack. I was so mad at Jack for interrogating me as a suspect that I went behind his back on a quest to find the real murderer. That only made things worse. I left town, broke Jack's trust, and was starting to fall under Tate's spell again. In my defense," I added, noting the scandalous intrigue that animated Giff's face, "he was dressed as a Viking."

"*No.*" Giff's dark eyes glittered with pleasure.

"You know my weakness," I said, sniffling. "We were getting along fine and suddenly our lunch turned intimate. That's when Jack arrived. It all degraded from there. I've mucked it up good this time and now ... now both men hate me!" I paused to stifle a sob. "I'm going to die alone! Hannah has Peter. Tay has Lance and I ... I have no one." I began to cry in earnest.

Giff jumped off the bed and glared at me. "Um, HELLO! What am I? Arugula? The bane of every salad and the pariah of the lettuce aisle?"

I stopped crying. "I like arugula."

"Nobody likes arugula," he said, trying not to smile. "You only said that because you're bitter, like arugula. Pick yourself up, Whitney. Dry your eyes and, for God's sake, throw on some fresh makeup. The Giffster's here and I'm not about to miss a Bloom family dinner because of two ridiculous men and an ex-ad girl wallowing in self-pity. By the way, angel, they don't hate you. They're giving you space. Not a bad thing when you're trying to find a murderer. Now hurry up. I'm famished."

The artists holding vigil on the front porch had gone, and all the rooms but for one at the inn were vacant. A strange emptiness had settled in the quiet hallways and foyer, in the locked dining room and barren breakfast nook, and on the empty bakery shelves of *Bloom 'n' Cherries!*. It was an emptiness quite foreign in the height of the tourist season. Mom and Grandma Jenn had worked hard to create a silver lining out of the inn's most recent calamity. The elegant Victorian manor was ours once again and they had claimed the beautiful patio, strung with white lights and fragrant with summer flowers, to host our family dinner. Three smaller tables had been pushed together for the occasion. The long table, awash in candlelight, had been covered with a red-and-white checkered cloth and set for only nine diners.

The two omissions had been startling. Jack and Tate, both being close friends of our family, had of course been invited. While I was napping, Mom had received a call from Tate. Then, just as she was getting over the shock that he wouldn't be coming to dinner, Jack had called as well. He let Mom know that he wouldn't be coming either. The news came as quite a shock to the family, particularly so because Mom thought Tate and I were back together, while Gran was certain that Jack and I were, to use her words, "having a fling." Apparently they were as confused as I was regarding my love life. Not a good sign. For the sake of my sanity, I decided to forget about men and concentrate on a matter that was just as confusing yet emotionally kinder: finding Silvia's killer.

As Mom and Gran were putting the finishing touches on the delicious smelling food, Giff and I crossed the patio to join Dad. He was talking with Hannah and Peter. They were all standing on the edge of the lawn, sipping cocktails while watching a breathtaking sunset. I wanted to enjoy the beauty of the coming night as well, but I was still reeling from the recent discovery Giff and I had made. On our way to dinner, we'd decided on a quick detour behind the front desk. All the keys had been returned except for three. Two from the Pine Suite, currently being occupied by Peter, and one from the Sailboat Suite, where Silvia had stayed.

Tay and I were concerned about Hannah and her growing fondness for Peter. Their unorthodox involvement, or lack thereof, in Silvia's murder was also disconcerting. Hannah swore that Peter had been with her all night, but if she'd been drinking, or doing other mind-altering things, or if she had just been very tired, she might not have noticed the all-powerful wizard sneaking out of her condo in the wee hours of the morning to do his nasty deed.

Hannah had provided him with the perfect alibi, but what if that was exactly what Peter had been counting on? The trouble was, I was also open to the possibility of ghosts, thanks to my brother. And thanks to reality TV. I was also certain that Sasquatch and the Loch Ness monster really did exist. However, vampires and voodoo magic were subjects I considered taboo, being too dark for my taste. Could a pot-smoking hippie with passive-aggressive anger issues really put a voodoo curse on his domineering employer? Or had Peter's most recent head-popping ceremony been an act, one to make him appear that he had real powers? In short, was Peter using Hannah to cover his vengeful misdeeds? It was this suspicion that kept Peter near the top of my suspect list.

"Hello," I said, and gave Dad and Hannah a hug. All I could muster for Peter was a weak smile. After a round of pleasantries I turned to Dad. "Has Silvia's room been thoroughly searched?" I asked.

"As far as I know," Dad replied. "The police were in there all morning. I don't know what they've found, but it's been taped off as part of the crime scene. Nobody's to go in there until they give us the okay."

"Fair enough," Peter chimed in. "The dead deserve their privacy, just as much as the living do." This was directed at me. The guy was miffed that we'd checked his room. "Even at an inn, it's a violation of privacy when someone enters your abode without permission."

"Right," I said, suddenly not feeling very charitable toward this man. "So you heard that we opened your door this morning. We didn't rifle through your things, if that's your concern. When we found Silvia, the police went to take a statement from everyone staying at the inn. When we came to your room and no one responded to our knocking, we were afraid that something might have happened to you as well. It's standard procedure to check on a guest when we feel that their safety might be compromised."

Peter shrugged, then grinned at Hannah. "I was otherwise detained."

"So we heard. I was unaware of the situation. I thought you were supposed to stay at the inn in case Silvia needed you?"

Curious about this direct line of questioning, Dad gave Peter a hard look and crossed his arms. Giff, standing next to Dad, took his cue and did the same, only with greater dramatic effect. Hannah, however, didn't care for my remark at all.

"You know that last night was the one exception." Her cheeks turned a bright crimson, whether from embarrassment or rage I couldn't tell. "I've already explained it to you. Peter and I have been dating behind Silvia's back. When you banned me from the inn he decided to rebel and spend the …" She looked at Dad and abandoned the explanation. "Anyhow, our alibis are sound enough … unlike some people."

That remark I recognized as spite.

Giff, unable to resist, jumped to my defense. "Is it a crime that some people like to sleep alone?"

"Dude," Peter cut in, "nobody likes to sleep alone—not if they have a better option."

Dad, having distinctly puritan views on the matter of sleeping with the opposite sex before marriage, especially where his daughter and her childhood friends were concerned, wasn't thrilled with the direction the conversation had taken. Before he could add his two cents, I jumped in.

"Oh! I have a question for you, Peter. Do you have both of your room keys?"

The soft, slightly unfocused gaze settled on me as he thought a moment. "Yeah," he replied. "Silvia insisted on having one. But I took it back Friday, after she had m'lady banned from the inn." He cast the m'lady in question a look that implied the simple act was heroically defiant.

"Do you also happen to have a key to Silvia's room as well?" I asked.

"Not on me," he replied. "Sometimes she would give it to me, but not, like, for keeps. Only to use, ya know, like when she needed me to fetch something from her room. I always gave it back, though." He grinned at Hannah. "I spent far too much time with the old soul-sucker. Why would I want her room key?"

Fair enough, I thought. I then asked, "But you do have the keys to her Escalade, right?"

Peter gave a nod before pulling a ring of keys from the pocket of his loose-fitting pants. "I keep the Lade keys. Silvia couldn't drive."

"Did you know a man by the name of Stanley Gordon?" I asked.

He shrugged.

"He's Silvia's ex-husband," I explained, watching his reaction closely. "He's the one who leased the car for her."

"Oh, him." He gave a lazy nod. "Poor dude. Married to that. Yeah, I heard she'd been married. I even went with her to pick up the new Lade, but I thought she signed the lease herself. The truck was already waiting for us when we got there."

"So you didn't meet Stanley Gordon? He's the owner of the dealership the Escalade came from."

"I might have," he replied, looking genuinely unconcerned. "How was I to know? But it wasn't the dude who gave us the keys. That dude was, like, eighteen if he was a day, and a bit too greasy for Silvia's taste."

Interesting, I thought. Silvia's ex-husband and the financier of her luxury SUV had been staying only a few rooms down from Peter, and he'd been totally oblivious, or so he said. Was Peter really as chill and laid back as he appeared, or was it all just an act, one that had fooled Hannah? The thought begged to be explored further, but for now I was more concerned about the missing key.

"I have another question for you," I said, offering a friendly smile. "Do you know of anyone that Silvia might have given her room key to?"

The soft, languid eyes sharpened a measure. "Got me." He gave another shrug of his straight, lean shoulders. "Aside from setting up her paints and easels, and carting her around the peninsula for her unveilings, I didn't really care what she did or who she did it with, as long as it didn't involve me."

I was processing this little tidbit of information when Hannah's eyes lit up. "Tay's arrived. Swingin' dingles! No," she uttered as Giff and I were about to spin around. "Don't turn around. Not yet. Let me warn you first." Hannah lowered her voice even further and whispered, "Tay looks fabulous, of course. But poor Lance looks as if he went head-to-head with a—"

"Mac truck," Dad finished for her, cringing slightly as he stared over our heads.

"And lost?" I asked.

"We don't know that," Giff chided. "We'd need to see the truck, of course. I take the fact that he's here and the truck isn't to be a good sign. Now, will one of you introduce me? I've never before had the pleasure of meeting a knight in, or out of, shining armor."

Twenty-One

There was no doubt that Lance had taken a beating. The poor man was covered in cuts and bruises and walked with a slight limp. His clothes were loose, his manner contrite, almost nervous, and anyone could see that he was putting on a brave face for Tay's sake. However, beneath the polite smile and dogged appetite, one got the feeling they were witnessing a man highly aware of his own spiraling descent to the bottom of his trade. Unfortunately, I knew precisely how that felt. My fifteen-second misplaced Super Bowl feminine hygiene ad had driven it all home for me. Unlike Lance, my wounds had been on the inside.

True to Tay's initial instinct, the tournament at the Renaissance fair had been a disaster. The notorious Black Knight had tilted against the best knights on the circuit, but from Lance's appearance, it didn't look like he'd bothered to raise his own lance, or his shield either. I knew Tay really liked this man, but the air between them was filled with palpable tension. It didn't take a genius to figure out the reason the couple had been late for dinner. Aside from the extensive number

160

of bandages required to keep the man on his feet, and a dosing of strong painkillers, Tay and Lance had been arguing.

Highly aware of this fact, the conversation at the table was kept light and superficial. Everyone raved about Mom's delicious fried perch and Grandma Jenn's fluffy biscuits and crunchy coleslaw. The grilled corn on the cob and cherry-melon salad were discussed ad nauseam as well. Dad gave us two updates on the orchard, both stating that the cherry crop was looking healthy and that the harvest would be good this year, in spite of the damage that had been done in May. Hannah talked about a new yoga routine and philosophized on working with goats again. Tay joined the conversation sporadically; Lance concentrated on keeping the appropriate amount of food in his mouth to deter others from asking questions; and Giff ... Giff was staring at Lance with the same interest and intensity as a thirteen-year-old girl discovering social media for the first time. In short, he was enchanted. Done with polite banter and waiting patiently for that small gap between the bob of Lance's Adam's apple and another bite, Giff pounced.

"*A Knight's Tale*," he said, pointing his empty fork accusingly across the table at Lance. All conversation stopped as Giff pressed on. "You're doing a classic Knight's Tale."

Lance, suddenly finding himself the center of attention, swallowed while painfully lifting a questioning brow.

Giff continued. "You've all seen it, right? It's a story about a young man of humble origins who masquerades as a knight. Suddenly this knight rises through the ranks until he's finally on the winning streak of his life. He's unseating all his foes to please the women he loves. But his lady wants real proof of his love. The only thing that will satisfy her is if our hero swallows his pride and loses every joust he's in. It's a big ask, but our hero does it. That's what you seem to be doing, only I can't understand why. Tay's hardly the type of woman who needs extravagant romantic gestures." This he punctuated with a playful wink at the lady in question.

Lance's face darkened behind a layer of bruising. "I'm not Knight's Tale-ing the tournament!" he cried, bringing his fist down on the table with enough force to make the dinnerware shudder.

"But you're good," Giff countered. "Tay's told us you are. So why the limp lance routine? Why become the pincushion when you could be doing the pinning? Clearly you're not 'ba da ba ba bah, LOVIN' IT,' are you?" Giff, never one to refrain from calling up an old ad jingle to make his point, looked at the sullen jouster. "The only other reason for such a masochistic tactic is apathy, but, in most cases, it doesn't cause such extensive bruising."

Lance noted the concern on Tay's face and gently placed a hand over hers. He then looked across the table at Giff. "I'm off my game," he admitted. "Call it apathy if you like. I've lost my edge and have been thinking about getting a real job." From the shocked look on Tay's face, this apparently was news to her. "The problem," Lance continued, "is, um, I've developed a skill set that's kind of hard to lateral out of. 'Oh, you can swing a sword on horseback and hit a shield with a lance?'" he mimicked in his best interviewer voice. "'Terrific! How are you with Excel?'"

Giff was about to laugh when a swift kick under the table from me brought him to his senses.

"Technical skills," the forlorn knight continued. "Mine begin and end with Yelp reviews. To get a decently paying job in today's workplace you have to know a bit more than that. And going back to college isn't an option. I can't take on any more debt."

Dad offered the beaten man a kind smile. "Look, I don't know what a Renaissance fair jouster makes these days, but I'd be happy to take you on at the orchard. Tay might have already told you that we've been left shorthanded. We can always use a strong fellow like yourself. We don't use horses, we use Gators, you understand. And in lieu of swords we use things like chain saws and pruning shears. Why, I'm even certain that Brock Sorensen would be happy to teach you Excel if you're interested."

For the first time since entering the inn, Lance almost smiled. "Mr. Bloom, that's a very kind offer, sir. But, um, I'm not so sure that working here would be a good idea at the moment." If there was a reason, Lance didn't elaborate. Hannah, however, believed she knew why.

"I don't blame you," she chimed in. "I'd think twice about working here as well. First, the murder of Jeb Carlson in the orchard, and now that nasty woman who bought it at the bottom of the stairs this morning. I'm beginning to think this place is cursed." As Hannah spoke the table fell silent. At least she had the decency to blanch before crying out, "Oh, come on, people! Don't look at me like that. We're all thinking it."

"Are we?" Mom asked, looking horrified. Dad clearly was none-too-pleased to have the word "cursed" bandied about at the dinner table after his kindly offer. Lance, however, appeared wary.

"So I've just heard," he said. "Tay forgot to mention it to me until we arrived. Apparently, judging from the fanfare on the front porch, the unfortunate woman had admirers."

"I'm sorry," Tay replied earnestly. "I should have thought to mention it to you before we came. I didn't think it really mattered, you know, considering all the pressure you've been under lately. It's not like you knew the victim or anything."

Grandma Jenn, studying the conversation with extreme interest, suddenly leaned forward. Looking squarely at the knight, she supplied,

"Silvia Lumiere, dear. She was a famous portrait painter who spent her summers in Cherry Cove. *Did* you know her?"

Lance stilled. Then, suddenly, he stood. "Excuse me," he said, and left the table. Tay, looking troubled, threw down her napkin and ran after him.

∞

"That was odd," I remarked again, a good while later.

Giff, Hannah, and I had been sitting on the patio enjoying our favorite post-dinner drinks while mulling over the evening's events. Dinner had ended shortly after Lance and Tay left, but not before cherry pie ala mode had been served. The table had been cleared and Mom, Dad, and Gran had retired. Peter, who'd been masquerading as a vegetarian but was, in reality, a fried perch junky, stated that he needed to lie down after gorging himself on such a delicious meal. Hannah remained with us once Peter left for his room.

It was a warm midsummer night. The sky was clear, black and full of twinkling stars. Giff still marveled at how many there were once away from the bright city lights of Chicago. It was too beautiful a night to retire so early. Besides, Lance's odd behavior was a subject worthy of discussion.

"I met him a while ago," I continued. "He seemed a great guy. Tonight, however, he looked positively hounded."

"Or haunted," Hannah said. "You saw him. That man was clearly spooked by the possibility of there being a curse on this place." Hannah, although sorry that her remark about the Cherry Orchard Inn being cursed had virtually ended dinner, was clearly convinced of the matter herself.

"Who knew he was so sensitive?" Giff shrugged and took a sip of his microbrewed beer.

"Sensitive? Are you kidding me?" I emptied my wineglass and cast him a theatric eye roll. "The guy works at a Renaissance fair and just took the beating of his life. This morning, when I talked with Tay, she was afraid something like this would happen. Lance has his own personal demons to battle." This was the real crux of the problem, I knew, recalling what Tay had said about Lance's beautiful armor being repossessed at the fairgrounds. I continued. "I hardly think something as silly as a curse is going to spook him—even if there was such a thing, which there's clearly not. No, what we witnessed tonight is something quite different. A man like that doesn't just fall out of love with jousting. In fact, when I first met him he was wearing a full suit of armor. He was so magnificently convincing in the role that I nearly believed I had actually traveled back in time."

"Cool." Hannah looked impressed. Then, suddenly, her face came alive with a thought. "Hey, what if Lance really is a time traveler? You heard him. He's a millennial and doesn't do technology. Maybe that's what's bothering him. Maybe he's trying to find a way back to the time he came from but can't because the portal's been blocked, and he's trapped here, with us."

Giff set down his beer. Dripping incredulity, he stared at Hannah. "Sweetheart, you really need to stop hanging out with that hippie of yours. Time travel doesn't exist. I know, because if it did I wouldn't be here. I'd be in ancient Rome driving a chariot and totally rocking a thigh-length toga."

"Good point," I said, and turned back to Hannah. "There you have it. A definitive answer on time travel. It doesn't exist because Giff is here with us and not in ancient Rome rocking a sexy toga. Okay, we know that Lance is a modern guy who's down on his luck. And I'm pretty sure I know why." I hastily told them about Lance's money problems and his embarrassment earlier in the week when his prized suit of armor had been repossessed.

"It's put a strain on their relationship," I continued, "one that Tay wants desperately to fix. She really likes this guy. As her friends, we need to find a way to help her."

"Okay," Giff replied prosaically. "But why did the name Silvia Lumiere set him off?"

I looked at him, suddenly thinking of several things at once. Lance, although appreciative of Dad's offer, was hesitant to work at the orchard. He'd said he was unaware of the murder at the inn, and yet didn't seem overly concerned by it. Most telling of all was Gran. She'd been watching Lance closely before offering up the victim's name. She'd also asked, rather pointedly, if he had known her. That was when Lance had stood up from the table and left.

"Holy cobbler!" I breathed, staring at my friends. "Could Lance have a connection to Silvia Lumiere that we don't know about?"

"I doubt it," Hannah was quick to say. "That would be a long shot. But you could always call Tay and check. Anyhow, I thought this was the guy's first visit to the Cherry Orchard Inn. My bet is on the curse. If I had money problems I'd have to think twice about hitching my wagon to a place that's been the site of two murders." She drained the last few drops of wine from her glass and checked her iPhone. "Okay, gotta run. I told Peter I'd stop by his room before I went home. FYI, he'll be staying at my place tonight. The inn's giving off a creepy vibe, being so empty and all. Also, he has the feeling that Silvia's disgruntled ghost is going to be staying here a bit longer. You might want to consult your brother on how to handle this one, Whit. It's more in his line of work than yours. Okay. Tootles."

We all stood. As Hannah and I exchanged a parting hug, she said quietly, "Call Jack. I know you two had a falling out today, but I need you to find out if he has any other leads on the murder. You and Tay know what Peter and I did last night. I know you don't want to believe it, and, truthfully, neither do we, but sometimes the weirdest explanation is the correct one. We weren't at the inn. There isn't any physical evidence to say otherwise, but if Jack gets wind of what Peter did, I'm afraid he'll charge him with Silvia's murder. Will you call him?"

"I'll think about it," I said, and let her go.

I wasn't going to call Jack. I had nothing to say to him, and as far as I was concerned, Hannah could make the call herself when she was ready. Instead, Giff and I continued to sit on the patio, discussing my suspect board. Half an hour later, we were both brought to our feet by a rustling in the bushes. We were spooked to silence, especially since the events in the orchard this spring still haunted me.

"Who's there?" I asked, staring into the darkness. A moment later a bright flaxen head appeared in the moonlight.

"Miss Bloom?"

It was Erik Larson. What the devil was the kid doing sneaking around the inn so late at night? He acknowledged Giff, then stepped onto the patio.

"Erik. What's going on?" One look at the boy's face and my heart sank. He looked troubled. I softened my tone and beckoned him forward. "Come here and have a seat. Then you're going to tell us what's bothering you."

"I, um, I need to talk with you," he said, nervously wringing his hands. "I knocked on the door to the family wing. Your mom told me you were here with Mr. McGrady."

I smiled kindly and urged him to go on.

"I, um, I have a confession to make. I lied to you about last night."

Twenty-Two

Erik Larson had been terrified of losing his job, and so he had lied. The confession hadn't come easy. He was more nervous than I had ever seen him, which was saying quite a lot. Erik was a young man who took risks, for better or worse. Apparently, whatever he had done last night, I was inclined to believe it wasn't for the best. In fact, it had taken two sodas to drag it out of him. When the kid was finally ready to talk, I had a sinking feeling. Part of me actually wished he had decided to carry his secret to the grave with him. Undoubtedly, he had considered this himself. However, given the fact that he was only eighteen and had a long life ahead of him, the obvious strategy he'd embraced was to get this misdeed off his chest.

"So, um, I came to tell you that I didn't leave the inn when I told you I did."

I looked at him through narrowed eyes. "You lied about leaving the inn after delivering room service to Ms. Lumiere? Why?" Erik cast a nervous glance at Giff and remained silent. "Okay," I said, "what time did you leave then?"

"Um, later. Much later."

"Do you remember what time that was?"

The boy shifted in his chair, clearly fearful of answering the question. Earlier, when I had gone to the Larson house to speak with him, I had the feeling that Erik had been hiding something. My suspicions had been confirmed, and yet his fear of coming clean and telling the truth was wearing on me as well. It wasn't like him to be so shifty. "Look," I finally said. "You came here for a reason, so you better just tell us. What were you doing here?"

Even in the soft lighting of the patio I could see his face flushing to an unhealthy blood red. He took a deep breath and boldly stated, "I, ah, I was in the elevator."

I turned to Giff, curious to see what he'd make of this. He too looked perplexed and answered my look with a questioning shrug. No help there. "Okay," I said, studying Erik closely, not quite sure what he was getting at. "So, you were in the elevator. Were you traveling to the second floor?"

Erik shook his head. "Nope."

"Okay, you were traveling to the first floor." Again, the boy shook his head. I was swiftly losing patience. "Look, Erik, there are only two floors here. This isn't rocket science. What the fudge were you doing in the elevator that late at night if you weren't going up to one floor or down to the other?"

Before the boy could reply, Giff suddenly grabbed my arm. One look and I could tell he'd figured it out, only he couldn't speak because his other hand was balled into a fist and pressed tightly against his quivering lips. Erik, noting the man sitting next to me, looked mortified.

"It, um, was stopped between floors," he confessed.

"Oh, for the love of cobbler! Were you trapped in there? Did it stop working? Did you try pressing the emergency button?" I was horrified to think the boy had been stuck in an elevator all night.

169

"No, ma'am. I wasn't stuck. I was the one who stopped it."

"What? Why on earth would you do that?"

Giff, removing his fist, turned to me. He'd been stifling a case of the giggles. "Seriously?" he asked. "An eighteen-year-old boy has just confessed to being in an elevator well after midnight that was stopped between floors, and you can't figure it out?" Judging from the look on my face, he decided to fill me in on the joke. "The young man was otherwise engaged."

Erik eyed Giff and confessed. "It's true, Miss Bloom. Kenna and I … we, uh, we use the elevator at night to—"

"WHAT!?" I felt as if my eyes were about to pop out of my head. Honestly, the thought had never occurred to me. "Stop right there!" I held up a hand in warning. "You and Kenna have been using the inn's elevator to … to? Oh, there are so many health violations in what you've just told me, not to mention the very real violation of common decency! I don't even know whether to scream or cry right now, I'm so flaming mad at you."

Giff squeezed my arm once again. "Angel, how about you just calm down and listen. I doubt Mr. Larson has come here to brag about his nocturnal conquests in the inn's only elevator, no matter how epic they might be. The point you're missing is that he was here much later last night than he originally told you. Isn't that right?"

Erik nodded.

"And you saw something, didn't you?" Giff asked.

Again, the boy nodded.

"Well, Mr. Larson, I've paved the way. Now's your chance for redemption."

"Okay," Erik began softly. "We did see something, but you're not going to like it."

Sparing us the details of his elevator exploits, he told us that when he and Kenna were between floors, someone had tried to call the elevator.

"It shocked us. It was nearly two in the morning. No one's ever wandering around the inn at that hour, and I should know."

"Right," I said, still miffed about the brazen misuse of my elevator. "Because you and Kenna do this all the time." Giff cast me a chiding look while urging the young man to continue.

"Ms. Lumiere liked to stay up late to paint, but she didn't wander around. Once she was in her room, she hardly ever left it. Anyhow, this person tried calling the elevator again, but by the time we were in a position to, um, unlock the elevator, whoever it was had already made for the stairs."

I looked at the boy, suddenly realizing what he was saying. He and Kenna might have witnessed Silvia Lumiere's murderer. If so, this little bit of information might change everything. I knew that Silvia was missing a room key, something a person not staying at the inn would need to enter the building. The fact that this person tried to use the elevator might indicate many things, the chief among them being that whoever was in the building was trying to be as inconspicuous as possible when traversing the floors. I looked at Erik. "When you unlocked the elevator what floor did it go to?"

"First floor. The doors opened, and we got out, but no one was there. However, we did see something." Giff and I both leaned in. Erik continued. "We saw, um, a ... a black shadow."

"What?" I asked, thinking I'd misheard him. "What do you mean by a black shadow?"

"A black shadow," he stated. "Look, Miss Bloom, I'm only telling you what we saw. It was dark in the foyer but Kenna and I both saw the same thing. We both saw a large black shadow sweeping up the staircase. It totally freaked us out. We ran back through the kitchen as quietly as we could and out of the inn."

I gave an involuntary shiver as Hannah's words sprang to mind. She had told me just before leaving to get Peter that sometimes the weirdest explanation was the correct one. None of us had wanted to believe it, but who was I to argue with an eyewitness? Was Peter as powerful a wizard as Hannah claimed him to be? Could he really have summoned up dark powers to murder his former employer? Giff, as if reading my mind, cast me a disparaging look and shook his perfectly coiffed head.

"Dark shadow?" he questioned with a sardonic quirk of his brow. "Why would a dark shadow need to use the elevator? For that matter, why would it need to walk up the stairs? Could you and Kenna have witnessed a person perhaps? Maybe someone wearing dark clothing or a black cape?"

With a little thought, Erik replied, "Yeah. It could have been a black cape. All I know was that it was dark, and it was super creepy. We just wanted to get the heck out of there, ya know? Okay, well, that's what I've come to tell ya. Sorry, Miss Bloom. If you want to fire me, I totally understand."

I wasn't about to fire Erik, at least not until he had scoured the elevator from floor to ceiling with our most powerful disinfectant. Instead I told him that he was on double-secret probation and would be until he accompanied me to the police station in the morning to correct the bogus statement he'd made to Jack. Hopefully, with this new revelation, Jack would remove me from the suspect list. Only then would I remove Erik from double-secret probation. How ironic, I thought, that the teenaged miscreant just might have provided the biggest clue yet in this case. Still, whoever it was Erik and Kenna had seen sweeping up the staircase in a black cape after two in the morning was still a mystery.

"I don't understand," Giff said half an hour later, lounging on my bed with arms crossed and legs crossed at the ankles. He was staring at the suspect board now residing on my vanity, puzzling over this latest piece of evidence. "Every indication is pointing to Peter Mc-Clellan. He has motive. He owns a black cape. He even admits to owing a decapitated voodoo doll of the deceased. How is he not the murderer?"

I turned from the board with a dry-erase marker clenched in my hand. Wrestling with the same thoughts, I shrugged. "Because he was with Hannah all night. She swears that he was."

"He could have drugged her," Giff suggested. "Knowing Hannah, she might not even realize it if she was."

"I've already thought of that," I said. "I haven't had the courage to ask her about the possibility. Being drugged by the guy you happen to be dating is not a pleasant thought."

"True. Okay. Let's think about Silvia's missing room key instead. We don't know where it is, but that doesn't mean the murderer had to use it. It could just be a coincidence, or Peter could have taken it to throw us off the trail."

"Or he could have used it to get into her room," I offered.

Giff shook his head. "No. He wouldn't need it. You told me that Silvia kept him close. She would have opened the door to him no matter what time of night he came calling."

"Maybe, but here's what we know so far." I turned to the suspect board with my dry-erase marker ready to underline the facts. "Silvia was murdered sometime between two and five o'clock in the morning.

I'm using the new time of two because when Erik and Kenna left the inn, Silvia was still in her room. At some point after they witnessed the black shadow sweeping up the staircase, Silvia was suffocated with a cherry scone and pushed down the stairs. The scones in question had been delivered to her room that very night by Erik Larson. I once publicly stated that I wanted to choke Ms. Lumiere with a scone, and I have access to the inn, including a key to every room. However," I continued, drawing a line through my name, "I didn't murder the woman. Which leads us to her ex-husband, Stanley Gordon."

"Right," Giff said. "Odd coincidence that he and wife number two just happened to be staying at the inn on the same weekend wife number one is murdered."

"But I talked with them. Jack did too. I'm inclined to think that it really was coincidental. Stanley genuinely appears to have no hard feelings toward his ex. In fact, he's been giving her money. Also, Erik witnessed Stanley and his wife entering their room around twelve thirty last night, the same time he was delivering the scones to Silvia. Stanley was staying just down the hall from her. He would hardly need to throw on a black cape and sweep up the stairs at two in the morning to kill her. Besides, the man's an upstanding businessman. I doubt he even owns a black cape."

"Which leads us back to Peter," Giff stated again, casting me an *I told you so* look. "He's a wizard ... or shaman ... or something. We *know* he owns a black cape."

"Right," I said, recalling the incident well. In fact, the image of Peter in his black cape sitting around a fire with Hannah and Erik was still burned in my memory, prompting me to add, "He was also convinced Silvia was a vampire—a soul-sucking vampire," I clarified. "He's a habitual pot smoker and clearly not dealing with a full deck.

But he does have an alibi. Besides, black capes aren't too hard to come by these days."

I walked around the suspect board and underlined another name. "There's also Fred Beauchamp," I reminded Giff. "Silvia's suspected lover, whom I still have to talk to, and Bob Bonaire, our head chef. He also despised the woman. But here's the thing. If Fred wanted to sneak back inside the inn after midnight, he'd need a key. Bob wouldn't. He has keys to the kitchen. He can enter the building whenever he wants to."

"Does he own a black cape?"

I shrugged. "I honestly don't know. But I don't think he'd use a scone as a murder weapon. He's got access to some of the best knives on the planet and knows how to use them. Besides, I have a feeling that the scone was a direct attack on me. Bob would never implicate me in that way. However, I still think we need to talk with him."

"Okay," Giff replied, then fell silent. A moment later he suddenly sat up. "Where would Peter keep his black cape?"

"In his room, I'm guessing. However, if he was with Hannah last night and they were down by the lighthouse holding their voodoo pow-wow, he would have brought it back to her place."

"It would only stand to reason." Then, with a pointed look, Giff remarked, "But don't you remember how upset Peter was when he learned that the door to his room had been opened?"

"I thought that was about something else." I set the marker I'd been holding back on my vanity. "Peter's been smoking in a nonsmoking room, and I'm not talking about cigarettes."

"Angel, he's a hippie. They all have a blatant disregard for authority figures and rules. But let's say it was about the cape. What if he'd used it to sneak back into the inn unnoticed and then left it in his room after the deed had been done? Since he's already staying here he wouldn't have to worry about being seen, and because he was staying here he obviously knows that his chances of running in to anyone at that time of night were slim to none."

"You really can't get over the fact that Peter has an alibi, can you?"

"Oh, I'll get over it, once we can prove beyond a shadow of a doubt that he didn't murder Silvia Lumiere. I say we sneak into his room and do a little poking around."

It was enticing, and yet I hesitated. Part of it was because I'd already been in that room once today and didn't feel like subjecting myself to that kind of skunky mess again. The other part was merely philosophical. If Peter found out we'd been in his room again without his permission, I could get in real trouble. Murder at the inn was bad enough, but a manager that snuck into rooms out of sheer curiosity wasn't the type of behavior that inspired customers to visit. I looked at Giff and offered, "We could just call Hannah and ask if Peter's cape is still at her place."

Giff, bristling with excitement, jumped off the bed. "Whitney, where's your senses of adventure? Sure, we could call Hannah, but the inn's empty and you've got a set of master keys. Also, and I'm just throwing this out there, angel, but, um, the Cherry Orchard Inn was the scene of a brutal crime last night. Aren't you the tiniest bit curious to have a look at Silvia's room?" With an inviting grin he opened the door. "I know I am."

Twenty-Three

With the master keys in hand, Giff and I walked into the empty foyer. It wasn't quite midnight yet, but the main lights had been turned off, leaving only the soft lighting of the wall sconces in the hallways and the glowing fixture above the front desk. I looked at the foot of the spiraling staircase and felt the hairs on the back of my neck prickle. Less than twenty-four hours ago the body of Silvia Lumiere had been there, neck broken, mouth stuffed with one of my cherry scones. The discovery of the body had left a haunting image. It took a cleansing breath and a conscious effort to shake the eerie feeling that had come over me.

"I suppose the elevator's out of the question?" Giff mocked with an impish grin.

"Too soon, and not funny," I hiss-whispered, then headed up the stairs.

The Pine Suite was tucked away at the end of the darkened hallway. I had never seen the inn so eerily silent and empty as it was now. Although we were the only two souls in the entire place, we moved with quiet reverence until we stood before the door to Peter's room.

"Ready," I whispered, knowing that I was about to violate the trust of a non-paying guest. As an innkeeper the thought disturbed me; as Hannah's best friend I was more than ready to do a little poking around. The key was almost in the lock when Giff stopped me.

"Wait. Knock first," he advised with a sudden look of caution.

"Why?" I asked in muffled tones. "It's not like he's in there or anything."

"Right. But you can't just open the door to someone's room without knocking. It just looks bad."

"There's no one here, literally," I reminded him.

"I'm here."

I looked at the idiot. He was serious. I was of half a mind to remind him that breaking into Peter's room had been his idea to begin with but decided to take a different tactic on the matter. With a well-placed sarcastic snarl, I turned to the door and slammed my fist against it with the force of an angry teen. The echoing sound made us both cringe. I'd hit it harder than I intended to, yet received a ripple of satisfaction from Giff's theatric *really?* glare. However, a heartbeat later, we both jumped when the door flew back on its hinges.

We were hit with a putrid cloud of smoke. Giff coughed and waved at the cloud with furry, cursing under his breath. I was choking too, and seething. The room wasn't on fire; it was filled with pot smoke—a flagrant violation of our non-smoking policy.

A slim figure appeared in the fog. "Hannah?" it asked, then coughed. A shaggy head broke through the cloud to peer into the hallway. "Dudes, like, you're not Hannah." Peter was about to shut the door when I thrust my foot in his room and stopped it from closing.

"What the heck are you doing here? Where's Hannah? Holy cobbler, could you please put on some clothes?" I shaded my eyes with a hand. The only piece of clothing the guy was wearing was a very skinny little thong made out of jungle camo.

Giff, never more delighted than when I was in an uncomfortable situation, replied, "His room, his rules, am I right, brother?"

"Dude. Totally. But I have some pants here … I think." Peter turned and stumbled back into the cloud of skunky smoke.

While Peter was searching for said pants, Giff and I went about defogging the place. We shut the hall door, opened the windows, and turned on the ceiling fan. The moment Peter was decent, I pounced. "Why are you here and not at Hannah's?"

Although the guy was still high as a kite and just as confused, he looked glum. His head dropped to his chest, causing the bushy unbound hair to swirl around him like a tuft of unruly weeds. "Like, Hannah left. I … um, really pissed her off this time."

If it was possible to feel sorry for a pot-smoking idiot with a blatant disregard for hotel rules, one who just might be a cold-blooded murderer as well, then the dejected puppy dog look was working for him. The guy was dazed and truly down on his luck, and that struck a chord somewhere deep within me. It was how I'd felt earlier in the day when the two men I cared about most had both dumped me.

We sat Peter on the bed and asked him to tell us what had happened. His movements were slow and lethargic. A part of me was afraid he was going to flop back on the bed, unconscious. To prevent that from happening, Giff fired up the en suite Keurig and began the process of brewing a cup of coffee while I kept Peter talking. Eventually, once enough caffeine had been administered, his brain engaged and he told us the reason Hannah had left the inn without him.

Apparently Hannah had made Peter promise to stop dabbling in the dark arts, and, more importantly, to stop self-medicating with his cleansing herb. Whatever they'd done on the beach beneath the lighthouse last night had freaked them both out, especially when they'd learned of Silvia's death this morning.

"She said that now Silvia's gone there's no reason to, ya know, cleanse. But, like, dude, there's always a reason to cleanse. Am I right?" This he directed to Giff, having a hard time focusing on me. The puppy dog look had vanished, and with it all my sympathy.

"Hannah finally figured out that this"—I waved a hand at the dissipating smoke—"isn't medicinal but recreational, and that you've been lying to her, playing on her sympathies and generous nature." I gave Giff a knowing nod. "So, Peter, what else have you been lying about?"

"Well, I came up here to rest up a bit after that delicious dinner, and that's not a lie. I really wanted to, but then I thought about Silvia and kinda freaked out again. I mean, *dudes*," he said, his glossy brown eyes staring intently at us, "I'm not really a shaman or a wizard. I just do that stuff because chicks really dig it." He brought his hand over his chest. "Like, I'm the biggest Harry Potter fan. Those books totally changed my life when I was a kid. Everyone wants to believe in magic, right? Especially when they're beholden to an evil soul-crushing pixy like Silvia Lumiere. It was my way of coping with her demands, that and the fact that I was little better than her slave. But I swear, I'm like a total pacifist. Is it a crime that I use a sweet combination of weed, art, and magic to lure hot chicks into bed with me?"

"Not a crime, per se," Giff remarked, as I was too angry to reply. He beheld the man with mild distaste. "The word I'd use is 'deceitful' ... and creepy."

"Dude. It's my thing," Peter said defensively. "But, um, last night everything went wrong. I was so angry with Silvia. I mean, the bitch, like, had banned my girl from the inn! Hannah's special. We're, like, soulmates, ya know? We both love yoga pants, quoting Harry Potter, taking long pumpkin spice bubble baths, and, like, watching videos of baby goats on YouTube." He giggled unsteadily. "Those little dudes are super cute and super bouncy."

As Peter smiled at the memory of baby goat videos, Giff, clearly still stuck on the pumpkin spice bubble bath comment, looked disturbed. He mouthed over Peter's head, "Is that even a thing?" and shivered slightly. I didn't know and didn't really care. All I was concerned with was the fact that Peter keep caffeinating. I handed him a second cup of coffee.

"Goats might be cute," I warned, "but they're the reason Hannah was banned from the inn to begin with. Goats, and certain people, can't be trusted."

"Silvia couldn't be trusted," he countered, his voice infused with passion. "That's why I took Hannah to the beach below the lighthouse. I told her we were going to hold a special ceremony. Like, it's spooky down there, ya know? I'm pretty sure it's haunted too. The fact that it was forbidden only made it better. Dudes, it's like the ultimate aphrodisiac. We got stoned and I put on quite the show. I was totally focused on taking revenge on Little Silvia." He gestured to a lump in his pocket, which I assumed was the eerie little doll.

As I explained Little Silvia to Giff, Peter paused to take a sip of coffee.

"I, like, snapped off her head," he told us, illustrating with his hands. Giff, still marveling that the man had kept a little doll of his employer in his pocket, shivered. "I might have even said that I wished the old bag would choke on a bone or, like, break her beefy neck. I even pretended to speak in tongues, purely to impress Hannah. But I totally swear that I had no idea my powers were real. It's freakin' me out. I killed Silvia," he uttered in a fear-stricken whisper. He then held up his hands, focusing on his wiggling fingers. "And, like, I don't even know what to do with these things. I've turned them into weapons of murder. Hannah was right to leave me."

"First off," I said, crossing my arms and sounding frighteningly like my mother, "I suggest that you stop smoking pot. It's not only a flagrant violation of our non-smoking policy, but it's also warped your sense of reality."

Giff, casting me a mildly reprimanding look, turned to Peter. "Were you, by chance, wearing a black robe last night?"

Peter nodded. "My wizard cape. It, like, sets the mood; creates the illusion. Hannah's got a thing for my cape."

Giff was clearly charmed by this piece of information. "And do you happen to have it here with you?"

Peter cast a look around the room, then shook his head. "Nope. I must have left it at Hannah's last night."

"Okay. Here's another question," Giff said. "Do you remember coming back to the inn last night at around two in the morning wearing that cape?"

Peter looked at him as if he were mad. "Like, that's not possible, dude. My wizard cape and I were otherwise engaged at Hannah's place until way past two in the morning."

Giff seemed mildly impressed, which fanned the flames of Peter's besotted grin. While Peter was momentarily lost in some wildly inappropriate memory, Giff turned to me. With a look that brought me back to my advertising days, he conveyed that he was finally satisfied that Peter had nothing to do with Silvia's murder.

"Well," he said to the swiftly sobering hippie, "I've got some good news and some bad news for you. The good news first. You didn't kill Silvia Lumiere with your mad wizarding skills. The bad news? Aside from an uncanny psychic moment, I'm afraid you're just a muggle like the rest of us."

"Whoa, dude. Are you sure?"

"Pretty darn," I said, looking at the slightly confused man. "Let me explain." I then told Peter about our earlier discussion with Erik Larson and his eyewitness account of a person wearing a black robe at the inn late last night. "So, you see? You couldn't have killed Silvia because there was someone else at the inn last night who we believe actually did the deed. But that's where I'm stumped. Who else might have a black cape and a reason to want Ms. Lumiere dead."

"Whitney, um, like, black capes aren't hard to come by." Peter drained the rest of his coffee and stood, clearly relieved that his imagined powers hadn't killed anyone. "And, like, she offended nearly everyone she knew. If I were you I'd start by looking in her room, not mine."

I turned to the shirtless, wild-haired man with the slowly sobering gaze and thought that Giff had been correct. Peter didn't have wizard powers, but he just might be a little psychic. He had, after all, read my mind. I was itching to get into Silvia's room, which was, ostensibly, off limits. I was now soundly convinced, as was Giff, that Peter wasn't at the inn last night when Silvia was murdered. But he was her assistant. He traveled with her, knew her habits, handled her paintings, and knew of the people she dealt with. He was obviously unaware of the fact himself, and perhaps the prodigious amount of weed he smoked was to blame, but Peter knew Silvia's killer. The problem would be getting him to remember a conversation he might have overheard or recall some small slight the woman had made to the wrong person. I looked at both men, one groomed and styled to perfection, the other unkempt as a Yeti. It was like staring at the perfect before-and-after photo of a clever men's hair product ad. I pushed the thought aside and pulled out the set of master keys I'd been carrying. I held them up, indicating that Silvia's room wasn't off limits.

"*Whitney*," Giff breathed, feigning shock. "Silvia's room is a crime scene. You're not allowed to go in there. *Legally*," he clarified. "If you thought Officer McHottie was mad at you before, think of how irate he's going to be if he finds out that you've been snooping around in Ms. Lumiere's room."

"But he's not going to find out. Because we're not going to tell him, are we? And we're not going to touch anything either. Silvia obviously had her secrets," I reminded them, "and I'd really like to look at her room. There are so many people she annoyed and stomped on; so many who have cause to shove a scone down her throat and push her down a flight of stairs, but only one person was unhinged enough to do it. Gentlemen, the sooner we find Silvia's murderer, the sooner the Cherry Orchard Inn can get back to business."

Twenty-Four

The Sailboat Suite wasn't our biggest room, but the airy cottage décor and spectacular view made it one of my favorites at the inn. Although Mom had a flair for modern Victorian, she had a real knack for creating unique and comfortable rooms of all themes. The Sailboat Suite boasted white beadboard wainscoting below walls of pale blue. A navy and white striped wingback chair sat beside a white-mantled fireplace with a painting above it of a historic ship at full sail. Near the window sat a small table with two chairs, and on the white-framed bed was a quilt in shades of blues, whites, and pinks. The floor was knotty pine, with striking area rugs beneath the bed and in the sitting area.

When Silvia had occupied this room, it was in a state of perpetual turmoil. Furniture had been pushed aside to make room for paintings and supplies, easels and blank canvases, clothing, wine bottles and luggage. Thanks to the crime scene unit, it appeared to have been raked over with a fine-tooth comb. The array of food trays, wine bottles, and used glasses that had accumulated over the past few days had all been removed, as had the sheets on the bed and any clothing that had been strewn across the floor. Most of the luggage Erik had hauled to her room when she arrived had also been removed. There were still some clothes hanging in the closet, but that was about it. The first thing we noticed upon crossing the yellow crime scene tape was the quiet stillness of the room, and the fact that there weren't any obvious signs of a struggle. No wine splatters on the hardwood floor. No scone crumbs on the table. No battered paintings, broken glass or scattered art supplies. Everything looked as it should for an elderly woman who collected unfinished paintings.

It was the paintings that drew us in, scattered haphazardly around the room in various phases of completion. "These are some of her new commissions," Peter offered, highlighting one with a flip of his hand.

"She liked to work on them at night," he added. "Too many distractions during the day, or so she always said. I think it was the wine. She drank a lot of it at night. It, like, loosened her up; got the creative juices flowing. She'd call me in at around eleven or so to set up her easel and mix the paints for the painting she wanted to work on."

"Were you in here last night?" I asked him, remembering my first talk with Erik. He had told me that he thought there was someone in Silvia's room last night when he delivered her tray of scones. Peter shook his head.

"Nope. I was mad at her. Told her that if she needed me to set her up, she'd have to let me know by ten. There was a little pushback on her end about that. She called me the usual names, 'useless bohemian drug-monkey' being my favorite." He smiled wanly. "But when she started in on Hannah, I, like, told her to stuff it. She found out that we, ya know, hang together. Silvia was weirdly possessive of my time, and I told her I'd had enough of it. She knew we were all supposed to be going to the Renaissance fair today, just as she knew I'd planned to spend the night with m'lady."

Giff, studying one of the unfinished paintings, was pulled back to the matter at hand by the archaic phrase. "Was your other m'lady perhaps jealous?" he asked, using a theatric voice. "Word on the streets is that she was quite the cougar."

"Dude, like, that thought right there? That's disgusting."

"So you and Silvia weren't...?"

Peter, looking remarkably sober, paled and shook his head. "She used to try when she first took me on. That's when I went full hippie on her. I stopped bathing, using deodorant, combing my hair, washing my clothes, and I started eating a lot of Doritos. In just weeks I totally repulsed her." He grinned. "After that we came to an agreement."

Giff, studying the paintings, turned. "Smart man," he said, then stilled. "Whitney, come take a look at this."

He'd found our family portrait. Although Silvia had just started it, I was amazed by the progress she'd made. And, quite frankly, I was awed to silence by what I saw. Her original sketch had been in charcoal pencil. But the strokes, the subtle lines capturing my father's thoughtful gaze, my mother's unfettered cheerfulness, my gran's wry demeanor and ageless grace were the marks of a genius. But it was the look of pure desire on Tate's face as he peered down on me that stopped my heart for a beat or two. There was nothing brotherly about that look, and I felt no artist could capture such an emotion if it wasn't real. As for me, again she'd been dead on. Although I smiled, she'd managed to tap into the micro-emotions behind it—a hint of worry in the creases of my eyes, a dimple of confliction marring the smooth surface of my chin, and a smile that was more forced than felt. It was nothing like looking into a mirror. A mirror is a reflection, changing and shifting with the movements of the observer. What Silvia had created was the truth. And sometimes the truth is hard to acknowledge.

"Dear Lord," I uttered. "I now understand why there's a shrine taking over our front porch. Maybe I was too quick to judge her."

"This is what I was talking about." Giff turned to me with a pointed look. "I told you that her talent is legend in Chicago. Just because you couldn't get along with her, cupcake, didn't mean you had to deprive me of the opportunity to observe this virtuoso."

"Dude," Peter said. "Cupcake did you a favor. It's better to view the art than to feel the sting of the artist. Besides, she would have liked you, bro … I mean, really *liked you*. Your clothes look costly. You've got sweet blond highlights in your dark hair. And, like, don't read into this, but you're a total dude. Whatever scent you're wearing is, like, dangerous. Sexually dangerous." This was punctuated with a cautionary look.

"Acqua Di Giò," Giff replied. "Giorgio Armani. My signature scent. And don't worry about me. I know how to fend off the ladies. Ask cupcake. She'll tell you."

"Yeah. I thought I did too, bro," Peter said, oblivious to what Giff was hinting at. "It was the flattery that undid me. Silvia told me that she liked my paintings and talked me into working for her. I thought I had scored big. Working for a painter like Silvia is an up-and-coming artist's dream. However, once she had me under her thumb I saw her for what she really was, a soul-sucking vampire. You put up with it, I suppose, because of moments like this." He gestured to the painting.

"It is remarkable. Whitney," Giff said, turning to me. There was a brightness in his eyes I didn't trust, and with good reason. "A small observation," he continued. "It appears Mr. Vander-licious has been elevated to god status by the hand of the recently deceased. That is art. You should really consider apologizing to the man."

I was speechless. That's when Peter chimed in. "But, like, aren't you and that police dude a thing? That's what Hannah told me."

Dammit if my heart didn't give a blood-draining lurch at the mention of Jack. I had mucked that one up good, and I doubted if Tate would ever talk to me again. "Nope," I said. "I'm quite single." I then turned my eye-daggers on Giff. "What you're witnessing, Gifford McGrady, is purely artistic interpretation. Tate was a stand-in for my brother. Silvia was supposed to switch out the face but obviously hadn't gotten that far." Before he could add a snappy reply, I changed the subject.

"Did I ever tell you what happened earlier this week? Silvia was really beginning to get under my skin. I was seething mad at the woman and of half a mind to toss her out of the inn when one of her admirers from the arts council approached me. Alexa Livingstone," I said to Peter, knowing he was familiar with the name. "She was so taken with Silvia's talent that she actually cautioned me against lashing out at her. She feared Silvia would leave Cherry Cove if she was offended. Ms. Livingstone instructed me to give Silvia a pass on her bad behavior—that her talent demanded it. I thought the woman was nuts. I thought they were all nuts. But now I think I understand."

"That's the effect she had on people," Peter replied with a nonchalant shrug. "Fawning and vicious by turns. It messes you up. I started smoking weed to cope with it."

"These paintings," I said, suddenly struck with a thought. Truthfully, I didn't know what I was looking for in the room. I was hoping something would jump out at me, but the only thing that had was Silvia's pile of unfinished paintings and an artful rendition of Tate. "What if one of these paintings holds the clue to Silvia's murder?"

"Okay," Giff said. "So what are we looking for?"

"I don't know. Anything odd, I suppose. Hopefully we'll know it when we see it."

We went through the ten paintings Silvia had been working on in her room, but there was nothing out of the ordinary about any one of them as far as we could tell. They were all unfinished portraits or land-scapes she'd been working on. When we were done inspecting them, I turned to Peter.

"I thought Silvia sold twelve sittings, not counting the portrait she was painting for our family. There are only seven portraits here, along with three landscapes."

"Right," Peter replied. "That's because she hadn't scheduled all her appointed sittings. She liked to spread them out over the summer."

"Could the person owed one of those sittings have gotten mad she was taking so long?"

Peter shrugged.

"Or maybe she was rude to one of these couples," I offered, "or a family member?"

"Could have been," he added. "You could call and ask. I have all the names. I keep all Silvia's records."

Giff and I looked at one another. We were thinking the same thing, a habit from our old ad days. "You have all Silvia's records?" Giff asked. "Does Jack MacLaren know?"

Peter shook his head. "He never asked. I didn't really think of it until now."

Filling with excitement, I looked at Peter. "Where do you keep them? Are they here? In this room?"

"Dudes, like, Silvia never kept her records in here. They were pri-vate; her secrets. And the woman would never hide her secrets in a hotel room."

"Where then?" Giff asked. "Your room?"

Peter shook his head, then reached into the pocket of his baggy pants. "The Lade," he said, triumphantly dangling the car keys. "Or, more correctly, the trailer behind the Lade."

190

Twenty-Five

After making a real effort to leave Silvia's room the way we had found it, the three of us quietly left the inn to walk across the dimly lit, eerily vacant parking lot. The behemoth of a trailer was still connected to the Escalade, and both were parked at the edge of the pavement near a row of tall pines. I thought the trailer had been disconnected from the SUV when Silvia arrived, but Peter confirmed that it hadn't been.

"I'm gonna be honest," he began, his loose flip-flops making muffled slapping sounds on the asphalt as he walked. "Like, I didn't realize the extent of Silvia's money problems. I mean, the woman was always cheap, and, like, never paid for anything she could get for free, my services included. But I thought it was just another one of her nasty ways. I probably shoulda realized she was in trouble before we left Chicago. The day before we left she hired a couple of movers to pack up all her paintings and some of her furniture, mostly the heavy antique stuff. I thought she was being eccentric, ya know, like, she couldn't be creative unless she was surrounded by all her stuff? Kinda in the same way that tormenting the young and promising, like Hannah, Erik, you, and me, made her feel superior and important. But packing up the old paintings and antiques, that's different. Silvia was in real trouble."

As he stood before the trailer, a flash of sorrow or possibly remorse crossed his face and disappeared. "Anyhow," he continued, brightening a measure, "Silvia insisted we take the white beast with us wherever we went."

As Peter went for the lock with his ring of keys, Giff and I pulled out our phones and engaged our flashlight apps to assist him. Although the back of the trailer was bathed in warm light, Peter's fine motor skills were still suffering the effects of his recent bender. It took close to a minute before he put the correct key into the lock.

"Okay," he finally said, throwing the double doors wide. "The records are in here."

Giff and I stood a moment in silent amazement. There were far more than just records staring back at us in the packed, cavernous space lovingly referred to as the white beast. Back in Chicago, after I had lost my job in advertising, I attempted to drown my sorrows in wine and sketchy reality TV. I had seen my share of compelling, unsolvable mysteries about ghostly encounters, Sasquatch sightings, the Loch Ness Monster, aliens, and angels. I had watched them all with suspended disbelief. It was what I lovingly referred to as my "dark period." Since moving back home to Cherry Cove I'd been so busy working at the inn that I didn't even have a social life, let alone time to watch any TV, reality or otherwise. However, peering into Silvia's trailer with the help of two smartphone flashlights, I felt like I had walked onto the set of one of those unsolvable mysteries, only this one was about the dead and the secrets that surrounded them. The thought sent a ripple of excited fear coursing through me.

"So, um, it's a bit crowded aboard the white beast," Peter warned in his languid hippie tone, utterly breaking the spell I'd been under.

"I've made an aisle on the right for easier access, so, like, follow me."
He stepped up into the trailer. Giff jumped up next and gave me his
hand.

The moment I was aboard, Giff whispered "Get a load of this" and
ran his phone light over the contents of the white beast. A jumble of
folded easels sat near the entrance along with an old wooden chest
containing a variety of high-end paintbrushes. Just behind this was a
long rack filled with rows and rows of paint tubes in every color under
the sun. Next to the paints and easels sat a stack of blank canvases in a
myriad of sizes, and directly next to these were what appeared to be
framed paintings, although each one was covered by a heavy black
cloth.

"Dudes. The record book's down this way." As Peter talked, he
continued down the darkened aisle. Clearly he wanted us to follow, or,
at the very least, he wanted our light. But Giff and I stayed where we
were, our lights trained on a stack of covered paintings.

"Are these all Silvia's paintings?" I asked his retreating form.

Peter stopped and poked his head around an antique floor-length
mirror. "Um, nope. Damn," he uttered. "I like almost forgot about
those."

"Short term memory loss," Giff whispered to me, his dark eyes twinkling with mischief. "Classic symptom of habitual self-medicating."

"Dude," Peter hissed, overhearing him. "I'm gonna stop. *Okay?*
And, like, I know what those are. They're what's left of last year's
commissions, only I forgot that someone's going to have to deliver
them now that Silvia's gone."

"These are the paintings Silvia hadn't gotten around to unveiling?"
I asked aloud, staring at the vertical stack of covered rectangles that
ranged in size from four feet high to a manageable two-foot by two-foot
square. I focused my phone light on the first in the row. As I ran my

hand over the black cloth covering the painting, I felt like an archaeologist who'd just discovered the burial chamber of an ancient queen. This metallic cavern on wheels housed the painter's last remaining possessions, a somber thought for a woman who'd spent a lifetime devoted to her art. Noticing that Giff was growing impatient, I peeled back the cloth and inhaled sharply.

Giff's reaction was just as violent. He jumped back a step while crying out like a wounded animal. "What the heck am I looking at?" Although he was horrified, his eyes were glued to the painting before him. "Is it just me or is that man ghosting himself on the pottery wheel?"

"Ghosting?" I questioned, looking at my friend.

"Yeah. Ghosting. It's a term used for those who find it humorous to recreate the iconic pottery wheel scene from the movie *Ghost*. Fred's a potter, so the impulse is there, but he's far from being a Patrick Swayze look-alike. And that's not Demi Moore he's got clenched between his thighs. Correct me if I'm wrong, but that looks like a younger version of Fred." It was then that Giff let out a long, pent-up hoot. Still chuckling, he asked, "What was the woman thinking, painting a portrait like this?"

"It's farcical," I added. "Mocking even." And it really was, because the portrait we were staring at clearly depicted a present-day Fred making a ghostly visit to his younger self on the pottery wheel, teaching his younger self his perfected technique. The subject was oddly disturbing, and yet no one could deny that it was beautifully executed. "It's astonishing," I uttered. "I'm not quite sure what to make of it."

"Hey, dudes. Can one of you throw some light over here?" Peter was still rooting around in the back looking for the record book.

Giff stood and held up his phone.

"Peter, we're looking at a painting of Fred Beauchamp," I said. "I didn't know Fred commissioned a painting."

"Yeah. Last summer. He's not rich or anything." Peter poked his head above a richly upholstered chair with a gilded frame. "I think he did it to impress her. Anyhow, his unveiling was scheduled for next Saturday. It's all here in the ledger." He held up a leather-bound book and wiggled it. "I keep it in the drawer of the big desk," he explained, walking back toward us. He opened the book, revealing a bookmarked page. "These are her new commissions. Pricing's over here, and on this page is the order of the unveilings. People pay a lot of money for her work. She liked to draw out the ordeal for dramatic effect. Those," he said, pointing to the row of covered paintings, "are in order."

"So Fred hasn't seen this yet?" I pointed my phone light back on the painting.

"Whoa!" Peter cried upon seeing it. "Dudes! Is it just me, or is old Fred ghosting a young Fred?"

"Is this the first time you're seeing this?" For some reason this intrigued me.

Peter, still staring at the portrait, started to giggle. A short while later he pulled himself together and replied, "Yeah. I mean, I'd totally remember this one if I'd seen it before. Silvia painted in her room at night. She always made sure I attend the sittings. After that I'd, like, catch glimpses of all her commissions in various stages of completion. But after Silvia worked on a painting she liked to cover it. She didn't want anyone looking at her work until she held the unveiling. It was just her way." Peter looked at the painting again and let out another wave of giggles. Giff, unable to help himself, erupted in laughter as well. "I was at Fred's sitting," Peter offered, stifling his laughter. "It was totally normal. This," he added, pointing to the painting, "is totally messed up."

I studied the painting a minute longer. It was either going to delight or feel like a slap in the face. Silvia was ether paying homage to Fred and his craft, or she was making a mockery of him by depicting him ghosting himself on the pottery wheel, guiding his own hands lovingly on the wet clay. If Fred had in fact seen this portrait, or somehow had caught wind of it, it might have been enough to throw him over the edge. Silvia had been publicly toying with his emotions for years. Was this meant to be another costly humiliation? Then another thought struck me. Silvia had been a sly woman. Maybe this painting was meant to be a challenge to Fred's devotion. By rejecting the painting Fred would be, in a sense, rejecting Silvia. And, as a member of the arts council, he'd surely catch flack for that.

If, however, Fred proclaimed to love the painting, the council would applaud him, but Silvia would be suspicious.

"What were you playing at, Silvia Lumiere?" I asked the portrait.

While I was mentally planning an unveiling and my inevitable talk with Fred Beauchamp, I was aware that Giff and Peter had wandered off. Giff, having an eye for antiques and oddities, couldn't help himself. I had just replaced the cover on the painting when he called me to the back of the trailer.

"Whitney! Quick, come here." Blond highlights poked through a press of luxurious fur coats hanging on a rack. The look of urgency on Giff's face made me jump. "Another disturbing discovery. You're going to want to take a look at this."

I worked my way to the back of the trailer, weaving a path through Silvia's personal belongings. To my annoyance, Peter and Giff were at the very back. I had just climbed over a large upholstered chair when Giff turned to me.

"I've found it," he said, his dark eyes glittering with excitement. "It's the legendary missing painting." He stepped back and focused the beam of his phone light on the canvas. For the second time since climbing aboard the white beast, I inhaled sharply. It was another exquisite painting done by the hand of Silvia Lumiere, only the subject of this one was a handsome young man wearing nothing but a fierce grimace. As shocking as this was, it wasn't what was causing my heart to pound away in my chest like a pack of greyhounds chasing a lure. No, that was caused by the unmistakable identity of the man himself, and even if I was in any doubt about that, the huge broadsword by his side should have given it away.

"It's Lance Van Guilder," Giff said, looking as shocked by the discovery as I was. "Dear Lord, Whitey. He's the man who tried to sue Silvia but was unsuccessful. He must be. Here's the proof."

It was undeniable, and yet I was gripped by a sickening fear. "Poor Tay. She's not going to like this one bit."

Twenty-Six

The discovery of the painting in the back of Silvia's trailer changed everything, and Giff, Peter and I were having a hard time trying to process what it meant. We decided to remove it from the trailer and bring it to my room for safe keeping. That might have been a mistake. Once there, the three of us couldn't stop from gawking at it—for a myriad of reasons—while trying to figure out what to do with this new and startling piece of information.

I shook my head. "And Tay was wondering why Lance was acting so strange lately. Now we know."

"It's not a bad painting," Giff remarked, assuming the attitude of an art critic. "In fact, it's highly flattering. I would have never suspected the guy was so ripped."

"*Right?*" Peter agreed with a bob of his head.

"It's not about the painting," I reprimanded. "And we really shouldn't be looking at this. It's ... it's indecent."

"It's art," Giff challenged.

Knowing that there was only one way to regain their attention, I replaced the black cloth. "Giff, when we talked over the phone, you told me that Silvia had a young male apprentice who claimed he was coerced into posing in the nude in exchange for money. When Silvia didn't pay him, he took it to court."

"Wait," Peter interrupted. "That dude used to work for Silvia too?"

"He must have," Giff replied. "How else would she have had this in her private collection?"

"Tay's only known Lance for about a year or so, but she's crazy about him," I told them. "He's a Renaissance fair jouster, but Tay also told me that he's a gifted metal artist as well. I nearly forgot about that, but that's got to be his connection to Silvia. How many years ago was this painting supposedly done?" I looked at Giff, seeing if he remembered.

"At least five," he answered. "That's when this particular lawsuit was thrown out of court." He turned to Peter and explained. "When Whitney asked me to look into Silvia's background for her, one of my discoveries was that Silvia had been named in a sexual harassment lawsuit."

"No doubt," Peter said, his face reminding us both that he had firsthand knowledge of Silvia's darker side.

"We found out that Silvia was having an affair with a young man named Jake Jones, but that was years ago. It led to her divorce. We also discovered that she'd been named in a sexual harassment lawsuit. The identity of the young man who brought the lawsuit against her had been protected. This man claimed to be Silvia's apprentice. He also said that Silvia made overt sexual passes at him and at one point offered him a sum of money to pose in the nude for a painting. When Silvia refused to pay him, he took her to court. However, when Silvia took the stand she must have put on quite a show, because she managed to turn the whole thing around on this poor man. She claimed that she was the one enduring all the sexual harassment, and basically dragged the apprentice's name through the mud. She also denied ever making such a painting, and since no one could prove that she had, the whole case was thrown out of court. The only concession to the whole ordeal was that this man's identity was stricken from all court documents, allowing him to remain anonymous. Whitney and I had no idea who he was until now."

I nodded. "I'm sorry to admit this, but it does makes sense. Tay told me that Lance had a client who owed him a substantial sum of money. That client must have been Silvia Lumiere. For some reason she'd decided to settle this debt, maybe because she got wind that Lance was in Cherry Cove. I really don't know. What I do know is that Tay told me how Lance purchased an expensive suit of armor when he received the money owed to him, but soon after the armor arrived the check bounced. Tay said it sent him into a tailspin. The armor was repossessed, and Lance started losing in the jousting ring."

"The soul-sucking devil," Peter breathed. "She destroyed the poor man. No wonder he killed her."

"Whoa, fella." Giff shot Peter a cautioning look. "We don't know that for sure. All we have is this painting and a hunch. As far as we know, the first time Lance set foot at the inn was at tonight's dinner."

I looked at Giff, my mind racing. "But Lance didn't know about a murder at the inn, remember? Tay hadn't gotten around to telling him."

"True," Giff concurred. "But when Jenn mentioned the name Silvia Lumiere, he got up and left. You saw her, angel. She looked right at him—as if she knew that name would illicit a response."

"She did," I said, vividly recalling the incident. "How did Gran know?"

Giff filled with admiration and shook his head. "I've told you, angel, that woman doesn't miss a trick."

"I've got to call Tay." I pulled out my iPhone, but before I could press her number the phone was snatched from my hand.

"No," Giff reprimanded. "It's one in the morning. She's sleeping, most likely next to that gorgeous hunk of a knight. And if we wake her to tell her about this, she'd just freak out. You know how in-your-face she can be when her back's against the wall. Plus, and don't forget, the man makes his money swinging a sword from the back of a horse, or so he says. We don't want anything happening to Tay."

"And that's exactly why I should call her—so she can get the heck out of there." My heart was racing just thinking about it. I made a grab for my phone, but Giff held it over his head, causing my swipe to fall short.

"No. We calm down and visit her in the morning."

"Dudes." It was Peter. His look of admonishment faded with a loud yawn. "Like, just let the police handle it. I'm going to bed." He made for the door, then stopped. "Can I, like, crash here tonight? It's spooky on the other side of the inn."

Giff graciously agreed to let Peter sleep in his room on one of the inn's roll-out cots. We were all tired and ready to turn in for the night, but not before agreeing that Peter's suggestion was the correct choice. Tay was my best friend, but the painting was a matter for Jack. I had planned to make a trip to the police station anyhow tomorrow. Erik needed to revise his original statement, describing to Jack how he and Kenna had seen a black shadow sweeping up the stairs at two in the morning—right before Silvia was murdered. There was also the matter of the odd, undelivered portrait of Fred Beauchamp, still in the trailer. However, it was the erotic painting of Tay's boyfriend that was really going to set his head spinning. There were so many new pieces of evidence to consider, so many people Silvia had toyed with and hurt. And yet as I climbed into bed all I could think about was Jack MacLaren, and how my heart and hurt pride were going to handle facing him again.

Twenty-Seven

I awoke at eight thirty, feeling remarkably refreshed under the circumstances, and stumbled downstairs in search of coffee. Mom was already in the family kitchen, dressed in navy capris and a cute floral top. She was humming along to Adele. Mom wasn't overly adept with cell phone technology, although she could answer her smartphone, send a text (although she preferred to call), and ask Cortana for directions or to place a call from her list of important numbers. She also, thanks to me, knew how to sync her phone to her car stereo and stream her favorite Pandora station through the speakers. But apparently she'd just added a wireless speaker to her burgeoning techy skills. I smiled and joined in on the chorus of "Someone Like You."

At the sound of my voice Mom turned off the music and spun around. "Good morning," she said. Her smile was bright and cheerful, just the thing I needed before facing what was certain to be a troubling day. As if by magic, a cup of hot black coffee found its way into my hands. Mom turned back to the stove and continued working as she remarked, "You were up late last night. I heard you and Giff

202

come in around one in the morning. Truthfully, I'm surprised you're up this early."

I watched Mom flip four perfectly round pancakes on her stove-top griddle before I replied. "I've been getting up so early to do the baking that I feel as if I've been lounging in bed all morning."

Mom smiled. "But with the inn currently shut down," she began, then stopped. Her face clouded and she couldn't bring herself to finish the thought. Instead, she poured more batter on the griddle. I understood just how she felt. Cooking was second nature, and far easier than contemplating a recent murder and the temporary shutdown of the inn at the height of the tourist season. It was no secret that Mom found solace in the kitchen. Because of her cheerful demeanor and kind smile I used to think she was seldom troubled by anything, but then I grew older and learned to look for the signs. The moment she opened the oven I could tell she was more than on edge. The inn was shut down, but Mom had made enough pancakes to feed a small army.

"Mom," I cried, my eyes nearly popping out of my head. "How long have you been up making pancakes?"

She immediately shut the oven, but not before removing a warmed plate with three perfectly stacked, cherry-bespeckled pancakes marinating in a drizzle of melted butter, and a side of thick-sliced, apple-wood-smoked bacon. Dammit, it smelled like heaven! I didn't have time for breakfast, but Mom wasn't one to take no for an answer. She set the plate down on the island counter, added a pitcher of warmed syrup and shoved a fork into my hand. "I'm used to getting up early too," she said breezily. "Cherry pancakes are you father's favorite. He wanted to get working early at the orchard today, so I thought I'd make him a good breakfast. He's already eaten. So, while I was here, I thought I'd make some for you and the boys as well. This is a bed-and-breakfast, after all."

The boys she was referring to were Giff and Peter, who weren't likely to be out of bed before noon. Giff, as a rule, was generally opposed to mornings. Of course, that didn't fly during the workweek, but on weekends and vacations it was a hard-and-fast rule he adhered to. Peter? I really didn't know what his habits were but was nearly certain he was going to take advantage of his newfound freedom. I apprised Mom of the situation and suggested she put the remaining pancakes in ziplock bags and pop them in the freezer for later use. I then made her join me at the counter with her own plate of pancakes and told her about some of the new discoveries we'd made last night.

"You'd better call Erik and let him know that you're coming to pick him up," she advised the moment I told her about his latest confession, while strategically omitting the reason he and Kenna were in the elevator so late at night to begin with. Mom then set down her fork and took a sip of hot coffee. "Well, this is good news. I'd rather have a menacing black shadow haunting the inn than a daughter wrongly accused of murder." Although that statement really made no sense, Mom shook her head, causing her long blonde braids to sway gently. "Bret always thought this old place was haunted. Anyhow," she said, waving off the very scary mention of ghosts with a cheerful smile, "this new statement of Erik's should certainly clear your name." Was it wrong of me to feel slightly discouraged by the fact that she looked more hopeful than confident?

"Mom," I softly chided. "Bret thinks everything's haunted. That is, in effect, his entire career." I rolled my eyes to better express just what I thought of my brother and his obsession with ghost-hunting. "Besides, Erik admitted that it could have been a person in a black cape, which, obviously, it was."

Mom agreed, yet her smile was slightly disingenuous. "I honestly don't know who'd do such a thing."

"I don't either. But believe me, Giff and I are looking into it. Last night he was convinced Peter was the culprit until Peter managed to convince us he wasn't."

"And do you believe him?" Although Mom had never been suspicious of Peter, she looked troubled.

"I do. And what's more, he actually helped us last night. He let us in to Silvia's trailer."

"Goodness, no! Silvia didn't want anyone but Peter going near that beastly thing."

"I know. But now she doesn't really have any say about it, does she?" Mom agreed. That's when I told her about the two paintings we discovered. "So, you see?" I said, getting up to refill our coffees. I filled both our mugs to the brim and returned the pot to the coffeemaker. "There's now two people I'm focusing on: Fred Beauchamp, who commissioned a portrait last year but still hasn't seen what Silvia has done to it, and Lance Van Guilder. However, I'm still not sure how the black cape Erik saw sweeping up the stairs fits into things."

"You think that nice man Tay's dating had something to do with this?" Mom was aghast. Although happily married to my dad for over thirty years, she definitely had a type, and that type was Vikingesque. She adored Tate, who was essentially a clean cut, modern day Viking. He was an expert sailor and not at all opposed to plundering things, like women. Lance Van Guilder had a similar build. The fact that he was an actual knight in a Renaissance fair was enough to make any woman swoon, even one in her mid-fifties. Mom shrugged. "Well, he is the Black Knight," she offered. "But I don't know if knights actually wear capes? I think any reference to color just comes with the title."

"Swingin' dingles!" I blurted as Mom mused over the puzzling facts of knights and capes. The thought of Lance being the Black Knight was stomach-churning. I suddenly felt very ill. "I almost forgot about that." I looked at Mom.

"The only way I know of it is because Tay mentioned it last night. Don't you remember? Also …" Mom lowered her voice as if what she was about to say was scandalous. "Char told me that he was. She's been talking about Lance for quite a while now and delights in telling us ladies in the women's league how muscular he is and how he's the famous Black Knight. She's even been to see him joust. Char's very fond of Lance and thinks he's the perfect man for Tay. At the very least, Lance keeps Tay occupied so she's not focusing all her energies on humiliating Todd. Char's a little sensitive about the fact that she's engaged to a man who could be her son. But who am I to judge? As Reverend Dahl says, 'Love comes in all shapes and sizes, in all forms under the sun.'"

"Even a mother and son," I quipped, only because I couldn't help it. Mom looked at me, then burst into a fit of giggles. I did too.

"You're terrible," she admonished with a grin.

I admitted that I was, then thought of something else. "I hope to God Lance isn't the murderer, especially for Tay's sake, but I have to ask. Do you know if he's ever been to the inn before last night? The portrait we found proves that he knew Silvia, but I've never seen him here."

Mom thought about that. "Come to think of it, I've never seen him here either. But you and I are awfully busy. You might want to ask your grandmother. Now that you've taken over the baking she's made it a point to mingle more with the guests. That woman's got eyes and ears for the both of us. Also, the fact that she keeps company with Edna Baker and Cecilia Cushman means that she's up on all the latest gossip." Mom shook her head. "I swear, nothing happens in Cherry Cove that those three don't know about. In fact," she began, easing herself off the high stool and picking up both our plates, "why don't you stop in and see her before you head out to the Larson place? She should be back from yoga by now."

"Good thinking," I said, and drained my coffee mug.

Mom put the plates in the dishwasher and turned around. "Also, and I don't mean to pry, dear, but have you given a thought as to what you're going to do about Tate? Cecilia Cushman called this morning and said that the *Lusty Dutchman* is gone. Tate must have sailed off last night and hasn't returned. He's an expert sailor, so she's not overly concerned, but she is worried. It's not like him to abandon his business without a word to anyone. I know you two had a falling out, but it's not the first time. And he's such a dear young man. Why don't you visit the marina after you drop off that painting with Jack? I know that you're a great crime-solver, dear. But you've done enough. Let Jack find the murderer. After all, that's his job. My goodness, you're twenty-eight years old. I was married and had two children by the time I was your age. Now that you're back in Cherry Cove, you really need to give some thought to settling down. Your father and I aren't getting any younger. We'd love to have some grandchildren before we're too old to enjoy them."

I loved my mom, but she was utterly oblivious to the struggles of my generation. Millennial dating was complicated. I wanted to settle down too. But I also wanted a career and financial security. I wanted to travel more and spend more time with my friends. Most of all, however, I wanted to find the right man to settle down with, and at the rate I was going that was never going to happen. Why did she have to remind me of all this now? Didn't I already have enough on my plate? Although I cared about Tate and always would, my first priority was the inn. An empty inn during the height of the tourist season wasn't a great way to build financial security. I needed to clear my name. I needed to get Jack to clear the inn so that we could begin calling our displaced guests and filling rooms again. Most of all, however, I needed to find Silvia's murderer. Staring at Mom as she openly nudged me toward Tate only made me realize how much I wanted the satisfaction of finding the person who'd shoved one of my scones down Silvia's throat. I deserved nothing less. Strictly for Mom's benefit, I acquiesced.

"I'll stop by the marina," I promised, then said, "Have Giff call me when he's up. I don't have time to wait around here all day for sleepyheads and prima donnas."

Twenty-Eight

With a covered portrait of a naked man in the back of my Escape, I headed for my gran's house, hoping she'd be able to give me a little more insight into Lance Van Guilder and why she had thought to mention the name Silvia Lumiere to him last night.

Grandma Jenn lived in a charming little cape cod less than a mile from the orchard. It was also on the way into town. She'd grown up in the old Victorian mansion that was now the Cherry Orchard Inn. After selling it to my parents, she decided to move into something smaller, something new and all her own. Although she made daily visits to the inn and was still an integral part of the business, I had to admit Grandma Jenn thrived in her cozy little house. I loved it too. It was light, airy, and smelled of everything good from my childhood.

I parked in the drive and found Gran on the back deck with Mrs. Cushman and her little dog, Molly, the adorable West Highland terrier she'd adopted when moving aboard the *Boondoggle II*. After being thoroughly greeted by a happily wagging tail and rapid-fire puppy dog licks, I joined the ladies on the deck. Gran and Cecilia were still in their yoga clothes, both enjoying the warm morning sun and refreshing cherry smoothies. They were Gran's specialty. The fact that she used vanilla ice cream as the base made them closer to milkshakes than fruit smoothies, but her secret was safe with me. Besides, both ladies looked as if they could use the calorie boost.

"Darling!" Gran called, shortly after Molly accosted me on the lawn. She smiled and waved me over to join them. "What a surprise! We've just come from Hannah's class and needed a little fortifying. She's a great instructor but seemed a little on the warpath today."

I smiled in greeting and took a seat. "That'll be because she's had a falling out with her new man."

"Hot Jesus?" Mrs. Cushman inquired from the rim of her cherry ice cream smoothie. She set down the tall glass. "Of course we all know his name is really Peter, but at the marina we call him Hot Jesus." She tossed me a wink that took all the muscles on half of her face to achieve. "We also know Hannah's nuts about him. It's all she can talk about. At yoga it's all 'Peter this' and 'Peter that.' We thought it was cute until she named a yoga move after him."

"The Hot Jesus," Gran added with a twinkle in her vibrant blue eyes. "Or HJ as we like to call it. It's essentially a warrior one pose with a hyper-extended back bend."

"I'll tell you what it is," Mrs. Cushman interrupted. Her kind brown eyes hardened beneath her soft silver curls. "It's blasphemous!"

"And quite impossible at our age, dear." Both older ladies were in agreement there. "However, I don't need to tell you that Hannah's remarkably flexible. But she's also very encouraging to those of us who aren't so bendy anymore. It's what makes her a great instructor."

"She really is," Mrs. Cushman agreed. She then locked eyes with me. Resting her elbows on the table, she leaned forward. "Seems that falling out's all the rage with you young people. First you and Tate, then Hannah and HJ, and Jenn's just told me about Tay and her hand-some knight. It must be something in the water."

"Cecilia's just filled me in on Tate," Gran said, manufacturing a grandmotherly look of concern. Although Gran was very fond of Tate, I knew for a fact that where my love life was concerned she was firmly on team Jack. Gran continued. "Apparently, he's cast off on a solo adventure aboard the *Lusty Dutchman*."

If they thought the news would be a shock to me, it wasn't. Mom had already filled me in on Tate's abrupt departure. The truth was, the *Lusty Dutchman* was the place Tate felt most at home. Over the years, I had spent my share of time aboard that boat as well, and most of that below deck. Just thinking about it made me blush. However, unless he was engaged in a wildly passionate night of wave-rocking love-making, which I doubted was the case, it wasn't like Tate to just unmoor ship and sail off in the middle of his busiest season at the marina. I was struck with a pang of white-hot guilt, because I knew that his sudden departure was a direct result of the careless way I had treated him yesterday. I might not have been madly in love with Tate anymore, but I still cared deeply for him.

I reached across the table and took hold of Mrs. Cushman's hand. She was a dear older lady whose regard for Tate went far beyond her humble housekeeper status. "He'll be okay," I assured her. "He's just gone off to think. He likes to drop anchor near the islands." And I should know, I thought bleakly as erotic memories began to flood in. I cleared my throat and pushed them aside. I then gestured to the lake just visible at the bottom of Gran's heavily wooded backyard. Far out in the bay, on the other side of the point beyond the lighthouse, was a string of five small, uninhabited islands. "It's quiet out there," I told them. "And peaceful. I'll tell you what. If Tate hasn't returned by this evening, I'll go out there myself and bring him back. There's one

211

island in particular he's very fond of. I'll bet he's there now, gathering his thoughts."

My promise was enough to placate Mrs. Cushman, allowing me to question Gran about what had prompted her last night to ask Lance if he knew Silvia Lumiere.

"Well, because I thought he did," Gran stated matter-of-factly. "At first I didn't recognize him, but then I remembered an incident last Thursday night. Silvia was holding court, as usual, on the patio with Fred, Edna, Alexa, and that knot-artist fella, Jeffery. It was after dinner. The sun was setting, you see, making it hard to make out the new-comer's face. In fact, he was more of an outline against the setting sun, but I clearly saw a young man with a striking build and a mane of shoulder-length, well-conditioned hair. He didn't come from the inn, just walked onto the patio from the back lawn. Silva was shocked to see him, and I could tell he was very upset about something. He was addressing her. He wanted to confront her, but Silvia wouldn't give him the time of day and waved him away like a pesky fly. Fred got up and escorted him off the patio. Eventually he left. I nearly forgot all about it until dinner last night. When Tay introduced me to Lance, I thought he looked familiar but I couldn't be sure. That's why I asked about Silvia."

"So you were working off a hunch?"

Gran nodded.

"Pretty good hunch," I told her.

"He's all right, though, isn't he?" Gran looked genuinely con-cerned. The fact that I gave a noncommittal shrug didn't help any.

"He used to work for her, Gran. I don't think anybody who ever worked for Silvia Lumiere came away without scars of some form or another."

∞

After leaving Gran's house I picked up Erik and headed for the Cherry Cove police station. If I was being totally honest with myself I would have acknowledge that neither the sullen Erik Larson nor the painting of a buck-naked Lance Van Guilder was the reason I was sweating. Nope, the sweat beading on my brow and trickling down my spine was entirely due to the fact that I was about to face the man I'd been stalking for weeks, flirted with, had finally worked up the nerve to invite on a group date, and then offended to the point of open disgust. Sure, I was still miffed that he had marked me as his prime suspect yesterday for the murder of Silvia Lumiere. But I felt that was a small hurdle to leap—a tiny bump in the road that could be overlooked once he came to his senses. I now had a car full of evidence in my favor, yet somehow the thought of facing Jack was a bit more terrifying than being a murder suspect. What I didn't know was if I would ever be able to look him in the eyes again. I gripped the wheel tighter, building courage as I turned into the police station parking lot, thinking that maybe Mom had been right. Maybe Tate and I really did belong together.

"Looks busy," Erik remarked, pulling me back to the task at hand. It was just after ten thirty in the morning and already the beach parking lot was full. The streets teemed with cars, jet skis and motor boats frolicked in the bay, and every patio table at Swenson's ice cream parlor next door was occupied. It was a stark contrast to the emptiness of the inn, so much so that I felt a sudden flash of anger and purpose.

I pulled Erik with me through the group of tourists blocking the front entrance to the police station. With phones and cameras pointed at the roof, they were antagonizing Thing One and Thing Two—or maybe it was the other way around. Either way, the cacophony was astounding. Children and adults called to the goats and laughed. The horned, disruptive duo screamed and leapt around their lofty vantage point. Clearly they were loving the attention. Since I had a soft spot for Jack's kids, I cast them a wave before ushering Erik through the front doors. I had strategically left the pornographic painting in the car, believing the boy had suffered enough without having to witness that expertly painted train wreck.

I was surprised to see Jack's mom, Inga, behind the front counter. She was on the phone bobbing her head as the person on the other end talked. She looked up, saw us, and cupped her hand over the mouth piece.

"Come on back," she said. MacDuff, aware I was in the building, shot through the gap below the front counter and sat at my feet. His whole back end was wiggling as he looked up at me with his big brown eyes. Unable to resist, both Erik and I knelt and gave the dog a big hug.

"I love this dog," Erik said, allowing the slobbery tongue to land on his unshaven, boyish face. I knew what a comfort MacDuff could be and gave the boy space as he hugged the dog.

"Jack's on his way back," Inga informed me and lifted the flip-up countertop, allowing us to pass through. "Tourist fender bender," she said. "Busy morning. Why don't you two take MacDuff and wait in the kitchen. I'll call Jack and let him know you're here."

Fifteen minutes later Jack came strolling through the door dressed in his police blues. It had been only one day, but I'd nearly forgotten how good he looked. Guarded and a little skeptical, Jack took off his cap, ran a hand through his lush ginger hair, and poured himself a cup of coffee. He then pulled up a chair and turned his honey-colored gaze on the two of us. "So, to what do I owe the pleasure of this meeting? Guilty conscience? Confession? Startling new revelation, perhaps?" His remark was as biting as it was condescending.

214

Rising to the challenge with a bold stare of my own, I said, "Startling new revelation, actually. And a bit of a guilty conscience as well. Last night Mr. Larson here made a visit to the inn to inform us that he'd left out a few important details from his earlier statement. I thought we'd drop by this morning and fill you in."

Jack's eyes shifted to the young man. "You lied to me?"

Erik paled. "I didn't mean to, Officer MacLaren, sir. Honestly."

"Just hear him out," I advised. "You'll understand why in a minute."

As Erik spilled his sorry tale of sexual misconduct and flagrant abuse of inn property, I watched Jack closely. Professionalism battled disbelief and ultimately lost the moment when Erik described the eerie black shadow he and Kenna had witnessed sweeping up the staircase at two in the morning.

"Whoa. Back up a minute." Jack looked sharply at Erik. "You're telling me that after a mythically long romp in an elevator you two came out only to witness a black shadow sweeping up the staircase … like in a ghostly sighting?"

"No," I said, speaking for the boy. "He was obviously light-headed. What he means is he witnessed someone walking up the stairs wearing a black cape. The point is, Jack, it couldn't have been me. I was fast asleep at two a.m., and I don't own a black cape. You can search my room if you don't believe me. And clearly it wasn't Erik. As he's just explained he was otherwise detained. Kenna can attest to that. Also, earlier in the evening we discovered that one of Silvia's room keys was missing. Aside from the Pine Suite occupied by Peter McClellan, the inn is empty. We should have both sets of room keys for every room, but we only have one for Silvia's. We've talked to Peter. He doesn't have it and has no idea who might. Silvia might have lost the second key, or it might have been taken for the purpose of entering the building after hours. Whoever called the elevator while it was turned off between floors was obviously trying to sneak up to the second floor unnoticed. When the elevator didn't come, they were forced to use the stairs."

Jack leaned back in his chair and crossed his arms. "I'm impressed, by both of you, actually. Erik, for coming clean with what was undoubtedly a difficult tale to tell, and you, Whitney, for not having killed the boy for what he's been doing to your elevator. Truthfully, you should be thanking Mr. Larson. Erik, I'm going to need to call Kenna to confirm what you just told me.

Jack excused himself to make the call. He returned a few minutes later and took a seat. "Okay," he began, looking relieved. "Kenna's confirmed Erik's story. Erik is now off the suspect list, having left the inn with Kenna at two in the morning. She also had a more concrete description of this mysterious black shadow. She said that not only did it sweep up the stairs, but she felt it was rather tall. Much taller than Ms. Bloom, to be exact."

"Exactly!" I said, looking vindicated. "So I'm off the suspect list too, right?"

One corner of Jack's mouth lifted. "Not exactly. But it does move you down a few notches. We also have a new timeline. We now know that Ms. Lumiere was murdered after two and before five in the morning. I'll call Doc Fisker with these details and see if he can confirm the new timeline. Thanks for coming in."

Jack was about to dismiss us when I reached across the table and touched his hand. It might have been a mistake. The move shocked us both. I quickly let go, as if burned. "Before you dismiss us, I have another piece of evidence you're going to want to see. It's in the back of my car."

"I'll get it." Erik sprang to his feet, clearly itching to get out of there.

"No. I'm sorry, Erik, but this is strictly a matter for Officer Mac-Laren."

Twenty-Nine

"What on earth is that?" Jack was holding the door as I lugged the large, cloth-covered painting into the police station.

The moment I'd insisted that what I was about to reveal was for Jack's eyes only, Inga had been quick to volunteer to drive Erik home. She took MacDuff with her, telling Jack that she'd had enough of answering phones and fielding tourist inquiries about leash laws and dining recommendations for one day. Jack regarded his mother's declaration with suspicion but nodded all the same. She then gave me a hug, placed a kiss on her son's cheek, and told him that he could pick up MacDuff when he came by for dinner. She turned back to me. "Or…" A sly grin fluttered across her lips and was suppressed. "If you have new plans for dinner, just give me call. You can always pick him up tomorrow." This was punctuated with a wink. That made Jack blush. I blushed a little too, but found Jack's high color—particularly the bright crimson on the tips of his ears—achingly adorable. Inga turned and ushered Erik out the door, leaving us with her parting request of, "Play nicely, now," as if we were still children. Her quick departure hadn't escaped either of us. But it was a little suspicious.

It also made me wonder if perhaps she'd received a call before my arrival—one from Grandma Jenn giving her the heads-up on the situation between her son and me. I loved my gran, but I also knew that she meddled as she pleased.

"And you call yourself a detective," I said, slowly shaking my head. "It's a painting."

He nearly grinned as he locked the door behind me. He then turned the sign, indicating that the station was now closed, and led me through the police station and across to his living quarters on the other side of the building. I set the painting down on the kitchen table. Jack stood across from me and eyed the black cloth.

"Intriguing," he remarked with a touch of cynicism. "Ms. Lumiere was a painter, after all. I've already seen the contents of her room. I'm going to assume, since it is a crime scene, that this wasn't taken from there?"

"Very good," I said, trying to look as if I'd never dare breach the yellow police tape plastered across one of the inn's doors. "Anything else you'd like to note before I lift the black cloth?"

He raised a cinnamon brow, accepting the challenge. "The black cloth, including the fact that you wouldn't reveal it in front of Mr. Larson, suggests one of two things. It's either a painting of the kid, or it's pornographic in nature. I hope to God it isn't both."

"Nope, but interesting all the same," I said, mildly impressed by his reasoning skills. I was also a little thrilled he was speaking to me at all after yesterday. Although he'd already guessed the real reason the painting was covered, I wanted to keep him talking for my own sake. Therefore I asked, "But why not include 'disturbing in nature' to the list?"

"For the simple fact that our young Mr. Larson has seen more disturbing things in his short life than you or I put together. Not only is he a gamer," Jack reasoned, "but he also has unlimited access to the internet and a mom who's too busy trying to keep a roof over his head to worry about what he's getting up to. It explains the fact that he was loitering at the inn well past two in the morning with his girlfriend. His mom assumed he was already fast asleep in his own bed."

I exhaled and shook my head. "Poor Lori. However, I'll bet nearly every mom in America with a teen and the internet must be going through something similar." I looked across at Jack, issuing a new challenge. "Okay. You feel that 'disturbing in nature' isn't a reason to want him out of here, stating he's been desensitized by the internet. Wouldn't 'pornographic in nature' fall under the same category? I mean, obviously Erik's no angel. Even his best intentions are often thwarted by his devious nature."

"I totally agree," he said, clearly enjoying the mysterious nature of the painting. "In general, you're correct—internet access, a working mother, a wildly devious teenage brain." He counted them off on his fingers. "However, I happen to know that you're a responsible adult, one that would never subject a kid to a pornographic painting." He pointed to the black cloth, his eyes suddenly alight with conviction. "It's pornographic in nature. It has to be."

I was still stuck on, "You think I'm a responsible adult?"

The moment the words had been uttered, excitement faded from Jack's eyes only to be replaced by a wariness that made him look much older than his twenty-eight years. "Look, before you remove that cloth, we need to talk, Whitney." His brow furrowed with consternation as his gaze suddenly dropped to his hands resting on the table. "I know you were mad at me yesterday. But I was mad too. Really, really angry," he added, looking up at me with an intenseness in his light brown eyes I'd seldom seen. "When I was called to the inn yesterday morning and found Ms. Lumiere's body like that, I felt ... well, I felt betrayed. The trouble was, in my heart I knew that you couldn't have

219

killed her. I know you. I've known you since we were kids. You're one of the most responsible adults I know, if a little overzealous at times. But you'd let Silvia get to you. You'd said those things about her in the bakery. How do you think I felt when I saw your scone in her mouth—that she'd been pushed down the stairs at your inn? And the fact that you couldn't give me an alibi…? That pissed me off." Emotion accentuated the fine lines of his face and he nervously raked a hand through his thick, cinnamon-colored hair again. "It pissed me off because it made you the prime suspect, and because I knew that if I named you, you were going to hate me for it."

"Jack," I said, unaware of the internal conflict he'd suffered. I wanted to tell him that he was wrong, that I wouldn't hate him. But I couldn't. He'd hit the nail on the head.

"Of course, I didn't mean that I wished you were with Tate," he added, his eyes creasing in distaste as he said it. "That was just petty jealousy. It flares sometimes, you know. What you might not know, and what I've never had the nerve to tell you before, is that it's always been there, even back in high school."

The revelation shocked me. "But… you were my friend," I reminded him.

His lips pulled taut in a grim smile. "Friends, frenemies, the girl I had a crush on but could never tell."

"Truly, Jack," I uttered, and fell speechless. My hand was over my heart. I feared it might flutter away or stop altogether. I was dumbfounded. "You… you liked me in high school?" Truthfully, I thought he merely tolerated me.

Jack let out a pained sort of huff. "Yes. Of course. But I could never tell you. Didn't have the nerve. Besides, I was a skinny, geeky, know-it-all kid. Tate was a—"

"Muscly football player," I finished for him, my heart still racing double-time. I had no idea what to say. The revelation was startling, and painful, and oddly uplifting. "It's all genetics, Jack," I blurted. "Tate blossomed young, and he was an upperclassman. I had no idea ...?"

"Well, that was the plan. There's only so much embarrassment a geeky kid can take. Same's true with a geeky man who works as a cop in a small tourist town. When you came back here, I knew there was little reason to be hopeful. Tate lives here too, so what's the point. Right?"

"But ... we were broken up," I argued, feeling him slipping though my fingers; fearing that the shadow of Tate was too much for him to live under.

Jack gave a little laugh. "Right. But how many times has that happened before? You two were always breaking up over something. I know what he did. We all do. And, in Tate's defense, women do tend to throw themselves at him. I never looked at it as a bad problem to have until you came home. He still has a thing for you, and I understand. But after Jeb's murderer was apprehended this spring, you came to the station and kissed me."

"It wasn't a mistake," I assured him, not really knowing what else I could say.

He nodded as if he believed me. "I really thought I had a chance." The raw expression in his eyes as he spoke belied the ironic grin. "Then Tate called, and you went running after him like always. And I kicked myself, because even I knew that it was just a matter of time before you would forgive him."

"But ... but—"

Jack held up his hand to stop me. "Please, just hear me out."

Captivated by his emotional confession, I nodded.

"It was too painful to see you after that. But you kept persisting. For my own self-preservation I knew that with Tate, you, and me in the same small town it was never going to end well for me. I was of half a mind to move back to Milwaukee but you softened me up, like you always do, and gave me hope again." His lips twisted in recollection. "You even asked me to the Renaissance fair. That was pretty cool."

I wanted to tell him that I too had been nervous. That he was the man keeping me up at night, not Tate. "Jack," I said, "listen." But he wouldn't.

"No," he said sternly, cutting me off again. "I'm not done yet. There was something about the murder of Silvia Lumiere that made me snap. As petty as this sounds, I was actually angry with you for letting it happen—for allowing yourself to be caught up in another senseless murder. I said some things I didn't really mean. And you surprised me again by fighting back. You don't take things sitting down, Whitney, and this picture here is proof of that." His eyes settled on the black cloth once again. "Unfortunately," he said, and slowly looked at me, "I've always found it easier to avoid you, or tease you, rather than admit how I really feel about you. Which brings me to yesterday. When I found out that you had gone off with Tate in search of suspects you shouldn't even have known about, all those old, insecure feelings I had suppressed came flooding back with force. Seeing you two having lunch confirmed that I'd been firmly thrust aside— shoved back to the friend zone again. It was only after I left that I realized you had asked *me* to the fair, not Tate."

"That's ... that's what I've been trying to tell you!" I cried, feeling anger nipping at my nerves. "You have no idea what I've been going through either. You and Tate are now friends and I'm in the middle, getting in between you both. Do you think it's easy being back here, knowing what a mess I'm making of everything? Tate's the reason I avoided coming home in the first place, but … but you're a big part of the reason I decided to stay. I thought you knew that?"

His face darkened. "How the hell would I know that?" he cried. "You never bothered to tell me!"

"Do you honestly think I started running because I like it?" I yelled back at him. "I did it just so I'd have a few sweaty minutes with you!" He looked astonished, as if the thought had truly never occurred to him. Humph, some detective, I thought. I rounded on him again. "But you're too bloody fast for me … and then work got really busy. But I tried, Jack, which is more than I can say for you."

Anger flooded his handsome face, and I'm sorry to think I enjoyed the way he was glaring at me. "What the hell?" he shouted. The goats on the roof heard him and began to scream. Jack ignored them, knowing they'd stop in a minute. "Why do you think I stopped by your bakery every morning? You know I'm health conscious. Did you really think I like eating so much sugar and fat? I ate your … your frickin' delicious cherry baked goods because I wanted to see you! Then, because I did, I had to run even more!"

His anger was approaching adorable levels. We were virtually arguing on the same side of the fence, only he was too torqued up to see it. If I was ever going to wow him with my sleuthing skills, and show him the painting I'd discovered, I was going to need to talk him down a bit.

"And I'm glad you do," I said in a much softer tone. It was then that I reached a hand across the table to his. The moment I touched him the tension drained from his face. "It's truly the highlight of my day. It took me weeks just to get up the nerve to ask you out on a group date to the Renaissance fair. Granted, it's not the most romantic place, but I thought it would be fun. And if there's one thing you and I have,

Jack, it's fun. You might also be interested to know that Tate sailed off last night on the *Lusty Dutchman*. The fact that I'm here in your kitchen, standing over a cloth-covered painting and not in the *Lusty Dutchman* should, if you were a really good detective, tell you everything you need to know. However, I should also probably tell you that Mrs. Cushman is very worried. It's not like Tate, but I think he'll be back. He's not used to rejection, just as I'm not used to rejecting him. It's new territory for all of us. But I think, if we're careful, we can all move forward from here. That is, if you want to move forward." I held my breath, waiting for him to reply.

"I would. More than anything."

I squeezed his hand. "Good. Now, let me show you what I found."

"Jesus," Jack uttered, trying to process both my confession and the naked painting confronting him. "That's not right." He shook his head as if to clear the larger-than-life image. "Do I know him?" he asked. "Why do I get the feeling that I do?"

"Because that's Lance Van Guilder, Tay's boyfriend."

He looked confused. "The knight? But why would Silvia Lumiere have this?"

"For the obvious reason that he was at one time her assistant too, only she'd been able to manipulate him into posing for this."

"What? I thought he was a jouster?"

"That's what he does now. But Tay mentioned that he's also quite a talented metal artist."

"Right," Jack said, nodding. "But when did he work for her? And does Tay know?"

"No. I don't think she does. And as far as when Lance might have worked for Silvia, it would have had to have been at least five years ago." I looked at Jack. "You know that Giff's been helping me, right?" He nodded. "Well," I continued, "he's really good at digging. Along with the fact that Silvia had been married, he also found out that she was named in a sexual harassment lawsuit. It was brought on by a young male apprentice who used to work for her. His name was stricken from the record once the case was thrown out of court. Did you know about this?" I asked.

"No," he said, shaking his head. "I've been too busy going through statements from hotel guests and people who knew her, working with the folks at Crime Scene Evidence, and handling petty tourist issues to do much digging."

"Well, it was bound to come up once you did," I soothed. "However, Giff's done it for you. Anyhow, this man—this apprentice— claimed that Silvia was always coming on to him and treating him like dirt. She'd even made him pose in the nude for a painting, promising him money if he did. The lawsuit was eventually thrown out of court and Silvia skated free, her reputation untarnished, primarily because the existence of the painting could never be proven until now."

"Jesus," Jack swore again. "Where did you find it?"

"I'll tell you in a minute. First I want to tell you what I know about Lance." I proceeded to bring Jack up to speed, telling him how that beautiful suit of armor we'd seen Lance wearing had gotten repossessed when the check he'd used to pay for it, drawing on funds from an old client who'd paid him a substantial amount, had bounced. I told Jack about Lance's humiliation, and how he'd been losing in the jousting ring ever since. I then told him how Lance had come for dinner at the inn last night with Tay. "However," I said, "aside from this painting and everything I've just told you, the most damaging piece of evidence against him is that Grandma Jenn actually witnessed him coming to the inn one evening to confront Silvia. I honestly didn't think he knew Silvia. And I had never seen him at the inn before last night. But you see, that connects him to the inn and to Silvia. I'm also pretty sure he owns a black cape. He is, after all, the Black Knight."

"Whitney," Jack said, trying to be stern. "You know that you're not supposed to be sticking your nose into police business, but I'm genuinely impressed."

"Really, Jack, the moment you named me suspect number one, I had no choice."

There was no arguing with this, and he knew it. "You do know what this means, don't you?"

I nodded. "Tay's going to freak. I only wish there was some way we could let her down gently."

Jack shook his head. "Silvia Lumiere," he breathed, staring at the incriminating painting. "What a mess you've made of my town."

Thirty

With a new understanding between us, and a nude painting as well, Jack and I drove the one block down Main Street to Cheery Pickers in search of Lance Van Guilder.

It wasn't going to be an easy visit. How was I to tell my best friend that the man she was obsessed with had just landed himself on the top of the police suspect list? Jack had swiftly informed me that Giff and I had made more progress than the entire police force had. I was about to give myself a high five but could see how his competitive nature chafed against the thought of two amateur sleuths having such success. No point flaming that fiery sharp tongue of his. Jack had paid me a compliment while schooling all sardonic comments he might have had. It was a remarkable show of restraint, and in its own small way had meant the world to me.

"So tell me, where did you find that painting?" he asked, parking his police-issue SUV in the crowded lot on the side of Cheery Pickers. "It wasn't in her room. Did McClellan have it?"

"No. But Peter did have keys to Silvia's white trailer."

He grimaced. "The trailer! I'd almost forgotten about that. It wasn't part of the crime scene. Anyhow, we didn't have keys to get in there, and Peter wasn't around."

I smiled at him. "Well, last night after dinner Giff was so convinced that Peter murdered Silvia he wanted to search his room."

"What for? The man had an alibi?" Jack looked confused. That's when I remembered that no one had bothered to fill him in on what Hannah and Peter had actually been doing before they went back to her place for the night. I reached over to the keys and turned off the ignition. I then handed them to Jack.

"Okay. Don't be mad, but Hannah and Peter held a little voodoo ceremony on the beach the night of Silvia's murder."

"What?" His bright amber eyes held mine. "And why am I just hearing about this now?"

I gave him a placating pat on the hand. "Better now than never, right?"

The scowl on his face was proof it wasn't. I quickly filled him in.

"So, you see?" I said once I had finished. "Giff thought Peter's story was highly suspicious. Then, when we learned Erik had been in the elevator and had seen a black-caped figure, Giff thought that if we could find the black cape in Peter's room, it would prove that Peter had been back to the inn after he and Hannah were supposedly asleep. Giff thought that Hannah might not even have known. The two of them have been, um, self-medicating due to Silvia and her soul-sucking nature. Anyhow," I said, breezing right along, "Peter was in his room when we went there. He was supposed to be with Hannah."

Jack looked confused. "Why wasn't he with her?"

Excessive pot smoking was the real reason, but to Jack I just said, "They had a falling out. However, as cold as this sounds, I'm glad they did. Otherwise we would have never gotten into that trailer."

Jack stroked is chin thoughtfully as he listened to what I had told him. "I'm going to need to get into that trailer as well. I take it McClellan still has the keys?" I nodded. "Good. But first, this." Jack looked out the front windshield at the brightly painted sign that read *Cheery Pickers*. "Listen Whit, I need you to talk with Tay. Divert her. Let me handle Van Guilder."

Tay's shop was abuzz with customers. The essence of calming, scented candles wafted above the underlying scent of complimentary coffee and a variety of perfumes that might have been applied a tad too heavily. Celtic-inspired instrumental music trickled softly from the ceiling speakers, accentuating the experience of browsing through the popular, eclectic shop. As I entered I cringed slightly, realizing that many of the faces browsing the goods were familiar.

"Officer MacLaren!" Edna cried the moment she spotted him. She and Gabby Gaines, the mayor's wife, had been fondling a hefty piece of pottery. I thought they were in danger of dropping the darn thing the moment Jack entered the picture. In fact, thanks to Edna, all heads swiveled our way; every pair of curious eyes settling on the man behind me. Apparently, I was chopped liver. Excited whispers circulated. Nervous giggling erupted. It had never occurred to me before, but Jack—tall, ginger, handsome, and cutting a fine figure in his police blues—had quite a fan club with the older women of the cove.

"Ladies." Although blushing from the attention, he was trying his hardest to look professional.

Tay spied us from the sales counter. She was ringing up a customer, but there was something wary in her silent greeting.

Char, in a far corner helping an elderly woman try on an Irish walking cape, called to Jack and waved. She was coming to greet us when another woman, partially hidden by a glass shelf, stepped in front of us.

"Ms. Bloom. What are you doing here?" It was Alexa Livingstone. Her taut face pulled into a look of puzzlement as she stood before us in fashionable white pants, a navy and white striped top with billowing sleeves, and a red ascot tied around her neck. The woman looked like an aging Ralph Lauren model and smelled like the perfume aisle of Neiman Marcus. She turned to Jack with a look of extreme displeasure. "Our beloved friend has been gone one day, and you think it's a good idea to parade the murder suspect around town?"

"Ma'am, please step aside," Jack warned.

Char swept in, the lovely Irish walking cape still in her hands. "Alexa, please." Obviously the last thing she wanted was a scene in her daughter's busy shop. "Murder in Cherry Cove is unsettling for us all. The fact that Officer MacLaren is here now with Whitney suggests the investigation isn't over. Don't you watch TV crime shows? Murder is never as straightforward as it seems. Isn't that right, Officer?"

Jack hesitated. Char was clearly trying to placate a customer but hadn't given any thought as to why Jack would be in the shop wearing his uniform. Tay suffered no such illusions and understood, her face clouding with concern. Alexa had picked up on the meaning as well.

"Oh," she said, as the thought dawned on her. She brought a hand over her heart. Alexa then looked at me, her eyes shifting between remorse and suspicion. "I'm … sorry. Does this mean that Ms. Bloom is, in fact, innocent?" She looked at Jack. The thought that I wasn't a heinous murderer had obviously never occurred to her. Jack, clearly uncomfortable with the whole situation, remained silent, prompting Alexa to add, "My dear, I'm so sorry. It was all so clear to me yesterday—all the evidence was pointing to you … but of course"—she looked at Char—"that would be too obvious."

Except for Tay, who remained steadfast behind the counter, everyone in the shop had pressed in, most of them hovering behind Jack.

230

Edna peeked around his trim waist. "That's what I've been telling the lot of you." Her face, with its beady black eyes and bulldog-esque wrinkles and jowls, turned to Alexa. "She's maybe a flighty millennial," she said, pointing a meaty finger at me, "but she's not a killer. Doesn't have it in her." She cast me a wink. We were, after all, co-Gilded Cherry trophy winners. "What she is, is a gifted baker. And from one baker to another, I know that Whitney would never degrade one of her cherry scones in such a way."

"I agree," added Gabby Gaines, peeking around Jack's other side. "We have to be kinder to our millennials. After all, they're our future. Hi, dear." Mrs. Gaines smiled at me. She then tilted her face up to Jack's and coyly ran a hand up his arm.

Jack immediately stepped away. "Everyone, please! Go about your business. Keep shopping, or I'll be forced to close Cheery Pickers down temporarily."

It was a serious threat, which seemed to remind everyone how serious the matter was. Tay came around the counter and placed a hand on my arm. "Come with me."

"What's going on?" Tay asked the moment she closed the door to her office. Something was bothering her. The fact that Jack and I had shown up at her shop unannounced only heightened her look of concern.

"I'm looking for Lance Van Guilder," Jack said. "Do you know where I might find him?"

Although they'd been friends since high school, that statement from Jack sent a visible shiver of fear running through Tay. She tried to wave it off as nothing, but she wasn't good at pretending. "Um, sure. He's out back taking a nap in the hammock. What's this all about, Jack?"

"Tay." I took hold of her hand and squeezed. "You and I will stay here. We need to talk."

The moment Jack left Tay's office, heading for the back door, she turned to me. "What...what have you found?" Her voice was deceptively light. Last night at dinner she'd been upset, not fearful like she was now. Something told me that she knew about Lance and had been waiting for the other shoe to drop.

I took a chance and asked, "Did Lance tell you that he used to work for Silvia?"

She plopped down in the leather desk chair and let out a long sigh. "He did. I thought this might be about that."

As I sat down opposite her, a loud meow echoed from under the desk. A moment later her plus-size, wine-loving cat, Izzy, appeared in her lap. Tay, grateful for the distraction, stroked his long, silky gray fur.

"Last night, after we left the inn," she began, "I knew he was keeping a terrible secret. It's not like him, you know, to be so sullen and glum all the time, or to allow his competitors at the fair to beat him to a pulp. These last couple of weeks have been particularly hard for him, and he refused to tell me why. He really takes his chivalric knightly code to heart." A half smile appeared on her lips as she said this. "Anyhow, he made it quite clear that he didn't want to bother me with his problems. It was as if he was protecting me from some great evil. Then, last night, he heard the name Silvia Lumiere and learned of her death." Her troubled brown eyes shot to mine. "After that, Whit, it was like the flood gates opened. We came home and he began telling me everything."

Tay paused to pull a half-eaten box of Double Stuf Oreo cookies from a drawer in her desk. She took one and offered the box to me.

The crisp chocolate cookie with an extra helping of sweet cream filling in every bite had always been our favorite nerve balm. Apparently, it was Izzy's as well. Tay, working on autopilot, twisted her cookie and mindlessly scrapped a nugget of creamy filling on her desk. Izzy pounced. With the hefty cat happily attacking the Oreo cream, Tay explained how Lance had been working as squire at Medieval Times in Schaumburg, Illinois, when he and Silvia had met.

"It's virtually, like, medieval dinner theater with a menu straight from the dark ages," she explained with an ironic twist of her lips. She twisted another top off yet another Oreo and shoved it in her mouth. "But folks don't really go there for the food," she said, still chewing. "It's the entertainment that draws them in. That's where Lance got his start as a knight. He was attending art school during the day and performed in the jousting ring at Medieval Times at night or on the weekends. It was after one of his shows that Silvia approached him. Her offer to pay for art school was too good to be true. Lance, of course, had heard of her. He was enchanted by her paintings and her reputation. It hadn't taken much to persuade him to hang up his sword and go to work for her. Once he did, however, he virtually became her slave. He worked in her studio for two years, and she gave him nothing above room and board. She owed him a lot of money," Tay added, focusing all her attention on Izzy. "Silvia was the person who mailed him that check, the one that bounced."

"I know," I said gently. "I assumed as much."

A helpless look seized her eyes. "He didn't even know she was in Cherry Cove. When the check bounced he called the bank that issued it, but they had no idea how to reach her. All her accounts had been drained. It plagued him, he said. It was almost as bad as when he worked for her. Then, last Thursday, when he was coming home from the fair, he saw her drive by. He had to do a double-take, he was so shocked. But there she was, sitting in the passenger seat of that big white Cadillac of hers. According to him, she had stared straight at him. Lance followed her. That's when he learned she was staying at the Cherry Orchard Inn."

I thought of that humiliating painting Silvia had coerced him into sitting for. I found it more than a little ironic that it had been stowed in the trailer behind the SUV when Silvia had driven past him.

"He came home, showered, changed, ate dinner with me, and then left to run an errand, or so he told me. He was really paying Silvia a visit."

"Grandma Jenn saw him," I explained. "I was unaware Lance had ever set foot in the inn before last night."

She gave Izzy a big hug and pushed him off the desk. The cat landed softly for his big size. He then pranced across the floor and disappeared into a closet. "Well, nothing came of their confrontation, just more humiliation. Silvia has quite the posse surrounding her. They're all fiercely loyal. Anyhow, Lance realized that he was never going to get any money from her. He was also really contemplating hanging up his lance." The silly pun made her smile. "But now he's reconsidering his options. Look," she said, "I should have told you the moment I learned, but I just couldn't. It was inconsequential, really, and very private. However, the instant I saw you and Jack walk in the shop, I knew you had found out." She closed the pack of Oreos, folded her hands, and leaned on the desk. "So," she began, curiosity igniting her eyes, "how exactly did you find out? How did you connect Lance to Silvia?"

"The painting."

Tay sat a moment, her pert little nose scrunched in contemplation. "What painting?"

"You know, *the painting*? The one that's not supposed to exist? Well, it does. Giff and I found it last night in her trailer."

Tay was a sharp cookie. She wasn't easily confounded by things, but the mention of the painting threw her for a loop. I suddenly realized that Lance hadn't told her everything. I took a deep breath and was about to explain the sensitive nature of the painting when the knight in question barged through the office door. Jack was fast on his heels.

Although bruised and still a bit wobbly from the beating he'd taken the day before, it was instantly apparent that Lance was back in fighting form. "Babe!" he cried. "Your friends have found something, and you're not going to like it. But I need you to tell them that I didn't kill Silvia Lumiere."

Thirty-One

"**O**h, my gentle Jesus," Lance breathed, staring at the painting Jack had brought in. The gilded frame had been propped against the wall. The knight's expression fluctuated between pain and relief as he studied his younger, naked self.

Tay, standing beside him for moral support, gawked with jaw dangling. A breathy sigh escaped her lips and was swiftly covered by a sudden clearing of her throat. "It's so wrong," she remarked. "And yet the artistry is undeniable."

Lance, ignoring everything but the erotic portrait, suddenly looked up, his eyes locking with Jack's. "I can't tell you how much sleep I've lost over this stupid painting. I thought the old witch had burned it. How ... where did you find it?"

Jack, with a deferential nod to me, explained. "I didn't. Whitney did. She brought it to the station this morning. It wasn't in Silvia's room, if that's what you were wondering."

All eyes shifted to me. "We found it in that big white trailer she's been towing around. Peter calls it the white beast. He keeps the keys. Look," I said, staring at Lance's bruised face, now two shades darker with consternation. "When I was named as the prime suspect in her murder I called my friend Giff and asked him to do a little poking around on the internet for me. He came across the sexual harassment lawsuit and learned of the painting that had never materialized."

"What?" Tay looked at Lance. "You never told me about a lawsuit."

The poor man blushed. "Babe, I never told you about the painting either, and I'm sorry. I told you how miserable I was working for Silvia. But this"—he gestured to his naked likeness—"this was too humiliating to even mention."

Jack, taking that as his cue, walked over to the large frame and replaced the black cloth. Everybody, with perhaps the exception of Tay, had had enough of it.

I continued. "After knowing Silvia for a few weeks, and learning from Tate how she'd tried to talk him into posing nude for her last year, we figured that if there was a lawsuit against her the painting had to exist. What we didn't know was the identity of the young man she'd coerced into posing for it. Last night, however, when we were poking around in Silvia's trailer and came across this, you can imagine our surprise. We were just as shocked as you are now."

"Lance," Jack began, looking at the man near his own age who'd definitely been made to suffer for knowing the painter, "you do understand that the discovery of this portrait links you to the murder victim? What this means is that I'm going to have to bring you to the station for questioning. I'm also going to need to get your fingerprints."

"Jack!" Tay cried, her inner mama bear released. She rounded on him, her soft brown eyes hardening like onyx-tipped daggers. "That won't be necessary. There's no way Lance could have killed Silvia, and I'll tell you why." Jack was all ears. Tay pressed on. "As you well know, that portrait is proof the woman was a Class A creeper. Yes, she had talent, but her cloying ways and faux assistantships were little better

237

than a Hollywood casting couch. If anyone has reason to want her dead, Lance would be at the top of that list. But he didn't do it. He couldn't have. Whit told me that Silvia was murdered sometime between midnight and five on Sunday morning."

That had been the case yesterday. Thanks to Erik, however, we now knew that it was sometime after two in the morning. But I kept my mouth shut.

"Do you want to know what Lance Van Guilder was doing at that time?" she cried, her voice escalating with anger. "I'll tell you what he was doing! He was sleeping and snoring loud enough to wake the dead. And I should know. I was right there next to him. That's what happens after a long day at the Renaissance fair," she spat, not wanting to break the flow of her tirade by taking a full breath. "Jousting, sparring, blocking blows with your body, and mucking about in a full suit of armor under the hot sun—all for the enjoyment of curious families, fantasy junkies, gamers, larpers, and the odd medieval historian. Lance is, quite frankly, too exhausted to even contemplate murder let alone finish a full episode of *The Office* without nodding off in the middle of it."

"What?" Jack, who'd been trying to write Tay's whole tirade down in his notepad, suddenly looked up. He tilted his head and stared at the man in question. "Dude, are you really sleeping through *The Office*? That's almost sacrilegious."

"I know," Tay interjected. "Right? We started streaming it at the beginning of June and we're still only in the middle of the first season!"

"Damn," he uttered. "I've never heard of anyone falling asleep in the middle of an *Office* episode." Jack flipped the page he'd been scribbling on and wrote two more lines. "Lance, is this true?"

The knight, looking utterly dejected, nodded. "It is. I'm so tired after a day at the fair that I can barely make it through dinner. Tay's being too kind." He looked at her and covered her hand with his own. "She deserves better than a beat-to-hell boyfriend who can't even stay awake through one episode of *The Office*. I was so poor working for Silvia that I didn't even own a TV. I'm trying to catch up on all the pop culture I missed, and Tay's been helping me, but the moment I come through that door, I'm pooped. You can imagine what it's doing to our sex life. That painting there …" He flipped an accusing hand at the black cloth. "That's the most excitement she's gotten all summer."

Jack, whose eyes were too damnably expressive for his own good, shot me a look after this last remark. I interpreted the look and nearly burst into giggles. But I refrained. Clearly, to Tay and Lance this was no laughing matter.

Jack cleared his throat. Looking utterly professional, he addressed Lance. "For the record, did you, Lance Van Guilder, murder Silvia Lumiere?"

"No," Lance said with utter conviction. Although I had wanted to shift the blame for the horrible crime to anyone else but myself, I had to admit that I was relieved. Jack, I could see, also believed him. Lance, however, was still miffed about the painting. "I didn't kill her, Mac-Laren, but after looking at that painting, and being made to relive the humiliation and violation I suffered at the hand of that woman, I really wish that I had."

Jack nodded. "I'm going to need both you and Tay to come to the station with me and sign a statement stating as much, omitting, of course, that last part."

Lance agreed. "And what about the painting? I've been sweating over it for all these years. What's going to happen to it?"

"I'm going to need to keep it for a while longer, just until we can find the person responsible for Ms. Lumiere's untimely death."

239

I could see that both Tay and Lance were uncomfortable with this. The painting was of a sensitive nature, and there was another fact to consider: since the death of the painter, it was likely worth a fortune. "Jack," I said, touching his arm. My touch startled him, but not in a bad way. His honey-colored gaze softened. "By stumbling upon that painting, I thought I had made a connection to Silvia's murder. But once again, it's just another red herring." I pointed to the black cloth trapped within the gilded edges. "There are so many people who had cause to want Silvia dead, but clearly Lance, like Peter and the Gordons, couldn't have done it. They all have alibis. Do you really need to keep the painting and record it as evidence? Up until a few hours ago, no one knew it existed. What harm would there be in keeping it that way?"

As Jack considered this, I noticed the look on Tay's face. I could see that she was grateful I'd asked such a thing. And why wouldn't I? Had that painting been of me or the man I cared about, I'd have done anything I could to make sure it stayed a private matter.

Noticing the tense looks on all our faces, Jack relented. "All right. It can stay here. I hardly doubt you're about to hang that on the walls of Cheery Pickers. Just keep it safe for the time being. I'll let you know if I need it again."

"Knock-knock!" A heartbeat later the door opened a crack and Char poked her head in. "Just thought I'd check in to see how you kids are doing."

"Fine, Mom," Tay replied quickly.

"Oh, is that our painting?" The door opened wider and Char stepped in, eyeing the gilded frame leaning against the wall. "Terrible about Silvia, but Todd and I were wondering when our painting—"

Tay, moving quicker than I'd ever before seen her, jumped in front of Char. "Not yours, Mom!"

"Oh?" Char forced a polite smile. "Well, then, whose is it?"

240

While we all looked to one another, trying to come up with an answer as to why a strange, covered painting sat in Tay's office, Lance jumped to the rescue.

"It's mine, Char. A little gift for Tay. Officer MacLaren, here, has kindly offered to keep it for her until she's ready to … um … ready to …" Lance, having gotten that far, came to a sputtering stop.

"Display it," Jack added, and stood in front of the painting.

Char's eyes shot wide with intrigue. "Well, before you take it away, how about letting me take a peek?" Char reached for the cloth. Jack batted her hand away.

"Sorry, ma'am. The painting's been placed into my care." Jack tossed a nod to Lance. Both men hoisted the painting and carried it out the door. For all my good intentions, apparently the safest place for Lance's painting was, after all, in the police station vault.

While Jack and Lance loaded the painting into the SUV, Tay had a quick word with her mom, putting her in charge of the store for the afternoon. We then climbed into the police cruiser with the guys and drove around the block to the police station.

Although Jack wouldn't report the discovery of the erotic painting, he would report the connection Lance had to the deceased. He and Tay would still need to make their official statements, but I, for one, was relieved that Lance Van Guilder had a lock-tight alibi. He was a good man. More importantly, he made my best friend very happy.

The discovery of the painting had been a shock, but it seemed the deeper we dug into the affairs of Silvia Lumiere, the darker her secrets. And she had more secrets, of that I was certain. We were back to square one, but that didn't mean we were out of options. Someone had killed the woman, someone with a link or a connection to her that we were yet unaware of. As Jack parked under the thick sod roof, I was struck with another thought.

Silvia was a painter of extraordinary talent, but that talent, as I had witnessed, was often bastardized by the need to humiliate or mock. So why had she mocked Fred Beauchamp? The fact that the painting was still in her trailer meant that he hadn't yet seen what she had done to it. I could only imagine the humiliation when that stunningly painted mockery was unveiled.

"Whit, would you mind getting my kids off the roof while I take Lance and Tay's statements?" The look Jack gave me as he asked this hadn't escaped my dear friend. As Lance and Jack gingerly removed the covered painting and carried it into the police station Tay turned to me and grinned.

"I thought that maybe all this was just a working relationship, you know, you and Jack putting aside your differences and putting your adorable little heads together to find the killer. But I don't think that it is? So what's happened?"

I smiled sheepishly. "I came to him with a painting and an apology. He apologized as well. We then had a little heart-to-heart." I shut the door to the SUV and beckoned for her to accompany me around to the back and through the garden gate. There I stopped. "He admitted to liking me ever since high school. Can you imagine that?"

"Duh," she replied with a grin. She then turned to the roof and whistled loudly. "And here I thought you had skills," she teased. "Some sleuth you are. All the clues were right under your nose all along, and yet you've ignored them. Well, I'm glad you two are finally being honest about your feelings."

While Tay marveled at my new discovery, I walked inside the goat pen and opened the gate to the steep little ramp that led to the roof. Thing One and Thing Two, bleating with joy at the sight of us, came trotting down, no doubt believing we had treats for them. I would have to go inside and get some carrots. As I gave the little brothers a much-appreciated scratch between the horns, Tay turned to me.

"It's like we're ushering in a new age here: The Age of Jack," she proclaimed. "I only wonder how Tate's going to handle the news."

By sailing off, I thought, but didn't say so. Instead, pushing all thoughts of Tate aside, I said, "Really? You just saw a painting of that hunk of a knight you're dating and you're talking about this? What I want to know is if any artistic liberties were taken, because if not, damn, girl!"

Tay flushed deep crimson, and we both burst out laughing. The little billy goats, for reasons all their own, joined in too.

Thirty-Two

While Tay and Lance sat in the police station giving their statements to Jack, I decided to stay out in the garden with the goats and do a little sleuthing of my own. I pulled out my phone. Giff answered on the first ring.

"I smell a guilty conscience. You've finally remembered that you left me in a room with a hippie. I awoke this morning to a skunky-smelling, Squatchy-looking creature shaking me, and asking if I had any three-in-one he could borrow—as in shampoo, conditioner, and bodywash all in one bottle. Can you imagine the horror?"

"Are you referring to Peter or the three-in-one?"

"In this scenario, angel, it's the three-in-one." His voice was chiding, as if I should have known.

"What's wrong with three-in-one?" I asked, having used it on occasion myself. My post-advertising Chicago days were a little lean. I saved money any way I could.

"What's wrong with it? Everything. If it were my account, I'd rebrand it Self-Loathing in a Bottle."

"That would make a catchy jingle."

He ignored my remark, adding, "Anyhow, I told him I have seven-in-seven—seven products in seven bottles—and proceeded to instruct him on the proper way to get gorgeous hair. I don't mean to pat myself on the back, but I've just made another convert."

"I hope you're representing all those products you're pushing, because no woman is going to thank you for coercing her man into tying up the bathroom any longer than needed. And I'll remind you again, no man should ever use seven products on his hair. That's, like, four more than your average woman." He gasped. I pressed on. "Products aside, I'm happy to hear that you and Peter are both awake and properly groomed. I'm going to need a favor."

Jack had just finished with the statements and was in the middle of a finger-printing session with Lance when Giff and Peter knocked on the back door of the police station. Peter held the door as Giff marched through, carrying another painting draped in black cloth.

"What's this?" Jack asked, closing his kit.

"Another curiosity we found last night," I informed him.

"Fred Beauchamp," he remarked, remembering our earlier conversation. "Bring it here. Let me see it."

We all crowded around the canvas as Jack peeked beneath the black cloth. "What the …?" he cried, then flipped the material over the back of the painting. Stunned silence all around, and then Tay erupted in a fit of giggles. The giggles were, unfortunately, contagious.

"No," she said, holding a hand over her quaking mouth. "This has to be some kind of a joke. He's a potter. I know the temptation's there, but this is … Oh, goodness. Fred's going to flip when he sees this."

"Right? It's not every day you see a potter ghosting his younger self." Then, because he couldn't help himself, Giff launched right in with the romantic ballad from the movie soundtrack, "Unchained

245

Melody" by the Righteous Brothers. The only blessing there was that he could actually sing.

Peter grinned. "Dude, like, that's got to be the bane of every potter. But on this canvas Silvia's managed to up the creep factor by, like, seven notches."

"Dear Lord," Lance uttered. "Did that man actually pay for this?"

Odd as it sounded, I believed he was relieved to see that he wasn't the only one subjected to Silvia's mocking brush. In all honestly, Lance's portrait had been highly flattering. Fred's was just plain wrong.

"He, like, commissioned this last summer," Peter explained. "Only I'm almost, like, a hundred percent certain he didn't ask to be ghosting himself on a pottery wheel." Peter stepped back, flipped his long hair and scratched his chin. "Silvia wanted the unveilings done in a certain order. Fred's was up next. I checked the schedule last night. His was to be Sunday afternoon. Like, the very day Silvia died."

I looked at Jack. "Do you think he got wind of this? Is there some way he could have seen this painting before the unveiling?"

Peter shook his head, sending a cascade of glossy brown waves tumbling over his shoulders and down his lean back. Giff might have been right to suggest so much product, I bleakly mused. Peter's hair looked amazing, touchable even. I was certain that if Hannah was to see him so clean and conditioned, she'd forgive him last night's little lapse in judgement.

"Nope," Peter continued. "The trailer's locked. I'm the only one with the keys. Hey, dude." He turned to Lance. "I saw your painting. You worked for her too." There was an undeniable Jesus-like quality to him, I thought, watching as the brown eyes softened with compassion while a kind smile appeared on his lips. Peter slowly opened his arms to the battered knight. "Come on, bro. Bring it in."

Thirty-Three

Although Jack informed me that he had already questioned Fred Beauchamp yesterday regarding Silvia's murder, and that Fred's statement hadn't set off any alarm bells, the discovery of the portrait demanded another visit. Jack was also curious about Silvia's ledger. Peter hadn't thought to bring it. Tay suggested they all go back to the inn and see what else they could dig up. It was a strategic move on her part, leaving me free to jump into the passenger seat of Jack's police vehicle. Oddly enough, he didn't complain.

Fred lived a little further north on the peninsula, near the quaint town of Ellison Bay. It was going to be at least a twenty-minute drive, and, since it had been a good long while since I'd spent any amount of time in a car with Jack, I was inexplicably nervous. I blamed it on the new understanding between us, that and the knowledge that Jack had liked me long before I ever realized it. Because of our easy friendship, conversation had never been lacking or forced. However, an unnatural silence had settled over the car, one we were both painfully aware of. We were heading north on Route 42 when Jack pulled his attention from the road and smiled at me.

"Hey," he said. "Thanks for coming along. I know it's not normal police procedure, driving a civilian to a suspect's house and all, but you're hardly an uninterested party. You've done some good work, Whit, but I'm going to ask you to let me handle Fred. Okay?"

"Of course," I said, having every intention of doing so. "Unless he's confessing, I'll just stand in the background and keep my eyes and ears open."

"Excellent." He grinned. "Are you okay with some music while we drive?" As Jack spoke he pressed a button on the SUV's touch screen, sending Mumford & Sons humming and thumping through the car speakers. "I know we've known each other a long time, but it's just dawned on me how much we don't know about each other. For instance, I can't listen to country music. Mumford's more my style." This was punctuated with a thumbs-up and a sly wink. "And, full disclosure, I'm mildly addicted to video games."

That much I already knew. I gave him a noncommittal nod. "Well, for the record," I said, playing along, "I also have a soft spot for Mumford & Sons." Which wasn't a lie. I liked a lot of other music as well, but there was no need to go into that now. "Also, and I hope this isn't a deal breaker for you, but I find video games pointless."

Jack feigned a look of surprise as well as a mild seizure. He brought a hand over his heart.

I placed a finger on his gaping jaw and turned his head back to the road. "Thankfully," I began, "I'm a firm believer that everybody has to have their hobbies. You enjoy gaming, and, full disclosure, I'm mildly addicted to online shopping. So many adorable things out there and all of it at my fingertips! I also share a surprising number of pointless things on social media."

"Urgh. Sounds boring, and expensive." He chanced a look my way.

"Well, I don't really have the money or time to pursue my shopping addiction, so no need to worry about that just yet. My main focus, and I think you'll agree with me here, is to find Silvia's murderer. We could just have that between us for now."

"Yeah. Okay," he said. "It's not very romantic, but it's probably a good deal more than most relationships have these days."

It wasn't long before Jack turned down a gravel drive, marked by a large sign that read *Beauchamp's Pottery Studio*. A moment later a rustic log cabin came into view. It was a charming little building, with a wide covered porch and a handful of overflowing flower boxes. Wildflowers filled the landscape requirements, somehow looking nearly perfect against the dark brown building. I was particularly fond of the giant wagon wheel casually propped against the front porch but thought Silvia might have found it too kitschy. This humble potter's studio was a far cry from a penthouse apartment on Chicago's Gold Coast.

As Jack parked I was pleased to see that Fred had other customers. There were a handful of cars in the parking lot, which had to bring a smile to any potter's face. I hoped he was selling a lot of pottery, because the painting Jack was about to show him might cause him to snap. And in a shop full of breakables, that might get messy.

A bell tinkled as we opened the screen door. Inside, the building was larger than I expected, lined with rows and rows of shelves, each one showcasing a handcrafted, beautifully glazed piece of pottery thrown on Fred's wheel. I was impressed and recalled seeing similar pieces in Tay's shop. I vaguely remembered her telling me that she carried Fred's pottery. As customers browsed the shelves, Jack, carrying the covered painting, walked over to the girl behind the register. There he inquired after Fred.

"He's in the back," she said and pointed to the studio door.

As Jack and I approached the studio we heard voices coming from inside, indicating that Fred wasn't alone. There was a discussion going on, one that stopped the moment Jack knocked and opened the door.

Three heads turned, all familiar and none of them surprised.

"Officer MacLaren, Whitney," Alexa Livingstone greeted us. She glanced at the painting in Jack's arms and smiled. Although she looked the same as she had earlier, in Cheery Pickers, her aging Ralph Lauren style appeared out of place in Fred's cluttered, mud-splattered workshop. She was standing between the potter and a younger man I recognized as Jeffery the knot-artist. "I drove out here to let Fred know that his pottery was flying off the shelves at your friend's store. I thought I'd see if he wanted me to bring more over to her shop. When I saw that Jeffery was here helping Fred, I decided to tell them the exciting news."

"Right," Fred said, taking off his clay-splattered apron. He folded it neatly and placed it on his worktable. "We understand that there's been a break in the case and that Ms. Bloom is no longer a suspect."

Alexa looked at me and bestowed a kind smile. "I feel just terrible," she continued, "having blamed you because the deed was done in your inn. As you can imagine, we're all still shocked by the murder."

"Still in mourning," Fred added. "A talent like Silvia's only comes along once in a lifetime."

"Oh, I don't know," Jack said, setting the covered painting against the leg of the worktable. "She could have been kinder. Talent's no excuse for rotten behavior. In my opinion, the woman's left more casualties in her wake than masterpieces. Which brings me to the reason for my visit. Fred, I'd like to have a word with you."

Fred, looking puzzled, forced a smile. "Sure. But I have nothing to hide. I told you everything yesterday. Silvia and I were on great terms. My friends can stay if they wish."

"Fred, really." Alexa placed a gentle hand on his sleeve. "We'll go and leave you and Officer MacLaren to talk."

"No," he said. "By all means, stay. MacLaren's brought a painting. It's mine, isn't it?" Jack nodded. "You were all invited to the unveiling yesterday. I closed the shop. I made drinks and hors d'oeuvres. I never dreamed Silvia wouldn't be alive to host my event." He turned to his friends. "I wanted the unveiling to be special, but now that Silvia's gone it hardly matters." He pointed to the black cloth. "I never imagined that this would be one of the last paintings she'd ever do. It's her parting gift to me." He turned to Alexa. "You were lucky to have her present you with yours. I only wish she was here to present me with mine."

Not quite knowing what to say to that, Alexa smiled gently and nodded.

"I told you yesterday, MacLaren," Fred continued, "that Silvia and I were good friends. But we were more than that. I'm not afraid to let the world know that we were lovers."

At that bold announcement, my heart dropped into my stomach. Jack, unsmiling as well, stood back and cautioned me to do the same as Fred lifted the painting. We watched as he gingerly set it on a long counter that ran the length of the back wall. The potter turned to his friends.

"I'm glad you brought this, MacLaren."

"Fred, I have to ask..." Jack looked at the potter with caution. "Have you seen this painting before?"

"What?" He looked shocked. "Of course not. I sat for this last year. As much as I begged her to let me see it, Silvia just laughed and told me to be patient. She didn't know then that she wouldn't be alive to deliver it to me herself." A sullen look crossed the potter's face.

251

"Fred, I'm cautioning you," Jack said. "You might want to view this in private."

"Nonsense." Fred was staring at the black cloth as if the painter herself stood before him. The poor man had no idea what he was in for. With a grin and a flourish, he yanked the cloth away, revealing Silvia's parting gift.

Alexa was the first to gasp. The shock on her face couldn't have been manufactured.

Jeffery let out a supplicating "Dude" and stared open-mouthed.

Fred, poor Fred, stumbled backward and crashed into his potter's wheel. "What the hell kind of sick joke is this, MacLaren?" he demanded. "That's not what I sat for! That's not Silvia's work! She would never..."

Fred, although in a full state of shock and denial, still had eyes, and they were telling him what his brain was unwilling to comprehend. While he backed away, Alexa and Jeffery came forward to study the exquisitely painted mockery. All three artists appeared to have arrived at the same conclusion at the same time, but it was Alexa who spoke first.

"It's her work, Fred. There are very few artists in the world who could replicate her style, and I highly doubt Officer MacLaren is one of them. This is an original." She looked at her friend with palpable empathy. "Only I don't understand why she did this."

Silence enveloped the studio as all eyes turned to the painting. My eyes were on the arts council members as they struggled to understand its meaning, or why the artist had targeted Fred for such a humiliation. Their behavior told me that the painting was unusual. Alexa and Jeffery were certainly aghast by it, but I had to wonder again if Fred hadn't caught wind of it beforehand. After all, it didn't require a membership in the Actors' Guild to master a look of shock and anger.

My eyes wandered the room, soaking up every detail until they settled on something very odd indeed. That's when Fred threw back his head and started laughing.

His laughter was loud and slightly unsteady. "The bitch," he cried, still laughing so hard that his eyes were wet with tears. "The cruel old bitch. She meant to humiliate me in front of all my friends. But the joke's on you, sweetheart. God love her," he said, sobering up enough to stare at Alexa and Jeffery. "So haughty, so full of herself, so talented, so cruel, and yet it makes me love her even more." And then Fred Beauchamp slumped onto his stool and burst into tears.

Thirty-Four

While Jack was dealing with the love-struck, tearful potter, I excused myself and went to inspect the back exit. I couldn't believe it was just dangling there, suspended on the hand-painted keyholder alongside a set of car keys and a plethora of keys to other doors. It's hard to miss a guest key from the Cherry Orchard Inn. The single silver key is unremarkable. The key ring, however, is a two-inch long oval with our logo printed on one side and the suite name on the other. It was the airy blue paint depicting the word *Sailboat Suite* that caught my eye.

It was the missing key to Silvia's room, and it just happened to be hanging on a hook in Fred's pottery studio. I wasn't exactly a trained professional, but I did know enough not to touch the key with my bare hands. I walked over to a box of tissues, pulled a few, and went to retrieve it.

Jack was still trying to console Fred when I showed him what I'd found.

"Jack—Officer MacLaren—this is a mistake." Fred, clearly unnerved that he was going to be taken to the station for further questioning, added, "I've already told you that I had nothing to do with Silvia's murder."

"But you have a key to her room," I said, and wiggled the tissue.

Jack, seeing the key for the first time, raised a ruddy brow. "Nice work. Where'd you find that?"

"Near the back door, hanging with the other keys. It also works in the lock on the side door of the inn," I informed them. "But Fred obviously already knows that, don't you?"

Fred, looking mortified, vehemently shook his head. "That's not my key!"

"Of course it's not. It's the key to Silvia's old room."

"I know what it is," he snapped. "But do you honestly think that the woman who did that"—he pointed to the painting—"would give me that?" Fred's angry finger was now pointing at the key clutched in a wad of tissue.

Jack pulled a ziplock bag from his pocket and handed it to me. I dropped the key in and zipped it up, feeling a little giddy with pride at having found the smoking gun, so to speak.

"Mr. Beauchamp." Jack addressed the distraught potter. "Sir, I don't want to have to put you in cuffs, but I will. I need you to calm down. I have to take you back in for questioning."

Fred, still unstable, stared at his two friends. "That woman was nothing but trouble," he spat. "We all knew it, and yet we let her walk all over us. For the greater good, my friends. Well, she sure showed us, didn't she? The old bat got what she deserved."

Alexa, her aging face flushed with anger, looked horrified. "Shut your mouth, Fred. Shut your stinking mouth."

Jeffery the knot-artist just shook his head and uttered a deprecatory, "*Dude.*"

Because Fred was a sensitive case—a little manic, a little angry, and in utter denial of having possessed the evidence I had found dangling on his keyholder—Jack called the station in Sturgeon Bay. He was instructed to take Fred there. Before he did, however, he thought it best to drop me off at the Cherry Cove police station.

Once there, Jack left the manacled Fred in the back of the SUV for a minute to accompany me to my car. It might have had the feel of a first date if a murder suspect wasn't leering at us through the tinted windows of the police SUV.

"So," Jack began, looking adorably nervous. "Um, I have to take Fred down to Sturgeon Bay, but I was thinking, you know, ah, since Inga has MacDuff and all, that you and I could grab a bite to eat somewhere for dinner?"

Yes! Yes! Yes! my inner voice screamed. For Jack, however, my cool Chicago girl persona kicked in and chose sarcasm instead. "Geez. I don't know. My baking schedule's so crazy right now, you know … now that the inn's been shut down due to murder."

Yet instead of grinning, Jack frowned. "But … you don't really have to bake, right? Or are you asking me to put pressure on the Crime Scene Unit to okay the inn for business? In which case you really will be busy baking." He was turning red and looked slightly confused.

Jack MacLaren was nervous. Apparently, his super-heightened sarcasm meter didn't work in such a state. "Yes." I told him, grinning. "I will have dinner with you tonight. I've been waiting for you to ask me all summer." This made him smile. "And about you putting the pressure on the Crime Scene Unit, we can discuss that over drinks."

The spark had come back to his eyes. "I'll give you drinks and an appetizer," he whispered flirtatiously. "After that, I'm going to demand your full attention."

"Mmm, I didn't know you were so needy, Officer MacLaren. But I like it."

Jack was about to reply when a muffled voice cried out from behind the tinted glass of the SUV, "Make an end to it, MacLaren! I haven't got all day."

I left Jack to his duties and got in my car, smiling as I did so. I watched as he pulled out of the parking lot, heading for Sturgeon Bay with lights flashing. I was about to follow him as far as the road to the inn when a niggling thought popped into my head. Fred Beauchamp. Murderers were good liars. Crime shows on TV taught me that. And yet the malicious painting had unhinged him. I didn't believe that had been an act; the man had truly flipped out. And the only possible explanation for that was because he'd never seen it before today. Then there was the matter of the key. The funny thing was, I'd assumed it was in Fred's possession all along. He was, after all, the woman's lover. So why the shock at seeing it there? Was that just an act? Or maybe, just maybe, Fred really didn't know it was hanging with his other keys near the back door. It was just a hunch, but I thought it best to ask an impartial party just in case.

Thirty-Five

Edna Baker lived in a mid-century ranch house two blocks from town. Apart from a lawn overrun by gnomes, fairies, and ceramic toadstools and the dozen mature trees sprouting from rings of colorful begonias, I imagined it looked much the way it had when it was built. I walked up the flagstone walkway and peered through the screen door, giving a little knock as I called out for the owner. A moment later Edna popped into view and came marching down the hallway in a sack-cut sundress to let me in.

"Whitney." It was said without any hint of surprise. "I imagine this'll be about the trophy." Edna turned and beckoned me to follow as she marched along the hallway. "It's like they say. Heavy is the hand that holds the great Gilded Cherry. Well, now with murder on your hands, I imagine it's even heavier. Don't worry. I've already made a spot for it on my mantle."

"This isn't about the trophy," I assured her, staring at the lonely, well-lit spot above the brick fireplace begging to be filled. "You heard it yourself. I'm no longer a suspect. Don't worry, you'll have your six months of cherry pie honors. What I've actually come to talk to you about is Silvia Lumiere and her relationship to your friends on the arts council."

I sat at Edna's linoleum-topped dinette table drinking a delicious cup of Earl Grey and nibbling on homemade peanut butter cookies. "These are really yummy," I remarked, and took another bite. "Did you make these special? Or is this a cookie you always have on hand?"

"You millennials." She peered over her half-moon glasses. "In my day the peanut butter cookie was a staple. We didn't have seven kinds of baking chips and exotic nuts to throw in our batter. But we always had a jar of peanut butter on hand. People forget about these until they take a bite. I'm trying to bring 'em back. The world is advancing too fast. What it needs is a nostalgic cookie from a simpler time." Then she grinned and confided, "Actually, I volunteered to bring a dessert to a couple of Silvia's unveilings and didn't have time to run to the store."

"I like it," I told her, taking another sip of Earl Grey. I then set my cup back on its saucer. "But aren't you afraid of serving them to someone with peanut allergies?"

Edna's wrinkles morphed into gullies. "Millennials!" she cried again. "Always have to ruin a good thing with allergies, or sensitivities, or … or some other nonsense."

"It's not nonsense if contact with a peanut might kill someone."

"Well, who would ever think that a cherry scone would kill a person? But one did. Don't sully my peanut butter cookies, Whitney, and I won't sully your scones."

She had a point. But it wasn't really the same thing. My scone had been used as a murder weapon, not an instigator of anaphylactic shock. However, there was no use arguing with Edna. Instead I told her that I was sorry and complimented her cookies once again.

"Thank you," she said in a distinctly self-righteous manner. "I have a whole giant Tupperware container full of 'em. You can take a dozen or so back with you when you leave. Just be sure to give one to Jenn."

"Will do. But she doesn't have an allergy to peanuts."

Edna looked affronted until she saw that I was teasing. She let out a hoot of laughter that had the ring of a cackle. "Good one. Anyhow, I've got peanut butter cookies to spare. I made them for Fred's unveiling." She paused a moment, visibly upset by the reason the event had been canceled. She swallowed and forced a smile. "And I was really looking forward to that one, too."

I didn't know much about Edna beside the glaring fact that she was the town's busybody. Truthfully, I'd given her a wide berth on account that she was Gran's frenemy. Although they traveled in the same circle of friends, Edna delighted in challenging Grandma Jenn and trying to get the best of her. I suspected it kept them on their toes and made them better at what they were, which was extraordinary older women. But for all Edna's brash, blustery ways, I was touched by her feigned indifference over Silvia's untimely death.

"Edna," I said softly. "I told you I was here to talk about Silvia and your friends from the arts council. You're the only person in Cherry Cove I know who's one of their members. What I really wanted to ask you about, however, is Fred Beauchamp."

Shock appeared on her perpetually intense face. "Fred? What's he done?"

"That's the thing. We're not sure yet, but we suspect he might be the person responsible for Silvia's murder. Were you aware that he was having an affair with her?"

"Oh, pah!" she spat, causing her double chin to quiver like Jell-O. "He was *trying* to have an affair with her. But everyone knew he was just after her money. Silvia saw right through him."

"But Silvia didn't have any money." The beady, bulldog-like eyes shot to mine in question. "I'm afraid it's true. We learned that she was bankrupt. Her pricey apartment had been foreclosed right before she came to Cherry Cove."

"Well, that ain't right. But I'm gonna be honest. I always sensed there was something of the flimflam about her."

"Well, I only learned of it yesterday. Do you think Fred suspected it as well?"

Edna frowned. "I don't know," she said, thinking. "I doubt that he did. Fred's nice-looking and all, and his pottery's not bad, but deep down inside he's an utterly self-centered chucklehead."

I smiled at her choice of words. "So, are you telling me that you don't think he was in love with Silvia?"

"He was in love with the *idea* of her," Edna said, lifting the pretty china teapot in her meaty hand. As she refilled our cups, she added, "It's the same kind of love an antique collector has for that one object he can't afford."

"Obsession, you mean?"

"Right!" Her head bobbed in approval. "Obsession, it was. Anyhow, Silvia played him like a nearsighted bull. Kept him on a short chain so she could tug him as she pleased."

As Edna talked of Silvia and Fred's relationship, the odd painting sprang to mind once again. To the outsider it appeared cruel. But Fred, after his initial shock and anger, had laughed. Had it been Silvia's way of letting him know that she was onto him? Or was it part of the twisted game they'd both been playing? "Edna, do you know if Fred had a key to Silvia's room?"

She shook her head. "She'd never go for that. Giving Fred a key would put him in control, and Silvia always had to have the upper hand on everyone, including yourself."

I thought a minute. "Could Fred have taken it?"

"Not if he wanted to marry her. That man isn't afraid of marriage. He's looking for wife number five, I think. Anyhow, crossing a woman like Silvia would be akin to putting his own neck in the noose. She'd cut him out of her circle in an instant, and Fred needed her approval as much as any of them did." Her eyes narrowed. "Hey. What's all this about a room key, anyhow?"

"One of Silvia's was missing. We found it in Fred's pottery studio."

"Where? Inside one of his pots or buried in a lump of wet clay?"

"No, nothing like that. It was just hanging there on his keyholder."

Her intense brown eyes narrowed. "Well, that doesn't make sense. If Fred took her key he'd hide it better than that. Sounds like someone's framing him."

I found it ironic that Edna had just uttered the one thing I'd been thinking. Somebody was framing Fred. I looked at her. "Could it be one of the arts council members?"

She gave a curt shake of her curly gray head. "Doubtful. You could ask them yourself, of course, but I'll spare ya the trouble. Even if one of them hated her, Silvia's presence was too important. It was all about appearances with that lot, and Silvia made them look good. If MacLaren's looking at Fred, well then, he's barking up the wrong tree. If you ask me, you should be looking a little closer to home."

"Who?" I asked. "Not my Grandma Jenn?"

"No, silly. Not your grandma. Try that hot-headed chef of yours. He and Silvia were at it like cats and dogs. Like cats and dogs, I tell ya."

"I know they were," I said, truthfully. "Bob's not a guy who's easily upset. He's cool-headed, but Silvia sure knew how to push his buttons." I paused to drink more of the hot tea. I drained the cup and returned it to its saucer. "Okay, let's say it was Bob. Why did Fred have

Silvia's extra key then? Bob wouldn't need it to get into the building. He had his own key."

"Right. But he's also clever," Edna reminded me. "He'd try to throw suspicion on anyone else but himself. I'll tell you one thing: if I were going to frame someone for Silvia's murder besides yourself— and you're the obvious choice—Fred would be my next choice. Silvia's room key wouldn't be hard to get if you already have carte blanche at the inn. Bob Bonaire has that, as well as a reason to want that old pain-in-the-ass dead. She criticized his steak, which was bad enough, but then she went after his signature fried perch. Even a man as evenly tempered as Mr. Bonaire has to draw the line somewhere."

"In general, I imagine that's true. Thanks for the tea, Edna." I stood up to leave, knowing that the task before me was going to be a difficult one. Bob was an old friend and a valued employee. Edna stood up as well.

"Hold on a moment. Let me give you some cookies."

As Edna filled a freezer bag full of her delicious treats, I thought to ask, "Alexa Livingstone also had an unveiling. How did that one go?"

"Fine," she said, handing me the bag. "But you might want to talk with her, all the same. She's terribly upset by Silvia's death. They were close, ya know. But if anybody can shed more light on Silvia Lumiere, it would be Alexa. She was the reason Silvia came to Cherry Cove in the first place. Alexa used to own a posh interior design firm in Chicago. Very high-end kind of stuff. Anyhow, rumor is she used to commission Silvia to paint original artwork for some of her wealthier clients. Silvia and Alexa go way back. The reason Alexa's the president of the arts council isn't any mystery either. Her connection to Silvia secured that office."

"I didn't know that," I said, thinking.

"Of course you didn't. You were too busy baking scones to pay much attention to anything. And speaking of lack of attention, you might want to stop by the marina and share some cookies with that boyfriend of yours if he's come back. I heard you two had quite the tiff and he sailed off, just like that. Men! Big bunch of babies they are. Well, nothing glues a strained relationship back together quite like a peanut butter cookie. I'll even let you tell him you made 'em yourself. And won't he be pleased. Peanut butter's a nice change from all that cherry-loaded gunk you serve at the inn."

Thirty-Six

Although I took offense to my life's work being referred to as cherry-gunk, Edna did have a point. Tate had sailed off yesterday in a huff, and I'd been so busy with this whole murder business that I'd nearly forgotten my promise to stop by to check on him. The marina was on the way to Bob's house, and I could use the diversion. I eyed the bag of peanut butter cookies in the passenger seat and actually considered passing them off as my own.

Nope. That would be wrong, I told myself. That would be lying. That would make Tate believe that I cared enough about him to bake him something other than my cherry-inspired baked goods—a treat that was second nature to me. I still cared for Tate, but I didn't want him to get the wrong message.

Once at the crowded marina, however, I thought differently and grabbed the bag off the front seat. Tate was undoubtedly still angry with me. The fact that the marina was hopping-busy wouldn't help his mood any either. Edna was right—no one could stay mad when they were given thoughtful, homemade cookies. Right?

I fully expected to find Tate hard at work, but there was no sign of the tall, blond-headed man bobbing about the many boat slips, or down by the rental hut. My eyes then went straight to his personal slip at the far end of the cement pier. My heart sank when I noted it was empty. A quick scan of the harbor told me he wasn't moored out there either.

"Ms. Bloom!"

I turned in the direction of the familiar voice and saw Cody Rivers, one of Tate's younger employees, and Erik Larson's best friend. "Cody," I replied with a friendly wave. "How are you?"

The kid cast me a harried look. "Could be better. I love working at the marina. Sure beats picking cherries and bussing tables." He flashed me an ironic grin. "However, it would be nice if my boss was here to help us out."

"Yes. I've heard. He's out on a little sailing expedition."

"Rumor is, you chased him away." The accusatory stare was a bit insulting, coming from the young man.

"Don't believe everything you hear," I countered, privately musing that Mrs. Cushman had obviously briefed the staff as to why their boss had sailed away in the dead of night. "He just needs some alone-time, you know, to sort things out."

"Right." The boy wasn't buying it. Tate was well-loved in Cherry Cove, especially by Cody and Erik. They were as loyal as lapdogs, but I understood. It obviously had to do with the bro-code.

"Listen. You have my word. Nothing's going to happen to Tate. He'll be fine. However, because I'm genuinely concerned"—here I held up the bag of cookies—"I'd like to have a word with Mrs. Cushman. Is she in?"

"On her yacht," he replied, and pointed to the *Boondoggle II*—as if it didn't stick out like an elephant amongst a pool of pygmy hippos as it rose and fell ever so slightly in its moorings. "But knock first," he warned as I headed for the behemoth. "She's entertaining a man."

∞

Charmed by the thought of Mrs. Cushman entertaining a man aboard her yacht, I decided it best to proclaim my arrival. I stood beside the gangway and called out, "Ahoy the *Boondoggle II*," to one of the open windows. At the sound of my voice Molly started barking. A moment later Mrs. Cushman appeared on deck and waved.

"Whitney, why, permission to come aboard, dear. We're just finishing our coffee."

I was always a bit unsettled by the magnificence of the yacht. It was a treasure trove of polished teak, brass fittings, tinted windows, and luxurious furnishings cleverly fitted into the curves of the craft like gentrified Legos. It was a penthouse on the waves, ultra-sexy and sleek. The fact that an elderly lady and her adopted dog lived aboard it never failed to delight me. In fact, the whole town had been tickled when Tate's housekeeper had packed up her bags and left the house, only to march down Tate's lawn, enter the marina, and climb aboard the abandoned yacht, swiftly claiming it as her own. As far as any of us knew, she'd never sailed a day in her life. The yacht hadn't left its slip since she'd gained control of it. And anyhow, it took more than one woman to navigate a craft the size of the *Boondoggle II*.

Once aboard, I followed Mrs. Cushman down a small flight of stairs to the spacious galley and eating area. The moment I did I nearly dropped my cookies.

"Angel." Giff smiled and languidly uncrossed his long legs. "What a surprise."

267

Was it? Obviously to him it wasn't. "What are *you* doing here?" I asked. It came off as accusatory, because it was. I knew Giff was insatiably curious about the yacht; he'd been itching to climb aboard since it was abandoned in the spring. Although I knew he would have preferred a guided tour by Tate, I could see that Mrs. Cushman was doing an excellent job in Tate's stead. But judging from the impish curl of Giff's lips, this wasn't about the boat. It was all about Tate. Gifford McGrady was moving in on my territory.

"When I heard about Tate this morning, I grew concerned. Poor Cecelia," Giff said, turning his sympathetic, puppy-dog eyes on Mrs. Cushman. "I would have thought you'd be here before now, Whitney, being the person responsible for his sudden departure."

Both sets of eyes turned on me. Mrs. Cushman was waiting for an explanation; Giff was waiting to see how I'd respond to the challenge, damn him.

"There's been a break in the murder investigation," I told them both. "Since the inn is still shut down, and since I am the acting manager, it's my duty to do all I can to move things along. Tate would understand. I stopped by because I thought he might be back." Feeling the weight of their silence, my hand automatically sprang into the air, revealing the ziplock bag Edna had given me. "See? I made him some cookies." It was a terrible lie. I'd just broken the baker's code, claiming another's delectable treats as my own. Dear God, what depths had I sunk to? I looked at Giff. It took all I had not to slap the sardonic grin off his face with the bag of cookies.

Beneath the dangling bleached forelock his black eyes glittered. "Whitney, you amaze me. When did you find the time?"

"She is amazing," Mrs. Cushman agreed, gracing me with a grandmotherly smile. She was utterly oblivious to Giff's sarcasm. "And that's a nice gesture, dear. But I'm afraid I must insist that you keep the cookies. There's been no word from Tate and he's still not answering his phone. I'm getting worried. I think you should take the cookies with you and go find him. I hate to even think it, but I'm going to insist you call Jack. He should go with you too, you know, in case there's been any funny business."

"What? You … you think Tate's in some kind of danger?" I suddenly felt a wave of genuine concern. "Mrs. Cushman. Tate left on his boat because we broke up. He's upset."

Her compressed smile was placating at best. "Well, of course. But, dear, you two have broken up before and he's always been back by lunch. This is different. There's a murderer on the loose in Cherry Cove. It would be just like Tate to take off and try to find the culprit on his own."

Could this be true? Could Tate have found out something about the murderer—perhaps even the person's identity? He'd told me himself, yesterday at Ed's Diner, that he was enjoying the investigation. That was before Jack had made his appearance. It had been an emotional day for us all. But what if Mrs. Cushman was right? What if Tate had channeled his hurt and anger in another direction—like I had— and kept digging? He'd taken his boat … or maybe somebody else had. If Tate had gotten close to the truth, he could be in real danger.

The thought was unsettling. I looked at Mrs. Cushman. "Did you happen to see Tate when he came home yesterday?"

She nodded.

"What did he do?"

"He stormed into the house."

"Did you see him leave?"

She nodded again. "He drove off in his truck. He was upset. I assumed he was going to the bar to have a few beers. I heard him come back, if that helps."

"It does," I told her. "Do you know if he was alone?"

Cecilia shrugged. "I can't say for sure. It was late, and I was getting ready for bed. The only reason I knew he was back was because Molly barked. She always barks when she hears his truck pulling in the driveway. Whitney, is Tate in danger?"

"I don't know. But wherever he is, we'll find him." I then took Giff by the arm and pulled him to his feet. "Look, no one's more concerned about Tate than we are. Do you mind if we have a quick look in his house before we go?"

"Yes," Giff cried, then lowered his voice in an effort to appear calm. "That's a superb idea. We'll need to search his house, probably from top to bottom, incase he's left any clues."

"Do you still have keys?"

"Of course I do," Mrs. Cushman replied, pulling a set from the pocket of her capris. "I may live like a queen aboard the *Boondoggle II*, but on land I still get paid to scrub that man's toilets."

Thirty-Seven

We followed Mrs. Cushman along the maze of docks, weaving through the press of boaters and guests as she headed toward the back lawn of the Vander Hagens' rambling, lannon-stone ranch. The back of the house faced the bay, sitting at a comfortable distance from the marina yet close enough to keep an eye on things, just the way Tate's dad had intended when he'd built it. Once across the patio, Mrs. Cushman opened the sliding glass door. Giff strolled in without a care. I felt slightly uncomfortable as I followed him.

"Wow," he remarked. "Much cleaner than I expected for a muscly bachelor, although the whole lakeside, boating theme is a bit overdone."

"Really?" I replied, scanning the airy room that was filled with sailing memorabilia. "The man owns a marina. And in case you hadn't noticed, the lake is right over there." I pointed out the sliding glass doors and continued through the family room to the kitchen. I immediately noticed a sprinkle of bread crumbs on a cutting board and a knife streaked with mayonnaise in the sink. A couple of empty beer cans sat on the counter beside the cutting board as well, which, under the circumstances, didn't seem so out of place.

"I cleaned this place up yesterday," Mrs. Cushman informed us. "Tate must have made a sandwich last night." She pointed to the beer cans. "And drank a few of those."

"Just two?" Giff shot me a pointed look. "I admire his restraint. Whenever I get dumped I go straight to the gin."

"Well, that's a good idea," Mrs. Cushman replied. "It's far more respectable than drowning your sorrows with these." She held up the beer cans, tipped them over the sink to force out the last few drops, and dropped them in the recyclable bin. The enchanted look on Giff's face faded to gentle amusement when she added, "I'm not one for the gym." Clearly she had misheard him. "I prefer yoga myself."

Giff wrinkled his nose in mock distaste. "I suppose anything's tolerable with a splash of tonic and a twist of lime."

Mrs. Cushman nodded thoughtfully. "Have you ever tried Jenn's cherry smoothie? That'll fortify a body." Thinking, she added, "It might even help mend a broken heart. I'll have to make one for Tate when he returns."

"Good thinking," Giff said and asked her to point him in the direction of the master bedroom.

While Giff meandered off down the back hall, I gave another thought to the two beers in the recycle bin. I took a quick inventory of Tate's fridge as well. He was never in the habit of keeping a lot in there, but I did know that he was fond of sandwich fixings. It was his go-to meal, convenient for a late-night snack and the perfect food for sailing. I turned to Mrs. Cushman. "It doesn't take two beers to make one sandwich, especially for a man adept at wrapping a couple of pieces of bread around nearly everything he eats. Did his fridge look this empty yesterday?" I swung the double doors wide so she could bet a better look. "Two beers might indicate he was in the kitchen longer than the time it takes to make and eat one sandwich. Could he have been stocking up? You know, preparing for a longer sail?"

She gave a little sigh. "It appears so. There was a lot of beer in there the other day."

I smiled gently. "I'll check the garage just to be sure. If there's a cooler missing, I'll spot it." I headed out of the kitchen, aiming for the garage, but then decided to make a detour to the master bedroom first, strongly suspecting that Giff was in there just snooping around for his own amusement.

I opened the door and was a little shocked to see him sitting on the unmade bed studying a framed picture. He looked up as I entered, but the impish grin never appeared. Instead I was met with a quiet, solemn expression. "This was on the nightstand. It was placed face down. Pity," he said, turning the picture to me. "You two made an adorable couple."

The picture had been taken years ago. Tay had gotten a new camera and had joined us for a sail aboard the *Lusty Dutchman*. She'd snapped a lot of pictures that day, but this one had been Tate's favorite. He was at the wheel and I was beside him, our heads pressed together, our happiness genuine. We looked as if we didn't have a care in the world, and back then we hadn't. How strange pictures are, I thought. Capturing emotions with the click of a button. I had been in love, but I didn't remember how much until I was forced to look at my own face. It was years ago, yet nonetheless my heart clenched painfully and every nerve in my body ached with renewed sadness.

Tate had obviously felt it too, finally understanding that our day in the sun had passed. It was over. He had laid any remaining hopes to rest. The picture sent a clear message. Tate hadn't been targeted by the Cherry Cove killer; I had chased him away. I had broken his heart.

I walked over and gently took the picture from Giff's hands. I then laid it back down on the nightstand. "We shouldn't be in here. The man deserves his privacy."

Giff agreed and followed me out of the room. Before we left I checked the garage. Tate's pickup truck was parked in one of the bays, and, just as I expected, a cooler was missing.

"Call me if he returns," I told Mrs. Cushman. "If I don't hear from you in a few hours, we'll try to find him."

∞

"You're driving," I told Giff, heading for his gently used, light gray, three-series BMW convertible. "We'll pick up mine on the way back." I threw the peanut butter cookies in the back seat and buckled up. The moment we pulled out of the Cherry Cove Marina heading north, I asked, "What the devil were you doing there?"

The picture on Tate's nightstand had given Giff a jolt, and at least he had the decency to look guilty. "The man's heartbroken," he stated. "And Mrs. Cushman was worried. Is it a crime to visit the poor woman and offer comfort?"

"Generally, no. But I know you. Your visit to the marina wasn't about Mrs. Cushman. It was reconnaissance. You want to get as much information on Tate as you can because you're infatuated with him. You're swooping in on my territory!"

With sunlight glinting off his blond highlights and the mirrored blue lenses on his black sunglasses, he turned to me and smiled. Damn him, but his teeth were blinding too. "Abandoned territory, angel. The man's vulnerable. I thought he could use a friend, one who understands exactly what he's going through. I used to work with you, remember? I have invaluable insight the man could use just now."

Maybe I wasn't totally over Tate, I thought, staring at Giff as we drove out of town toward our next destination. Fighting the sudden impulse to squeeze his neck, I offered instead, "He's one hundred percent hetero. You know that, right? I mean, you can't get any more manly than Tate Vander Hagen."

"Angel," he soothed, grinning at my discomfort. "Your imagination delights me. But this isn't what you think it is. Yes, I'm curious about that Adonis, and I'm also concerned. But I'm also a wee bit suspicious as well. Think about it. Tate knew Ms. Lumiere. You told me yourself that she tried to get him to pose for her in the nude. He has access to the inn, and I'm sure he could get a black cape if he wanted one."

"What are you saying?"

"I'm not saying anything. But I've been thinking. Peter McClellan's an obvious choice for a murder suspect, isn't he? He's got motive, access to the inn, and he's riddled with vices. He has an alibi, but it's not without its flaws. Tate knows all this too. Both of you stumbled on Mr. McClellan when he was holding one of his little voodoo ceremonies on the beach. You said that Tate was beyond angry when he found out that Peter was supplying young Mr. Larson with weed. After Mr. Larson's checkered recent past that had to have been quite a blow to a man like Tate, being a mentor to the boy. Another thing to consider. He's still in love with you. What if he was trying to protect you from Silvia's misplaced wrath and devised a way to make that happen? He wasn't at the inn the night of her murder, but he could have entered the building late at night without anybody knowing. He probably still has a key to the place, and nobody's bothered to look at him as a suspect. I doubt he even has an alibi."

Giff kept driving while I thought about what he was saying. I didn't really believe Tate would do such a thing, but Giff did make a sound case for further questioning. The moment I spied the narrow road flanked by trees, I instructed Giff to make a sharp left. He made another sharp left down an equally narrow gravel driveway, bringing us to our destination. As Giff turned off the car, I asked, "Do you think his sudden disappearance has anything to do with Silvia's murder?"

Giff shrugged. "I did until I saw that picture. Honestly, I'm just as confused as you are. By the way, where are we?"

"Another man we need to talk to," I said, peering at the rustic, ramshackle cottage before us that was clearly in need of a new roof. "Bob Bonaire. As much as it pains me to admit it, I don't think we have the luxury of ignoring anyone who had a serious issue with Silvia Lumiere. Over the past month, that woman made Bob's life a private hell. Clearly he's not much of a housekeeper, but the man can cook. He's one of the best on the peninsula, and that woman made him doubt it at every meal."

"Let me guess. He also has keys to the inn?"

I looked at Giff and offered a wan smile. "Probably owns a black cape as well. I'm told they're all the rage."

Thirty-Eight

I knocked on the old screen door as Giff peered inside. "Damn," he uttered. "Looks like he could use a dumpster in there as well."

"Hush," I whispered and knocked again. A heartbeat later a giant, shaggy figure of a man appeared at the screen, a smile on his face and a drink in his hand. It had only been two days, but Bob already had the appearance of a bear emerging from a long winter's hibernation.

"Whitney!" The greeting erupted like a car horn. "And your fancy city friend! Well, don't just stand there. Come on in."

Bob, somewhere in his mid-forties, was a tall man, barrel-chested, mustachioed, and with hands the size of catcher's mitts. His demeanor was laid back, efficient when it needed to be, and highly protective of his reputation as a chef. He was also a bit wacky, which was part of his charm. Bob stared at Giff. Unsure of what to do next, he cleared his throat and shoved out his hand. "PBR?" he asked.

"Ah, no thanks," Giff politely demurred, staring at the opened can of Pabst Blue Ribbon beer. "But by all means, keep drinking. It's what I'd do if Whitney showed up on my doorstep unannounced."

Bob, apparently liking this answer, grinned. He turned and indicated for us to follow as he walked through the war zone of his living room toward the back deck. "Don't mind the mess," he told us. "I'm taking advantage of *that woman's* murder by doing a little home improvement."

The deck was also in need of a good scouring, but Bob was a bachelor and worked long hours at the inn. The whole house might have needed a little loving care, but no one could improve upon the view. Bob's cabin was right on Cherry Cove Bay, with a little half-moon sandy beach and a pristine white dock. At the end of the dock was a covered boat hoist where his speed boat was currently parked.

Aside from the industrial-sized grill, the only furniture on the deck was an array of colored plastic deck chairs that had seen better days. He indicated for us to take a seat and said, "I assume you're here because of Tate. Saw him at Shenanigans last night and we had a little chat. Whitney, Whitney," he admonished. The deep-set brown eyes, full of accusation, settled on me.

I was taken totally off guard by his remark. Truthfully, I hadn't come to talk about Tate and was a little disturbed he thought that I had. It was a small town, but as far as I knew, Bob and Tate weren't particularly close. The fact that they'd been drinking together did beg to be explored.

"Did you and Tate make arrangements to meet at Shenanigans?" I asked.

Bob shook his head. "Nope. Again, I was just taking advantage of my time off." The playful wink he used to punctuate this statement fueled my suspicions. "I went there for drinks and to meet some ladies," he added. "Tate was already there. The lucky bastard was surrounded by a group of vultures. They were buying him drinks and giving him hugs. I had no idea you'd broken up with him."

It was a difficult subject, being so fresh. Words failed me. Thankfully, Giff had plenty for the both of us. "These young vultures, did you know them?"

Bob opened another can of PBR. "I didn't say they were young. I said they were vultures. It's a ladies' book club. Books and Brews, they call themselves. Don't know what they read, but they sure can drink. I go on their meeting night because Francine Smith is in the club." Bob's bushy eyebrows wiggled as a wide grin appeared below his prickly mustache.

I perked up. "The woman who owns the knitting store?"

Bob nodded. "Recently divorced and the right age. I'd worked up the nerve to finally ask her out but found her hugging Vander Hagen instead. Sucked the wind right out of my sails." He gave a sorry shake of his head.

Giff, filling with his own form of jealousy, frowned. "I think what Whitney would like to know is if he was hugging this woman back."

Damn him. I didn't want to know. I shot him a look as my insides curdled like sour milk on a hot day.

Thankfully, Bob laughed. "Nope. He was polite, but largely ignoring the lot of them. However, he was talking with Alexa Livingstone for a while. She's in the book club too. Such a nice woman. I really don't know how she got mixed up with that despicable painter. Obligation's my bet. Too bad she's not a little younger or I'd be all over those old bones." He tossed Giff a knowing wink and raised his PBR.

Attempting to wipe the image from my fertile imagination, I blurted. "Bob. Do you happen to own a black cape?"

The bushy mustache quivered in question as Bob's dark eyes narrowed. Giff cleared his throat, adding, "What Whitney means is, did you have any reason to go back to the inn Saturday night?"

This Bob understood. "Do you think I had something to do with that woman's murder?" he cried angrily. "Do you honestly think I'd jeopardize my career by killing that pretentious food snob? Look," he said, and turned the full force of his bearish intensity on me. "I was extremely insulted when that woman sent that first perfectly prepared meal back to the kitchen. But I handled it professionally. When it became an everyday occurrence, I was outraged. I would have given that woman a piece of my mind if Alexa and Fred hadn't come to the kitchen to talk with me. They knew she was a handful, but they urged me to look beyond it. They swore she'd be a benefit to the inn, and she was. Whenever Silvia was dining with us the restaurant was filled to capacity. I still didn't like it one bit. Sure, I wanted to strangle her. Who didn't? But we all had our reasons to hate her. Right, Whitney?"

"I wasn't fond of her, but I didn't murder her," I told him.

"Well, neither did I. But I took out my revenge same as you. You brought the goats. That was brilliant!" he said with a chuckle, as if I'd had something to do with them getting loose and wreaking havoc on the back lawn. "Us chefs, we have our own saying in the kitchen. *Don't bite the hand that feeds you.*" Beneath the mustache, Bob grinned like the devil. I didn't like that one bit.

Giff and his darkly subversive nature were, naturally, enchanted. "Are you suggesting that certain liberties were taken with her food?"

"Liberties?" Bob hooted.

Before he could reveal just what he'd done to Silvia's food, I held up my hand. "Look, you're a respectable chef and employed in our kitchen. This is a dangerous line of questioning."

"Right," he said, and cleared his throat.

"You've obviously given a statement to Officer MacLaren yesterday. Is there anything else you can think of that might be of interest on this case?"

"Are you trying to find her murderer, Whitney? Is that what this is about?"

"The sooner we find the killer, Bob, the sooner I can get Jack to clear the inn for business. You want to get back to work, right?"

Bob cast a critical look at the mess that surrounded him, then glanced at his docked boat with something akin to longing. "I do," he said. "All right. I didn't want to mention this to anyone, because I like the guy. But you might want to talk to Fred Beauchamp. The crazy loon was trying to get into the old witch's pants. Don't know why. She treated him like dirt. But Saturday night, when I was alone in the kitchen, I heard a knock on the kitchen door. It was Fred. Silvia had kicked him out around midnight. Said he drove around for a bit, then decided to come back and surprise her. He wanted to sneak through the kitchen door, so I let him in. Thought he was going to pop the question. Terrible idea, but I was feeling particularly spiteful. Fred's a good man, but that woman could make even the most docile lapdog turn into a rabid Ol' Yeller."

Thirty-Nine

"Keep heading north," I told Giff as I took out my iPhone. "I'll get directions from Tay. I also need to call Jack and tell him what we've just learned."

As Giff navigated the congested traffic through Sister Bay, I made a few calls. The first was to Tay, who told me that Peter had unlocked the great white beast again. "We got a tarp from your dad and started unloading the whole trailer," she informed me. "I'll say one thing about the woman, she had great taste in furniture. The stuff we're unloading would fetch a fortune at auction, not to mention at any antique shop. If these are the pieces she kept, I hate to imagine what she had to leave behind."

"I'm glad you appreciate them. You and Giff are probably the only ones in Cherry Cove who understand their value." Hearing his name, Giff perked up. "Antique furniture," I told him, then addressed the phone once again. "Tay, have you guys come across anything of interest, something that might lead us to the person who actually killed her?"

"Nothing obvious. The paintings are interesting, though." Tay described the handful of framed portraits yet to be delivered, omitting her mother's. Peter had inspected that one, she had told us, insisting that only he and Jack view it before the unveiling. Most of the others I had seen myself last night. "Peter and Hannah are going through the books while Lance and I tackle the heavier furnishings and antiques," she added. "Who knows, maybe Peter and Hannah will come across something odd in there."

It was terrible of me to even think it, but I didn't have a whole lot of confidence in those two being able to detect an oddity in the ledgers. Peter, until last night, was a stoner. And Hannah, although brilliant in her own way, was never one to suffer tedious numbers. "Don't get mad at me, but maybe you can have Brock Sorensen take a look at the ledgers and notebooks. He may be a faux-bearded beta male and a closet carnivore," I added, mostly for Tay's benefit—she and Brock had once shared an embarrassing evening together and the memory still haunted her—"but he sure can make sense of numbers."

"That requires me to go to his office, doesn't it?" Tay quipped teasingly.

"Bring Lance with you," I suggested. "Show him what a real meat-eating man looks like." Tay laughed at this. I then told her about our visit to Fred Beauchamp's studio, including the missing key we found hanging there.

"And Jack has him in Sturgeon Bay for questioning? Good," she said. "So what are you and Giff doing now?"

"We're heading up to Alexa Livingstone's place to see if she can help us any. Edna suggested it. And she's right."

"Of course," Tay said. "Silvia's biggest fan and the only person on the entire peninsula who doesn't have a reason to want Silvia dead. Oddly enough that singles her out, don't you think?"

"She's got a solid alibi," I told her. "She has a live-in housekeeper who confirmed she was home the entire night. Besides, why would she murder the woman she idolized?"

"Maybe for the same reason Fred Beauchamp might have done it. Silvia humiliated the man with that ridiculous portrait. What if Alexa's unveiling was equally as embarrassing?"

"The thought did occur to me," I told her. "But Edna Baker was at her unveiling. She claims that Alexa's portrait was just fine."

"But you're heading there to see for yourself, because you, by nature, don't trust Edna!"

I glanced at the peanut butter cookies in the back seat of Giff's convertible. It was true that not long ago, Edna had stooped to bribery with Giff, tantalizing him with a home-cooked chicken pot pie dinner if he voted for her cherry pie, not mine, to win the highly competitive cherry pie bake-off. But Edna wouldn't lie about a portrait. Still, there was something about Alexa that begged to be investigated. Worshipping someone as horrible as Silvia had to wear on a person, I thought. Then I asked Tay for the woman's address.

"It's in the ledger. Alexa's portrait was the last one Silvia delivered. Just a minute and I'll text it to you. Oh, I have to ask, any word on Tate yet?"

"He's still missing," I said, then gave her more instructions before ending the call.

As Giff heeded the directions on Google Maps that would take us to Alexa's house, I made another call, this time to Jack. The moment he answered I told him what we had learned from our visit to Bob Bonaire, particularly the part where Bob had let Fred back into the inn through the kitchen door well after midnight.

"What?" Jack cried over the phone. He sounded furious. "That clay-sniffing weasel. He never mentioned a thing about entering the inn again once he'd left Silvia for the night. He obviously never thought we'd find out."

"Well, that's ridiculous. Bob works at the inn, and he's not the most tight-lipped man on the planet. What did Fred tell you, if you don't mind me asking?"

Jack gave a little laugh on the other end. The mere sound sent a bubbly tingle of pleasure shooting through me. I couldn't help but smile. "Of course I should mind," Jack said. "But I'll tell you anyhow. Fred never veered from his original statement, including his utter denial at having Silvia's room key in his studio."

"Do you believe him?"

"Well, given what you've just told me, I might believe him about the room key. If Bob let him in through the kitchen door a little after midnight, Fred wouldn't have needed the key."

"True," I said, thinking about it. "But what if Fred took it while he was visiting Silvia for the second time? Maybe she upset him. Maybe he had no intention of causing her harm until that moment. He could have taken the key, planning to come back even later to finish the job."

"Three visits to the inn in one night?" Jack's voice sounded skeptical. "That's a bit much, even for a groveling potter like Fred." The voice on the other end fell silent a moment. "You know what?" he finally said. "Maybe now I do believe him, but only about the key. What the devil was he doing back at the inn after midnight?"

"Really? You have to ask?" I shot Giff a look and rolled my eyes. "Booty call, Jack. The man was after a good old-fashioned booty call."

Silence, and then a loud "Blagh" erupted over the phone. I could almost see Jack quiver in disgust. "I'm trying not to picture it, but it keeps popping into my head. Thanks, Whit."

"Well, I don't know if he was successful, so the imagery you're suffering is all your own doing. Actually, Erik did mention that someone

285

might have been in her room when he delivered room service, but he couldn't be sure. Now we know his suspicions were correct. Fred was in there. Also, the Gordons might have seen Fred go in there as well but kept quiet about it. I don't think they had a hand in her murder, but I also don't think they were terribly upset by it either. Silvia cost them money. When I spoke to Stanley and Carol, Stanley mentioned that Silvia was seeing a man, one who couldn't afford her. He obviously meant Fred."

"Well, he swears he didn't know about the portrait just as he swears he didn't know about the room key. It'd been wiped clean of fingerprints anyhow, so we couldn't link it to him. However, re-entering the inn and not mentioning it? That demands another visit from me. Poor Fred. He won't like that one bit. If I can get Bonner to make a statement I just might have something to hold our besotted potter on. Nice work, Bloom." This was said in a mildly flirtatious way.

"Thanks." I was blushing with pride. Thank goodness he couldn't see me. "Just want to get the inn back up and running. Also, Jack, I hate to do this to you, but I'm going to have to take a rain check on dinner tonight. Instead I want you and MacDuff to come to the inn. Tate's still missing. I know where he is, but I think it would help if all his friends came out in force to find him. Tate's still a very important part of Cherry Cove."

I'm not afraid to admit that I found the silence on the other end unnerving. At length Jack replied, "Yeah. Okay. I'll grab Duffy and head on over, after I've dealt with Fred Beauchamp … for the second time today."

"Whoa. Whoa. Whoa!" Giff exclaimed the moment Jack had ended the call. He'd just turned off the main road and was now driving his little crop-topped beamer down a spotless brick driveway. The house waiting at the other end was a shock to us both. It was the kind of over-large, stately dwelling one saw springing up on the lawns of the newly monied, dotting the north shore of Chicago. Sister Bay had its share of beautiful homes as well, but this hidden gem stood out even among them.

"Toto," he said as my own reflection stared back at me on the surface of his impenetrable blue lenses. "We're not in Kansas anymore. Don't take this the wrong way, angel, but I think I've just met my new best friend."

Forty

We stood before the arched slab of oak that answered for a door, wondering if Alexa was in residence. A moment later our question was answered by a youngish woman in yoga pants and a bright pink tee. She was the housekeeper, she explained in a Polish accent. She stood in the foyer with us while she sent a text to her employer. A moment later she looked up from her screen. "Come to the sitting room. Ms. Livingstone will be with you in a moment."

The room we were taken to was like a small cathedral. A network of thick, arched beams held up the vaulted ceiling while light poured into the room from tall arched windows. Aside from exquisite furniture and tasteful decorations, the focal point in the room was the giant fieldstone fireplace. Giff, marveling at the grandeur of his surroundings, grinned impishly and plopped down in a leather chair fit for a king. I ignored him and chose a spot on the upholstered couch. Although the walls were covered in fine works of art, I couldn't detect Alexa's recent portrait among them. I was about to comment as much to Giff when Alexa swept into the room. Her housekeeper brought up the rear, carrying a tray of refreshments.

"What a pleasant surprise," she said, although she looked more shocked than pleased. I noticed that she'd changed from her nautical-inspired outfit of the morning to a more relaxed ensemble of loose-cut capris and billowy sleeveless top.

"I've been on pins and needles waiting for news about Fred. Oh, hello," she said as Gifford appeared from behind the leather chair. "I thought you'd come alone, Whitney. I heard about Tate last night," she added coyly. "But I see you have a new friend with you today." With a look of appreciation, she turned her attention to the fashion-forward male beside me.

"Old friend," Giff clarified, extending a hand. "Gifford McGrady. And, for the record, I'm not into girls." A quick head-bob to me and he jumped right in with, "Women, however, are another matter. Correct me if I'm wrong, but you look like a woman who thrives in luxurious surroundings. I believe we're kindred spirits. Is there, by chance, a Mr. Livingstone?"

Whatever Giff was doing, it was working like a charm. Alexa was a tall woman and could meet Giff eye-to-eye. Her youthful appearance may have been manufactured, but her smile as she looked at him was genuine.

"He died years ago, I'm afraid. I never remarried."

"I'm certain you've had plenty of offers, though. Am I correct?"

Alexa giggled. "I did. But I had the money to protect, you see. For my daughter. I've heard stories of women getting remarried only to be fleeced by their new husbands. Besides, I was too busy running my own business."

"You worked in Chicago, didn't you?" I asked.

Alexa directed us to sit back down as her housekeeper set the tray of refreshments on the coffee table. She picked up the pitcher of iced tea and began filling three glasses. "I had my own interior design firm in Chicago," she affirmed. "I started it when Evie, my daughter, went off to grade school." She took a long sip of her iced tea and leaned back in her chair, reminiscing. "I've always had a knack for interior design and did it more as a hobby. Then, finding myself with a little more time on my hands, and encouraged by my late husband, I decided to open a shop."

Alexa paused a moment to soak in her surroundings. "It still amazes me, the fact that I had come from virtually nothing to all this. But it wasn't without hard work. And it wasn't until I started attracting more high-end clients on Chicago's Gold Coast, plus the North Shore people, that it really started to take off. The company grew by leaps and bounds. When I was finally ready to retire, it was worth a fortune."

"I'll bet," Giff said, hanging on her every word.

Classic Giffster, I thought, and caught myself before I shook my head in disapproval. "Is that where you met Silvia Lumiere?" I asked.

Alexa's attention shifted to me. "Yes. Silvia was just starting out then too. It was a man's world back then in Chicago, but we had our own gifts and knew how to go after what we wanted. The moment I met Silvia I knew we were destined to work together. She was marvelous. Her mere presence oozed class, but it was nothing compared to what her portraits and paintings did for my clients. I helped her build her name and reputation. She helped me by working with my clients to create original works of art for their stately homes. We had the perfect partnership."

Recalling the magnificent antique furniture Tay had been drooling over in Silvia's trailer, I asked, "Did you decorate Silvia's home as well?"

"Of course. She had marvelous taste. When she was married she spent quite a lot of her husband's money on rare antiques and costly décor."

"And did you know about her penchant for younger men?" I asked.

Alexa's glossy brown head tilted as a puzzled expression appeared on her bright red lips. She might have thought of lying, but ultimately decided against it. "There were a lot of things about Silvia that I didn't particularly care for. But it was none of my business."

I studied her as she said this, and offered, "Because yours was more of a business relationship, wasn't it?"

Her injected lips curled slightly, but the smile never appeared. "If you're asking were we kindred spirits like Mr. McGrady here and myself, then the answer would be no. We were friends, but you are correct. Business was our common ground. Truthfully, I don't really know if that woman was capable of making any deep friendships. I always found it a bit sad."

"But you put up with her anyway," I ventured, believing I understood how she felt, "because she was good for business."

"Remember the little talk we had at your inn?" she asked me. I recalled very well how she'd told me to turn a blind eye to Silvia's bad behavior for the greater good. "She had you in tears," Alexa gently reminded me. "I can't tell you how many times the same happened to me. But I realized very early on in my career that sometimes people come into your life for reasons we can't explain. Silvia always challenged me. I could have shown her the door many times. But my own style and business would have suffered terribly for it. She pushed me to be better."

"And you suffered her friendship for the greater good?"

Alexa smiled. "No. For my own good. But Silvia stopped working on corporate accounts years ago. Then around six years ago I ran into her again. She confided to me how she was struggling financially. I had just built this place here and was about to retire. That's when

I thought that maybe I could do something good for the old girl one last time."

Giff leaned in. "You brought her here and introduced her to the arts council," he remarked. "You wanted to make Silvia feel important again."

"Exactly," she said, smiling at him. "I suppose I thought she'd be grateful, and she was. We were nearly on our way to becoming the friends I always imagined we could be. But then she was so brutally murdered." Her brown eyes, cradled in fine lines, shot to me. "I was so angry with you, Whitney. I thought for sure you'd done it. It was the scones. Silvia loved them so."

"Well, I have to admit that I was very close to snapping. But I'm not a murderer." This I proclaimed with confidence, totally omitting the few hours when I'd feared I might have done the deed in my sleep. "The reason we came here, Alexa, is because we'd like to look at the portrait Silvia painted of you. Yours was the last one delivered before her death. It might be helpful to take a peek at it."

Her expertly painted on brows rose. "Oh? Well, I'm afraid that's not possible. It's not here."

Giff rested his arms on the thick armrests and leaned forward. "Where is it?"

Alexa smiled breezily. "Out there." She pointed to the back of her house. "It's on my boat. Silvia's death has shaken me to the core, so I thought I'd get away for a week or so and visit some friends on Mackinac Island. I'm packing the boat up now. I couldn't bear to leave the portrait here, so I'm taking it with me."

Giff, charmed by the thought of a visit to Mackinac Island, jumped to his feet. "Need a first mate?" he offered.

Alexa stood as well. "Tempting. But I prefer to sail alone with a very small staff. "Now, if you'll excuse me, I must get back to packing. Paulina will walk you to the front door."

Just then, the Polish housekeeper appeared. "Follow me please."

Seized with panic, I jumped to my feet. "Can I please just take a quick look at your portrait?"

Alexa shook her head. "Too messy, I'm afraid. The galley is being stocked, fresh linen has just come aboard, and the engine room is currently undergoing a preventive tune-up. I'll be happy to show it to you when I come back, though. Good day," she said, and walked out of the room, disappearing toward the back of the house. I started after her, catching a glimpse out the back windows of the magnificent house—of the broad stone patio, the expanse of green lawn and the long white pier with a stately mini-yacht moored beside it—when a strong grip seized my arm.

"Follow me, please," Paulina said in no uncertain terms, pulling me back the way I had come. "The lady said, no look at painting now."

Forty-One

"Swingin' dingles!" I exclaimed. "I want to see that painting now more than ever!"

Tay, holding the other end of the giant cooler, shook her head. "Yeah, I get that. But it's private property, Whit. Alexa literally doesn't have to show it to you if she doesn't want to, and there's really nothing you can do about it. Besides, Peter just told you that Alexa's unveiling went smoothly. Great food, lots of friends, silence when the portrait was revealed, and then applause. He said that the painting looked fine to him, and that Alexa was the perfect hostess."

We were all back at the inn preparing for operation *Tate Night*, as Hannah was now calling it. Although Mom, Grandma Jenn, and Dad would stay at the inn while we sailed in search of Tate, Mom and Gran had stuffed two giant coolers full of enough food and drink to last an entire week. Dad had gassed up his newly repaired cabin cruiser and made sure everything was perfect for our evening mission. While my family did their part, the rest of us loaded supplies onto the cabin cruiser while waiting for Jack to arrive.

The boat was all packed and everyone was aboard, nibbling on Gran's homemade Chex Mix and drinking bottled sodas, as the sun sank lower in the western sky. We were still moored to the dock. I was in the captain's chair with Giff sitting next to me, mulling over our recent visit to Alexa's McMansion. Giff's take on it all was entirely different than mine. He assured me that the woman was still upset by the painter's death.

"It's natural to want to get away," he told me. "And who wouldn't want to get away on a sweet baby yacht like that?" The fact that she was taking the portrait with her was a good sign. He then pointed out that it was the last commission Silvia would ever paint for Alexa, and it must have very special meaning for her.

"You're just mad she didn't let you snoop around her palatial home." He grinned spitefully before downing another fistful of Chex Mix. "And you were being snoopy," he said accusingly. "You pulled a full-out Nancy Drew on her. Some people don't find that as charming as we do, angel. You're not a cop, and it's obvious she doesn't trust you. Maybe because you baked the scone that killed Silvia."

"That's ridiculous." I shot him a look, then relented. "Well, maybe you're right. Truthfully, I'm so confused by Silvia's murder I don't even know what's up anymore. Hey," I said, changing the subject while jumping to my feet. Jack stepped out of the inn with MacDuff trotting beside him. "Jack's here. Let's make ready to shove off."

It would have had the makings of an epic outing, having all my friends aboard Dad's boat, had we not been on a mission to retrieve my ex-boyfriend and the onetime love of my life who ran away because we'd finally broken up for good. Although Jack had changed into a pair of lightweight hiking shorts and a sporty tee—looking uber hot—there was still a professional air clinging to him that he didn't even try to shake. Maybe it was because of Fred Beauchamp and the lie Giff and I had caught him in. Fred had made two visits to the inn on the night Silvia was murdered. Filled with both love and loathing for the woman he'd been courting, the man had been a wreck when he was taken to Sturgeon Bay for questioning. According to Jack, Sargent Jensen was now escorting him back there for yet another round. Jack was convinced the man was hiding something, but hard evidence linking him to the crime scene was still to be found.

And now we were motoring through the dark, glossy waters of the Green Bay in search of the wooded island Tate had been fond of sailing to. It was the perfect place to disappear for an afternoon, or weekend. A one-hour's sail on a breezy day from Cherry Cove, and yet remote enough to give the illusion of being at the end of the world. Maybe Jack's reticence, I silently mused, was due to the fact that I knew the way to Tate's island so well.

I looked at the man standing next to me as I guided the powerful boat through the black water. MacDuff was lying at his feet. Although the sun had dipped below the horizon, the sky was still luminous, glowing in shades of indigo and purple. It had been another breathtaking sunset in Cherry Cove. "Thank you for coming with us," I said to him. "I know it's not ideal, but I really do appreciate it. It was a bit of a disaster for all of us at the diner the other day. You and I, we're going to be just fine. But Tate …?" I shook my head. "He's been gone too long this time. We're still his friends, Jack. That's why we're all here. Tate needs to know that Cherry Cove wouldn't be the same place without him."

"I agree," he softly replied. "And I'm proud of you, Whit. Only, you know, you're going to have to make this up to me, right?" For the first time all night an impish grin appeared on his face. "Look, you broke our first date," he exclaimed. "I'm not saying that this isn't a good reason. All I'm saying is that you're going to have to make it up to me. Duffy agrees. Don'tcha, Duffy?"

The dog lifted his floppy-eared head, looked at me, then laid it back on the rumbling deck. The poor pooch looked exhausted, or maybe just utterly uninterested.

"Okay," I said, grinning a little too, then. I turned, looking behind me, and called out for Tay. She and Lance were sitting with Hannah and Peter on the wraparound seating in the stern. "Can you pass along a couple of those roast beef and Havarti sandwiches? Officer MacLaren and MacDuff are faint with hunger."

"He always looks like that," Jack remarked, casting a loving glance at his dog.

A moment later Jack not only had a giant sandwich in his hand, but a bag of chips and a fizzy beverage as well. MacDuff was gobbling one of his own. It might not have been the romantic dinner Jack had envisioned, but even he couldn't deny how delicious and timely the food was.

"There," I said, giving MacDuff a pat on the head. "Just a small token of what's to come. Never doubt me, Jack MacLaren. I got your back, buddy."

It was dark by the time the island came into view, looming before us in the darkness like a forested humpback whale. I throttled back the motor to a soft purr, causing the boat to settle in its own wake as I rounded a familiar rocky outcrop. A moment later the protected horseshoe bay came into view, and with it the skeletal outline of the *Lusty Dutchman* at anchor.

"Bingo!" Hannah whispered near my ear. "Gotta hand it to you, my friend. You really know your lusty dutchman. I didn't want to say anything back there, but the moment we left the dock I had a terrible feeling in the pit of my stomach, like, we weren't going to find him.

I'm not exactly psychic or anything, but Peter thinks I'm a sensitive."
Answering my questioning look, she clarified. "It means that I have
paranormal potential." She cast a loving glance at the man who was
not only sober but sporting a man bun, cutoffs, and Jesus sandals as
well. "I'm relieved," she added, suppressing a troubling look that still
lingered on her pretty features. "Now, let's see if we can't convince
him to come back home with us."

Until then I'd never given a thought to the possibility that it might
be difficult.

As Hannah returned to Peter's side, I maneuvered the boat as close
to shore as I could and dropped anchor. It was a wet landing, but
thankfully one above a sandy bottom. MacDuff was the first one in,
leaping from the back deck into the water like a canine long-jump
champion. He wasted no time swimming to shore as the rest of us
waded through the thigh-high water with flashlights in one hand and
our footwear in the other.

"Tate!" I cried before hitting the beach, hoping he'd hear me. His
name became a battle cry, erupting from every mouth as we stood on
shore, dripping. None of us wanted to voice what was obviously apparent. The beach was empty.

"I found the fire pit," Jack called out a while later. Giff and Lance
had accompanied him down the beach with their flashlights.

"It's littered with beer cans and sandwich wrappers," Giff called
out. "The same brand we saw on his counter, Whit. Oh! I found a
cooler!"

"He was definitely here," Lance added. "He made a fire, but the
ashes are cold."

"Maybe he's hiding?" Hannah whispered beside me. I don't know
why she whispered.

"Yeah. Probably saw us coming and dove for the woods," Tay quipped from my other side. "Jilted men are known for their desperate, hairbrained antics." She was trying to lighten the mood, but even she wasn't fully committed to the task.

I nodded in the darkness, mostly to convince myself. "He's probably spent with exhaustion and is sleeping somewhere. There's no dingy that I can see, so he's probably back on his boat. In fact, I'm sure he is." I wasn't sure of anything, but it was better than staring at the look on Hannah's face. In the aura of my flashlight she looked troubled. I dismissed it and asked, "Where's Peter?"

She pointed to a light bobbing away in the woods. "Investigating," she said bleakly. "Told him I was staying here. Thanks to you, I'm now terrified of woods. Bad things happen in the woods."

"Good things too," Tay remarked impulsively. She didn't say so, but Hannah was freaking her out as well. Tay brushed it off, adding, "I mean, if the legend is correct, this is where Whitney and Tate used to come to make out. It wasn't spooky back then, was it?"

I shook my head as the hair on the back of my neck began to prickle. "Not particularly," I said, watching the bobbing lights come toward us again. "What's going on?" I asked Jack.

It wasn't like Jack to look nervous, but he was. "I want you all to stay here and keep searching the island. It's not large. Break into groups so we'll cover more ground. I'm going to swim out to the *Dutchman* and see if Tate's fallen asleep in there." We all turned to the shadowy boat bobbing gently at anchor. Lights from our cabin cruiser glowed across the water, but the sleek sailboat with the tall masts was utterly dark. Tate, if he was aboard, would at least have his mast lights on, I thought.

"Cry out if you find him," Lance said, and headed off with Tay.

"We'll go this way." Giff pointed his light on the other side of the woods.

I stayed where I was, close to Jack and watching as he prepared for a late-night swim. Unaware that I was still staring at him, he began undressing on the beach. He removed his shirt first. Then his watch, cellphone, and wallet were removed. His shorts came next. In a flash, those too were on the beach, pooled at his ankles. Jack was about to remove his briefs when he said very softly, "It might be best if you turn around now."

Caught off guard, I inhaled sharply and spun to face the woods where the others were heading. I could feel myself blushing to the roots of my hair. "Sorry," I blurted. "I ... I didn't mean to ..." There was no good answer to that. Stop talking, idiot, I told myself. Honestly, I'd had no idea he knew I was staring at him.

"It's not that I mind," he added, whispering very close to my ear. "But I'm a bit old-fashioned, not to mention superstitious. It would never do to reveal the goods before we've had our first date."

"Right," I breathed, my heart pounding with the same fear and intensity as a thief fleeing the scene of a crime. "I ... um, was just about to turn around myself."

"Good," he replied, teasingly. "Knew we'd be on the same page. I have a favor to ask. Keep Duffy with you until I get back, okay?"

There was a big splash, and then the soft pearling of water as it lapped over a smooth body gliding through the water. I turned to the lake once again and saw that Jack was swimming. He was a powerful swimmer.

"Come on," I said to the spaniel at my side as my heart pounded away a little erratically. "Let's go find Tate."

MacDuff and I caught up with Giff and Hannah. They'd been holding hands as Giff pulled her along through the woods with him, swinging his flashlight in a wide arc. He stopped when he saw me, and grinned. "Nice view of the moon tonight." The way it was said I knew he wasn't referring to the one orbiting earth.

"I wouldn't know. I wasn't looking."

A flash of white teeth appeared in the darkness. "Pity," he said. "I was. And for the record, it was a very nice, very fit moon."

"Guys!" Hannah reprimanded. "Seriously. Stop talking about the moon! Tate's missing, and now Peter is too. The last time I was in the woods I was nearly abducted. I still have nightmares about it. So, stop fooling around and keep looking for Tate!"

With MacDuff in the lead sniffing the air and the ground alike, we continued searching the densely wooded island, following narrow, winding footpaths and exploring the rocky shoreline. More than a few times we were startled by the screech of a bird, or the sudden rustling of bushes. In those cases, MacDuff sprang off to investigate, leaving us alone in the eerie woods. Hannah, not liking that one bit, had strategically placed herself between Giff and me. Although MacDuff always came back with a wagging tail, Hannah was beside herself with fear. Thankfully, it wasn't long before we met up with Tay and Lance, who'd come from the other direction.

"Find anything?" I asked.

"Nothing," Tay replied.

"I don't understand it," Lance added, shaking his head. A rogue piece of hair had come loose, which he quickly secured behind his ear. "Tate's a large man. It's like he's just disappeared. I hope for all our sakes he fell asleep on the *Dutchman*."

It was the one hope we all clung to as we headed back to the horseshoe bay where Tate had made camp. We'd no sooner come out of the woods than we saw Jack and Peter. Although his coppery hair was dripping as it clung to his beautifully shaped head, Jack was already dressed. Peter was beside him, staring at a limp object in his hands.

"What's that?" Hannah cried. She ran toward them with the erratic intensity of one being chased. Earlier she'd voiced the fear that Peter had gotten lost, which was a hard thing to do on a small island.

Surrounded by the glow of flashlights, Jack looked up. The look on his ashen face stilled my heart. "It's a black cloak," he informed me. "Peter found it in the cooler. I didn't think to look in there before. Thankfully, Peter did. And that's not all. He's left a note. Dear God, Whitney. I'm so sorry."

Forty-Two

"It's not possible," I said, shaking my head as tears streamed from my eyes like water over a breached dam. "No, Jack. I refuse to believe it. It makes no sense at all."

We were traveling back from the island, towing the *Lusty Dutchman* behind us; the boat appearing in the darkness like the skeletal remains of some poor lost soul. It had been hard leaving the island. All the evidence we had found on the deserted beach had been conclusive, but it made no sense at all. The mood on Dad's cabin cruiser was positively dour and hopeless, so unlike the mood when we'd left. We'd been so hopeful then. Our goal had been to cheer Tate up and bring him back home, making sure he was aware of how much he was needed and loved in the cove. Instead we had found a scene of unspeakable sadness. The note, hastily scrawled in Tate's hand, was a confession to the murder of Silvia Lumiere. It was also an untimely farewell, the tipping point not being guilt but heartbreak over losing me.

I could maybe just believe that he was capable of murder—if he was pushed to his very limits. But suicide from a broken heart? Not likely. Not Tate. I absolutely refused to believe our breakup had anything to do

303

with it. The truth was, Tate hadn't been in love with me anymore than I'd been in love with him. Sure, there was mutual attraction. We'd always had that. But Tate had his flings on the side. It was a direct response to me chasing a career in Chicago. Once Tate was no longer the center of my universe, he'd felt abandoned, or so he had once said. Part of me regretted that, but there were no do-overs in real life. We had both made our mistakes. However, once I was back in Cherry Cove, I believe we both began to fall in love with the idea of us, and that was a totally different beast than being in love. Tate, I believed, understood this too.

But still, the emptiness was haunting.

Lance and Tay had the helm and were driving the boat back to the marina. I'd been sitting in the cabin with Jack, trying to make sense of the senseless. Jack, although trying to remain professional, was falling apart at the seams. He'd been cradling his face in his hands, tears visible in his own eyes, when he gently looked up. "I'll call Sturgeon Bay. They'll want to send out divers in the morning."

"Divers?" I sniffled and attempted to dry my tears with the backs of my hands. It wasn't very effective.

Jack nodded. "There was no sign of the body on the island or sailboat."

"It was dark," I reminded him. "He could …" I cleared my throat and started again. "He could still be there."

"We had flashlights," he said. "And MacDuff. If there was a body on that island, he would have found it for sure. A dead body gives off a particularly nasty odor. It's like a rotting—"

I held up my hand to stop him before he got carried away with gruesome descriptions of dead bodies. Jack had seen quite a few in his days working in Milwaukee, and he had a real gift for vivid imagery. Such clinical talking might put him at ease, but I couldn't hear it. Not now; not ever. "Point taken," I said. "So you think Tate drowned? You know he's the most powerful swimmer in Cherry Cove."

Jack's honey-colored gaze held mine as he gently spoke. "Whitney, when someone is desperate enough to take their own life, they go to desperate measures. Tate was a powerful swimmer, which means he might have swum out very far into the lake in a purposeful attempt to exhaust himself. I have no idea how he did it. All the note said was that he didn't want to live in a world where you no longer ..." Jack stopped, then let out a pained gasp. "Jesus, Whitney. What have we done?"

"Jack." I forced him to look at me. "This isn't about us. If you'll recall, Sunday at the diner, both you and Tate were quite done with me. I screwed this up, not you. And that's another thing that doesn't make sense." I furrowed my brow. "You know Tate as well as I do. He's not the type of man to harbor a lot of guilt. In fact, when he left my car he said, and I quote, 'You know where to find me if you need me.' That doesn't sound like a man who's ready to end his life due to guilt and a broken heart."

It was then that Jack's eyes clouded with sorrow. "You don't know that, Whitney. No one does. That's what makes this kind of behavior so tricky to diagnose. People are good at hiding their true feelings, especially those with suicidal tendencies. We all knew Tate as a larger-than-life, happy-go-lucky guy. But something made him snap. Something made him want to kill Silvia."

"Wait," I said, and sat up a little straighter. "Did Tate have an alibi for his whereabouts on Saturday night?"

"Nope. Same as you. Said he was asleep. Mrs. Cushman lives on the yacht now and couldn't confirm it."

We both fell silent then, mulling over our own thoughts as the powerful motor hummed beneath us. Poor Jack. He tried to hide it, but I could see how the guilt of Tate's sudden disappearance consumed him. Hours ago we'd both been positively giddy, swept up by the fact that after a month of tap dancing around the issue, we'd finally come clean with our feelings for one another. It was akin to skimming a toe in a fathomless pool of earthly delights, heady and all-consuming. Tate, poor Tate, had been the sacrificial lamb in our newfound happiness. And though my head refused to believe what Jack and all the evidence was telling me, maybe, just maybe, I'd hurt Tate more deeply than I'd ever imagined.

I heaved a sob in despair. I was a terrible person.

"Tate didn't have any issues with Silvia, though," I said softly, as much for myself as for Jack. "He knew how to handle the woman. He had her in the palm of his hand." My voice grew stronger. "She adored him."

Jack took hold of my hand and nodded. "She trusted him. She'd open the door to him." He shook his head, as if he was the biggest idiot in the world. "No. If anyone had the means to kill Silvia, it would have been Tate." He pulled me to my feet, then wrapped me in his strong arms. "I'm sorry, Whit," he whispered, clinging to me as fiercely as I was clinging to him. "It's one hell of a first date. I'm the one who needs to make this up to you. And I promise, if it takes me a lifetime to do it, I will make this up to you."

A few minutes later, the door to the cabin opened and Giff's head appeared. "The marina's in sight."

Jack thanked him. With one final squeeze, he released me and walked out the door. Giff, looking as forlorn as an abandoned puppy, came into the cabin. He pulled a tissue from the dispenser and plopped down on the edge of the bed.

"You're crying," I remarked stupidly, and sat beside him.

"This is the worst day of my life," he said, and perhaps it was the most honest thing Gifford McGrady had ever uttered. Reflexively I wrapped him in my arms, like a mother comforting her precocious son. "Such a waste of a beautiful man."

"I agree. A horrible waste." Then, as I was still holding Giff, a silent rage consumed me. "The coward," I seethed. "The stupid idiot. What the devil did he do that for?"

The dark head with the trendy bleached highlights lifted. "You're angry with him?" Giff clearly felt this was off base. "*Whitney*," he chided. "The man's dead."

"He better be," I said, abandoning Giff to the bed as I headed for the door. I spun back around, filling with self-righteous anger. "All of us gathered at the inn this evening. Dad lent us his boat. Mom and Gran stuffed coolers full of delicious food, just so that we could go out to the island and show Tate how much he meant to us—and he does this!" Giff, hovering between sorrow and fear, tilted his head. I ignored him and continued my tirade. "Death, Gifford McGrady, is the coward's way out. I'll tell you one thing. If Tate isn't dead and I find him? He's gonna wish that he was."

Forty-Three

Mrs. Cushman, watching the *Lusty Dutchman* glide into its slip without her captain at the helm, was beside herself with grief. Young Cody Rivers, who had stayed well past the end of his shift to be with her, broke down in tears as well. Tate had been that male presence Cody and Erik had needed in their lives, and with his one last, selfish act, he had shattered their worlds forever. I wouldn't blame them if they never forgave him. But they would. They were good boys.

"I ... I need to call Erik," Cody uttered when he could.

"Yes," I told him, giving him a long, life-affirming hug. I released him, adding, "Please do that. And let him know that the body's still missing. If he has any information that might be of help, tell him to call Officer MacLaren."

While Jack was talking with Mrs. Cushman and the other employees of the marina, I walked over to where my friends had gathered. This was Jack's show now, and all we could do was watch helplessly as he tried to explain what we'd found and didn't find on the island.

"Are you going to be okay, Whit?" Tay, her dramatic eye makeup in drips and smudges, offered a pained smile.

"Really, Whit. I don't even know what to say." Hannah, the most excitable among us, had cried herself out of tears, and was still shaking. "It's so ... it's so not like him."

"I know. Is it wrong that I'm really angry with him right now?" They all shook their heads while I made another attempt to dry my tears.

"No. Not at all," Hannah hiccupped.

"It's perfectly natural." Tay, remaining stoic as the burden of getting us all safely home had fallen to her and Lance, nodded. "I know the feeling," she added, looking at the man beside her. "I was livid when I learned that Lance here was allowing himself to be used as a pincushion for the other knights as punishment for his shortcomings. You and Tate have a long history together. What you're feeling is betrayal. It's just as powerful as grief, only arguably healthier. Grief deflates us and makes us helpless. Anger is far more empowering. But it's okay, Whit, if you flip between the two, as you will. We're all shocked to the core about Tate. It just doesn't seem like him, but then I thought the very same thing about Lance."

Lance agreed, and although he hadn't known Tate very well, he expressed his sadness over the whole affair.

A short while later, Tay and Hannah decided it best to walk home with their respective boyfriends. The marina was a short walk for them both, and it was late. The day had been long and heartbreaking. They'd pick up their cars from the inn tomorrow.

Jack, after promising Mrs. Cushman that he'd do everything in his power to find Tate's body and wrap up the case, climbed back aboard the cabin cruiser. It was going to be a long night; his job was far from over, and he looked more troubled and downtrodden than I'd ever seen him. He hugged MacDuff before taking the seat beside me. Giff, after unmooring the boat, had disappeared down the small set of stairs into the galley. I'd driven the boat halfway across Cherry Cove Bay before he appeared again, bearing a tray with three mugs of coffee heavily laced with Irish cream. Leave it to Giff to know just what we needed.

"Are you going to be okay?" Jack asked. His light brown eyes, now glossy and dark under the night sky, were full of concern. It touched me, especially since I knew how hard the whole ordeal had been for him as well. The fact that my name had been mentioned in the suicide note was troubling to us both. It was also something that would haunt our relationship for a long time if we let it. And I was just mad enough at Tate not to let it. Jack, the dear man, didn't deserve that.

"I doubt I shall ever forgive him," I told him honestly. "But you and me, we're going to be just fine, if that's what you're worried about."

It was, but it was hardly a thing he'd admit to. Instead he finished the last of his coffee and headed for the galley, volunteering to clean the mugs.

Mom and Dad had waited up for us. They'd clearly been expecting a happy, boisterous crowd embarking from the large motor boat and not the glum skeleton crew that emerged. Mom, who I was certain had been harboring visions of a rekindled romance between Tate and me, had been holding a tray of fresh baked cherry chocolate chip cookies as she met us at the head of the pier. Dad was standing beside her, looking puzzled.

Jack quietly told them about Tate and wisely took the tray from Mom's hands, lest she drop it on the hard planks beneath her feet. The news was hard to swallow. Tate had killed Silvia Lumiere, then had taken his own life when the world seemed to be crumbling around him. Mom had a hard time believing what Jack was telling her, which was natural. Dad, however, seemed more hurt than saddened by the news.

"Dear Lord. Dear Lord, I better call his parents," Mom offered as Dad stormed off toward his boat.

"Better hold off on that a bit longer, Mrs. Bloom. At least until I have all the details. I'll call you tomorrow. If you still want to make the call, I'd be grateful."

After Jack had answered all Mom's questions to the best of his ability, Giff escorted her inside. I walked with Jack to his Jeep. He opened the door, letting MacDuff jump in first, then turned to me.

"I have to admit, this evening I wasn't too keen on boating to the island with you and the others. Tate had run off and part of me was actually grateful. As I drove here, so many different scenarios played out in my mind as to how the evening might go, some good but most were disastrous for me, given your history with Tate. But never in a million years would I have imagined this. I'm at a loss, Whitney. I don't know how to make sense of it all, and that seldom ever happens to me."

I took his hand and said the only thing I could. "It would never have worked out badly for you, Jack. I never would have let it." And just to make my point I placed a gentle kiss on his lips. It was all the encouragement Jack needed. A heartbeat later I was in his arms. The kiss I'd been fantasizing about ever since taking up residence in Cherry Cove was upon me, but the circumstances were hardly ideal. Neither of us could shake Tate from our heads, and we both knew it. At least Jack had tried. But the kiss came too soon, too suddenly, and it ended shortly after it began. "I'm sorry," he whispered and released me, failure and sadness clinging to him like an unshakable parasite. He then got into his Jeep and drove out of the parking lot.

I just stood there, my heart aching as I watched his taillights fade in the darkness.

"For what it's worth, I approve," came a soft voice from behind me.

I spun around only to find Giff standing there. "Two hours ago, I was firmly on team Tate, purely for my own selfish reasons. But Officer McHottie, he's a real solid kind of guy, angel."

A fresh stream of tears began then. I couldn't help it.

"Oh Whitney. You know I hate it when you cry." But as he spoke, I could tell tears were forming in his own eyes. "Come. Let's get you inside. It's been a long day, and not a good one."

Forty-Four

Giff and I had always worked well together. He'd been a dream of a coworker when I'd been in advertising with his witty remarks, his silly antics, and his creative mind. Giff was never afraid to voice his thoughts, no matter how crazy they might sound. And I appreciated that. Especially now, when I didn't want to think about Tate, or that note, or the senseless death of Silvia Lumiere. It was late, but I couldn't sleep. Giff couldn't either. Instead he came to my room with a bottle of cherry juice and a head full of questions. It was just the distraction I needed.

"If you think about it, it really makes no sense," he said, handing me a glass. He sat on the bench of my vanity and took a sip of the fortifying tart juice as he studied our suspect board. With the glass still in hand, he stood and pointed to a name. "Fred Beauchamp," he remarked. "The man had a key to Silvia's room. He lied about it, too, as well as sneaking back into the inn through the kitchen door. Silvia toyed with his emotions. And that portrait she'd painted of him? Utterly abominable! If anyone had a reason to want Ms. Lumiere dead, it would be Fred. So what's his connection to Tate?"

"What do you mean?" I asked.

"Look, angel. You know I think the world of you, but I know men. I didn't want to say anything back there, mostly because I didn't want to appear the insensitive ass. But, honestly, you're hardly the type of woman that would make a man end it all, especially a man like Tate."

"What?" I stared at him as anger and incredulity collided. "He wrote it in his note!" I stated, heatedly. "It was in his own hand, albeit sloppily written. And what do you mean by I'm not the type of woman? Hello, Gifford! Men like me."

His answer to this was a sardonic arch of his brow. "I'm not saying they don't, princess, but you and Tate were hardly dating. Your rekindled relationship was merely smoke and mirrors, thanks to Officer McHottie. However, I don't doubt that you upset the poor man. You two had a long history together and when a long-term relationship ends, it's crushing. Consider this as well; he's a sailor. Why would he abandon his business, including that gorgeous boat of his? What I'm getting at, sweetheart, is the fact that Cherry Cove is a small town. Everyone around here seems to know about you and Tate. What if somehow Fred learned about your breakup and decided to use Tate as his scapegoat?"

I sat a little higher at the end of my bed contemplating the validity of what Giff was saying. The wheels in my head engaged. "You think Fred might have something to do with Tate's disappearance? For your theory to work, Fred would have had to have known that Tate had sailed to that particular island. Mrs. Cushman was aware that he had sailed off but had no idea where to. Also, Fred would need a boat or access to one."

"We can easily check that out," Giff replied. "According to Mrs. Cushman, Tate sailed off Sunday night. Who else knew about it?"

"Mom knew and so did Grandma Jenn." I pursed my lips together as I mentioned another name. "Edna Baker knew about it as well."

"There you have it!" Giff declared, looking triumphant. "You've just named the four women upon which the Cherry Cove gossip mill is built. So we can pretty much assume that everyone in town, and very likely the whole peninsula, knows that the spurned owner of the Cherry Cove Marina hoisted sail and took off to some nearby island to lick his wounds."

"True. I'll give you that. But even if Fred went to the island with an intent to frame Tate for the murder of Silvia Lumiere, he'd still have to convince a man twenty-years younger, five inches taller and with a whole lot more muscle to write that note."

Giff gave a meditative nod of his head. "Tate is quite the specimen. Normally I'd say you're correct, but even our Vikingesque friend is no match for a gun. With a gun pointed at his head, he'd write the note."

"Fred's a potter. He doesn't look the type to own a gun. Also, doesn't it strike you as a little odd that Tate just happened to have a black cape with him? Tate doesn't own a cape. I'd almost bet my life on that fact."

"Peter!" Giff turned from the suspect board with dark eyes blazing. "I don't know why, but Silvia's death always seems to lead us back to Peter McClellan. Think about it, Whitney. Peter disappears on the island as soon as we land, ditching his fear-stricken girlfriend. We all pair up, you and I getting Hannah by default, and begin searching the island in different directions. But the island is deserted. Tate's sailboat is also empty, and then voilà! Peter appears on the beach and magically finds the cape and the note."

I had to admit, it was strange. Out of habit and impulse, I pulled my iPhone from my jeans and called Hannah. It was just after eleven o'clock. She'd still be awake.

"What are you doing?"

"Calling Hannah." As Giff anxiously looked on, Hannah answered.

"Sorry to bother you so late," I said, "but I have to ask you a question. Is Peter's wizard cape at your condo?"

"Oh no!" she cried on the other end. "You seriously still think Peter had something to do with all this?" There was no doubt Hannah was angry.

God help me, I didn't want to keep pushing, but for the sake of murder I had to. "Please, Hannah," I begged as my heart began to pound painfully against my rib cage. "I just need you to check and see if Peter's cape is at your place." I waited in silence as fear began to plague my nerves.

"Dangit, Whit! Normally I'd tell you no. But under the circumstances ... because it's been a difficult night for us all, I'll check." I held my breath until her voice came back over the phone. "Yeah. I got it right here," she said. "Now, do me a favor and erase Peter from your suspect board. I'm serious, Whitney."

"I will. I promise. But first can you please put him on the phone."

A moment later a distinctive, "Dude," floated out of the speaker. "Like, what is it now, Whitney?"

"Just a quick question. When we got to the island you disappeared. Where'd you go?"

"Um, like, I'm not exactly sure where? It was dark and woody. But if you want to know why I skedaddled off, that's easy. Since Hannah had stayed on the beach I like decided to find a quiet spot for a poop." He lowered his voice. "I had to go. It's something I prefer to do in private. Anyhow, by the time I came back to the beach, like, everyone was gone. Then I saw the cooler. I figured from all the beer cans on the beach that there likely were more in there, but I was wrong. Vander Hagen drank it all. All that was in there was some black material and the suicide note. Really sorry about that, Whitney. I didn't know it was a cape either because it was the same material Silvia uses to cover her portraits for her unveilings. But when I held it up, poof! It was a cape."

"Wait. You recognized the material?"

"Yeah. Though it's hardly scarce. You can buy it at any fabric store. Silvia bought bolts of the stuff."

"So you're saying that the cape was handmade?"

"Totally. Machine stitched. A really sweet job too. Vander Hagen has skills. Okay, well, I've got to go. Can't keep m'lady waiting." I thanked him before he ended the call.

Giff looked intrigued. "Okay," I said, thinking. "I'm sorry to inform you, but Peter's not our guy. It's been confirmed. His cape's at Hannah's place. But he did mention something very interesting. He said that the one he found in the cooler was handmade." I turned to Giff, a terrible thought dawning on me. "Holy cobbler!" I cried. "Bob Bonaire saw Tate at Shenanigans last night, remember?

"Bob has a boat," Giff chimed in, looking excited. "A really nice one at that. It's the kind of boat that could run out to the island and back under a half an hour."

"No," I said, getting off the bed. I walked over to the suspect board and picked up a marker. "Not Bob. It was something Bob said—about a group of women from a book club. They were talking with Tate, trying to cheer him up. And one of those women was Alexa Livingstone." I wrote her name on the board, a name that until now had been overlooked.

"What? You think it was that stunningly rich woman who adored Silvia? *Whitney,*" he chided, although I was happy to note that the wheels of his mind were also spinning.

"She's an interior designer. Peter said that the cape was sewn, not bought, and I'd bet my life Alexa knows her way around a sewing machine. Also, she has a very large boat and seemed in a hurry to cast off." As I spoke, a press of thoughts and images of Alexa came tumbling into my head.

"I saw her in Tay's shop this morning while you were still sleeping." I told him. "Jack and I had gone in there to talk with Lance about that portrait of him we found in Silvia's trailer. Alexa was there. It's where she learned that I was no longer a suspect in Silvia's murder. A while later Jack and I found her at Fred's pottery studio. That's when we found Silvia's room key dangling by the back door. Alexa didn't look to be in too much of a hurry when we found her there. What changed that suddenly made her anxious to motor off to Mackinac Island?"

"She could be in mourning," Giff pointed out, clearly not happy with the way the conversation was going.

"Or she could be hiding something … like a portrait! Peter said her unveiling went fine, but I sure got the feeling Alexa didn't want us to see her portrait." Jumping to my feet, I grabbed my car keys off the dresser and turned back to Giff. "Come hell or high water, my friend, I'm going to see that portrait."

Forty-Five

Our plan, hastily devised in my car as we raced down the deserted highway, was simple. Giff was to create a diversion by going to the front door while I snuck around back and climbed aboard Alexa's mini-yacht. He was to flirt with her, something he'd been shamelessly doing earlier in the day. It wouldn't come as a huge surprise to her, I reasoned, when he showed up on her doorstep at midnight with a bottle of cherry wine in hand. She'd be flattered.

"That's a terrible idea," he said, shaking his head as he stared at me.

"It's a brilliant idea," I countered. "She already knows you like her."

"Correction. I like her money. The whole possibility of her being a murderer, however, has ruined the romance for me. For instance, what if she invites me in?"

"Then you go in."

"You're a monster."

"Look, you don't have to stay long, just long enough for me to get on that boat and have a look around. There must be something wonky going on with that portrait. I'm sure of it. All along, Giff, I've had the feeling that Silvia's murder is directly connected to her paintings. You've seen them for yourself. There has to be a connection there."

"Why don't I climb aboard the yacht and you give her the wine? You know I have a better eye for art than you do. And we both know how you love wine."

I turned onto the long drive and cut the engine, coasting silently to a stop on the far side of the three-car garage. Once the car was parked, I turned to Giff and whispered, "Because you're a handsome devil and a shameless bootlicker. Now go. I'll buzz your phone when I'm ready to leave. If there's something amiss we go straight to Jack. Got it?"

"Got it, boss."

I watched as Giff quietly walked down the brick walkway toward the front door with a bottle of wine taken from the inn. Once he was on his way, I snuck around the side of the garage and headed toward the back yard. I was struck with a terrible thought—if the yacht was gone, the portrait would be gone with it. I held my breath as the yard and lake opened before me, then slowly released it.

The yacht was still moored to the dock.

Feeling emboldened, I ran for it, as swift and silently as I could. However, the moment I hit the back lawn the darkness gave way to a burst of blinding light. It had the same effect as a bomb going off, only without the noise. I had tripped the floodlight sensors, something I hadn't even considered. I should have stopped and crouched behind a bush. It would have been the smart thing to do. But I couldn't stop running. Adrenaline coursed through my veins, my heart was pumping double-time, and I felt like a super-charged superhero as I bounded for the yacht. The moment I leapt aboard I crouched low, frantically trying to catch my breath. A moment later I got to my feet and peered over the railing to see if anyone had detected me. Aside from the bright lights, all was still and silent.

My heart slowed to a pace just above normal. It was time to get to work. I pulled out my phone and hit the flashlight app, then entered the main living quarters of the boat. Like the house that towered over the back lawn, the craft was spectacular. The smartly fitted furniture and seaworthy décor were done in shades of light blue and white with accents of gold. The wood was lighter than the on the *Boondoggle II*, but just as finely polished. Alexa's manageable yacht appeared both elegant and livable. It was impressive, and the thought struck me that if I should ever be so lucky, this would be the exact yacht I'd have. It was regal and sexy; it was just the thing Jack and I needed to sail the Great Lakes.

Yep, just my hot cop boyfriend and me … and his dog. Possibly the goats as well. Nope. Not with this décor. I'd have to put my foot down about the goats. It would be MacDuff, Jack, and me sailing the fresh water in our boat. As I studied the room, the fantasy took life in my mind. How great would it be? How hot would Jack look captaining such a huge craft? I would bet there was a rockin' master bedroom aboard her too. I was just about to go there in my mind when Jack's face popped into my head. And it wasn't his handsome, smiling face either. It was his angry face—the exact stern, unbending look he'd have if he ever found out that I was here, illegally trespassing on a wealthy woman's yacht. That face was a real fantasy-crusher.

However, all thoughts of Jack faded the moment my light touched on a gilded frame. Reality struck. Not only would I never be able to bake enough cherry pastries to afford a yacht as grand as Alexa's, but there was no doubt in my mind that I'd found Alexa's commissioned portrait.

It was still on its easel but had been turned to the wall. The long black cloth that had once covered it was also gone. I walked across the elegant room and turned the portrait around. Then, with my light shining on the glossy, oil-covered canvas, I stared.

For a brief moment I felt the presence of the painter beside me. It was a whiff of a scent, a vision of the mischievous pixy smile. The light I cast on the portrait seemed to grow brighter, then fade as I stared at yet another work that was as brilliant as it was masterful. Before me was a four-foot portrait of Alexa Livingstone, with every nuance of her form and personality laid bare for the casual observer. It brought to mind my earlier conversation with Char and Todd.

It was during the high tea reception for Silvia Lumiere. Alexa Livingstone, as head of the Cherry Country Arts Council, had just come to the microphone to introduce the guest of honor. Todd had described her portrait sitting. He had called her the White Lady, then proceeded to describe how the tall, elderly woman, still pretty in a manufactured way and wearing an outdated white gown, had arrived for her portrait. She had chosen to stand beside the trunk of a gnarled old oak, and I couldn't help but notice how the two shared a striking familiarity. They were both tall, a bit weathered, and yet proud and wise with age. Alexa's eyes were still vibrant and sharp. A compliment to the handsome woman if ever there was one. I searched every corner of the canvas, thinking there must be some mistake—some travesty hidden in the purposeful brushstrokes. But the longer I searched, the more I realized that Silvia Lumiere had painted a masterpiece for the only woman who dared call her a friend.

It was a stunning blow because I'd been so certain. Tate's suicide note and confession had thrown me over the edge. I couldn't accept it. I wouldn't accept it. And so I had done the unthinkable. I had stolen aboard an innocent woman's super sexy yacht.

Tate, dear Tate. What have you done?

Defeated, and feeling a new wave of hurt and anger, I turned off my flashlight app. I was about to send Giff a quick text when I realized that the portrait was still illuminated.

"It's hideous, isn't it?"

I spun around. The woman who confronted me was so strikingly similar to the one in the portrait that I flinched. The only difference was the murderous look in her eyes and the gun in her hand pointing at my head.

"Alexa," I uttered, both fearful and confused.

"I had a feeling you'd figure it out sooner or later," she said. "You're a smart girl, Whitney Bloom. Pity. Under different circumstances I'd take you under my wing, cultivate that drive of yours and give your life real purpose. But I can't, you see. That terrible woman has made a murderer out of me."

I stood in silence as my mind raced to find a reason why this woman would have killed the portrait painter. I was coming up with nothing when I offered, "I... I thought that you and Ms. Lumiere were friends?"

"Nearly friends," she countered. "But when she presented me with this—this travesty," she seethed, flicking the barrel of her gun at the portrait, "I was outraged."

Alexa had a gun trained on me, yet her remark was the thing that made my jaw drop. I closed it and shook my head. "I... I don't understand. That portrait's a masterpiece."

"A masterpiece?" she cried, looking utterly unhinged. "Look at it!" she demanded. "Look at it, Whitney! Look and see what that old pixy hag has done to me!" Her voice was quaking with anger, and I was a little afraid some spastic nerve in her trigger finger was going to snap as well. It didn't. But I was still at a loss as to why the painting angered her. I turned, because she wanted me to, and stared at the stunning portrait once again. When I didn't reply she answered for me.

"Don't you see it? Don't you see it?" she cried in an escalating shrill. "She's gone and made an old woman of me! That... that stranger in the portrait, that's supposed to be me! But it's not. Look at me, Whitney!

Look at my face. My skin is flawless. There's not a wrinkle on it," she declared, pressing her age-gnarled fingers to the firm skin of her high, round cheek.

There was no doubt Alexa had gone to great lengths to make herself look younger, but somehow Silvia's brush had captured more than any of us dared notice. In this new light of hysteria, Alexa's eyes looked more desperate than vibrant as they stared from their tight sockets, her face as gray and weathered as the oak she stood against. I didn't know what to say to her. The fact that anger now consumed her made her look even older than her likeness in the portrait.

Alexa wiggled her pistol at the canvas. "Those careless brushes of hers, they've stripped me of my youth and beauty. She's stolen my vibrance. That wrinkly-necked creature staring out with the haunted eyes, that's what she thinks of me! That! I was a model before I was married! I was a beautiful, successful business woman! And she had the nerve to tell me that I was wrong. That this—this ghost of skin and bones—is what I am … is how the world sees me."

I finally understood. Alexa Livingstone was mad and delusional.

Tears streamed from her old brown eyes then, and I actually felt sorry for her. I should have taken the gun from her hand, but I was too dumbfounded by what she was telling me.

"You confronted her?" I asked, recalling that Alexa's unveiling had taken place Saturday afternoon.

"Not at the unveiling, of course. I have better manners than that. But afterward. Late, late at night, well after Fred would have gone. You see, I couldn't sleep I was so upset."

"But you had an alibi," I said. "Your housekeeper confirmed you'd been there all night. She lied to Officer MacLaren!"

"Of course she did. Dear Paulina, she says whatever I tell her to. A very loyal employee, she is."

"And you had Silvia's spare key, didn't you?"

"Very good, Whitney. Yes, I had her key, the very one you found hanging on Fred's keyholder. I didn't want anyone to see me, so I made a black cape out of the veiling material, like the one her hippie assistant wears. I didn't mean to kill her. I just wanted an apology and to make her admit to her mistake. But that insolent old bitch! She wouldn't budge. She told me to look in a mirror and get over myself—that the brush of an artist never lies." Alexa growled at the memory. Redoubling her anger, she continued. "She ... she had the nerve to tell me that I might have been young and beautiful once, but that I was just as old and wrinkly beneath all the plastic surgery as she was. I was the one lying to myself, she said." Alexa paused for a moment to flick on the light, illuminating the whole stunning room.

"I was only trying to shut her up," she admitted. "There was a plate of scones on the table. I grabbed one and threatened her, but she just laughed in my face. My anger amused her. She was getting a good laugh at my expense. I've suffered the woman for nearly forty years. Forty years of it, Whitney! I wasn't about to take it any longer."

"You stuffed the scone in her mouth," I said, able to picture the horrible scene all too clearly.

Alexa nodded. "The beast was still trying to laugh, so I picked up the other one and stuffed it in too. That finished the job."

"Why did you push her down the stairs?" I asked, trying to keep her talking. It suddenly occurred to me that Giff was still up at the house while Alexa was here. I needed to get word to him. As she talked, I slyly slid my thumb over the screen of my phone, trying to write the word HELP.

Alexa, seemingly unaware of my phone, replied, "I panicked. Like I said, I really didn't mean to kill her, only to teach her a lesson. I wanted to make it look like an accident. Or at the very least ..." She suddenly crossed the room and yanked the phone from my hand. "You little sneak!" she cried, looking at my phone. She then walked to the door.

"No!" I pleaded, real fear gripping me. "Please," I begged, feeling a welling of panic. "My whole life's in there!"

"Too flipping bad." She flashed a rueful smile and tossed my phone into the lake. The sound of a splash confirmed my deepest fears. "Your life, I'm sorry to say, is about to end as well. Just like your ex-lover's. Pity about him." Before I could react, she yelled out an order to someone called Adrik. A moment later the engine engaged, and the boat shifted beneath my feet. I was seized with panic.

"And that's the thing I find most troubling," she continued. "I didn't intend to murder Silvia, but I did. However, I absolutely refuse to take the blame for it. I'm an upstanding citizen and a credit to my gender. Of course, because they were your scones, I tried to pin the murder on you, but that didn't last very long. When I learned that your name had been cleared, I panicked. I had Silvia's room key. I needed to get rid of it, and Fred, that poor, pathetic man, was the obvious choice. He thought Silvia was the ticket to the art world he needed. He convinced himself of it, even though she saw right through him. Oh, she had a good laugh over him as well. Poor Fred. I hung the key in his pottery studio, certain you'd find it, and you did. But framing Fred was a hollow victory. I'm actually quite fond of him, you know."

I glanced out the window. The lights on shore were swiftly getting smaller. "Tate!" I cried. "What have you done with him?"

"Let me tell you a little something about that ex-boyfriend of yours. I met Tate at Shenanigans last night. He was very drunk, and very talkative. So sad about you two. But what really got my goat was what he told me. You see, he nearly had it all figured out. I knew that after a few quiet hours on that island he was sailing to, he'd have it. I couldn't risk it, so I sent out two of my employees. Tate provided the perfect solution. A murder confession and a suicide note in one fell swoop!" She clapped her hands as she said this, an unhinged look flashing in her eyes. "My boys are a bit rough but they know how to get the job done."

Fear gripped me again. Two armed men going after Tate ... and after I had dumped him? "You ... you killed Tate?" Pure white-hot hatred flared within me.

"Did I have a choice?" she screeched, turning on me like a rabid dog. "No, I didn't. And I'm afraid, Whitney, you're to meet the same fate—you and that hideous painting. You shall both meet your end at Porte des Morts."

"Death's Door?" I cried, recognizing the old French term for the watery place of death. Every boater around these parts knew of it. Death's Door sat at the end of the peninsula and was the navigational passage between the Bay of Green Bay and Lake Michigan. The swirling currents, high winds, and raging waves had given it the dubious distinction of being the world's most deadly fresh water passage. "You're ... going to toss me overboard? With your painting?" It was a horrible thought to entertain. I was a decent swimmer, but I was no match for Death's Door.

"Yes." It was said with little emotion. "I'm dusting my hands of two embarrassments at once." Alexa then turned to the door and cried, "Riley! Take Ms. Bloom away!"

The cabin door burst open, revealing a man larger and with more bulging muscles than Tate.

"Lock Ms. Bloom up but do be kind. We're not animals, you know."

Forty-Six

 $\mathcal{I}$ was sobbing uncontrollably when Riley, the bald, muscly giant, escorted me to a set of stairs that descended into the belly of the yacht. What had I done, I thought? Dear Tate. She had drowned him too. He didn't deserve to die like that. And now I was about to follow him on that dark, lonely journey.

The corridor we traveled down was dim and narrow. A moment later the man unlocked a cabin door and thrust me inside. I tumbled forward, tripped and crashed to the carpet-covered floor. And there I stayed, too helpless with anger and sadness to move. I was going to die—to be left to drown in a cold, wet, terribly haunted place—at the hands of a super-rich madwoman. Odd as it sounded, I might have been safer had I stayed in crime-ridden Chicago.

It was only a second before I heard the rustling, indicating that I wasn't alone in the room. My heart dropped to the pit of my stomach. Giff, I thought. The crazy woman had snagged him too.

"Babe. Is that you?"

I sat up and found myself staring into the confused face of none other than Tate Vander Hagen. "Tate!" I cried, scrambling to my feet.

"Mother-loving fudgeballs! You're not dead!" Without thought I launched myself at the bed, wrapping my arms around him. Although his arms were bound behind his back and his legs were tied together as well, his lips were working just fine.

"Babe," he said, pausing for a breath. "Happy to see you too. I knew you'd find me. I knew you'd take one look at that note and figure it out."

"Figure what out?" I sat up on the bed and stared down at his rope-bound, prone body.

"The clue I left you. Sure, I was mad when I left your car, and heartbroken," he added. "But I knew you'd come to your senses eventually, like you always do. I mean, MacLaren? Really? I figured you'd know where I'd gone off to. You'd cool down eventually and come out to our island and join me. We'd have a heart-to-heart and make up, like we always do. But our plans got ambushed by Alexa and her lackeys. Her two men came to the island before you, and they made me write that stupid suicide note. I knew that once you saw it you'd see right through it. I mean, seriously, why would I take my life when I have everything in the world that I want right here in Cherry Cove?"

"What?" I said, quickly coming to my senses. "You sailed off to the island knowing I'd come running after you?" It was not only incredulous, it was the height of arrogance. "My God, I was worried sick about you! We all were. And when I finally did see that note I really thought you'd killed Silvia and took your own life as well. I was so … so mad at you! How could you!" I cried and brought my hand down as hard as I could manage on his bare chest.

"Ouch!" He flinched. "Hey, babe, I'm defenseless here. How about another kiss instead?" He looked incredibly confident.

"No, Tate. I'm not making up with you."

"Really, babe? Because a moment ago you were doing a very convincing job of it." He flashed his cheek dimples.

No, my heart screamed. Look away. Think of Jack. Think of Jack at the helm of this uber-sexy yacht. "Tate," I said again, this time squeezing his face between my hands. "I'm not here to make up with you. That ship has sailed. I'm here to rescue you," I stated confidently, having no idea where that came from. "Alexa is heading for Death's Door," I told him. "She means to throw us and her portrait overboard there before continuing to Mackinac Island."

He stared at me a moment, then uttered, "Well, crap," noting the serious look in my eyes. "All right. So what's your brilliant plan, Whit?"

And that was the funny part, because I didn't have one. But Tate was alive, and seeing him in the cabin looking so healthy had given me confidence. Embracing that confidence, I said, "I'm going to untie you, and then you're going to …" I looked at the door. It was locked, but it wasn't the most solid thing in the universe. It was a cabin door on a private yacht. I was pretty sure they weren't designed for prisoner containment. I shot Tate's muscly thighs a look next and made a decision. "Fortunately, Alexa's henchman was in a hurry. He must have thought this room would be enough to contain us. Silly henchman. I'm going to untie you, and then you're going to kick down that door."

As the yacht motored along through some truly choppy water, I sat on the bed with Tate and wrestled some very intrepid knots.

"Jesus," he uttered, listening to the boat's engine while making some quick calculations in his head. "We should be arriving at Death's Door soon. Alexa will send her goon down any minute."

"And that's why you need to kick this baby down now!" I declared, pointing at the door.

A moment later, with back braced against the solid frame of the built-in bed, Tate's legs sprang to action. He kicked the door with all his might, nailing the sucker and stripping the small bolt from its seating. The door flew wide. That was my cue. The moment I heard footsteps pounding down the stairs I shot out of the cabin and ran the opposite way. Riley took the bait and raced after me. The moment he came to the cabin door, Tate jumped out and punched him square in the face.

Riley went down like a stone.

I stopped and turned back around. Our objective was the stairs Riley had just bounded down.

"Come on!" Tate cried. I was just about to leap over the prone body when it suddenly sprang up and grabbed hold of my leg. Tate, bounding for the stairs, turned in time to see me land on top of Alexa's henchman.

"Crap!" he uttered. He took a few purposeful steps back, growled like a Viking and gave the man a hard kick in the teeth. Blood poured from Riley's nose and mouth as his head crashed back to the floor. Then, without hesitation, Tate grabbed me and tossed me over the large body blocking the narrow hallway. He kicked the man again and followed me up the stairs.

"Quick," I cried. "To the dinghy." For I had visions of lowering that little boat into the water without Alexa finding out, but the thought was absurd. And we were too close to that dangerous passage to make a swim for it. The lake was cold, and the wind had picked up. Due to the darkness, I wasn't exactly sure where we were.

None of that mattered, however, when we burst into the large living room. Alexa was already there, standing beside her painting and waiting for us with her gun.

"No!" she cried and took aim.

Tate pushed me to the deck, falling on top of me as the gun went off. The large window behind him shattered, causing an explosion of glass to rain down all around us. Alexa, angered that she had missed, aimed the gun again. Before she could pull the trigger, we were back on our feet, this time scrambling for the door behind us.

"Go on deck," Tate ordered, slamming the door. We were in a little antechamber that led both to the galley downstairs and the wheelhouse upstairs. There was also a door leading to the outer deck. "I'm taking the helm."

"I'll help you," I insisted, frightened of Alexa and her gun.

"Babe. I got this. Hang on to whatever you can until I give the order. By my calculations we're now very close to Death's Door Bluff," he said, looking grim. "I saw it when the glass broke."

Another shot rang out, this time whizzing through the shut door and striking he wooden frame of the galley stairs. It narrowly missed us. There wasn't any time to argue. "Got it!" I cried, unwilling to stay put while a madwoman had a gun.

As Tate ran up the stairs to the wheelhouse, I felt safest heading for the outer deck. The moment the cabin door shut behind me, I realized that might have been a mistake. The decking was narrow and covered in ice-cold water, making it slippery as well. But I had no choice. I started to work my way forward in the darkness, praying that Alexa wouldn't follow me. But the woman was unhinged.

I hadn't gone far when the cabin door burst open again. Alexa appeared, silhouetted by the light from the cabin. She looked around wildly, then shouted a warning to the man at the helm. I couldn't tell what happened next, but the boat suddenly lurched to the right, causing Alexa to tumble and me to look up. My heart sank again when I saw that Tate was already there, fighting not only the captain of the ship but also that other big brute, Riley. Unfortunately, I didn't have time to worry about Tate. Alexa was on her feet again, aiming her nasty little pistol at me.

As Tate was fighting for all he was worth, I was going around with Alexa, slowly working my way toward the bow of the ship as she fired shot after shot at my head. The bow was crashing into the waves, sending spumes of cold water leaping over the side. My clothes were getting soaked as I clung to the little rail for dear life.

I knew what Tate was trying to do. When rounding Death's Door, a sailor was faced with a dangerous outcropping of rock and shoals. One wrong turn and a ship could be flung upon the rocks or scuttled by a rogue wave. Alexa, unfortunately, was totally oblivious to anything but killing me. I, however, was preparing myself for the worst.

The boat was picking up speed. I looked out over the dark water and saw the lights high on the bluff getting closer. It wouldn't be long now.

"Alexa!" I cried, peering over the rounded decking of the bow. "Please put the gun down and listen to me."

"No!" she cried. "I'm not going to prison, not for the death of that horrible woman."

"Okay. But seriously," I cried, poking my head a little higher. She aimed her gun and shot. "For the love of Pete! How may bullets do you have in that damn thing?"

"Enough to finish the job. Stop moving!"

The engines on the boat roared even louder as the yacht picked up more speed. I looked up and saw Tate in the wheelhouse. The other two men were nowhere in sight. Tate gave me a thumbs-up, then disappeared. It was my cue but I hesitated.

"Alexa, please listen to me. Drop the gun and head for the back of the boat. Look!" I cried over the crashing of the waves. "Look over there."

"Oh my God," she exclaimed, anger gripping her voice. "You're trying to ground my yacht!" She shot her gun off one last time before throwing it into the water. Alexa might have been mad but she wasn't a fool. Taking my cue, she began gingerly making her way along the narrow decking on her side of the boat, heading for the back of the yacht.

I scrambled down my side and beat her, finding Tate already there. He tossed me a life jacket. I hastily put it on, then tossed one to Alexa, who was stumbling toward us like a befuddled toddler.

"We're going to have to jump!" I told her.

"In there? Never!" she yelled, but I was pleased to note that she put the life jacket on in spite of her words. "Those waves are too high, and lake water ruins my hair."

"Suit yourself," Tate cried, and took hold of my hand.

I was terrified. Jumping off the waters near Death's Door was akin to suicide. Staying on the boat as it crashed into the swiftly closing rocks, however, would be worse. Seeing my trepidation, Tate gestured to a spot on the lake. Above the roaring of the motor and the crashing of the building waves I saw what Tate had pointed to. It was another boat racing through the darkness with lights flashing.

"Coast Guard. We can do this. Ready, babe?"

"Ready," I cried and squeezed back. And then we ran to the back of the yacht, over the seat cushions of the plush bench seats and into the shocking cold water off the bluffs of Death's Door. The moment we surfaced in the building waves, pulled up by the buoyant life jackets, we heard Alexa scream. A moment later, the sound of metal grinding upon solid rock hit our ears. The beautiful yacht had made its last voyage.

Forty-Seven

ate and I weren't in the water long before the small Coast Guard cutter that had been chasing us came to our rescue. But it wasn't a member of the Coast Guard that stood on the back platform ready to fish me out of the cold water. It was Jack. And the look he gave me as he assisted me onto the boat was one of confounding contradictions. He was both elated and angry at once. I suppose I deserved it, but I had to be honest, the sight of him sent my heart fluttering away like the wings of a butterfly in a particularly succulent garden.

The moment I was firmly on deck his expression broke. A blanket came around my shoulders and I found myself wrapped in his arms. "Jesus Christ, Whitney," he chided, holding tightly, cradling my head against his warm, fleece-covered chest. "This is the second time I've pulled you from the water in the dead of night since you've been up here. And I don't mind telling you that I don't like it one bit."

Tears sprang to my eyes as I held him back just as tightly. "I'm sorry," I said, sniffling. "But ... but I had a hunch. About Alexa's portrait."

"I know. Giff told me all about it. I heard how you roped him into your madcap plan by sending him to the house to create a diversion

335

while you went to search Alexa's boat. The moment Alexa saw him, he said, was the moment you set off the floodlights out back. She knew instantly that something was up. Her housekeeper tried to detain him while Alexa, her yacht captain, and her groundskeeper went after you. Thankfully Giff escaped, or else ... Christ, Whitney, I don't even want to think about it. But you should have called me," he reprimanded. It was then that a small, pain-stricken groan escaped his lips. "You do realize that before you showed up, Cherry Cove was a quiet, boring, sleepy little village?"

I forced a smile. "It was never boring, Jack. But I will give you quiet. It might not be so quiet now that I'm here. Are you really mad at me? I did find Tate, after all, just as I found Silvia's murderer."

"Quiet's better than boring," he breathed, tightening his grip on me. "I'm just happy you're here, safe in my arms."

I looked at the partially sunken yacht, now awash in floodlights. The once sleek hull was a tangle of metal grinding against the jagged rocks. Alexa, looking like a drowned rat trapped in an extra-large life jacket, was bobbing in the waves twenty feet off the bow of the cutter. She wasn't enjoying a minute of it. And she certainly wasn't going to love what the lake water had done to her hair and makeup. She was currently being towed to the boat by two men from the Coast Guard. Her lackeys were still aboard the sinking yacht, waiting for the second Coast Guard cutter to arrive and take them off.

"Alexa Livingstone," I uttered, and shook my head. "I never saw that one coming."

"Neither did I ... not until Giff called me. He explained your suspicion of the black cape we found on the island. He also said that you were obsessed about getting a look at her portrait. I'm curious. What did you find?"

"Nothing," I told him honestly. "It was a stunning piece of artistry. But I learned that it wasn't really about the painting, Jack. The whole senseless murder took place because Alexa's portrait didn't look anything like she assumed it would. It depicted her as she really is, an older woman. Due to her ego and pride, Alexa refused to acknowledge that the old woman staring out from the painting was her."

Jack looked across the water at the woman now in the spotlight, floundering in the waves. "In general, I'd say there's nothing wrong with clinging to one's youth. Growing up and getting older is a part of life, but sometimes not an easy one. You and I, we've grown up a bit, haven't we? And I have to be honest, there are days I feel very old."

"You're far from old, Jack."

He smiled gently. "We're all in denial about something. As long as it doesn't lead to murder, I suppose it's harmless enough. Good work, by the way."

"Thank you."

"Hey! MacLaren!" Startled, we both turned in the direction of the voice. It was Tate, standing on the other side of the cutter with a blanket draped around his shoulders and a mug of hot coffee in his hand. I felt a welling of relief at the sight of him. An hour ago, we'd all believed he'd committed a murder-suicide. It had been a horrible night, but the fact that he was still very alive and very innocent of murder made us both smile. "Dude," Tate continued, staring at Jack. "For the love of God. Stop hugging my girlfriend!"

Jack fell silent as he studied the dripping, blond-headed man. A look, part confusion, part terror, seized him, and I could feel his grip on me begin to slacken.

"Tate," I said, gripping Jack tighter. "I believe I made it quite clear back there on the yacht that I'm not your girlfriend."

The look on his face was pure challenge as he stared at Jack. Jack stared back. Then, suddenly, Tate's face broke into a dimpled grin. "Right. Just checking. Thought maybe you changed your mind." He winked and took a sip of coffee.

"Nope. I haven't," I said. "But you do know that we all still love you, right?"

"Of course. I mean, look at me. I'm practically the embodiment of Cherry Cove, and who doesn't love Cherry Cove?"

It was then that Jack released me and walked over to Tate. "No hard feelings?" he asked, extending a hand.

Tate stared at him a moment, then grinned. "No hard feelings, bro. Actually, I'm a bit relieved. Ever since her return to Cherry Cove, Whitney's been hazardous to my health."

Forty-Eight

lexa Livingstone was arrested for the murder of Silvia Lumiere as well as the kidnapping of one Tatum Vander Hagen of Cherry Cove, Wisconsin. Although it was a beautifully done portrait that had finally thrown her over the edge, the truth was that after years of putting up with the difficult, snarky, and unduly mean painter, Alexa hadn't been able to take one more insult from the woman. It was doubtful that Silvia had even been aware of the level of Alexa's narcissism or her fear of aging. The artist had simply done what she did best: she painted what she saw. Only in Fred Beauchamp's case had she veered from that path. Why Silvia had chosen to mock him was a secret she'd taken to the grave.

It was a sad ending to what had been a surprisingly lucrative few weeks at the Cherry Orchard Inn. Jack wrapped up the paperwork and gave the okay for us to open for business, now that Silvia's belongings had been removed from the Sailboat Suite and the place had been deep-cleaned. Yet in an unexpected twist, things continued to get better for us financially, since the murder of the portrait painter was creating quite the sensation.

Greta Stone, the sexy reporter from Baywatch News (Grrrretah!), certainly had a hand in generating the buzz. She thrived on scandal and murder, and the savvy advertiser in me understood her value. Giff did too. After a short chat, we'd decided to call Greta up and offer an exclusive interview. We explained our role in hunting down the real person responsible for the murder of Silvia Lumiere. And while I felt that my performance was good, I couldn't deny that it was Giff who really stole the show. The man had never met the portrait painter, but that little detail wasn't about to deter him. His descriptions were animated, his mannerism dramatic, and best of all he planted the notion on live TV that Silvia Lumiere's restless spirit still lingered at the inn, particularly around the last step or two of the grand staircase. He then highly recommended the sour cherry martini (Ms. Lumiere's favorite) to really summon her spirit—or just to enjoy, because it was a house specialty. By that afternoon, the phones were ringing again.

Things were about to get better for Hannah too. Due to the fact that Silvia didn't have a next of kin and had never bothered to make a will, her ex-husband was left with her worldly belongings. Stanley Gordon and his dear wife, Carol, did what they could, but in the end, I believe, they just wanted to wash their hands of the whole business. After careful consideration they decided to give everything over to Silvia's poorly treated assistant, Peter McClellan. No one could deny that Peter hadn't earned the windfall of paints and canvases, antique furniture, and vintage costume jewelry. But the thing that excited him most was Stanley Gordon's generous offer to let him keep the huge Cadillac Escalade for the duration of the lease. Peter also committed to finishing the work Silvia Lumiere had started, and part of that task was to proceed with the scheduled unveilings.

Mom, harboring a soft spot for Silvia's hippie assistant, agreed to let him stay in the Pine Suite for as long as he wished, with the one stipulation that he couldn't smoke in there. Peter, thrilled with the offer, agreed and presented Mom with one of Silvia's prized antiques as payment. Mom didn't require payment but loved the gesture all the same. Besides, it was a beautiful eighteenth-century cabinet, which Mom brought straight to the breakfast room. Somehow it looked perfect in there.

"Dude," Peter said to me as I ran down the front steps of the inn carrying a tray of finger sandwiches stuffed with cherry chicken salad. "Jump in the Lade, Whitney Bloom, or we're gonna be late."

"Right," I said and climbed into the back seat with my goodies. Giff, occupying the seat beside me, shot me a deprecatory look while tapping the face of his watch.

"Always running late," he said. "And you're the one who insisted on removing the black veil of this highly awaited portrait."

"Sorry," I apologized.

Hannah, sitting in the front seat next to Peter, looked back and shot me a grin. "Buckle up. Tay's just texted me. She says half of Cherry Cove is already there, anxiously awaiting the big reveal of"— she paused to put up air quotes—"*Mother and Son*."

Peter laughed, then quickly suppressed it.

"What? Have you seen it?" Hannah cried, shooting an accusatory look at him. "You're not supposed to look at the portrait until it's *revealed*."

"Dude," he said, this time addressing his girlfriend. "Like, it's my job. I have to look."

"Oh, do tell us," Giff chimed in mockingly. "I'm on pins and needles." I cast him an eye roll, secretly thankful that he had stayed on at the inn, helping wherever needed and eating plenty of Grandma Jenn's food. Giff had also spent a good deal of time at the marina. Although his motives were purely selfish, Tate genuinely enjoyed his company. I believed this was because Giff had been regaling him with stories of Chicago, including my most embarrassing moments. It might also have been because Giff was a great guy and fun to hang out with. He didn't come from Cherry Cove but had plenty of connections to it, and that was just what Tate needed. I'd never let on that Giff had been enchanted with him from the moment he'd spied a picture of us sitting on my desk.

It was a short drive to Char's house, but Hannah was right. Cars lined both sides of the narrow street, and people were still arriving. The moment we walked through the rose-covered trellis to the backyard, Tay and Char, with wineglasses in hand, trotted over to greet us. Lance, with a bottle of microbrewed beer, came over as well. His bruises were healing nicely. His face was almost as handsome as on the day we'd met outside Tay's shop.

"Is that it?" Char asked excitedly. Peter nodded but kept walking until the covered portrait was brought to its place of honor on the patio.

"She's been giddy as a schoolgirl all day," Tay informed us with a grin. She took the tray from my hands, adding, "Todd too. But that's not unusual considering he's still going through puberty."

"Tay," Lance chided, though clearly just for show. Having hung up his sword for the summer, the Black Knight had been forced to spend more time with Tay's mom and her fiancé. He got along fine with them both but couldn't keep from laughing at Tay's jokes.

"Oh, by the way, somebody else has been anxiously awaiting your arrival and it's not Edna Baker," Tay said. I looked to the patio and saw Jack standing there. Our eyes met, and he smiled. Tay continued. "Word on the street is that it's a big day for you as well. First an unveiling, and then your first date with Jack. Any idea where he's taking you?"

"None whatsoever," I said. I was about to wander over to where Jack stood when Hannah appeared.

"You're up," she said, pulling me to the opposite corner of the patio where Peter and the painting awaited.

Peter introduced himself before giving a little talk about his former employer, one that highlighted her strengths and her gifts, in order to help perpetuate her legacy as well as her legend. While he talked, I stood beside the covered portrait and studied the crowd.

They were all there—our friends, our neighbors, our little community of Cherry Cove. Mom waved. She and Dad were beside Dr. Engle and his wife, Diane, standing on the left side of the spacious patio. Gran and her group of friends, Cecelia Cushman and Edna Baker among them, stood by the food table sampling the offerings and, no doubt, discretely judging them. I was especially tickled to see old Doc Fisker, the county coroner, and his wife, Ginger. Although I was currently banned from the morgue at Door County General, it did nothing to mar our relationship. Old Doc Fisker, with a plate full of Gran's award-winning cherry pie, smiled and gave me an encouraging thumbs-up.

Most surprising of all was the group of women, young and old, that flocked around Giff and Tate as they stood near the back of the patio. Although both men appeared utterly oblivious, wrapped in their little bro-cocoon of microbrewed beer, bacon-wrapped cocktail wieners, and laughter, the women were always at hand when the snacks ran out. I was aware of Giff smiling at me as he whispered something to Tate. I had no idea what was said, but apparently it was hilarious.

Amongst the crowd I was surprised to see Fred Beauchamp. He was standing beside the younger artist, Jeffery, both men looking sad and humbled as they watched the proceedings. I felt quite sorry for them. Clearly they'd worshiped the deceased portrait painter, and both had been knocked off their feet by how the Cherry Country Arts Council president had let them down.

Then my eyes settled on the tall, lean form of my old high school friend and nemesis. He looked good, dressed in khakis and a summer-weight sweater in navy. Sunlight glinted off his hair, turning it to sparks of flaming copper. I found that I couldn't look away and was lost in a fantasy all my own, wondering where our first date was to be. First dates were important. They were memorable. They set the precedent on which the entire relationship would be built.

"Whitney!" It was Peter. He was hiss-whispering my name.

"What?"

"Now! Now, dude. Like, throw back the cloth!"

I took a deep breath and smiled. The honor of revealing Char and Todd's long-awaited portrait was all mine. I took hold of the black cloth and flung it over the back of the painting.

The crowd fell silent. A flash of nerves seized me then, and I feared something might have gone wrong. I looked at the painting too. At first glance it was stunning, an outdoor portrait with the rich, satu-rated colors of nature—the cool green of lush summer grass, the vi-brant blue of a cloudless sky, the deep indigo of the wind-swept lake beyond. Char, standing beside the young man soon to be her husband, looked magnificent in her long, bare-shouldered, form-fitting black gown. Todd, for his part, looked almost princely with his carefully brushed dusky-blond hair, his trim-cut black suit, and his flashy gold and black striped tie. The happy couple, for clearly that's what they were, were cast in a glow of sunlight, but most remarkable was the tender look Silvia had managed to capture as Todd gazed down upon the woman he loved. He looked nothing like Tay's brother, just as he looked nothing like Char's doting son. What he looked like was a man in love.

What was I missing, I wondered as the silence continued. Then, finally, Todd's voice rang out, breaking the silence.

"By God, it's a masterpiece! That's my future wife, people! And doesn't she look magnificent! Happy engagement to us!"

The crowd erupted in thunderous cheers and clinking glasses.

It was extraordinary, I thought. At long last, from beyond the grave, Silvia Lumiere had finally managed to capture the hearts of the entire village of Cherry Cove.

The crowd had dispersed, yet some still mingled in the garden as Char and Todd celebrated their new portrait and their future life together.

"Whitney Bloom," Jack said, appearing beside me. He looked into my eyes as a quiet smile graced his lips. "You promised me a date, remember? And since you took liberties with both my nerves and my profession, I'm going to insist you come with me." Before I could answer, he took my hand and escorted me to his Jeep.

Once I was buckled in, he started the engine. "We have to stop by the station first, I'm afraid. I need to take the kids off the roof. They weren't cooperating earlier, the little hellions. Will you help me?"

"Of course," I said, thinking it an odd way to start a first date. But this was Jack MacLaren. Nothing about Jack was ever straightforward. I flashed him a smile. "You know that I love your kids."

We pulled into the station and went straight to the garden. There Jack grabbed a covered bucket and handed it to me. He took one as well and said, "Sliced carrots. It's like goat-crack." He then called out to the thick grass of the roof, but no little horned heads appeared.

"Damn. I guess we're going to have to go up there and drag them down ourselves. Ready?" he asked, opening the gate to the ramp. He took my hand and pulled me along with him up to the thick sod of the roof. And there I saw it.

"Oh my God, you didn't?"

"Oh yes, I did," he said, and gingerly led me to the blanket he'd placed on the gentle slope of his roof-lawn. Jack had set up a romantic picnic for two on his roof, complete with china and candles ready to be lit. As for the goats, thankfully they were nowhere to be seen.

"They're at Inga's," he informed me, taking the bucket from my hand. He pulled back the cover, revealing four little bottles of wine sitting in crushed ice. His own contained a variety of wrapped cheeses, crackers, and thinly sliced meats. "The way she spoils those two, you'd think they were real kids. Duffy's there too, but he clearly wanted to be here with us. Call it selfish, but I didn't want to compete for your attention tonight." He grinned before gently assisting me to the blanket.

The moment he was seated beside me, he asked, "Do you like it? It's my special place, and it's got the best view in town." He pointed across the bay to the opposite shore. There, on the far wooded hillside, the roofline of the Cherry Orchard Inn could be seen poking above the trees.

Touched beyond words, I whispered, "It's perfect, Jack. Absolutely perfect."

Whitney's Cherry-Tastic Recipes and Other Delights

The Cherry Orchard Inn's Sour Cherry Martini
Makes 1 serving

Bring the taste of Cherry Cove to any occasion with the Cherry Orchard Inn's signature drink. For the twenty-one-and-over crowd, this is the perfect cocktail to kick off the evening or to pacify a cranky guest. No one can frown when cherries are in the mix. And with the added health benefit of tart cherry juice, there's even more to smile about.

Ingredients

1 fluid ounce of tart cherry juice (available in the juice aisle of
   most grocery stores)
2 fluid ounces of vodka
Splash of triple sec
1 slice of fresh lemon (for squeezing)
1 cup of ice (for chilling)
Sugar for rim of glass
Tart cherry or maraschino cherry for garnish

Directions

To prepare the martini glass, wet the rim of the glass with tart cherry juice, then immediately coat with sugar. Add the cherry to the bottom of the glass and chill in freezer if desired.

Combine the tart cherry juice, vodka, splash of triple sec, and a squeeze of lemon (approximately 1 teaspoon of juice) in a cocktail mixing glass. Fill with ice and stir until chilled. Strain into prepared martini glass. Enjoy!

Whitney's Famous Cherry Scones

Makes 6 servings

So good they're to die for!

Ingredients

For the Scones:

2 cups all-purpose flour

4 teaspoons baking powder

¼ cup sugar

½ teaspoon salt

5 Tablespoons cold butter

1 cup unsweetened dried Montmorency cherries

½ cup toasted pecans

¼ cup sour cream

½ cup + 1 Tablespoon heavy cream

1 egg

1 Tablespoon milk

For the Glaze:

2 Tablespoons tart cherry juice

1 cup powdered sugar

Directions

Heat oven to 350°F. Place pecans on baking sheet and bake 10 minutes or until lightly toasted. Remove from oven and set aside. Increase oven temperature to 450°F.

In large bowl or mixer, combine flour, baking powder, sugar, and salt. Cut in butter using a pastry blender or mixing attachment until butter is the size of peas. Add cherries and toasted pecans.

Mix the sour cream into the heavy cream and stir until blended. Pour over the dry ingredients and mix gently until well blended. Be careful not to overwork the dough or scones will be tough.

With floured hands, remove dough and place on floured surface. Form into round ball, then gently flatten into round disk approximately six inches in diameter and one inch high. Using a sharp knife, cut into six wedges.

Place scones one inch apart on parchment-covered baking sheet.

Beat the egg with the tablespoon of milk. Brush the top of each scone with the egg wash.

Let stand ten minutes.

Bake 15 minutes in heated oven until tops are golden brown. Remove from oven and let cool.

For the glaze, stir two tablespoons of tart cherry juice into the cup of powdered sugar. Pour over scones and let sit until glaze is set.

The scones are ready to eat! For an extra tasty treat, serve them with clotted cream and lemon curd.

Grandma Jenn's Delicious Cherry Chicken Salad
Makes 16 tea sandwiches

A delightful salad and a perennial favorite. It can be enjoyed on a bed of crisp greens, stuffed into a flaky croissant for a delicious sandwich, or spread on a dinner roll and served with tea.

Ingredients

4 cups cubed cooked chicken breast

2 celery ribs, finely chopped

1½ cups dried tart cherries

1 teaspoon fresh rosemary, finely chopped

¼ teaspoon ground pepper

1 teaspoon salt

1 cup real mayonnaise

1 cup chopped pecans, toasted

Leaf lettuce, washed and dried

16 dinner rolls (I use King's Hawaiian)

Directions

In a large mixing bowl, combine first six ingredients. Stir in mayonnaise. Mix well, cover, and refrigerate until ready to use.

Slice rolls in half and line with a leaf of crisp lettuce.

Remove chicken salad from fridge, stir in toasted pecans, and spoon onto lettuce-lined rolls. Enjoy with a cup of your favorite tea!

Acknowledgments

As a writer, coming to the end of a book is like arriving home after a long, marvelous vacation, one that began with a spark of an idea, required meticulous planning, took on a life of its own, and ultimately ended too soon, leaving behind cherished memories and a yearning to revisit that special place again. Cherry Cove is that special place for me, and one I can't wait to return to. But like with all great adventures, I wasn't alone on this journey. I'd like to thank those special people who paved the way and enriched the experience.

Sandy Harding, who believed in my Very Cherry Mysteries as much as I did, and who taught me what it means to be a cozy mystery writer; Terri Bischoff, for taking a chance on Whitney Bloom and her very cherry adventures; Sandy Sullivan, for her good judgment and excellent editorial skills; the generous people of Door County, Wisconsin; Jane Boundy, for the friendship, laughter, and cherry pies; Robin Taylor, a wise friend, gifted artist, and all-around cherry-tastic person; Dana Allen, for her kindness, support, and vast knowledge about cozy mysteries; Tanya Holda, for the friendship and amazing writer's quilt; Brandi Tambasco and all my lovely coworkers at the Howell Carnegie Library, for letting me share my cherry enthusiasm; Todd and Debbie Coy, for the dinners and the laughter; my wonderful parents, Jan and Dave Hilgers, for absolutely everything; my amazing sons, Jim, Dan, and Matt, who inspire me every single day; and to my fabulous husband, John, who's not only up for cherry-tastic adventures but is truly the wind beneath my wings. Thank you!

And a special thanks to all you wonderful readers who took a chance on this book. I hope you enjoyed your visit to Cherry Cove as much as I did.

About the Author

Darci Hannah is the author of *Cherry Pies & Deadly Lies* and two works of historical fiction, *The Exile of Sara Stevenson* and *The Angel of Blythe Hall* (Ballantine). When she isn't whipping up tasty treats in her kitchen, she's hard at work writing. *Cherry Scones & Broken Bones* is the second book in her Very Cherry Mystery series.